ANGELS UNLIMITED

the Cosmic Collection

Three heavenly adventures in one book!

Look out for these other titles in the
ANGELS UNLIMITED series

ANGELS UNLIMITED

the Cosmic Collection

Calling the Shots

Fogging Over

Fighting Fit

ANNIE DALTON

An imprint of HarperCollinsPublishers

Calling the Shots first published in Great Britain by Collins 2002
Fogging Over first published in Great Britain by Collins 2002
Fighting Fit first published in Great Britain by Collins 2003

First published in this three-in-one edition by
HarperCollins*Children'sBooks* 2004

HarperCollins*Children'sBooks* is an imprint of
HarperCollins*Publishers* Ltd
77-85 Fulham Palace Road, Hammersmith
London W6 8JB

www.harpercollins.co.uk

1 3 5 7 9 10 8 6 4 2

Text copyright © Annie Dalton 2002, 2003

ISBN 0 00 716645-1

The author asserts the moral right to be
identified as the author of the work.

Printed and bound in England by
Clays Ltd, St Ives plc

calling the Shots

*To Maria with love and thanks
for invaluable help*

CHAPTER ONE

When I was alive, I had totally the wrong idea about Heaven.

Each time I heard the word, this spooky film footage came up on my mental screen. I'd picture myself wandering ankle-deep in little fluffy clouds through a vast empty waiting room. Apart from the heavenly muzak playing over the PA system, there wasn't a sound. No swoosh of traffic, no pounding hip hop beat, no chatting, laughing or crying. *Nada.* Omigosh, I'd think, if this is Heaven, what must that other place be like!

Then, twenty-four hours after my thirteenth birthday, I was knocked down by some youth in a speeding car and BAM! I was checking out the heavenly facilities for real.

Not only that, I had been talent-spotted to be a trainee angel! I have no idea how that happened and I don't really care. The good news is you can all relax. There *is* no cloud-filled waiting room.

I live bang in the middle of a big, buzzy, beautiful city, filled with shops, cafés and the loveliest gardens you ever saw. The beach is like, minutes away. Lola and I go there constantly.

It's weird to think that if I hadn't died, Lola and I would never have met, because originally she's from the twenty-second century. Her full name is Lola Sanchez, also known as Lollie. We met on my first day here and I'm not exaggerating, we are total soul-mates. We love the same fashions, the exact same music, and are both deeply dedicated shoppers.

I've shocked you, haven't I? You had NO idea it was possible to go shopping in Heaven! But like Lola says, "Well, duh! Who do you think invented shopping malls in the first place!"

Don't go thinking my new life is one long heavenly beach party. I still go to school, remember. The sole purpose of the Academy is to train us to be celestial agents; angels in other words. This means the Agency (that's like, Angel HQ) is constantly monitoring our progress. Plus my teacher, Mr Allbright, doesn't let us get away with a thing. I have never studied so hard in my whole existence as I do in that guy's class.

To be honest, I never saw the point of school when I was alive. My teachers made everything SO boring. Even history, if you can believe that? The Angel Academy takes a much more hands-on approach. We don't just memorise dates and read books. We genuinely experience history.

Yes, I'm talking actual time-travel! This is not mere time tourism, OK? We're training to be celestial trouble-shooters, so we have to do everything the professional agents do. Lola and I are now so hooked that we signed up to study Earth history as our special subject. It's like I finally found what I was created for.

And yet... I still didn't totally believe I was an angel.

Oh, I *looked* the part! When I checked in the mirror there I was, glowing with that rosy angel glow, in my favourite school casuals with the cool Academy logo. I had my new ID in my wallet. I had my official angel name (it's Helix). Plus I already had several angelic missions safely under my belt.

But somewhere inside I still thought of myself as the same old Melanie Beeby, the insecure girl I used to be, before that joyrider booted me out of the twenty-first century into the Afterlife.

Then something happened which completely changed my attitude.

Lola and I were in our favourite department store on an urgent mission to buy her the ultimate pair of biker boots. We sailed up the escalator, yakking away, when with absolutely no warning, the entire store started rushing away from me; sort of like a tidal wave in reverse.

In the blink of an eye, all the shoppers, bright lights and displays of cute celestial handbags were miles below, looking exactly like a pretty pattern in a kid's kaleidoscope.

My actual body was still travelling up the escalator. I could feel my fingers clinging on to the handrail. But my inner angel or whatever stared down with interest from its new perch in outer space.

Snatches of conversation zipped past. There was a gale of girly laughter, so close it tickled. Someone was plonking out a tune on an old-fashioned piano and someone else started singing, "Put another nickel in, in the Nickelodeon." And the whole time, I could feel this unknown force pulling and tugging at me.

Then like a cosmic rubber band, I pinged back to the department store. I staggered off the escalator, totally weirded out.

"Boo, are you OK?" Lola was asking anxiously. I don't know why she calls me Boo. Lola is constantly giving her mates weird nicknames.

"I'm great," I gulped. "We'll find you those biker boots if it's the last thing we do!"

Lola shook her head. "Change of plan, babe."

She steered me firmly towards the down escalator. Minutes later we were sitting at one of Guru's outdoor tables in the sun. Mo brought our smoothies, waving away my ID. "It's on the house," he insisted. "You look like you need them. I bet you skipped breakfast, am I right?"

I gave him a feeble grin. "Yeah yeah, it's the most important meal of the day."

"You said it," called Mo and he disappeared into the kitchen.

Guru's strawberry smoothies are really something else. After a couple of sips I felt new strength flowing through my veins.

"That's better," said Lola. "You had me worried, Boo. You went white."

"Don't be such an old lady," I growled. "It's like Mo said. I had low blood sugar or something."

As a trainee angel, I'm constantly exposed to paranormal events when I'm on duty. But when I get home, I expect life to putter along in a happy heavenly groove. The idea that an unknown force could like, *toy* with me any time it fancied, totally confused me.

Two days later it happened again.

We were having a class martial arts session. Lola and I were in a three with our buddy, Reuben. Mr Allbright had just shown us this cool move called the Waterfall. To get it right, you have to unplug your mind and become pure angelic energy, something I'd always found impossible. But this time I was a bit too successful, because three, four, five times, I went whirling through the air, chanting, "I am pure angelic energy. I am pure angelic energy..." Then – WHOOSH! I completely left my body.

Once again I was floating past stars and planets, to the tinny soundtrack of that bizarre Nickelodeon song.

Then Reuben and I banged heads and all three of us fell in a heap.

Lola rubbed her nose. "Ow! What happened?"

"I think that was me," I said. "I kind of lost my concentration."

Lola and Reuben exchanged meaningful looks. "Then she must be punished," said Reuben gleefully.

Squealing with laughter, I joined in their play fight, until Mr Allbright made us break it up.

I know, I know, I should have told my mates. But I couldn't somehow. Once I said the words out loud, I'd be admitting my terrifying experiences were real.

That night I was afraid to go to bed in case the mysterious force snatched me out of Heaven the minute I fell asleep. Once I dozed off in my chair and I literally felt myself rising out of my seat, but I got a grip just in time. And that creepy Nickelodeon song was going round and round my head until I thought I'd go nuts.

Finally I did what I always do when I'm having a disturbed night. I stuck my headphones on and listened to the special CD that Reuben had burned for me.

Unlike Lollie and me, Reuben is pure angel. He's not like, a saint or anything. He's actually a bit of a party animal. When we first hooked up, Lola and I played him all our favourite Earth tunes and he went into this major rapture! After that, he refused to give us a moment's peace until we agreed to give him DJ lessons.

But like Lola says, our work is totally done! Our buddy turned out to be a natural angel DJ. We've actually adopted one of his mixes as our theme song. There's a bit which goes, "You're not alone. You're not alone." And I swear it has healing powers, because I played it over and over until the sky was growing light outside my window, and suddenly the lyrics genuinely got through to me.

I'm NOT alone, I thought. We're the three cosmic musketeers, like Lola says. There's nothing I can't tell those guys.

I decided it was now officially morning. I showered, dressed and went to knock on Lola's door. She came to the door in her PJs, looking unbelievably frazzled.

"Get moving, sleepyhead," I teased. "If we hurry, we can grab breakfast at Guru, on the way to school."

My soul-mate was in a strangely crabby mood. "Honestly, Mel, can't you do anything by yourself?" she snapped.

"Hey, I offered to buy you breakfast," I said huffily. "No need to bite my head off."

"Sorry, babe," she mumbled. "Just had a bad night. Later, yeah?" She closed the door, leaving me in the corridor.

I felt like crying. I had no idea why my best friend was being so mean.

Then things got worse. When I got to school, Reuben, normally the sweetest boy in the universe, practically blanked me! And Lola made it offensively obvious that she wasn't interested in anything I had to say. For some reason my mates had completely gone off me. I must have done something terrible without realising.

Unfortunately I had no chance to find out what, because Mr Allbright kept us slaving away all morning. My problem would have to keep until the evening. It was Wednesday, and on Wednesday afternoons angel trainees go off to do their own thing: talk to trees, go scuba diving or whatever.

Chase, one of Reuben's weirder buddies, hangs out with the tigers in a wildlife park. Reuben spends his private study time improving his martial arts. And every Wednesday my soul-mate goes down to the beach where she sings her heart out to the wind and the waves. Lollie has a brilliant singing voice.

I used to get SO depressed on Wednesdays. It seemed as if everyone but me had some special talent. Also I *hate* being by myself. I sometimes get really scared when I'm on my own, as if I'm actually going to dissolve or disappear or something.

Then one day some little nursery-school kids found me on the seashore and took me back to school. And I discovered that I do have a talent – for hanging out with pre-school angels! I go there most weeks now to help out Miss Dove with her class.

This particular afternoon we were making a class collage of my old solar system. Everyone got stuck in, using scrumpled tissue paper, masses of shiny gold and silver stars and about a ton of glitter.

Then for the third and final time, my heavenly surroundings dropped away. *This* time all my resistance had gone. This time I longed to go where the mysterious force wanted to take me. This time the force and I were like, *one*.

I floated through the glittering void in total awe. I swooshed through pearly swirls of new-born galaxies, past silent planets crusted with ice and hot hyperactive planets spewing out rainbow-coloured gases. Finally I saw Earth far below, with its shimmery blue oceans and jewel-green forests. And then across time and space, I heard someone calling to me.

"Who are you?" I whispered. "What do you want?"

Then the cosmic elastic twanged me back to the classroom. I think I'd fainted at some point, because Miss Dove had pushed my head down between my knees and all the little angels were gazing at me with fascinated expressions. Omigosh, I'm really ill, I panicked. I've caught some rare cosmic disease that no-one ever talks about.

But Miss Dove just beamed down at me, as if my weird fainting spell was like, an Oscar-winning achievement. "It is disturbing the first time you get the Call," she said calmly. "But you get used to it."

"The Call?" I quavered.

She gave me a warm smile. "You'd better run along. The Agency will want to brief you before you leave."

I seemed to have turned into her echo. "Leave?" I repeated in bewilderment. "Where am I going?"

"Tell her, someone!" said Miss Dove.

A little boy stepped forward. "Someone on Earth needs a guardian angel, Melanie," he said shyly. "And there's absolutely NO time to lose."

CHAPTER TWO

I had been at the Angel Academy over three terms now. If I had to, I could find my way around blindfold. I was equally at home off-campus. I could tell you where to go for the ultimate breakfast (Guru, obviously), the coolest place to go dancing (the Babylon Café) and the place to find that very special outfit (the Source).

Yet I was so ignorant of the basics of angel existence, I had mistaken a natural cosmic phenomenon for like, an imaginary disease!

"You have got to finish reading that Angel Handbook, Melanie," I scolded myself, as I headed into town. "You are a total disgrace."

But I have to admit I was secretly thrilled. I have always wanted to be a guardian angel. OK, that's not strictly true. Back on Earth, I was desperate to be rich and famous. But then I died and the rich and famous scenario seemed kind of passé, and my guardian angel fantasy gradually took over. I'd never told anyone, obviously. The training takes like, aeons, and anyway, I'd look a real twit if it didn't happen. I think I might have mentioned that I was not exactly a big success at my old school? My teacher, Miss Rowntree, thought I was a complete ditz. "An airhead with attitude," she called me once.

Luckily I didn't need to worry about Miss Rowntree's opinion any more. I started to dance along the street. "I'm an angel!" I sang out. "A real, live, bona fide angel. I got the Call. Woo! I got the Call!"

I recognised a familiar figure up ahead; a honey-coloured boy in faded cut-offs. Tiny dreads whipped around his head as he hurried downtown. It's Wednesday, how come Reuben isn't doing martial arts? I thought. Then I got it!

"Hey, wait for me!" I ran to catch him up. "You got the Call, didn't you?" I panted. "That's why you were being so weird in school."

Reuben's eyes opened wide. "You mean you...?"

"I thought I was going nuts!" I admitted. "I had this spooky song going round my head."

"Hey! I'm the hotshot DJ," he objected. "Why didn't I get a song?"

"Do you think anyone else—" I began.

I heard footsteps flying along behind us. "You might have waited, you monsters!" Lola gasped.

"This is *so* sublime," I breathed. All three of us had been Called.

Lollie looked guilty. "Boo, about this morning – I'd had this weird night and I—"

"Forget it," I grinned. "Everyone stresses out the first time, Miss Dove says."

"This is happening, right? I'm not just dreaming I'm going to be a guardian angel?" Reuben was in a daze of happiness.

Lola patted his back, laughing. "It's happening, Sweetpea!"

"I can't take it in," he burbled. "I'd never even been to Earth until last term. Now I'm going solo."

My stomach totally looped the loop, and Reuben's words echoed round my brain. *Going solo, going solo...*

I mean, I was still honoured and everything. I simply hadn't expected to be doing the full-on guardian angel thing so soon. In my guardian angel fantasies I'd been calmer, and wiser and well, *older*.

We had almost reached the Agency building. In a city of gorgeous buildings it's still a major landmark; a soaring skyscraper built from some special celestial glass which constantly changes colour, almost as if it's alive. We turned the corner as the building was turning from shimmery hyacinth to a sparkling cornflower blue.

My eyes were still dazzled as I followed the others through the revolving doors. The guy at the desk waved us towards the lifts without even glancing at our ID.

"That's a first," Lola whispered.

A scary first, I thought. This is how they treat grown-up agents.

We made our way to the hall where we have our briefing sessions. To my surprise it was packed with angel trainees, including Amber, a girl from our class, and Reuben's mate Chase (the kid who hangs out with tigers). I'd been congratulating myself on breaking into some cosmic elite. But apparently angel trainees were being Called constantly. I just hadn't known about it.

Amber waved and we went to sit with her and Tiger Boy.

A bunch of junior agents came in. "Michael says sorry to keep you, but he's on his way," one said apologetically.

Chase gave me a grin. "Must be having trouble with your century again, Mel."

"There are other centuries," I said huffily.

We started chatting amongst ourselves. It turned out we'd all been freaked by our first experience of the Call.

"It just seemed way too huge," Amber confessed.

"I know," I said eagerly. "You think no-one else could understand."

Michael arrived at last and everyone instantly stopped talking. Michael is our headmaster, but if you're picturing an old buffer with elbow patches, forget it. He's an archangel, one of the advanced beings who keeps the cosmos running smoothly, plus he's a major player at the Agency.

From the outside, he's just a big tired guy in a crumpled suit. But as he scanned along the rows of trainees, his eyes met mine and I shivered with awe. Even in that crowded hall, Michael knew exactly where I was. If he wanted to, he could see right into my soul.

His voice was matter-of-fact. "No doubt you're all wondering why your teachers didn't warn you about your recent ordeal."

"Don't say it! 'Some things can't be explained in words', wah wah wah," Lola called out daringly.

Michael smiled. "Precisely. They have to be experienced. For a short time each of you felt confused and alone. You couldn't understand how such a thing could occur in Heaven. You worried that you were imagining it, or what's the phrase, 'losing it'?"

"Boy did I lose it," muttered Reuben. "I could hear creaking sails and ocean waves."

"I got thundering hooves," Lola hissed. "Anyone else get that?"

"I just got a bizarre little song," I hissed back.

There was a buzz of voices as trainees eagerly swapped strange experiences. Michael waited and eventually everyone went quiet again.

"Some of you even decided you must be in the wrong business," he went on. "After all, real angels never 'lose it'. Real angels are unfailingly beautiful, calm and serene and know all the answers. Isn't that right?"

"Well, yeah," said someone.

"Rubbish," said Michael cheerfully. "An angel who has never experienced a second's doubt, an angel who never made a mistake, or was never tempted to tell a lie, would not be suitable for guardian angel training."

I sat up. Wow, I thought, I am SO suitable!

"Your experiences were actually proof that you are ready to watch over a human being. With appropriate supervision, of course," he added, smiling.

My hands went clammy. "But this isn't like, our own personal human? I mean, we still have to work in teams, right?" I asked him.

Michael shook his head. "Guardian angels work strictly one to one."

"But you're always going on about team work," I blustered. "'No stars or heroes'. Isn't that what you're always saying?"

"That's exactly what I'm always saying," he agreed calmly. "I'm delighted it's finally sinking in."

I was not in the mood to be teased. "So – so how come you changed the rules?" I stuttered. "How come now it's about going to Earth all on your own, and babysitting some human stranger single-handed? Not to mention, ooh, protecting them from the Powers of Darkness! Frankly I don't think anyone in this hall is ready for that much responsibility." My voice was squeaky with fear.

Michael ignored my drama-queen tactics. "No-one ever feels ready," he said firmly. "Angels become ready, by taking risks, by trusting that we will receive the help we need, exactly when we need it."

I rolled my eyes. "Oh yeah, the Angel Link, how could I forget. Have you actually tried to access the Link on Earth with the PODS, erm, I mean, the Opposition, breathing down your neck?"

"Many times," he said quietly. "Which is why we're issuing you all with these."

A junior agent stepped forward. Without a hint of a smile he held up a dinky little mobile phone. In a bored voice, he began to demonstrate its various functions, which I have to admit were quite impressive. Actually having something technical to concentrate on really helped calm me down. I didn't exactly stop being scared, but my panic definitely subsided into the background.

It was early evening by the time we left the Agency Tower. We were being sent off on our separate missions early next day. None of us felt like going back to school, so we stopped off at Guru. Lola and I were too nervous to eat an actual meal, so we just ordered smoothies. But when our order came, Mo unloaded heaps of goodies from his tray.

"You'll need more than smoothies where you're going," he said firmly.

All the other customers were smiling at us and I went totally hot all over. That's the one thing about Heaven I can't get used to. Everyone knows your private business!

It didn't help that Orlando was sitting at the next table. Orlando literally looks like an angel, the dark-eyed kind you see in Italian paintings. He's also the school genius. Unfortunately I only tend to run into him when I'm breaking some major cosmic law, which doesn't exactly give a good impression.

With a little help from the boys, Lola and I managed to demolish most of Mo's tasty titbits. I was going to ask her if she fancied sharing some of Guru's special passion-fruit pud, when my surroundings flickered out of focus. I blinked but it got worse. I thought I might be getting some kind of weird angel migraine so I decided to call it a night.

"Have fun tomorrow, you guys!" I told my mates. "Miss you already," I whispered to Lola. I meant it. I felt as if part of me was drifting away from her, like a kite with a broken string.

I closed the café door and the voices and laughter faded behind me. From now on, it's just you and the cosmos, Mel, I told myself.

I heard the door open again. Someone came out and I went tingly all over. "Mind if I walk back with you?" Orlando asked.

I gave him my coolest shrug. "I don't mind."

He peered up at the sky where the sunset had left streaks of tawny gold. "Feels like trying to watch two movies at once, doesn't it?" he commented sympathetically.

I was stunned. "How did you know?"

"It's a side-effect of GA work. You've become tuned to your human's wavelength. That's how you heard the Call. Now the vibes of his or her time and place are all mixed up with your reality."

"No wonder I feel so spaced," I breathed.

With humungous concentration, I managed to

ignore my flickery visual disturbances and walk in a more or less straight line.

"So, have you done much erm, GA work?" I said, as if I habitually talked in initials.

"About four modules now."

I flashed him a cautious smile. "So if I pass this module, you know, without breaking any cosmic laws…"

"Like whacking a world-famous playwright," he grinned.

"Hey," I said. "How was I to know it was William Shakespeare? Like I was saying, if I get through the first module without a major screw-up, they'll give me tougher GA assignments, right? Is that it?"

"Why, do you think you'll like GA work?" Orlando seemed genuinely interested.

I tried to sound nonchalant. "Maybe. Ask me again when I get back."

We were walking past the Sanctuary. I glimpsed shining beings moving to and fro between the pillars. The Sanctuary angels devote their entire existence to healing. I could feel their tender vibes streaming through the twilight. It was so lovely I could have cried.

"Remember the first time you saw injured agents coming back from Earth?" Orlando said softly. "You asked me what kind of human would hurt an angel."

I'd been shocked to the core when Orlando told me about the evil forces which deliberately try to sabotage our work on Earth. The Agency refers to them as the Opposition. My mates and I just call them the PODS, short for Powers of Darkness.

"I guess I'm the type who has to learn the hard way," I said ruefully.

Orlando's eyes were gentle. "You were just innocent."

I felt a little ache of loss. "You're right. I was. Until I met Brice."

The truth is, Brice and innocence don't exactly mix. It's like, even before we met, we had this embarrassing history. He worked for the PODS, at least he used to. To complicate things, he looked exactly like this boy I used to fancy at my old school. Until you saw his eyes, which were totally empty.

I ran into him on my first ever field trip to Earth, and by complete beginner's luck, got the better of him. Unfortunately bad-boy Brice wasn't your forgive-and-forget type. Like the Demon King in a tacky pantomime, he popped up during our mission to Tudor times and gave our buddy Reuben a horrifying beating. Lola and I only just got to Reubs in time. Thanks to the Sanctuary angels, Reuben recovered from his injuries, but the memory still upset me.

"The guy's a total outlaw," I told Orlando angrily. "He isn't even a real PODS. He's an angel who changed sides. Can you believe that?"

His expression was annoyingly serene. "I heard he had his reasons."

I snorted. "Oh, please. We ran into him in the future, remember? He told us this big sob story and I wish he hadn't."

Orlando looked genuinely bewildered. "Why?"

"It's too confusing. I mean, is Brice a good guy who temporarily went bad, an evil joker pretending to be good, or just a lost little puppy who needs a home?" I tugged at my hair. "Aargh! I just want to forget about him."

Orlando has this unnerving ability to read my mind. "But you feel responsible for him at the same time," he suggested.

"I suppose," I admitted. "I mean, he sold his soul to the PODS purely to save his little brother from their evil Mafia-type family."

He succeeded too, with a bit of angelic co-operation. It's a long story, believe me. But just as Michael and everyone arrived to tie up any loose ends, Brice totally vanished. It's like he was ashamed to show his face. Obviously I hated the jerk as much as ever, but I couldn't help worrying about what would happen to him. When I tried asking Michael he just went into Yoda mode, something about taking the long-term view and trees eventually turning into diamonds.

I sighed. "Brice blew it with our Agency. He's blown it with the PODS. Where else is there?"

Orlando didn't answer and I realised we'd arrived back at my dorm.

"So erm, where are you off to now?" I said awkwardly.

Orlando looked down at his trainers and I sneaked the opportunity to admire his beautiful eyelids. "I'm due down at the Angel Watch centre."

"But that's in the complete opposite direction!"

"I know." Giving me one of his sweet enigmatic smiles, Orlando strolled off into the dark.

I stared after him wonderingly. Was it possible, after all our fights and misunderstandings, that this incredible boy actually *liked* me? A soppy smile spread over my face.

Then a chilling thought brought me back to reality. In a few hours I was going on my first GA assignment and I had absolutely nothing to wear!

I hurtled up to my room and tried out every look you can think of: streetwise, funky, cute 'n' fluffy, until my bed was totally buried under clothes. Finally I plumped for my shocking pink Kung Fu Kitty T-shirt, teamed with bootleg jeans and suede sandals. I'd created the perfect look for today's guardian angel; stylish yet girly, caring yet seriously feisty.

I knew I wouldn't be able to sleep a wink, so I perched on the edge of my chair, clutching my flight bag and listening to my headphones. "You're not alone," I sang bravely. "You're not alone."

At last the Agency limo purred into the car park. I ran down, jumped into the front – and almost had a heart attack. Michael was in the driver's seat.

"Hi," he said calmly. "I thought we could talk on the way down."

I gulped. I could only think of one reason for Michael playing chauffeur. He was going to haul me over the coals for my outburst earlier that day. "If it's about my attitude," I quavered, "I'm really—"

He shook his head. "I wanted to talk about Brice."

Yeah, well I don't, OK?

"Oh, right," I said aloud.

Michael explained that he'd managed to track down my old enemy to his obscure cosmic hideout. Since then they'd met up several times "on neutral ground", as Michael put it. I pictured the two of them sitting on some little rock out in space, the archangel and the boy with beautiful empty eyes, having some major discussion about good and evil.

To my surprise, I was OK with this. I was glad Michael was keeping an eye on Brice. That meant I totally needn't worry about him any more.

"The dilemma is, what now?" he sighed. "We knew when we accepted him into the Academy that it wasn't going to be easy. But his soul scan was outstanding, so we decided to take the long-term view."

"Oh yeah, trees and diamonds," I remembered. "Too bad it didn't work out."

I love Michael to bits as you know, but I really wasn't in the mood to play cosmic agony aunt. In a few minutes I'd be alone on Earth, with just my wits and my mobile phone for protection, and the thought made me weak at the knees.

Michael suddenly looked apologetic. "Sorry, Melanie, you'll be wanting to know where you're going."

"Well…" I began doubtfully.

Then he told me and I screamed my head off!

"Omigosh, omigosh!" I burbled. "That is so cool!"

He smiled. "It is a fascinating period. An era of massive change and contradictions. You could say it's when modern times properly began."

I was trying to take it in. I couldn't believe it. I was going to what has to be the most exciting country in the world, during its most stylish era ever – 1920s USA!

Chapter Three

It was three o'clock in the morning and I'd expected Departures to be deserted. But to my surprise hundreds of trainee GAs were milling around with their luggage.

I felt a rush of pride. We were all in this together. We had all been summoned by the same awesome cosmic force, and I felt so honoured that I kept smiling at complete strangers!

Can you believe I had to join four separate queues to pick up all my Agency stuff? My 1920s info pack, my special Agency watch, my mobile and finally my angel tags, the platinum discs we wear when we're on official Agency business.

Lola and I usually help each other fasten them, but this time I had to manage on my own. I was so nervous that I was still struggling with the clasp when the door of my portal slid shut. Al, my favourite maintenance guy, rapped on the glass and made me jump. "Ready?" he mouthed.

I gave Al and Michael a shaky thumbs-up. Next minute the portal lit up like the Fourth of July and I was catapulted out of Heaven.

I've done heaps of time-travelling since I've been at the Academy, but it's always a total miracle to witness Earth's entire history stream past in a matter of moments.

While I waited to land, I had a squint at my information pack, and discovered I was heading for the city of Philadelphia to watch over a girl called Honesty Bloomfield. I felt a happy little zing inside my heart. I just *knew* that Honesty was going to be really special. I sort of suspected she might be some kind of celebrity, like a child movie star or whatever.

Hang about, I thought, have they invented movies yet?

I riffled through my notes and was thrilled to find out that movie-making really took off in the Twenties. That's it! I thought excitedly. Honesty's this feisty girl who has dreams of being a big star, but she's from totally the wrong side of the tracks, so she needs my help to overcome her many obstacles and make her dream come true.

The colours outside the portal grew intensely clear and bright. Any minute now, I'd be touching down. I counted under my breath. Four, three, two, ONE!

With a final burst of light, the portal vanished and I found myself all alone on planet Earth.

I gazed around at the sunny silent street with its flowering cherry trees and manicured gardens and my heart sank into my suede sandals. How could they DO this to me? Everyone knows I'm a city girl. Suburbs, especially posh suburbs, are just not my style.

I squashed my negative thoughts. So what if it's the right side of the tracks, I scolded myself. Probably Honesty hates it too. Probably she's this major square peg, and you're here to help her find the courage to defy her uptight family and become an all-singing, all-dancing star of the silver screen.

This was such a cool scenario that I instantly cheered up.

My Agency watch beeped and I started to run through my landing procedure. I was just checking the prevailing thought levels, when I heard someone singing. I felt a tingle of angel electricity as I recognised the Nickelodeon tune.

Two girls were coming down the street. The younger girl was lolloping along like a playful puppy, really belting out the song, hideously off-key. Her sister was peering at a book through a pair of owlish spectacles, reading as she walked. They both wore dowdy school uniforms with hems trailing around their ankles and round felt hats like pork pies.

For the first time I got a good look at the first girl and felt the strangest chime inside my heart, as if two pieces of a puzzle had finally come together. At least, that's how the angel me was feeling. My inner bimbo was like, yippee! It's my future film star!

Honesty unfastened some white gates and gave her sister a nudge. "Rose," she prompted. "We're back."

"Uh-huh," mumbled Rose. She trudged up the drive, still reading, and Honesty lolloped happily after her.

They were heading for the grandest house in the

street. It was one of those painted clapboard houses with a front porch, and it had a huge garden. I'm talking swimming pool and tennis courts, that kind of huge. Piano music was pouring from a downstairs window.

At this point, my angel self was going, it's not Honesty's fault she was born into a humungously rich family, she could still be a really worthwhile person! But a doubting voice said – if she's got so much going for her, why would she need me?

Honesty opened the front door and Rose headed upstairs still reading, apparently finding her way by some kind of personal radar.

Honesty dumped her school bag down in the hall. She went bounding into a front parlour where a woman was playing the piano with a far-away expression. Honesty called to her over the torrent of sound. "Hi, Mama. I'm home."

The music stopped. "Well, hi, sweetheart!"

Honesty's mum was exceptionally pretty, with her fair hair swept up in smooth coils. She held out her arms and Honesty walked into them.

"How was your day, sugar?" Her mum's voice had a smoky southern lilt, like Scarlett in that old film *Gone with the Wind*.

"OK, I guess. Only got a B+ in my maths test though."

I stared at her. Only got a B+! I personally am ecstatic if I get a C!

"Never mind, sugar," said her mum. "Everyone has off days." Her fingers strayed towards the piano keys, and I could tell she was dying to continue playing. "Why don't you run and ask Cissie to get you some milk and cookies?" she suggested.

Oh, wha-at! I thought. These people have servants!

Honesty hovered as if she had something on her mind. "Mama, did Papa say any more about buying a car? Every time I ask him, he says he's thinking about it. I don't understand what there is to think about. It's not like we don't have the money!"

Her mother gave a husky laugh. "Sweetheart, men are like mules. They won't budge unless they think it's all their own idea. Give him a few more weeks and he'll come round, I swear."

"It's not fair," Honesty complained. "We're the only kids in Philadelphia whose father is still stuck in the nineteenth century."

"Honesty, that's enough," said her mother firmly. "Your father is the hardest-working, biggest-hearted man I know and I will not allow you to criticise him this way."

Honesty turned bright red. "Sorry, Mama."

"You run and get those cookies," smiled her mum. "Dinner might be late tonight."

Honesty clomped off down the corridor, clearly annoyed at not getting her own way. I followed, sniffing the air. Mmnn, vanilla and cinnamon, my all-time favourite aromas!

In the kitchen, trays of newly baked cookies were cooling by an open window. A tall black woman was helping a curly-haired little boy cut circles from leftover dough. There was a flour smudge on his nose and the tip of his tongue stuck out while he worked. I grinned. He looked just like my little sister does when she's concentrating.

The kitchen was pretty and homey in a retro kind of way, with its gleaming pots and pans, an old-fashioned range and a low sink with a scrubbed wooden draining board. A corner of the kitchen was occupied by a monster refrigerator. I had the feeling fridges were like, the latest hi-tech invention.

The little boy suddenly caught sight of Honesty. His face lit up. "You're home! I baked cookies for you, look!" He peered anxiously at the lumpy grey shapes on his baking tray. "Cissie says they'll look better when they're cooked, didn't you Cissie?"

She grinned. "They're fine, Clem honey. You want me to finish these off for you?"

"OK," Clem said promptly. He slipped off his chair and ran to bury his face in his sister's stomach. "I missed you, sis," he said happily.

"Quit it, Clem," Honesty complained. "You're getting flour over me. Anyway, little boys don't do baking. That's for little girls."

I understood exactly why Honesty was being so mean. She hadn't got her own way about the car, so now she was taking it out on Clem. And I know it's not very angelic, but when I saw her brother's hurt little face, I wanted to smack her one. Doesn't this girl know how lucky she is? I fumed. Doesn't she realise some kids would kill to be in her position?

I'm not saying I wanted to actually like, *be* Honesty, being welcomed home by a piano-playing mother, a cookie-baking maid and a cute little brother. It was *my* family I wanted. My mum and my funny little sister Jade and my lovely step-dad, Des. What I missed was being human and alive.

But I couldn't exactly criticise Honesty, because

when I lived on Earth I was just the same. There was always that mysterious missing 'something' which stopped my life being perfect. That gorgeous little skirt from Top Shop, or a must-have CD.

It's agony seeing someone make the same mistakes you made, so I took myself off to explore the rest of the house.

The minute I was alone again, it struck me that Honesty's house had a really unusual atmosphere, intensely sweet and peaceful. It might sound stupid, but I felt as if the house was *waiting* for something. The feeling was disturbingly familiar, but though I racked my brains, I couldn't seem to remember why.

I passed through the parlour where Honesty's mum was still playing her Beethoven or whatever. There was a vase of lilacs on the piano. I stopped to breathe in their gorgeous scent and noticed a photograph of Honesty's parents' wedding day. *Aah*, I thought. They both looked desperately young and nervous and totally head over heels in love.

There was a fancy studio portrait of an older boy I guessed to be Honesty's big brother. Mmn! I thought approvingly. Definitely inherited his daddy's looks.

I flitted invisibly up the huge staircase and went into the girls' bedroom, where Rose sat on her bed, glued to her book.

I peeped over her shoulder. What's got her so gripped? I thought. A fruity love story? A juicy diary? But Rose's reading material totally took me by surprise. It was all about ancient Egypt; old tombs and mummies' curses, pure Indiana Jones! I was so impressed!

I roamed around the girls' bedroom, nosing into cupboards and peering at shelves. I told myself that I was not snooping, but simply gathering information. Somewhere in this room was the evidence which revealed Honesty's secret intention of breaking out of the 'burbs and into international filmstardom.

Except that it wasn't. My search revealed precisely *nada*. No tap shoes, sheet music or inspiring movie posters. And the dreary garments in Honesty's wardrobe betrayed no hint of a creative spirit trying to break free.

You'd think she'd have *one* little drop-waisted Charleston dress, I thought crossly.

I heard a metallic jangle somewhere in the house, and Honesty's mum started talking to someone. I got the feeling she was incredibly excited about something, because her intonation became heaps more southern.

I sighed. I had now inspected all Honesty's worldly possessions, except for a stash of notebooks at the back of a drawer. To judge from the threats on the covers (KEEP YOUR NOSE OUT OF MY STUFF OR YOU'LL DIE IN AGONY. YES, ROSE BLOOMFIELD, THAT MEANS YOU!), they were Honesty's journals and there was no way I was stooping to read someone's secret diaries, thank you very much.

I was now officially flummoxed. I had no idea what a real guardian angel would do next. I thought of calling the GA helpline and asking for tips, but I'd only just got here. So I settled down at a little old-fashioned bureau, dug out my fact pack and did some research.

I found out that only a few years ago the First World War was blasting the old world to smithereens. The western world had witnessed too much horror and people couldn't handle it. You can't exactly blame them. They didn't want to feel guilty for surviving when so many millions had died. They didn't want to know how terrible humans could be to each other. They wanted to forget all that. They wanted to have fun. So when the Twenties arrived, everyone went crazy. Good girls hacked off their hems, painted their faces and turned into bad but gorgeous flappers. People danced for days without sleeping, and held mad competitions like who could shove the most sticks of gum in their mouths, or swallow the most live goldfish. In America this urgent need to party was complicated by something called the prohibition law. In other words, alcohol was basically banned. Of course, this only made people more desperate to get hold of it.

If I shut my eyes, I could actually feel that frantic glittery Twenties spirit, surfing on a sea of darkness and chaos. I'd always imagined the Twenties to be like one long frothy bubble bath. I'd never thought about the deadly PODS vibes under the froth. Omigosh, the poor things, I thought. They're all living for the moment like beautiful butterflies.

And then I thought, yeah, right, butterflies! In Hollywood maybe. But I was stuck in some stodgy Philadelphia suburb with a little diary-keeping rich girl who, let's face it, was not ideal butterfly material.

I heard footsteps pounding upstairs. Honesty burst in, her face blazing with excitement. "Rose! You'll never guess what happened. Papa just called Mama on the telephone, and—"

"And obviously you eavesdropped," said Rose drily.

"Rose! I'm telling you the most thrilling news since the invention of moving pictures! He's actually gone and bought—"

Rose jumped up so fast, her little spectacles actually fell off her nose. "I don't believe it!" she shrieked. "Papa's bought a car!"

"He's on his way to pick it up. He's driving it home!"

The girls threw their arms around each other, squealing happily.

I wanted to be thrilled for them, but the strange sweet vibe was growing steadily more intense and I was having my two-movies-at-once sensation again. Something was happening to someone in this family. I could feel it with every one of my angel senses.

"You have to pretend to be surprised," Honesty was saying. "Daddy will be so disappointed if we don't act surprised."

"Act! I won't have to act!" laughed Rose. "I'm ecstatic."

Honesty flew over to an old-fashioned gramophone with a shiny brass horn and cranked a handle. A scratchy voice floated out of the horn. "Put another nickel in, in the Nickelodeon." This was obviously their fave tune of the moment.

The girls started dancing the Charleston, flouncing their skirts and showing their big white knickers. Clem and Cissie rushed in to see what on earth was going on. Honesty grabbed her brother and whirled him round the room. Rose grabbed Cissie, and instead of being annoyed, Cissie kicked up her heels and did this wicked little dance step.

When movie characters get over-excited like this, something terrible always happens. But I tried to tell myself that this was real life, not Hollywood. There was no reason the Bloomfields couldn't live happily ever after. But by this time, I think I'd sussed that 'happy ever after' was not an option.

As the tragedy inched closer, I felt an invisible cosmic gateway opening. The sweetness grew unbearably beautiful and I suddenly knew when I'd felt it before. It was during my last day on Earth, as

angels gathered like invisible birds to guide me
back to Heaven.

I knew then that someone was going to die. I'd
got here just in time to see Honesty's old world
blown to smithereens. And there was nothing I
could do about it.

CHAPTER FOUR

The girls cracked car jokes right up to dinner time. How Mr Bloomfield was so old-fashioned he was probably still figuring out how to hitch the new Model A Ford to the horse, or how he was so thrilled with his new toy, he'd gone for a spin via the Rockies on his way home.

But when eight o'clock came and went and he still failed to appear, the atmosphere started getting strained.

"You'd better dish up, Cissie," said Honesty's mum.

But no-one could manage to eat Cissie's good roast chicken and mashed potatoes, and in the end she took the food away, shaking her head.

I found their reactions slightly surprising. My step-dad could have been like, five hours late and no-one would have raised an eyebrow. Des is the world's worst timekeeper. Mum used to say he operated on 'Desmond time'. But I got the feeling that if Mr Bloomfield said he'd be back by eight, then he was back.

It was dark when the police car drove up. Two grim-faced cops came to the door and Cissie showed them into the parlour. The children clustered around their mother. Clem was shivering like a puppy. He knew something terrible had happened.

They'd sent a young cop and an old cop, just like in the movies. The young guy was looking everywhere but at the Bloomfields. The old cop cleared his throat. "Mrs Grace Bloomfield, I'm sorry to have to—"

Rose burst into tears. Honesty went white and ran out of the room.

In those days, they didn't make you take a test before they let you loose on the road. Drivers just picked up the necessary know-how as they tootled along in the traffic. Sadly, Honesty's father never got the chance. He hit a truck ten minutes after he left the Ford garage. The cops said he died instantly.

Honesty's mother roamed around the house all that night, sick with grief. Once she came into the girls' room in her nightdress and watched them as they lay sleeping. But that was the one and only time I saw Grace Bloomfield lose control. When she came down to breakfast next morning, she was deathly pale but totally composed. "I can get through this so long as I don't let myself think," I heard her tell Cissie.

"That's right, Mizz Grace," agreed Cissie. "You got your whole life for thinking. Right now, you got to survive."

I'd spent the night radiating angelic vibes to everyone in the household. In my opinion the entire family needed heavenly support.

Later I wondered if I'd got it wrong. If I'd concentrated on Honesty like I was supposed to, I might have been quicker to spot the signs. That first day when she came down to breakfast and said in a toneless voice, "Oh, great, waffles!" – that wasn't normal, but I refused to see it.

Rose had been crying so hard, her face looked as if it had been stung by swarms of bees. And Clem clung to his mama's skirts as if he was terrified she'd be next to disappear. But Honesty heaped her plate with ham, eggs, and hash browns, drenched her waffles with maple syrup, shovelled it all down like a zombie, and said, "See you later," and pushed back her chair.

Rose peered out between her swollen eyelids. "What are you doing?"

"Going to school," said Honesty in her new zombie voice. "Same as usual."

Her mother put her arms around her. "That's very brave, sugar, but you don't have to go to school today…"

Honesty wriggled free. "I do. I've got a test in Geography."

Grace stood firm. But by the end of the day, I bet she wished she'd let Honesty take her stupid test after all, because she was a complete nightmare.

When Honesty heard that her brother Lenny was coming back from medical school for the funeral, she just said, "Great. We've got to share the house with Lenny's stinky socks." Rose said they'd have to go into town to buy clothes for the funeral and

Honesty snapped, "You can dress like a Sicilian widow if you want to. It's not like Papa's going to care. When you're dead you're dead."

Honesty had had a total personality change. She was hardly recognisable as the sweet goofy girl who hugged her mum, yelled at her baby brother and flaunted her big knickers dancing the Charleston.

And there was another thing. When I first met Honesty, her thoughts were so easy to read, she might as well as have yelled them through a megaphone. But now she was putting out no thoughtwaves whatsoever.

Lenny came home for the funeral and everyone else rushed to the door to meet him. They cried and hugged each other and generally behaved like human beings. But Honesty didn't even bother to come downstairs.

When the family met up for the evening meal, Lenny tried to put his arms around her, but she pulled away. "People die every day, you know," she said coldly. "You don't have to make a big production out of it."

That night I took my mobile out of my flight bag. I got as far as punching in the GA code. Then I thought, I'll give it until after the funeral. Then she'll start to grieve properly and she'll be really sad but basically OK.

Honesty's dad must have been well respected in Philadelphia, because absolutely loads of people came to the funeral. Though I didn't see any members of their families as such, like cousins or grandparents. It was more business associates with their wives.

Grace kept glancing anxiously round the church as if someone important was missing.

I heard Lenny whisper, "Probably he's sick."

"Then why didn't he call?" Grace whispered back. "He didn't even send flowers. He's meant to be his best friend for heaven's sake."

Honesty had this annoying nervous smirk on her face.

Finally Rose couldn't stand it. "What's so funny?" she asked.

Honesty shrugged. "I was wondering what Papa would make of being buried in a church."

Rose hissed, "You know Papa didn't care about all that stuff."

Honesty gave her a poisonous look. "We don't know any such thing *actually*, Rose Bloomfield. Papa's ancestors must be turning in their graves."

She made it sound as if her father was a vampire or something. Funeral or no funeral, this girl is getting too weird, I thought uneasily.

After the funeral, Grace invited all the mourners back to the house. Everyone stood around the front parlour, making agonising small talk.

I noticed Grace was still watching the door. I heard her ask Lenny, "Did you try Jack Coltraine's number again?"

He nodded. "Still no reply."

This news seemed to worry Grace. "I'd appreciate it if you could just keep trying, will you?"

"Of course, Mama," he said.

Jack Coltraine never did pick up the phone. That's because he had taken off for Havana with all Honesty's father's money. Next day, the family lawyer confirmed Grace's worst suspicions. Jack had been creaming off the business profits, stashing them in safety deposit boxes in his wife's name. In a matter of days, the Bloomfields' lives had totally turned upside down. They'd lost everything, including their home. All Grace stood to inherit now was her husband's debts.

That night Lenny came into the girls' room and I heard him and Rose talking. Honesty stayed huddled silently under her covers, giving off such minimal vibes, I don't think they even remembered she was there.

I was shocked to hear Lenny say, "I'll really miss Papa, but in a weird way it's set me free. Being a doctor was his dream, not mine."

"So what's yours, Len?" Rose's voice was still snuffly from crying.

"Don't laugh," he said awkwardly. "I want to be a stuntman. I met this actor on the train. He said there are great opportunities in the film industry for young guys like me, who aren't afraid to take risks."

Rose was disgusted. "You've had this expensive education and you want to throw it all away just so you can fall off horses and get brain damage! Have you any idea how lucky you are to be a boy? I'd do anything to go to college. But I'm a girl, so everyone assumes I'll just marry a nice doctor. Aargh!"

"You won't have to get married for years yet. I'm sure Papa would want you girls to finish your education."

Rose gave him a bleak smile. "Nice theory, Len. Where's the money coming from?"

"I think Mama should ask her family for help. They own some big plantation in the south, don't they? They must have loads of dough."

Rose shook her head. "Mama's family is a taboo subject. Remember how she used to clam up when we asked about them?"

"I know, but it's the best I can think of," Lenny said miserably.

But the next day, to their astonishment, Grace brought the subject up herself.

"I have reached a very difficult decision. I have been lying awake, racking my brains, and I can *not* see an alternative. I have a little jewellery, enough to buy train tickets with some over for emergencies."

"Mama," said Rose. "What are you talking about?"

Grace seemed to be talking to herself. "I was so young when I left home. People can change. Whatever happened, you're still his flesh and blood. I'm sure when your grandaddy actually sees you, he'll want to help. We'll pack a few necessities, and the lawyers can see to the rest."

I noticed Honesty slip out of the room while her mother was still talking. I hurried after her and found her in her bedroom removing her diaries from the drawer.

She tore the pages from the notebooks, stuffed them into the tiny fireplace and dropped a lighted match into the grate. When her diaries were reduced to a heap of curling black ash, Honesty lifted down a suitcase from the top of the wardrobe and started to pack.

She folded bloomers, chemises, blouses and pinafores; put them into her case and carefully fastened both catches. Then she put on her horrible coat and hat, seated herself on a hard wooden chair and stayed there, staring into space, until the taxi came and the Bloomfields left their home for ever.

I left with them, so I saw that Honesty didn't once look back. She just stared straight ahead, humming tunelessly. I knew then that this was going to be the toughest assignment of my angelic career.

CHAPTER FIVE

In Honesty's day, a first-class train carriage looked exactly like your great granny's front parlour, right down to the tablecloth with fancy fringes. They look cute in movies, but in reality they ponged of dust and coal fumes and men's cigars, not to mention human sweat. People weren't too big on personal hygiene back then.

After he'd stashed everyone's luggage, Lenny went into the corridor. He pulled down the window and watched the Philadelphia skyline disappearing into the distance.

Grace had brought a pack of cards and started to build a house for Clem. Rose was curled up in a corner seat, reading as usual. Honesty stared at her fingernails, then muttered, "I'm going to get a soda."

I hurried after her along the swaying corridor. The soda was just an excuse, because Honesty walked right through the dining car and out the other side. These carriages were crowded with tired men and women sitting on hard benches instead of plushy upholstery, and there were ratty cardboard suitcases on the luggage racks instead of leather.

I was surprised to feel my skin prickling like crazy. This usually means there are other angels in the vicinity. Sure enough, two carriages down, I spotted that giveaway cosmic glow. An earth angel was sitting calmly amongst the paying passengers. She wore a shabby Twenties coat and a cute little cloche hat trimmed with a faded silk rose. I felt so proud of my profession, I can't tell you. The humans had no idea they were sharing their railway carriage with an invisible celestial agent, but from their peaceful expressions I knew they were responding to her angelic vibes.

The angel and I gave each other a brief wave, one agent to another. Then I hurtled breathlessly after Honesty.

Our train shook and juddered as another train roared past. There was a flash of fire, and I glimpsed the driver furiously stoking the boiler. Steam billowed past the windows, like special FX on pop videos.

I heard snatches of talk from the passengers. An old man was complaining, "You know the thing about America? Everyone is always rushing someplace else." And I heard a salesman boasting, "Nowadays it's not enough to sell sausages. You got to sell the *sizzle* too!"

In the last carriage, tough-looking hoodlums in slouch hats were playing cards. Honesty stood watching until one of them noticed her and said humorously, "Beat it, kid. Didn't your mama tell you gambling was wrong?"

Honesty rolled her eyes. "I'm just watching. Anyway, what my mama doesn't know won't hurt her."

He made her a mocking bow. "Step inside, sister."

The old Honesty wouldn't dream of behaving like this, but the new Honesty seemed determined to walk on the wild side. Occasionally, the guys passed around a brown paper bag, and took swigs from a bottle concealed inside. They jokingly offered it to Honesty, but she said coldly, "Haven't you heard? That stuff is illegal."

"I was just going to send Lenny to look for you. What took you so long?" Grace asked her when we returned.

"I was talking to some interesting people for a change," Honesty said rudely. "You don't think I'm going to stay cooped up in here all the way to Georgia, do you?"

After lunch, Honesty went to sleep and I watched the vast landscape flow past. Occasionally a shabby little railroad town flew by. Ragged kids waved from the fields. Clearly our train was the big event of their day.

For no apparent reason the train began to slow down and eventually came to a standstill. At first, I thought we'd stopped beside some kind of massive garbage dump. Then I saw it was a little hobo town, a settlement of tumbledown shacks and improvised tents that had grown up beside the tracks. A couple of guys were having an argument. An older guy was slumped by a camp fire with his head in his hands. I could see his toes sticking through the broken ends of his boots. Dirty little kids ran around half naked, despite the cold. One of them was still just a baby. A woman was stirring a pot over the fire. She was so thin her clothes hung off her shoulders like a sack. Desperate feelings welled up inside me. The kind that make you go, "Why bother? This life is just too hard."

Fortunately, I'm an angel, so I soon sussed that these weren't my personal feelings. They weren't anyone's personal feelings, in fact. Originally they were probably an evil freebie from the PODS. Now deadly PODS vibes hung over the makeshift settlement like fog, and the wretched inhabitants had no choice but to inhale and exhale them with every breath. The PODS really have some sick strategies for making humans do their work for them.

The baby toddled up to the woman and pulled at her skirts. The train gave its mournful wail and she picked up the baby and turned to gaze at us as we moved off, as if all her hopes and dreams were leaving on our train.

As the train gathered speed, I did something I should have done days ago. I got out my Agency mobile and called up the GA helpline.

I couldn't help smiling as I waited for someone to pick up. It would be so cool to say, "Hi, it's me, I'm on a train!" Then I heard the helpline worker's voice and went hot to the roots of my hair.

"Finally!" said Orlando. "We've been expecting you to call for days."

Did it have to be him? I thought. Couldn't I just once talk to Orlando when everything is going well?

I reminded myself that I was a bona fide celestial trouble-shooter, and calmly updated Orlando on everything that had happened.

"I sit up all night, beaming her vibes," I finished up. "But nothing seems to get through. She's totally locked inside herself and I'm scared she's going to do something stupid."

"You think she's a suicide risk?" he asked.

I felt a stab of worry. "I don't think she'd deliberately—"

Rose dropped her book with a crash. I saw that people were running out into the corridor. I looked to see what had got everyone so excited and gave an unprofessional shriek. "Yikes! I've got to go!"

Thundering down a hillside towards us were hordes of Indian braves. As I reached the corridor, a mob of cowboys came galloping from behind the trees and they started having this major shoot-out. Horses reared and cowboys and Indians fell sprawling on the ground in horrifically gruesome positions.

This is terrible! I thought. People are killing each other, and I'm the only angel in the area. I must do something!

Then an old truck came in sight with an old-fashioned movie camera on the top and I went limp with relief.

A tubby little man got out of the truck. He started bellowing through a megaphone and suddenly the whole scene rewound itself. All the dead horses, cowboys and Indians miraculously came back to life and went scrambling back to their original positions, and the truck reversed madly out of the shot.

I felt like *such* a ditz. I could see now that the braves were nothing like real-life Native Americans, just white stuntmen in crude costumes and make-up.

The other passengers went back to their seats, but Lenny couldn't seem to move. He stayed glued to the train window until the actors were microscopic dots. Then he leaned his forehead on the dirty glass and closed his eyes, as if he was replaying the stuntmen's cheesy death throes in his mind.

The train tracks curved and divided and began to run along beside a river, a river that was totally unlike any I'd ever seen in England. It was vast, like the sea. Huge steamers chugged along like floating palaces, their paddles churning up the muddy river water. I've never seen anything so romantic as those riverboats. Their glitzy big-hearted names sounded like song lyrics to me: *Delta Queen*, *Heart of Georgia*, *Memphis Belle*...

The sun had started to set, and a path of gold and crimson rippled across the surface of the water. Honesty's mother pulled down the window, letting in the hot, damp, sweet-smelling air. From the expression on her face, I knew we had reached the south. Grace seemed delighted to be back in her home state – but I could sense the tension underneath, as if she secretly dreaded meeting her parents again after so many years.

My mobile went off in my bag. It was Orlando checking if everything was OK. I explained sheepishly about the shoot-out being a movie stunt, and he said, "What's that in the background?"

The train had just let out one of its plaintive wails, so I said, "You mean the train?"

"No, the music."

"Oh, it's some guys on a riverboat playing jazz." I held the phone up to the window so he could hear.

"Wish I was there," he said. "It sounds amazing."

I gazed out at the boat chugging past in the southern dusk. Suddenly its decks lit up with hundreds of tiny fairy lights. And I said softly, "It is so sublime you would not believe..."

Next morning the sun rose over cotton fields. It was barely dawn, and already sweating black men and women were working among the rows of fluffy cotton plants. A look of strain came over Grace's face.

Lenny and Rose were in the corridor talking in low voices. Rose looked upset so I went out to see what was going on.

"I'll make sure you get there safely, then I'm going to find those film makers and make them give me a job. I'm going to get into the movie business, Rose." Lenny sounded desperate. "You see if I don't. I'm a man. It's time I made my way in the world."

She gave a bitter little laugh. "A big man, playing cowboys! Bang bang you're dead! Oh, a really big man!"

I could see she was trying not to cry. Lenny said earnestly, "Rosie, we're not so different. You're crazy about the past. Well, I'm just as crazy about modern times. Movies are where it's all happening. I've got to do it, sis!"

And Rose sniffed bravely and patted his back and said, "It's OK, Len. It's OK. We'll be OK."

Lenny kept his word. He came with them to the gates of the fine old plantation house where Honesty's mother had been born and brought up, then he hugged them all.

Everyone else watched forlornly as Lenny trudged back down the road in the shimmering noonday heat. But Honesty kept her head down, kicking sullenly at the dirt.

Grace took a deep breath. "Let's go meet your grandaddy," she said to Clem. "See if time has improved the old buzzard any."

And then she gasped, "Oh, my stars, it's Isaac!"

A barefoot black man with tufts of silver in his hair was coming down the porch steps. He looked as if he couldn't believe his eyes. "Mizz Grace?"

Grace ran and threw her arms around him. "Isaac, I have missed you SO much!" Both of them had tears on their faces. "So how's Celestine?" she said eagerly.

Isaac's voice was so sorrowful, he almost seemed to be singing. "She passed, Mizz Grace. She passed. It's just me and the children now." He tried to smile. "Got me eight little grandbabies, can you believe that? Two of the girls work for your mama and daddy." He yelled into the house. "Dorcas, come out here." And Isaac's granddaughter came running out.

In my opinion, she was way too young to be working as anyone's maid, but apparently they did things differently down here. Dorcas was wearing a prim white cap and apron, but like Isaac she didn't seem to have any shoes.

"Mizz Grace is back," Isaac told her. His granddaughter gasped and a look passed between them. I thought, uh-oh.

Dorcas showed Grace and her children to a sunny terrace where Grace's parents were having breakfast.

Grace said nervously, "Hello Mama, Daddy."

There was a moment when any normal parent would have jumped up and hugged their long lost child, but there was just this electric silence. Then her father dabbed his mouth with a napkin and said, "Why Grace, this is most unexpected. What brings you here?"

Honesty stepped forward. "If you must know, my papa got hit by a truck," she said in her zombie voice. "And his sleazeball partner vamoosed with all Mama's money."

Rose looked appalled. "Honesty, for Heaven's sake."

"But that *is* why we're here," she said, all innocent. "You don't think we'd be sponging off our rich relations if we had a choice?"

Grace gave Honesty a look which would have reduced any normal child to a quivering jelly. "Please forgive my daughter," she said quietly. "This is not an easy time for us."

Her father ignored her and turned to Rose. Suddenly he was all folksy southern charm. "So what's your name, pumpkin?"

"She's Rose," piped Clem. "I'm Clem and this is Honesty."

"And honesty is obviously a quality dear to your sister's heart," said their grandfather, as if Honesty was invisible. "But when she grows a little wiser, I hope she will also learn the value of simple southern courtesy."

Grace's mother tinkled a bell and Dorcas ran in and bobbed a scared curtsey. Someone ought to tell these old relics that slavery's over, I thought angrily.

"Get my grandchildren's room ready," Grace's mother drawled. "They can have Miss Grace's old room for now."

Rose looked puzzled. "But where will Mama sleep?"

"We'll talk about that later, dear." Their grandmother dingled the bell again and an even younger maid rushed in. "Take my grandchildren upstairs and run their baths," she said in that same languid tone. "They want to freshen up after their long journey."

The children reluctantly followed the maid into the house. Something felt distinctly off, so I thought I'd better stay with Grace and find out what was going on.

It's a good thing I did. As soon as Grace was alone with her parents, her father said coldly, "I'm sure you understand that it is quite impossible for you to stay here." He made it sound as if this was a reasonable thing to say to your own daughter.

Grace looked as if he'd struck her. "You're sending us away?"

"Just you, Grace," he said in the same cold

reasonable voice. "The children can stay."

Grace opened her mouth but couldn't seem to find her voice.

"It's not as if they look Jewish," Grace's mother said brightly. "No-one need ever know."

Oh, no *way*, I thought incredulously. No wonder she never came back home. These old monsters disapproved of Grace for marrying a Jew!

"I suggest you leave tonight, after the children are in bed," her father went on. "That way you'll avoid distressing them with overly emotional farewells."

Grace was breathing fast. "*Avoid* distressing them? My children have already lost their father, you can't possibly—"

Her father talked over her. "We'll simply tell everyone that you and the unfortunate Mr Bloomfield died in the same tragic car wreck." He opened a drawer and pulled out a cheque book. "Don't worry, I'm not sending you away penniless."

"We can give them so many advantages, you see," wittered her mother. "Education, money, breeding."

"Yes, everything, Mama," Grace whispered.

"Yeah, right," I muttered angrily. "Everything but love."

Personally, I'd have just emptied the pitcher of orange juice over their heads, ice cubes and all. Grace was normally a very strong-minded woman, but now she was back in her childhood home, all the fight had suddenly gone out of her. She'd lost faith in herself, and now she was starting to believe their poisonous lies.

That evening Grace came to kiss her children goodnight.

Honesty said pleadingly, "Mama, I don't like it here. Can we leave in the morning?"

She said it in her real voice, not the zombie one, but Grace didn't seem to hear. Actually Honesty's mother sounded like a sleepwalker herself. "It's bound to be strange at first, sugar, but you know your grandaddy can give you all a great deal."

"I've seen what he can give me, Mama," said Honesty, "and I would personally prefer to have rabies." And she pulled the covers over her head.

On an unconscious level, Grace's children totally sussed that their mother was planning to leave them. But they didn't know it for sure, so they couldn't beg her to stay. There was just all this silent agony going on. I beamed angel vibes at that family like crazy, but despite all my efforts, Grace Bloomfield crept out of the house about an hour later.

I know Clem felt her go because he immediately woke up and started to cry. Rose took him into bed with her. Without a word, Honesty climbed in beside him, and the three children huddled like orphans in Rose's king-sized bed. Eventually Clem went back to sleep still quivering with sobs. But both the sisters lay awake under the slowly rotating blades of the ceiling fan, completely unable to mention that their sole surviving parent had just left them for ever.

I was desperately concerned for Honesty. If her father's death had turned her into a zombie, then losing her mum would probably tip Honesty right over the edge.

I groped in my flight bag, trying to find my mobile – and then I noticed some branches outside the window starting to shake. The window creaked open and someone climbed over the sill.

I heard a soft laugh. "I used to climb up and down that old magnolia all the time. Papa would lock me in and I'd be out of this window and cycling off to meet some boy, before he'd even reached the foot of our stairs."

Rose snapped on the light. "Mama? Have you gone crazy?" she said shakily. Clem sat up rubbing his eyes.

"No, sugar, I have just regained my sanity," said Grace. "I got as far as the crossroads, then I said to myself, 'Grace, those old dinosaurs have got you hopelessly confused, just like they always did. You know you can't live without those precious babies. Now go and get them out of there'."

She gathered her children into her arms and Clem clung to her tearfully.

"Mama, how will we manage?" said Rose anxiously.

Grace seemed to have it all worked out. "Remember my cousin, Louella, in San Francisco?"

"The one who was mixed up in that big scandal!" Rose sounded shocked.

"I admit that Louella is a law unto herself," said Grace. "But she runs a successful dressmaking business and I'm sure she'll give me a job. Will you take your chance and come to California with me?" Her voice faltered. "Unless you'd rather—"

Rose flung her arms around her mother. "Of

course we're coming with you, Mama!"

Clem's eyes went wide. "We're going to California – without Lenny?"

Grace gave him a hug. "Your brother's a smart boy. He'll find us when he wants to."

The children scrambled into their clothes. Grace climbed out of the window first and they tossed down their bags to her. Clem slithered down the magnolia like a little monkey and Grace caught him at the bottom. Rose and Honesty went next, then me.

In the darkness the smell of magnolias was suddenly overpowering. The night was shrill with crickets, sounding exactly like tinny wind-up music boxes.

I saw Isaac watching from a shadowy veranda as Grace and her children crept around the side of the house. He didn't say anything but I sensed he'd known all along that his Miss Grace wouldn't abandon her babies. Actually I got the feeling Isaac knew too much about what went on in this family. So much he could hardly sleep at nights, just sat up in his creaky old rocker, looking at the stars and humming softly to himself.

Chapter Six

On bad days we walked. On good days we hitched a ride in the back of some farmer's truck or rickety horse-drawn wagon. Most days we did a bit of both. Just once, the Bloomfields accepted a lift in a shiny new Model A Ford. But after five minutes Grace had to ask the driver to stop. They barely got out in time before Honesty spewed her lunch everywhere. I wasn't totally surprised. She'd turned white as chalk the moment the driver pulled up. Being Honesty, she denied that her travel sickness was in any way connected with her father's accident, just as she denied that she screamed out in her sleep night after night. But I think Grace knew the real reason, because after that the family stuck purely to wagons and pick-ups.

But one sweltering afternoon, Clem was too tired to walk, and no-one had the energy to carry him. So Grace and the children waited in the lengthening shadows of some lime trees, in the hope they'd get a lift to the next town. But no vehicles passed.

The first stars were coming out as a horse-drawn farm wagon pulled up. A young black guy looked down at them. He seemed oddly alarmed to see the family standing there in the dark. He glanced around. "I'm bettin' you ain't from around these parts," he said in a low voice. "Else you'd know it's dangerous to be out here after sundown."

I could feel pure physical fear pulsing off him. Omigosh, I thought. They must have some southern serial killer round here or something.

Then I got it. This man wasn't scared of some mad axe murderer. He was scared of Grace. He was terrified that someone would see him talking to a white lady and jump to the wrong conclusion. On the other hand, he felt totally unable to leave her and her kids stranded out in the sticks at the mercy of any passing local nutter.

"I'd better take you folks into Bournville. Better hide yourselves in the back though," he added in a humorous voice. "Won't do your reputation no good to be seen with a negro."

I saw him wonder if he'd gone too far. But Grace gave him one of her warm smiles. "I think our reputation can stand it," she told him. "But the back of the wagon will suit us just fine."

For over an hour we bumped over potholes in the dark, which gave me plenty of time to digest what had just happened. I don't mind telling you, I was finding racial attitudes in the American south of the Twenties deeply bewildering. I mean, slavery had been made illegal here like, decades ago, yet this guy clearly expected nothing but trouble from mixing with whites.

The man stopped his horses on the edge of town. He came round to the back, holding up a storm lantern. "Where you folks headed?"

"California," said Clem, blinking in the sudden light.

"I meant where you stopping tonight?" he asked Grace.

"I have no idea!" She saw the man's concerned expression and laughed. "We'll be fine. We always are. Erm, thank you for the lift, Mr...?"

The guy looked startled. I could tell he wasn't used to white people calling him mister. "Glass," he said. "The name's Nathan Glass."

"Are we at California yet?" Clem whimpered.

Nathan sighed and I could see him wondering what he'd got himself into. "Guess I'd better take you to Peaches' place," he said reluctantly. "That's if you don't mind walking some?"

I could see Clem droop at the very thought. Nathan handed the lantern to Rose. "But you can ride, little man!" He swung Clem up on to his shoulders, laughing, then took back his lantern.

We followed him across a field and into the woods. If it hadn't been for Nathan's lantern it would have been pitch dark. We must have walked for half an hour, hurrying in and out of the trees. It was marshy in places and the local frogs kept up this monotonous backing track, interrupted by the occasional eerie cry of a night bird.

So far as I could tell there wasn't a house for miles. Don't tell me Peaches lives in a tree, I thought. Then I stopped in my tracks, frowning. I was in the middle of nowhere, but I was picking up an incredibly buzzy vibe, the kind you get when loads of people are grooving to the max.

Uh-oh, I thought. This is not a good time to start hallucinating, Melanie.

Nathan gave a throaty chuckle. "What can you hear?"

"Crickets?" said Rose in an exhausted voice.

"No, it's music!" said Clem, jigging about on Nathan's shoulders.

"The blues," Grace corrected him softly. "Someone's playing blues."

"Peaches runs a speakeasy out here," Nathan explained. "Just a shack and a few barrels of moonshine. But we reckon the music is as good as anything they get at the Cotton Club."

"Will there be any food?" asked Clem hopefully.

A few minutes later we emerged in a large clearing and I saw a rickety wooden shack. Hazy light leaked out from between the planks. I couldn't just hear the blues by this time – I could feel it, tingling up through the soles of my feet and into my belly. The shack was literally vibrating from the exuberant partying inside!

There was a break in the music and I heard a woman's teasing voice, then a roar of laughter. Nathan rapped on a little barred window. It slid open and an eye squinted out through a fog of cigarette smoke.

"Tell Peaches she's got company!" said Nathan.

The door opened and he bundled us inside. There was a moment's astonished silence. Then someone said sarcastically, "Sup'n wrong with your eyesight, boy? Or did you just forget to mention they was white?"

Black men and women of all ages were staring at the Bloomfields with stony expressions, plainly not too thrilled to have a white lady and her kids in their backwoods hangout. I saw Nathan talking and gesturing earnestly to a big curvy woman I guessed was Peaches. She sauntered over, looking perfectly serene. "Hi, honey," she said to Grace. "Nathan says you need a place for the night. Sit yourselves right down and I'll send someone to get you some food."

The customers blinked at this. I could see them think, well, if Peaches thinks it's OK… And gradually everyone forgot about the white strangers and got on with having a good time.

Someone appeared with food, and Grace and the children gratefully tucked into pork and greens and cornbread.

Peaches was telling her customers about two prohibition agents, Izzy and Mo, who travelled around America trying to catch anyone breaking the law by making or selling illicit alcohol.

"There's nothing those devils won't do to get their man!" she chuckled. "They'll dress up in stupid disguises. Play mean tricks. You know one of them actually stood out in the snow until he was blue with cold this one time? His partner dragged him into a bar and begged them to give him some brandy to revive him. The poor fool brought it, and you know what Izzy says then? 'Dere's sa-ad news!'"

"Why'd he say that?" asked someone in a puzzled voice.

"Mo and Izzy always say that, when they bust someone," she explained, laughing. "I told you, those guys are devils!"

Clem gave a drowsy giggle. "Dere's sa-ad news," he repeated. Minutes later he was asleep on Grace's lap.

Someone started to play a guitar in a style and rhythm I have never ever heard before and an old man began to sing in a cracked growly voice. I can't explain why, but it was beautiful. It was raw and filled with human pain. But it wasn't like the singer was just bellyaching about his own personal troubles. He was singing for every human on Earth who'd ever suffered.

I found myself picturing all the faces I'd seen since I'd been in America: Cissie baking cookies with Clem, Grace watching her children's sleeping faces the night their father died, the yearning eyes of the woman in the hobo town by the railway tracks, and old Isaac rocking in his chair.

I saw Honesty watching intently. There was a new softness in her face and I knew that for just a moment, the pain and longing in the old blues singer's voice had reached her too.

It was past midnight when the last customer left. Peaches gave the family some clean flour sacks for blankets, then she and Nathan went home. Grace and her girls put their sacks on the floor and were fast asleep in minutes. And I thought, how come an illegal speakeasy in the middle of the woods feels so safe and peaceful?

We made good progress over the next few days, travelling up through Alabama and Mississippi and into Arkansas. The Angel Academy began to seem like a far-off dream. I occasionally wondered what Lollie and Reuben were getting up to, but only in a detached sort of way. Sometimes I felt as if I'd been travelling across the United States of America for ever.

One morning a farmer dropped us off at a town called Freshwater. Grace and her children went into the drugstore to buy breakfast. And standing at the counter, buying about a zillion cups of coffee, was Lenny!

The Bloomfields had a highly emotional reunion. Even Honesty gave her brother a wintry little hug.

"So have you gone into the coffee business?" Rose teased.

But Lenny proudly insisted he was in the movie business now. "I might be fetching and carrying at present, but eventually it will lead to bigger things. Come with me and I'll introduce you to the crew."

We found the film people in their truck, waiting morosely for their morning caffeine fix. The director seemed to be having a major temper tantrum about their sloppy attitudes or whatever. He caught sight of us, and his expression changed so dramatically I thought he was going to have a stroke.

"Mr Mantovani, are you OK?" Lenny faltered.

The director got out of the truck. He was gazing at Rose as if he was in some kind of trance. He held up his hands, forming an imaginary camera lens, and panned this way and that, peering at her startled face. "What's your name, doll?" he barked suddenly.

Rose looked annoyed. "Rose Bloomfield."

He shook his head, frowning. "Sounds like a firm of hick florists. Suppose we call you Rosa Bloom? Now that's classy."

"Maybe, but I'm happy with the name I've got," said Rose.

Mr Mantovani reached out and removed Rose's little owl glasses.

"Hey!" she protested.

"I knew it!" he said triumphantly. "Under those hideous spectacles, you have the face of an angel. I promise you, with make-up and fancy clothes, you'll be sensational!"

Omigosh, I thought. Little Rose has been discovered! I looked at her with new interest, and I thought the director had a point. Honesty's sister only needed a string of beads to twirl and she could have been one of those enigmatic 'It' girls I'd seen in Honesty's mum's magazines. In the Twenties, 'It' meant sex appeal. Girls like Clara Bow and Louise Brooks had 'It'. And according to Cissie, Rudolf Valentino had 'It'. But having seen a picture, I personally prefer my heartthrobs *without* eyeliner.

I could see Rose felt totally naked without her spectacles. She grabbed them back. "What's he talking about?" she asked.

Lenny looked envious. "I think he wants to put you in his movie."

Rose gave a nervous laugh, realised Lenny was serious and turned as pink as a tulip.

Mr Mantovani acted offended. "Girls would kill for this opportunity, doll. I'm asking you to be my new leading lady."

"Oh thanks a bunch," said a girl in film make-up. "What am I now? Chopped liver?"

"You're a very nice girl, Ingrid," Mr Mantovani said patronisingly. "But Rosa here is the mysterious beauty I've been searching for my whole life."

It went on like that for ages, with Rose insisting she wasn't interested, and Mr Mantovani totally refusing to take no for an answer.

Suddenly Rose said, "How much do you pay?"

"Ha!" snorted the former leading lady.

Mr Mantovani looked shifty. "Doll, what is money, compared with the birth of a new art form?"

"Then forget it," said Rose firmly. "I need to get my family to San Francisco."

The director frowned. "I can't give you the money, doll," he admitted. "But I could definitely get you to California."

She briskly extended her hand. "It's a deal."

I was SO proud of her. Acting and film-making were completely not Rose's thing, yet she had decided to go with the flow just to help her family.

Mr Mantovani's style people gave Honesty's sister a radical makeover. They took away her tiny owl spectacles and cut her long hair into a swingy, mischievous-looking bob. They plucked her bushy eyebrows until she was left with just two startled little crescents. The make-up artist painted Rose's sharp clever little face with Twenties-style film make-up, which instantly made her look v. mysterious and geisha-like. Finally the dresser buttoned her into a low-waisted Charleston dress with exquisite beading on the hem.

When they finally let Rose see herself in the mirror, she gasped and I felt genuinely moved. I had seen about a zillion TV makeover shows in my time but I've never seen such a miraculous transformation. Rose Bloomfield had totally vanished, and in her place was Rosa Bloom, a smoulderingly sexy movie star!

Boy, Melanie, I told myself, the Agency certainly moves in mysterious ways. In my scenario it was Honesty who got talent-spotted. Never in a million years did I think it would be geeky little Rose!

Clem got a part too. He played the cute curly kid with the puppy. Honesty could have been in the film if she played her cards right, but she was in full zombie mode, which didn't exactly make the film people warm to her, and eventually they left her well alone.

Can you believe it only took a week to make Mr Mantovani's film! Actually, compared with film making in my time, the process seemed really amateurish. Movies were silent then, so the actors just did loads of cheesy miming and face-pulling. To be honest, Rose didn't have that much to do in *Dangerous Pearls* (that was the name of Mr Mantovani's movie), except look scared and pretty while the hero rescued her and her precious pearls from a string of evil villains. I know, I know, it wasn't much of a plot, but like Mr Mantovani said, the film industry was in its infancy.

I have to admit to a bad moment when they tied Rose to the train tracks. OK, it wasn't so dangerous as it sounds. Lenny was crouching just out of shot, with a pen knife ready to cut her free, in case an express train suddenly came roaring out of the tunnel. But to be on the safe side, I crouched beside the rails too and surrounded Rose with protective angel vibes.

A funny sound made me look up and I saw that Honesty was trembling uncontrollably. I realised that she was totally convinced her sister was going to be horribly mashed by a train. She started moaning, "Cut her free. Quick, quick! Cut her free!"

Deep down I'd known that sneery zombie girl wasn't *my* Honesty. That's why I'd sat up with her night after night beaming vibes, trying to reach her. But now for the first time I glimpsed the terrible vulnerability she'd been trying so desperately to hide, and it shocked me right to the core.

On the last day of filming, Mr Mantovani held a party at the town's only hotel. Officially everyone was drinking fruit punch, but I glimpsed the inevitable brown paper bag doing the rounds and everyone started getting a bit flirty and giggly. I'd noticed that banning alcohol seemed to have made it more thrilling and desirable than ever.

Just as things were getting a teensy bit out of hand, a tow truck pulled up outside. A guy in dungarees came in and peered around the crowded bar. "Is there a lady called Rosa Bloom here?"

Rose turned in surprise and her short shiny hair swooshed across her rouged cheekbones. "I guess that must be me!" she laughed.

"Sign here please and print your name clearly underneath," he said. "Oops, nearly forgot to give you the keys!"

Rose pulled a comical face at the other Bloomfields, like, "What is going on?"

They all followed him outside, totally bemused. The delivery man unhitched a battered old pick-up from his vehicle. "Okey dokey, she's all yours!" he said cheerily and climbed back into his cab.

Rose stared at the pick-up with a stunned expression. Mr Mantovani came up behind her. "Don't look so surprised, doll," he chuckled. "You kept your side of the deal, now I've kept mine!"

"I thought you were going to give us the train tickets," she said wonderingly. "Not our very own truck." She looked doubtful suddenly. "It isn't stolen, is it?"

"Don't insult me, Rosa! I called in some favours is all."

To everyone's surprise, Rose kissed him on both cheeks. "Why thank you, Mr Mantovani," she said. Then she yelled, "Honesty, Clem, Mama – grab your bags, let's go!!"

Lenny was looking down in the mouth. "But you can't even drive," he said.

Rose's eyes sparkled. "No, but you can, Len! Hollywood is in California too, you know. What better place to be a stuntman than Hollywood?"

Yess! I thought. Hollywood was only just starting to be known for making films in Lenny's time, so he'd be arriving at exactly the right time.

"And when all those other directors come knocking on your door, doll, tell them Tony Mantovani saw you first!" the director called plaintively.

Rose laughed. "I told you, I'm not interested in movies. When we get to California I'm going to college and one day I'll be a famous archaeologist."

She climbed into the back of the old pick-up, put her glasses on and started to read. I had to smile. With her new confidence and 'It' girl haircut,

Honesty's bookworm sister looked gorgeous, even in her hideous specs.

Lenny, Grace and Clem climbed into the front of the truck. Lenny started singing, "California here I come!" and Grace and Clem joined in.

I suddenly felt desperately sad vibes coming from somewhere close by. Honesty had seated herself as far away from Rose as humanly possible. She had her usual grim zombie expression, but for the first time in weeks, I heard her thoughts.

Everyone is following their dreams. Everyone but me.

I had a terrifying insight. It wasn't that Honesty didn't have a dream. She did. A totally impossible one. She wanted everything the way it was before her father died. She wanted to be living with her mama and papa in suburban Philadelphia, scoring As and Bs at school. And if she couldn't have that, she didn't want anything. In other words, she was going to stay a zombie for the rest of her life.

I experienced the sickening sensation I get when I'm seriously out of my depth.

Admit it, Melanie, you are a hopeless guardian angel, I told myself unhappily. You have beamed so many vibes at this poor girl, she ought to glow in the dark by now. But not only is she not getting better. She's actually getting *worse*. You've got to hand her over to the professionals, before it's too late.

I called up the GA hotline as we bumped along in the back of the truck. It was hard to talk, partly because of the truck, partly because I was trying not to cry, and also because bits of my hair kept blowing into my mouth.

"Orlando," I snivelled. "You'd better tell the Agency to send someone else. I'm just not getting through to her."

"You are," he insisted. "You being there is helping her more than you know."

"I just don't understand her," I wailed. "To be honest, I don't even like her that much." It was the first time I'd admitted this even to myself, and I felt a rush of shame. What kind of guardian angel *dislikes* her human?

As usual, Orlando was serenely unshockable. "Give her time. Honesty hasn't come to terms with her father's death, that's all."

"Come to terms!" I wailed. "Orlando, she hasn't shed a single tear!"

"Of course not. She's completely frozen inside. That's how the PODS like it."

I felt myself turn cold. "Omigosh!" I gasped. "The PODS got to her when I wasn't looking!" I'd got so used to the dark powers operating on a huge scale – world wars, famines, famous authors and whatever – I had stupidly forgotten that ordinary individuals were equally at risk.

"I don't think they targeted her deliberately," Orlando was saying. "But it's easy for someone as vulnerable as Honesty to tune into a PODS wavelength. Now she's getting blasted with toxic vibes twenty-four hours a day."

I had also stupidly forgotten that we're not the only cosmic beings who broadcast vibes. I am SO useless, I thought.

As usual, Orlando read my mind. "Don't beat yourself up, Melanie," he said calmly. "Honesty Bloomfield called *you*, remember?" And he hung up.

But I knew I had failed her just when she needed me most, and I was disgusted with myself.

I was crying seriously by this time, and I'd got to the crucial stage when you need a really good blow. I scrabbled in my bag on the off-chance I'd brought some tissues and was astonished to find a bulky paperback.

How weird, I thought. I completely didn't

remember packing my Angel Handbook. It must have fallen in when I wasn't looking. Then I whispered, "Omigosh, it's a sign!"

I shut my eyes tight, then quickly opened the Angel Handbook at random and read, "It is said that it is better to travel hopefully than to arrive."

I looked up and saw Honesty staring emptily into space as if she had no idea where she was going and couldn't care less if she arrived. And I remembered her singing the Nickelodeon song, and suddenly I felt this ache inside my heart.

Orlando's right, I thought. She called me and I mustn't let her down.

CHAPTER SEVEN

All through Texas and into Oklahoma, I stuck to Honesty like glue.

I didn't just beam vibes, I chatted to her non-stop. I even sang to her. I figured, if it works with coma victims, it could work with Honesty too. Assuming Orlando was right, her fragile energy system was getting a twenty-four-hour battering from PODS FM. Our vibes are designed to make humans feel stronger, so they can get on with whatever they came to Earth to do. But the vibes the PODS put out literally poison human minds and hearts, making their lives seem totally meaningless.

Humans have free will as you know, so I couldn't disconnect Honesty from the PODS, even if I knew how. She had to do that herself. My job as Honesty's guardian angel was to remind her there were other cosmic vibes available: uplifting, inspiring, groovy, feel-good vibes.

We sat in the back of the pick-up, rattling across huge empty prairies under an equally huge empty sky. Oklahoma weather is really something else. One minute we'd be driving along in a blizzard, the next we'd be basking in hot sunlight. In one place we ran into the tail end of one of those midwestern twisters (that's like a cyclone). To everyone's horror, it started raining frogs! Rose and Honesty shrieked and threw the icky things out as fast as they landed. But I totally refused to let a local frog storm distract me from my mission. And when I was quite sure frogs had stopped falling out of the sky, I settled down beside Honesty, and told her the story of my own short, sweet but incredibly cool life on Earth. Oh, and I set her straight about that cloud-filled waiting room, in case she was worrying.

"Heaven won't be the same for your papa as it is for me, obviously," I explained. "For one thing,

I was only thirteen when I died. But if he has half the fun me and Lollie have, I promise he'll be having a ball!"

I also apologised to Honesty for dissing her the way I did, when she turned out to be just a regular person instead of some precocious child star.

"You're really special, Honesty," I told her. "And you have your own special path to follow. But your dad's death really shocked you and the PODS took advantage. I am your guardian angel and I'm going to help you through this, OK?"

One afternoon the Bloomfields picked up a Mexican woman with a baby. The woman had obviously been walking for hours, and was completely exhausted. Rose immediately put down her book and took the baby, so his mother could sleep in the back of the truck. He started grizzling and she hushed him in her arms, and started to sing a Twenties ballad about true love and apple blossom, only she made it sound like a lullaby. She had a surprisingly tuneful voice.

I was completely charmed. It was the first time I'd seen this side of Rose. Honesty was watching her too. She had this new alert expression in her eyes, almost as if she was making mental notes.

Since they'd left Georgia, Honesty's family had been living a hand-to-mouth existence. But I happened to know that Grace wasn't completely penniless. She still had a valuable diamond ring which her husband had given her. She kept it wrapped inside a blue silk scarf inside a secret pocket inside what Americans call a purse, and I call a handbag. Once I saw Grace take it out when her children were asleep, and touch it to her cheek. I didn't blame her for not wanting to part with it. The ring was the only thing she had left of her husband.

Sometimes Lenny managed to earn a few dollars, helping out at farms or country homesteads along the way. But they often went to sleep hungry, and most nights they slept under the stars.

The Bloomfield kids were scarcely recognisable as the same people who had left Philadelphia. They looked browner and wirier and somehow tougher, even little Clem. And their Philadelphia clothes were starting to get faded and raggedy around the edges. It wasn't easy to keep clean on the road, and any time the Bloomfields came to a public washroom, they dived inside and made the most of the free soap and hot water. I could only look on with envy. That's one big drawback to being a celestial agent. We can't use earthly facilities. Our molecules are too subtle or something. For the same reason, we can't tuck into the local cuisine. We have to make do with a kind of angelic trail mix, which luckily is quite sustaining.

Despite the tough conditions, Honesty's mother still managed to keep herself looking good. Grace Bloomfield struck me as one of those natural celebrities. She wasn't snooty or superior, yet she had this real air about her. Our fellow travellers noticed it and treated her with respect.

And we met all kinds on the road, I can tell you. 1920s America was positively heaving with colourful characters with weird Twenties-type occupations. As you probably guessed, quite a few of the occupations had to do with booze. Rum-runners smuggled it across the state line, bootleggers sold it, and moonshiners were the people who manufactured the stuff. But there were also holy rollers, preaching hellfire and damnation to anyone who would listen, quack doctors selling miracle cures for every known ailment (yeah, right!), and flashy salesmen hoping to make a quick buck. We also ran into a smooth-talking land speculator. This conman was trying to dupe people into buying 'building land' in Florida. But Lenny said it was probably pure swamp.

One evening Lenny stopped the truck to give a lift to a man called Caleb Jones. He said he was heading west hoping to find work as a fruit picker. It was getting late so Grace invited him to share their supper. "That's if you don't mind bean and potato stew," she said apologetically.

"Sounds like a regular feast to me," he said.

They all sat by the camp fire, eating stew and listening to the howling of a pack of nearby prairie wolves.

"Couldn't help noticing your truck seems to be developing a problem with its exhaust," he said shyly. "I'll fix it for you, if you'll let me."

As Grace said later, Caleb was a guy you could pass in a crowd without noticing. He wasn't tall or good-looking or exceptionally ugly. Yet he gave off this completely peaceful vibe, which is something you rarely find in humans.

I heard him talking to Grace when the others were asleep. "Your younger daughter seems troubled," he said. "Was she always that way?"

Grace shook her head. "Just since her daddy died."

He nodded as if he'd suspected something of the kind.

"I've been telling myself she'll come out of it," Grace said. "But lately I've been thinking, what if Honesty just goes deeper and deeper into herself and never comes out?"

I felt my skin prickle with sympathy. But I noticed that Caleb didn't immediately try to make Grace feel better. He just sat there, turning over what she had said, and for a few minutes there was no sound except the crackling of the fire and the familiar night sounds of the prairie.

Then he said quietly, "Sometimes I think the strongest people in this world are those who go down into the dark and come out the other side."

"Are you talking from experience, Mr Jones?" Grace asked him.

"Fifteen years in Singsing," he said calmly, "and a whole bunch of other penal institutions before that. But hell, I was a prisoner long before they put me away. In here." He tapped his head.

I saw Grace register that she was alone in the dark with a violent criminal. Then she took a good look at Caleb's peaceful face, and seemed to relax. "But you got out – of both prisons?"

The man gave her an extraordinarily sweet smile. "Once you're free inside, ain't a thing in this world anyone can do to you."

Caleb Jones went on his way at first light, while the family was still sleeping. I saw him go to the truck and fix its damaged exhaust with some wire and a piece of old bandage. Then he picked some yellow wiry-stemmed flowers, some kind of prairie daisy, and left them where Grace would see them as soon as she woke up.

Rose was horrified when she heard about their midnight conversation. "He could have murdered us in our beds, Mama!"

But Grace said, "I don't care what he used to be, Rose. It's who he is now that counts. And the man I talked to last night is one of the finest gentleman I have ever met."

Oklahoma had been gradually morphing into New Mexico, a dreamlike world of mystical mountains, tumbled red rocks and weird flowering cacti. Pink adobe houses nestled on slopes, and goats, pigs and chickens wandered about outside.

I felt as if we'd strayed into a totally foreign country. On the road, we passed dark-eyed men and women in vividly coloured woollen clothes, struggling under loads of avocados, knobbly chilli peppers or limes. The people called out to the Bloomfields and their voices made me briefly homesick for Lola. I wondered where she was and what kind of human she was looking after. Wherever she was, I really hoped my soul-mate was having fun.

Soon after midday, Lenny stopped at a gas station. An absolutely ancient guy in dungarees came out to fill up the truck. "Where you headed?" he asked.

"California," said Lenny.

The garage guy pointed to a figure slumped beside the petrol pumps, apparently sound asleep. "Got a feller here needs to get to Santa Fe."

"We're going over that way," said Lenny.

The old man gave a piercing whistle. "Gideon, you got yourself a ride!"

The man tipped back his cowboy hat, yawning. When he saw the Bloomfields, his face split into a lazy grin and he got to his feet. "Well, thank you kindly!"

I think it was Gideon's eyes that made me feel uneasy. They seemed to be everywhere at once, flickering over faces, purses and pockets as if he had some spooky X-ray vision. He acted so sleepy and benign, yet I found his vibes totally chilling. I suspected that Gideon was one of those humans who had come a *leetle* bit too close to the PODS for comfort. I tried to tune into his thoughts, but it wasn't like tuning into a normal adult human. Gideon was more like some hyperactive little kid, constantly going "gimme gimme gimme". I could tell the Bloomfields didn't like him either, but they generously took him all the way to Santa Fe.

That night the family set up camp. Clem wandered around collecting firewood, which was his special chore. After a few minutes, he came trailing back and drooped against Grace. "Mama, I don't feel so good."

She felt his forehead and looked dismayed. "Oh, my stars!" she murmured. "The child's burning up!" I saw her frantically thinking what to do. "Lenny, I know you've been driving all day, but we've got to find this little boy a doctor."

Everyone piled back into the truck and Lenny drove for another two hours in pitch darkness, on a narrow road with hair-raising bends. Clem had started muttering nonsense to himself. Grace stayed calm but I could feel Honesty silently freaking out.

We came to a small town called Sweet Rock, perched on a rocky hillside above the river. The Bloomfields checked into a Spanish-style inn called *The Laughing Horse* and Grace asked them to call a doctor.

They went up to their rooms and Grace undressed a weak trembling Clem. She lifted her little boy on to the bed and I saw his eyes roll right up into his head.

Honesty looked scared. "What's wrong with him, Mama?" she said in a small voice.

"He's just delirious," said Grace. "Could you fetch me a bowl of water, Rose? I'll sponge him down while we're waiting for the doctor."

"How are we going to pay for all of this, Mama?" Rose said anxiously. "Hotels and doctors cost money."

Grace tried to smile. "It's all right, I still have your daddy's ring." She reached into her bag and pulled out the blue silk scarf. She unwrapped it tenderly, then stared in horror at the dirty pebble inside.

"I am so stupid," she said in a harsh voice. "I knew Gideon was a phoney and I let him go right ahead and make a fool of me."

"You think Gideon stole your ring?" said Lenny incredulously.

"There is not a doubt in my mind."

Grace crouched down beside her open suitcase and started hunting for something.

"Clem is going to die, isn't he!" Honesty was chalk-white and trembling.

Grace stopped her rummaging. She took hold of Honesty and forced her to look into her eyes. "No, Clem is not going to die. He's got a high fever, that's all. Once it goes down, he'll be better in no time."

Grace went back to her seach. Suddenly she gave a sigh of relief. "He didn't get this at least." She held up the cheque her father had written all those weeks ago in Georgia.

"The Lord surely works in mysterious ways," she said gratefully. "I never did understand why I didn't just tear up that old buzzard's money. But I am truly glad I didn't."

The doctor came and clicked his tongue at Clem's condition. "Your son is exhausted and badly dehydrated. He needs fluids, bed-rest and most of all, a calm, stable environment," he told Grace as he wrote out a prescription.

After he'd gone, she paced up and down the room, looking totally haunted. "Why didn't he just come out and say, 'You are a terrible mother, Grace Bloomfield. You made your little boy ill, by dragging him selfishly all over America'?" she said despairingly.

Grace was unnaturally quiet all the rest of the evening. I wanted to read her thoughts, but didn't feel as if I should intrude on her privacy. I could tell she was trying to work out what to do for the best.

Next morning she announced that they were staying put in Sweet Rock, until Clem had recovered. I thought Grace's instincts were totally sound, and decided to do everything I could to back her up. Angels aren't supposed to interfere with human destinies, but as you know, there are times when a teeny cosmic nudge can make all the difference. I dialled up the GA hotline and asked Orlando for help.

"Hi, it's Mel! Sorry to hassle you, but the Bloomfields need to crash for a while," I rattled off breathlessly. "Do you think the Agency could find them somewhere to rent around here? Plus it would be helpful if Lenny could get work locally. The way I look at it, we're just helping them to help themselves, right?"

"I'll see if I can pull a few strings," he promised.

I never found out what cosmic strings Orlando pulled, if any, but the Agency definitely delivered the goods. The very first time Rose and Lenny went house-hunting, they found the coolest little cottage to let on the edge of town. It was built out of rose-coloured adobe, a kind of local mud, and it looked exactly like those houses in Luke Skywalker's hometown in the *Star Wars* movie. Rose and Honesty set to work making it homey, leaving Grace free to look after Clem. And the day after they moved in, Lenny found work on a neighbouring ranch.

I can't explain why New Mexico felt so right. Maybe it was all those angel place names: Angel Point, Angel Canyon, Angel Fire. But I was absolutely certain this was the perfect place for Clem to grow strong and well again after all his weeks on the road.

And guess what! It turned out to be perfect for Lenny's love life too!

Clem was getting better by this time, so when the circus arrived in Sweet Rock Lenny took the girls along for a treat. Naturally I tagged along. We filed into the tent and squeezed ourselves on to one of the front benches overlooking the circus ring. The locals were merrily turning their circus outing into a major fiesta. Children threw coloured streamers and tooted horns. Mothers kept handing Lenny and the girls delicious New Mexican goodies. Old grannies pinched Lenny's cheek and told him how handsome he was. And the grandpas insisted on giving him swigs of the local hooch which, being macho New Mexicans, they didn't even bother to hide.

Once again I saw that alert little gleam in Honesty's eyes as if she was amused despite herself.

It wasn't the most sophisticated circus: a couple of clowns, some brave geriatric elephants and a wobbly trapeze artist in grubby pink tights. Then the ring master bawled, "Presenting the one and only, magnificent Ruby Rio!" and I felt that prickle of angel electricity which means something is going to happen.

A golden-skinned girl rode into the ring on a palomino pony. She had flashing dark eyes and her glittery scarlet costume left little to the imagination. The pony began to trot faster, and suddenly Ruby Rio stood upright on the pony's bare back. She gave a whoop of triumph and struck what had to be the sassiest pose the people of Sweet Rock had ever seen.

Without warning, she let herself fall backwards. But just as it seemed she was sure to hit the sawdust, she casually reached out to save herself, and continued to ride round the ring, *underneath* the pony!

There was a collective gasp and Lenny's tortilla fell from his hand. Omigosh, I thought. The girl is pure dynamite! Plus her dress sense is totally slamming! Honesty was obviously mesmerised. So was Rose.

Ruby and her pony clearly had some telepathic link, because no matter how high she leaped, or how many times she spun around in the air, or how far she slid under its belly, Ruby effortlessly got back on to her horse. She even rode around the ring standing on her head. The audience went mad, clapping and stamping and yelling out in Spanish. The atmosphere was electric!

When the show was over, Lenny said huskily, "You girls go home."

"Why, where are you going?" asked Rose. For someone so clever, she could be really dense sometimes. Hadn't she heard of love at first sight?

Ruby Rio turned out to be half Native American and half New Mexican cowgirl, so you could say she was always destined to be out of the ordinary. But what I think is so sweet is that this incredible girl had spotted Lenny in the audience, and instantly fell in love with *him* at first sight too! Can you believe that she and Lenny even shared the exact same dream of going to Hollywood as famous stunt persons?

So when the doctor gave Clem the all-clear at last and the family was able to continue on their journey, Ruby Rio came too, bringing her impressive collection of costumes.

"Next stop Arizona!" Lenny said happily, putting the truck into gear. "In a couple of days we'll be in the City of the Angels!"

Oh yeah, I thought. Duh! I'd never actually registered the true meaning of Los Angeles before.

I have to admit that as we got closer I was getting totally over-excited. I was like, I can't BELIEVE I'm going to be in Hollywood at the dawn of moving pictures. I might see Charlie Chaplin or Laurel and Hardy, or my own personal favourite Harold Lloyd – stars that were like, *legends*.

It's a pity no-one was filming our arrival in Hollywood, because as we chugged into Sunset

Boulevard, Mr Mantovani's faithful truck spluttered, choked and died spectacularly. The truck obviously wasn't going anywhere, so everyone got out.

I immediately ran up to the Sunset Boulevard sign, going, "Woo, we're in Hollywood! Oh, wow, this is so cool!" I was fizzing with happiness.

Lenny whispered to Ruby, "I'll make you proud of me, you'll see."

I saw Honesty shiver in the California sun. She wrapped her arms around herself, scowling. "None of this is real," she said. "Not a single thing. They imported the palm trees from Hawaii. It's all totally fake."

I knew this wasn't Honesty talking. It was just Honesty under the influence of PODS FM. She felt lost and scared and she didn't even know why.

She's going to need my input more than ever, I thought. Being on the road is one thing. Now she's got to make a new life in completely strange surroundings.

My mobile rang. Yippee! I thought, I can swank to Orlando about being in Hollywood. "You'll never guess where I am—" I babbled.

"I know exactly where you are," he said. "And now it's time to come back."

All my fizzy happiness drained out of my feet. "But I'm just getting the hang of being a guardian angel!" I wailed.

"I know, and everyone thinks you're doing fine, but it's time you had a break."

"I don't want a break!" I fumed. "It totally doesn't make sense for me to leave Honesty now."

Orlando sounded annoyingly serene. "I know it seems that way," he agreed. "But the Agency is generally good on cosmic timing."

"Cosmic baloney!" I raged. "They send me to look after this damaged girl, then just when she needs me the most, they tell you to pull me out!" I was practically yelling into my mobile. "I *know* Honesty, OK? And she's still really vulnerable! You've got to let me stay!"

And I only just got to Hollywood, I screamed silently.

"Sorry Mel, rules are rules," said Orlando. "Don't worry. They'll have her on twenty-four-hour Angel Watch."

And before I had a chance to say goodbye, a beam of light came down and I went blasting back to Heaven.

CHAPTER EIGHT

My homecoming felt completely unreal.

I sat in the limo, watching familiar landmarks flow by in the velvety dusk, and breathing the celestial air with its haunting scent which is almost, but not quite, like lilacs. But I wasn't really here.

I kept seeing Honesty in the middle of Sunset Boulevard, shivering in the California sunshine and dissing everything in sight.

Back at the dorm I found a note on my door.

Wake me the instant you get in,
Big love
Lollie xxx

I hadn't let myself miss my soul-mate too much while I'd been gone. It would have been way too painful. But I was now totally desperate to see her.

I badly needed a shower and change of clothes, but I couldn't possibly wait that long, so I immediately banged on her door. There was a long pause. Eventually this mad curly bed-head poked out.

"Ta da!" I said.

"Omigosh, Boo!" she shrieked. "It feels like a lifetime!"

We jumped up and down, hugging each other and squealing excitedly.

Lola said, "I'm going to give you two options, *carita*. Option A, you catch up on your beauty sleep like a good sensible angel, or Option B, you, me and Sweetpea hit the Babylon right away and you do the beauty sleep thing later. What do you say?"

I slapped her palm. "Option B for Babylon! I'm beautiful enough already."

Lola sniffed the air. "Beautiful yes, but also strangely stinky."

"I've been hanging out with hoodlums and hobos," I said. "What do you expect?"

"Ooh," said Lola. "Tell me more." She followed me into my room and we yelled scraps of news to each other as I showered.

Over the sound of rushing water, Lola told me about the tribal princess she'd been minding in ancient Persia or wherever. "Her tribe breeds herds of fabulous horses and they travel with them from place to place. When they're not killing people from other tribes, the men are really spiritual and romantic. They give their sweethearts roses and recite Persian love poetry. The women are as fierce as the men," she explained. "They all ride like demons, even tiny kids."

"I met a girl who can ride like a demon too," I yelled, thinking of Ruby Rio.

"Is she your human, Boo?"

"Uh-uh. Erm, actually my human is kind of complicated," I said lamely. I found that I totally didn't know how to put my 1920s experiences into words. I put on my fluffy robe and blow-dried my hair, and I didn't say another word about Honesty. Probably Lola guessed how I felt, because she flung open my wardrobe door and said cheerfully, "OK, girlfriend, what are you going to wear?"

I threw on some jeans, a T-shirt which said *Little*

Miss Naughty (when in doubt go for the classics!), splashed on some Attitude, my fave heavenly fragrance, and I was ready to go.

Lola and I headed down to the Babylon Café, arm in arm.

We found Reuben at our favourite outdoor table. I thought my buddy looked unusually tense. I reckoned his Earth experiences might have been a shock to his system, so I said sympathetically, "Was it really tough?"

"Actually it was great," he said. "I'm looking after this little cabin boy who got mixed up in the Napoleonic wars. Erm, Mel, before I get into that, I've got something to tell you."

I was trying to figure out which delicious fruit punch to have. The Babylon does about a zillion varieties. "Yeah," I said vaguely. "What?"

"Orlando thought you'd rather hear it from me."
Reuben sounded so worried that I looked up.

"Brice is back," he said.

I put down my menu. I was so shocked, I could hardly get the words out. "Back here? No way!"

"Yes way," said Reuben. "He's practically the first person I saw when I got back to school."

"They let him back into our school?"

Reuben nodded unhappily. "I knew you'd be upset."

"I'm not upset, OK! I'm shocked, I'm sick to my stomach, I'm, I'm…"

"Upset," Lola supplied helpfully.

All my feelings burst out in a rush. "It's outrageous! Brice can't just waltz back and call himself an angel after the things he's done. After the things he did to you, Reuben!" I reminded him angrily. "OK, so we saw a different side to him when we met him in the future. And OK, so he's not one hundred per cent evil, but that hardly qualifies him to be an angel!"

I saw Reuben absently fingering his scar under his tunic, a souvenir of the savage beating Brice gave him in Tudor times. The Sanctuary angels could have healed it totally, but Reuben insisted on keeping it. He said he wanted to show all his mates that he was hard. But I think it was really a reminder to stay focused. You know, an angel warrior kind of thing.

I was still waiting for my friends to show me some sympathy, but there was just a long awkward silence.

Then Lola said, "Who knows, maybe Brice has changed? Maybe he's gone through his evil PODS phase and come out the other side, and from now on he'll be an absolutely incredible celestial agent."

"Oh *please*," I said. "Are you one of his little groupies now or something?"

She looked hurt. "Hey, Boo, I'm your best friend, but don't push your luck."

"Let's not talk about this now," said Reuben quickly. "We've only got a couple of days off. Let's just have fun, OK?"

It's all right for them, I thought. Brice hadn't been their cosmic stalker. They had no idea how insecure it made me feel, knowing I might walk into one of my favourite heavenly haunts and find my worst nightmares looking back at me.

When I finally climbed into my economy-sized bed, I was still freaking out inside. I didn't have the most restful night, I have to say. I kept dreaming I was back on Earth. I saw Ruby hanging up her costumes in the new apartment, and Lenny came in and gave her a kiss. Honesty was at the window staring down into a sunny courtyard, and I got the weirdest feeling she was missing me. I tried to tell her I was coming back, but the instant I heard my own voice, I woke up.

I must have been doing some unusually hard thinking in my sleep, because I didn't feel nearly as anti-Brice as I had the night before.

You're such a hypocrite, Mel Beeby, I scolded myself. You don't go riding in on your high horse every time a human makes a mistake. That Caleb Jones must have been into some heavy stuff to get put in Singsing, but he came out of it, and now he's this streetwise guru.

I found myself remembering what Michael said. That we couldn't be effective guardian angels, unless we were like, *flawed* and understood human suffering. Well, Brice was flawed all right and he'd suffered for it in ways I'd probably never know.

Maybe one day Brice would evolve into a streetwise guru angel. Maybe not. Either way, it was his and the Agency's business, not mine.

I was just getting dressed, when Lola came to find me. We decided to pick up some picnic goodies from Guru and spend the day on the beach, getting our strength back for phase two of our GA assignments.

We lay on sparkling white sand in our bikinis, soaking up the rays, and listening to the soft hush hush of the heavenly waves.

Suddenly Lola said, "I love being a guardian angel, but have you noticed how you're never off duty, even now you're back home?"

"Even when you're asleep!" I said ruefully.

She sat up. "Did you dream about yours too?"

"Only all night long! Actually I'm kind of missing mine."

"Me too," Lola admitted. "It's weird. I didn't even like her at first!"

"Ditto," I giggled.

See what I mean? Lola and I are total soul-mates. We can say anything to each other, and the other person will understand.

Her expression changed, and she reached out and patted my hand. "Michael would never have let him come back, if it wasn't right," she said softly.

She didn't have to say who she meant.

"I know," I said. "I'm trying to be more mature, babe. That's what the angel business is all about, right? Evolution. Trees and diamonds and whatever."

By the time I got back to school, I was totally at one with the cosmos. Orlando was right, I thought. I had needed a break. But now I was going back and I was going to be the best GA Hollywood has ever seen!

I was figuring out what to pack, when the phone rang beside my bed. It was Michael. "Sorry, I should have called, but I've been tied up."

"I know, don't say it. My old century," I sighed.

"Could be," he said humorously. "But I'm here now. And in your opinion, how is Honesty doing?"

I took a breath. "In my opinion? Not great. Orlando thinks she accidentally tuned into a PODS wavelength. She's totally withdrawn inside herself and I don't think just sending vibes is going to bring her out."

There was a pause. Then Michael said, "I think you'd better come down and pick out a suitable outfit, Ms Beeby."

I gasped. "You are kidding! You don't mean...?"

"You're saying that Honesty needs a friend. I happen to agree with you, which is why I'm giving you official permission to materialise."

CHAPTER NINE

I'd only materialised twice before. The first time I stupidly did it without permission, and almost got myself chucked out of the Academy. The second time I even more stupidly dived through a wormhole into the future and materialised by pure accident.

Now for the first time I was materialising with the Agency's blessing, which is practically unheard of for a trainee.

The Agency style adviser showed me and Michael all the delicious clothes I had to choose from, and I got totally over-excited. We picked out two authentically aged outfits, one to wear and one to pack in my real 1920s suitcase. After that I had to choose chemises and stockings and whatever. I think it was the underwear which suddenly made it seem real.

"Michael, I don't think this is going to work," I panicked. "As far as the Bloomfields are concerned, I'm a stranger. I can't just like, move in with them."

"We've been doing this for quite a while, you know," Michael assured me. "I think you'll find it will all work out."

But when I stepped on to planet Earth a couple of hours later, my knees felt weak with stage fright. Can you believe I found myself outside the exact same Spanish-style apartment building I'd seen in my dream? I could hear a dance tune playing on a crackly radio: "Not much money, oh but honey, ain't we got fun!"

A warm breeze rattled the fronds of the palm trees. The wind was surprisingly strong. Suddenly a red feather boa came snaking through the air and wrapped itself softly around my head.

I disentangled myself and saw Ruby and Honesty running out of the building. They started picking up pieces of glitzy circus clothing. I was just about to rush up to say hi, when I remembered. DUH! They didn't actually know me yet!

Then quite spontaneously, Ruby said, "Could you hold this a moment?" and dumped a heap of clothes in my arms. "I was airing my costumes, and the wind blew them off the balcony," she grinned.

I took a couple of microseconds to assimilate the good news – that I was now 100% visible to the human race. Ohh, this is better, I thought happily, and my nerves totally melted away. I was so thrilled to be able to chat to them in visible form like this, that I spoke right from the heart. "I can't believe it! I've always dreamed of going to Hollywood, and finally I'm really here!"

I saw Ruby register my lonely little suitcase. "Got any folks?" she asked sympathetically.

I shook my head. "I guess you could say I'm kind of a free agent," I said, which wasn't exactly a lie.

"Stop with us, till you get fixed up," she said impulsively. "Your mama won't mind, will she, Honesty?"

Honesty took a faltering step towards me. I was astonished to see wondering recognition in her eyes. "Have we met before?" she said softly. "I feel like I know you from somewhere."

I suddenly felt really shy. "I don't think so," I told her. "I've probably just got one of those faces."

But inside I was going, omigosh, this is so sweet! Honesty recognised me!

I had totally new respect for angel vibes after that, I can tell you. I didn't even have to try to win Honesty's confidence. It's like she just knew she could trust me.

Honesty even said I could share her little box room, if I didn't mind nocturnal gurgles from the hot-water tank. She thoughtfully emptied out two of her drawers and made some space in her closet, and while I put my things away, she told me what everyone in the family was up to these days.

Even allowing for differences in earthly and heavenly time systems, the Bloomfields had got work really speedily.

Rose was doing modelling, would you believe? (Don't panic, she kept her clothes on! It was her 'It' girl face everyone went crazy about.) Grace had landed herself a magic job, playing the piano at a Hollywood movie theatre called the Golden Palace Picture House. Ruby and Lenny worked in a Hollywood night club called the Top Hat Club. Honesty told me that the club was run by two brothers, Carlo and Luigi Franco, who owned a string of clubs all over LA.

Ruby was actually performing in the nightly cabaret. Lenny was just waiting on tables at present, but Honesty said he was sure to get his break really soon.

And guess what! Next day I got a job too! Over breakfast, Ruby offered to wangle me a few hours at the club doing washing up. Suddenly Honesty coughed and said, "What about me?" And Ruby just said, "Sure."

So four nights a week, Honesty and I washed dishes at the Top Hat. This was way more cool than it sounds because we got to see all the cabaret acts for free, including Ruby's. With Lenny's help she had worked up a v. exotic acrobatic routine, with some fire-eating thrown in for added excitement.

On the club's quieter nights, Lenny hung out with us, watching the other artists' acts. He wasn't very impressed with any of them, I have to say. But he really *really* hated the girl who played the musical saw.

"That stuff belongs back in the nineteenth century along with the – the barrel organ and horse-drawn carriages," he insisted. "Times have changed. People today need danger and daring! They need speed, novelty and excitement. More than that, they need magic!"

Lenny's eyes went all misty. I could tell he was picturing himself and Ruby drawing oohs and aahs from the crowd with some death-defying manoeuvre. Lenny might have to work as a waiter, but in his mind, he was a stuntman-in-waiting. He and Ruby spent every spare moment down in the courtyard devising weird and wonderful stunts.

"I like that mad stunt you do with the bicycle," I said shyly. "That's magic. It's funny too!"

Lenny's face lit up. "You really think so? Do you think maybe we could make the big time?"

"I know so—" I began.

A voice yelled, "Lenny! Get over here. Luigi's got an urgent message needs to be delivered."

I saw Lenny tense. "I'd better go."

"Let them wait," Honesty hissed at him. "They pay you to wait on tables, not to be Luigi's dogsbody."

I agreed with her. The Franco brothers treated Lenny like their own personal slave, constantly making him run their stupid little errands for them. They were really picky too, like Lenny had to go to this one particular florist even if it was like, after midnight.

Lenny patted his sister's shoulder. "You're a good kid. But I know what I'm doing." He was smiling but I noticed that he couldn't quite meet her eyes.

Violet was what the Agency had decided I should be called. But like Shakespeare said, "What's in a name?" My name might be bogus, but my friendship was totally genuine. And I know it showed, because now that we were finally hanging out together, like one to one, Honesty started to come out of her shell.

They weren't so big on security back then, so in our free time we would wander into the studio lots, and roam around the empty film sets. One was a ballroom with fake marble pillars. Cissie had taught Honesty a cool little dance routine, to *Puttin' on the Ritz*. Honesty showed me the steps and we danced up and down the ballroom, singing out the lyrics.

On non-work nights, we went to the movies. The projectionist at the Golden Palace let us go up into the projection box, so we got to see all the latest films for free.

Honesty and I didn't always share the same tastes. Like, I totally didn't get the Keystone Cops and she was a big fan. But no matter what movie they were showing, I was happy to go along. I just adored that whole Twenties movie experience. I loved being up in the projectionist's room, listening to the atmospheric whirr of the projector. And I loved watching that flickering ghostly light streaming down into the dark auditorium, and miraculously transforming itself into moving pictures on the screen. But more than anything I loved the audience's excitement. When the lights dimmed and the titles came up, I could literally feel people letting go of their troubles as the movie took them away from their hard-up, humdrum lives, into another more thrilling world.

One night we went to see a new Buster Keaton film. Honesty's mother was in the auditorium playing the piano as usual. I thought she did a fantastic job. She had to keep one eye on the screen the whole time she was playing, ready to switch styles at a moment's notice. She had to play comical plonky sounds for the funny parts, mad thunderous chords for the action scenes, and heart-rending music for the sad bits.

It was really warm and cosy up in the projectionist's box. Honesty and I sat on the floor, absentmindedly stuffing our faces with popcorn, totally caught up in Buster's antics. Suddenly we heard a loud snore. The projectionist was quite old, and he'd just dozed off. Unfortunately he'd done it during the most thrilling part of the movie! There was a mad clattery unravelling sound, as the reel of film ran out. The screen went totally blank and the audience started to boo and catcall. Grace totally saved the day, luckily. She stopped playing comical Buster Keaton music, and switched to a soothing classical piece – the Moonlight Sonata, Honesty said it was – while the old guy frantically replaced the reel.

On the way home that night, I caught sight of two figures on the other side of the street. They were sheltering in a shadowy doorway, and one was handing over a bulky package. He looks a bit like Lenny, I thought in surprise. Then I looked again and he'd gone.

I suddenly got a really iffy vibe. "Did you see those guys over there?" I asked Honesty.

She shook her head. "Uh-uh. And if you've got any sense, you didn't either." She sounded deadly serious.

I felt a shiver run through me. "How come?"

"He was probably delivering bootleg booze. Next time look the other way," she said solemnly, "or you could get yourself into trouble."

Honesty explained that America's prohibition laws had led to a humungous crime wave. "Gangsters like Al Capone are making millions of dollars every year, selling alcohol illegally."

"Al Capone!" I squeaked. "Al Capone lives in these times?"

She gave me a startled look. "Why, what other times would he live in?"

Yikes! I had just committed a major time booboo. I did one of my speciality airhead giggles. "I am such a ditz! My old teacher used to say I had pink fluff for brains. Sorry babe, you were telling me about the gangsters."

"The real trouble starts when they think other gangsters are muscling in on their business," Honesty explained. "After we got here, a famous LA mobster mysteriously 'disappeared'. They found him at the bottom of the river. There was some big war going on between rival gangs over who ruled which patch. The government is so worried that they employ special government agents to hunt down anyone making, buying or selling illegal liquor."

Honesty let out this incredibly infectious giggle. I giggled too, but out of pure shock. It was the first time I'd heard her laugh since she left Philadelphia.

"What's funny?" I asked her.

"I was remembering something I heard about these insane prohibition agents, called Izzy and Mo. They're so crazy to catch bootleggers, there's nothing they won't do. Play tricks, wear ridiculous disguises, they're like – like comic-book characters almost. And do you know what they say every time they bust someone?"

I had to bite my lip so as not to spoil her story. "No, what?"

Honesty rocked with laughter. "'Dere's sa-ad news'! Isn't that hilarious! 'Dere's sa-ad news'!"

"Sounds like a sheep!" I spluttered.

We walked along still giggling. On impulse I said, "You're so smart, Honesty."

She blinked with surprise. "How come?"

"You know all this stuff, and you take an interest in the world. You notice all the juicy little details, which pass other people by. You should be like, a reporter or something."

Honesty looked really spooked. "You scare me sometimes, Vi. I get the feeling you can actually read my mind."

Whoops, I thought. "Hey, I get the odd psychic flash," I said aloud. "It's no biggie, honestly."

Honesty shook her head. "It's a bit more than a psychic flash, or you couldn't know my secret ambition." She took a breath. "Up until last spring, that's exactly what I wanted to be, this hotshot news reporter. You know the kind that report back from dangerous war zones?"

I was scared to breathe or change my expression.

Honesty's voice cracked. "Papa never took Rose's dreams seriously. It's one of the things I feel bad about. But he really encouraged me. We used to discuss the news when he got back from work, and he'd buy me these notebooks. I'd record all the things I saw and heard, sort of training myself for the day I could be a real reporter."

Keep talking, I prayed.

She swallowed. "I'd give anything to have those books back."

"Why? What happened to them?" I said casually, as if I hadn't watched her diaries turn into a heap of curly black ash.

"I burned them. I couldn't stand to look at them, after he, erm, after he…"

Say it, I thought.

"After he… he… he died," she managed finally.

WHOOSH!

I felt a surge of cosmic power go shimmering through our energy fields, as if for just a moment, Honesty Bloomfield and I were one.

She had done it! Honesty had somehow found the strength to disconnect herself from PODS FM. And I had this involuntary mental image of all the angel trainees on the GA hotline, clapping and cheering.

I could tell Honesty had no idea what had just happened. She just looked really spaced suddenly. I took her arm, and said gently, "Let's go home."

That night I heard a funny sound coming from her bed. I listened to her trying to muffle her huge racking sobs, then I went to sit beside her.

"It's OK," I said, "it's totally OK to cry when your dad dies. It's normal. Actually it's necessary."

"You don't understand," she wept. "I'm not just crying because he's dead. I'm crying because I killed him."

"Don't be stupid," I said gently. "The poor guy was hit by a truck."

"You don't understand. I was a spoiled brat, Violet," she burst out. "I knew I was his favourite and I used it. I knew exactly how to twist him around my finger. Papa didn't want to get a car, but I kept on and on, like Chinese water torture, until he gave in. I killed him! I murdered my own papa and now I'll never see him again."

I ached to comfort her – but then I thought of Caleb Jones saying how people sometimes need to go into the dark and come out the other side. So I just sat with her quietly, until she cried herself to sleep.

And then I took my mobile out on to the balcony. I sat down in a calming yoga pose in the Californian darkness, and with pink, green, purple and yellow advertising signs flashing all round me, I punched in the number of the GA hotline.

Honesty had remembered how to laugh and dance and have a good time. She'd started to grieve for her dead papa. She'd even remembered why she was here on Earth. In my opinion my work was done. I waited for Orlando to pick up. "Come on," I muttered.

"Mel, hi. How are you doing?" said a cool voice.

I was so horrified, I actually dropped my mobile.

I imagined it, I told myself frantically. I'm so paranoid about Brice being back in Heaven, I actually imagined I heard his voice.

I held the phone shakily to my ear. "Orlando?"

"I'm afraid lover boy's buzzed off on some secret mission, sweetheart," the voice said calmly. "You'll have to make do with me."

It was him. A fallen angel was manning the GA hotline. The entire cosmos had turned upside down!

Calm down, I scolded myself. You're OK with this, remember? Trees, diamonds, evolution and whatever? Now act like a professional.

Unfortunately, when I'm shocked, my voice shoots up about two octaves. "Do you think you could ask the Agency to send me home?" I squeaked. "Honesty is pretty much sorted."

"You reckon?" Brice sounded so disbelieving that I wanted to smack him one.

"I'm telling you, she's back on track," I said sniffily.

"Oh yeah? And how long will that last if her big brother screws up?"

I felt an unpleasant sinking feeling. "I don't get you."

"Sure you do," he said. "All those harmless little deliveries for the Top Hat's special customers. Those late night trips to the florists, hint, hint."

I found myself picturing the Lenny lookalike in the doorway. "Omigosh," I gasped. "That guy didn't just look like Lenny. He *was* Lenny!"

I had been so wrapped up in Honesty, I had totally failed to notice that the Franco brothers were dangerous gangsters!

"I am SO dense!" I groaned.

To my astonishment, Brice said, "You're not dense darling, you were just being focused. Luckily you're an angel, so you still absorbed the relevant info. Think back. What have Lenny's vibes been telling you?"

This is an exercise we do in class to develop our angelic intuition, but I have to say that doing it with Brice felt deeply disturbing.

"I think Lenny feels like everyone's doing much better than he is," I said slowly. "Ruby's doing her cabaret act and he has to wait on tables and see loud-mouthed customers throwing dollars around, like they're big somebodies. I think Lenny wanted to make some fast cash so he could be a big somebody too."

Then Brice said something really chilling.

"He forgot his dream," he said quietly. "And when humans forget why they're on Earth, the PODS are never far behind."

Chapter Ten

It was the week before Christmas and fairy lights had gone up along Sunset Boulevard. But instead of beaming peace, good will and whatever to humankind, I was in the depths of despair.

My mission was about to go pear-shaped. Lenny had stupidly got himself mixed up with rum-running racketeers. If I didn't find a way to help him, he'd probably get thrown in jail, Honesty would almost certainly go back into zombie mode, and the cosmic scoreboard would read PODS: two, Melanie Beeby: absolutely *nada*.

As I washed and dried endless glasses at the

club, I racked my brains, trying to think of a solution. Maybe I should confront Lenny, tell him I knew what he was up to and advise him to clean up his act, before it was too late? That's definitely what the human part of me wanted to do. But my inner angel told me to wait and see just a little longer.

One night, Honesty and I were up in the projectionist's box at the Golden Picture Palace. Harold Lloyd was doing his mad stunts outside the top-floor window of a skyscraper, while Grace frantically kept up with the action on her plonky old piano. But neither of us were laughing that much, and I suddenly heard Honesty give a deep sigh.

"What's up?" I whispered, as Harold Lloyd almost, but not quite, plummeted to his doom.

"It's Mama," she whispered back. "She's worried she'll be out of a job now the talkies are coming in."

I'd heard customers talking about the new-style 'talking pictures' in the Top Hat a few days ago. They were getting incredibly over-excited, as if movies with soundtracks were some mindblowingly futuristic invention. I couldn't help wondering what they'd make of Dolby surround-sound! To me, the 'talkies' (as Honesty called them) were totally inevitable. But like with all new scientific advances, there were going to be casualties. Once films had soundtracks of their own, the movie houses would no longer need pianists to provide dramatic mood music.

I broke my Reese's Peanut Butter Cup into two and gave Honesty half. I had become totally addicted to this rather weird American sweet. "Your mother is a born survivor," I said. "She'll find a job which pays heaps better, I bet you."

Honesty looked grateful. "You're always so positive, Violet. No matter how low I'm feeling you always make me feel better. I used to feel low all the time." She started saying all these really flattering things, but for some reason it was really hard to take it in. I seemed to be getting this weird disturbance in my energy field. *Omigosh, Lenny!* I thought, and I jumped to my feet.

Honesty stopped in mid-compliment. "Violet, what's wrong?"

"We've got to go to the club." I pulled Honesty to her feet. I knew I was spooking her again, but I didn't have a choice. "I've had one of my psychic flashes. Lenny's in danger!"

We were just a block away when I saw the prohibition agents. OK, so I'd never seen a prohibition agent in my life, but I have watched no end of Sky TV, so a fleet of parked cars full of guys in raincoats and slouch hats naturally made me think the worst. Not to mention the humungous number of cops warily making their way towards the Top Hat.

"There's going to be a bust," I told Honesty.

"That's terrible," she gasped. "If the cops raid the club they'll put everyone in jail!"

We'd been working at the club for a while now, so we knew all its unofficial exits and entrances. Honesty and I dived down an alleyway, and managed to sneak in through the Top Hat's cellars without being seen. Ruby was just coming out of her dressing room. I could hear her muttering a prayer in Spanish, psyching herself up to do her act.

She looked startled. "What's up? I thought this was your night off?"

"You and Lenny have to get out of here!" I panted out. "There's like, an army of cops and agents outside."

Ruby wasn't the kind of girl who needed things spelling out. "Quickly, we've got to find Lenny!"

We found him in the kitchens, lighting about a zillion sparklers on a customer's birthday cake. To my surprise, he totally didn't think of himself when we broke the news.

"This is terrible," he said anxiously. "Harold Lloyd just came in with his friends. We've got to get him out of here."

Lenny peered through the swing doors into the club and gave a moan of despair. "He's right down by the stage. It's jam-packed in there. The cops will be all over us like a rash, before I can get anywhere near him."

"But there's two of us!" Ruby reminded him softly.

She and Lenny exchanged glances.

"Are you thinking what I think you're thinking?" he asked.

She kissed her fingers to him, and without a word, they ran up the steps and burst through the swing door into the club.

Someone was in the middle of a raunchy dance routine to *Second Hand Rose*. Honesty and I arrived in time to hear all the musicians stop playing in a jangle of discordant notes.

The Top Hat Club had a high church-like ceiling. A double row of chandeliers hung over the tables, their crystal drops trembling and tinkling with the tiniest vibration. With breathtaking confidence, Ruby and Lenny leaped on to a table and made a synchronised leap for the chandeliers. The customers gasped as Lenny and his sweetheart soared high over their heads, using the chandeliers for their trapeze!

"This is totally luminous!" I said to Honesty excitedly. "See what they're doing!"

Suspended from the Top Hat's ceiling was an enormous net, containing thousands of party balloons, which were due to come bobbing down at the end of the night's entertainment. As Lenny and Ruby swung crazily from one chandelier to another, they gradually pulled the net with them, in the process releasing brightly coloured balloons, streamers and glittery confetti over the astonished and delighted customers. Everyone began to clap and whistle, thinking it was all part of the show.

They reached a startled-looking Harold Lloyd. When they were performing, Lenny and Ruby were so in tune with each other that they read each other's minds. Without exchanging even a glance, they both hooked a foot around a chandelier and flipped upside down. And still dangling like a bat, Lenny whispered in Harold Lloyd's ear.

I saw the star's expression change as he took in the news. He nodded. Lenny and Ruby held out the net with a flourish, and the star sprang into the air and clung to the meshes for dear life.

Honesty's brother and his feisty girlfriend swung Harold Lloyd back across the club at electrifying speed. The trio did a graceful dismount, waved cheekily to the customers, and made a lightning getaway through the swing doors and out of the back of the club.

We caught up with Lenny and Ruby, just as Harold Lloyd dived into a cab and went screeching off in the totally opposite direction to the advancing law enforcement agents. I couldn't believe what had just happened. I had come *this* close to meeting a world-famous movie star!

Lenny was staring at a card with an incredulous expression.

"Was he grateful?" Honesty asked.

"Oh, yeah," said Lenny in a stunned voice. "Yeah, he was."

"He was only drinking root beer," said Ruby dreamily. "But it would have looked really bad for the studios if one of their big stars was involved with a bust."

"So what did he say to you?" Honesty asked eagerly.

Lenny still seemed overwhelmed. "He said, erm…" He cleared his throat. "He said we were the hottest stunt duo he had ever seen, and he told us to call him at the studios tomorrow."

"Omigosh, he *didn't*!" I screamed. "That is SO fabulous, Lenny!"

"Just as well," Ruby said calmly. "After tonight, it looks like we'll be needing new jobs."

I saw that the Top Hat Club was now totally surrounded by law enforcement agents. Violent battering sounds came from the front of the building. A cop was bellowing through a megaphone, ordering everyone to come out with their hands in the air.

I put my mouth to Honesty's ear. "Do you think Mo and Izzy are in that crowd somewhere, in a couple of cheesy disguises?" I said wickedly.

At the same moment we bleated, "Dere's sa-ad news!"

And we all linked arms and walked away from the mayhem, still laughing.

It was Christmas Eve, and I was helping Honesty stow the last of her luggage in the back of a rented car. Honesty, Rose, Clem and their mother were finally travelling on to San Francisco, where Grace was going to run a boutique for her scandalous cousin Louella. I'd got Honesty to give me the juicy details by this time, so I can tell you that by the standards of my century, Louella was disappointingly tame. Know what her big crime was? She had the nerve to marry a really dishy Chinese guy!! I'm serious! Unfortunately in the American south of the Twenties, this was enough to give her a reputation as a serious scarlet woman. But something told me she was going to be an excellent friend for Grace.

Rose was going to find work in San Francisco until what I called the autumn, and she called the fall. Can you guess what little Miss Smarty Pants was going to do then? Yess! She was actually starting college, just as she'd always dreamed. Like Michael said, things work out.

Honesty squished in the last bag and shut what she called the trunk and I called the boot.

"And you'll really be all right?" she asked me for the tenth time.

"I told you, I'll be fine," I said softly.

She shifted her feet, suddenly shy. "I don't know if I'll ever get used to Christmas in Los Angeles.

Don't you think it feels unnatural, Violet? I mean, sleighs and Santas, when the temperature is in the nineties?"

I smiled to myself. I had a different take on Christmas. I knew that this City of the Angels was Christmassy in every way that mattered. I could feel every sleazy glitzy inch of LA shimmering and tingling with joyful cosmic vibes, like peals of bells only I could hear. "I almost forgot," I said. "I've got something for you."

I handed Honesty the Christmas present I had bought for her with my wages from the Top Hat. "Go on, open it!"

She unwrapped the layers of tissue paper and gasped. "Ohh, Violet! It's the most beautiful notebook I've ever seen,"

"Yeah, well use it, Bloomfield," I told her. "Stick everything down. All the hobos, hoodlums and holy rollers. The bootleggers, rum-runners and speakeasies. The whole shebang."

The shimmery Christmas vibes were growing so intense that that it was overwhelming, even for an angel. I saw Honesty's eyes fill with awe. She almost seemed scared. "Who are you, really, Violet?" she whispered.

I kissed her on the cheek. "I'm your friend, nutcase. Any time you need me, just call, OK?"

A beam of heavenly light strobed down, and as Honesty watched, dazzled and amazed, I stepped into it and went home.

CHAPTER ELEVEN

A few days after I got back from my GA mission, I dragged my soul-mate along to the school library.

"I want to see if I can find any mention of a hotshot news reporter called Honesty Bloomfield," I explained. "I want to know if things turned out OK for her."

Lollie just looked at me with her knowing brown eyes, and I sighed and owned up.

"I suppose, what I really want to know is if I made the grade as a guardian angel."

She gave me a hug. "You don't have to justify yourself to me, Boo," she said. "Being a guardian angel is pretty intense. You can't switch off and stop caring just because your assignment is over. You need closure."

"Hey, that's right!" I said.

I needed to know that I'd made a difference to Honesty Bloomfield. After her dad died, her life was like this scary and depressing movie, one that was scripted and directed by the PODS. With the Agency's help, she'd found the courage to break free. But I wanted to know what happened next. Did Honesty get to direct her own life movie? Did she finally become the kind of person who called the shots?

Lollie and I went on with our search. Can you believe that we found about a zillion mentions? We could see that we were in for a long session, so we got comfortable on the floor between the stacks, and updated ourselves.

Lola gave a low whistle. "Boy, Melanie! Your girl really got around!"

She wasn't exaggerating. Honesty went everywhere. She was over in Europe covering some of the major events in the Second World War. She also went to Singapore and Cairo and sent back some brilliant reports.

It was Lola who found the photographs, black and white and slightly out of focus. In one a taller, skinnier Honesty was posing in front of the Pyramids. She wore her long hair in that brushed-back Thirties style. I thought she looked amazingly elegant in her army camouflage gear, screwing up her eyes against the sun.

In another picture, Honesty was at an old-fashioned typewriter. Tropical sunshine streamed through a slatted window. She wore her camouflage shirt open at the neck and her sleeves rolled up. She wasn't doing one of those cheesy celebrity smiles, just looking coolly back at the camera, with that interested gleam in her eye. Honesty had made it.

By this time I was on a roll, so I went into the film history section to see what the movies buffs had to say about Tony Mantovani's movies. To my disappointment, I drew a complete blank.

"I don't get it," I said to myself.

"Hi, Mel. How's it going?" Brice came mooching round the stacks, looking distinctly dangerous in a way you totally don't expect in an angelic library.

I decided to play it cool.

"I'm trying to find Tony Mantovani," I said carelessly. "He made a movie called *Dangerous*

Pearls, and Honesty's sister played the heroine, but no-one seems to have heard of it."

"Did you check through their old movie collection?" he suggested.

I didn't tell him I hadn't known our library possessed an old movie collection. I just rushed off to ask the librarian, and a few minutes later she pushed a heavy metal spool across the counter. "Director's cut," she said proudly.

My mouth fell open. "This is the actual film!"

"The original copy of *Dangerous Pearls* was destroyed in a warehouse fire, not long after it was finished," said the librarian. "But as you know, we keep copies of every film ever made."

"*Omigosh*!" I shrieked.

Several angel trainees looked up from their books and said "Sssh!"

I wandered around until I found Brice. "But how will I watch it?" I said pathetically. "It's like, really old technology."

He gave a deep sigh and took me to a door near the library's spiral staircase. I peered wonderingly into a dinky retro movie theatre, which I had completely never noticed. It had plushy seats, red velvet curtains, a screen, and best of all, an old-fashioned movie projector.

"Have fun, sweetheart," said Brice and he mooched off again, doing his dangerous bad-boy walk. As he went, I thought, well that wasn't so bad, Melanie. Providing you only meet him in totally public places.

That night I took all my mates to the movies. We did it American style, with popcorn and Hershey's Kisses and Reese's Peanut Butter Cups.

Chase started up the projector, and I heard it starting to whirr in the dark. I hugged myself happily. It was almost as good as being in the Golden Palace Picture House. The film had been remastered to recreate the full Twenties film experience. As the title *Dangerous Pearls* came up, humungously dramatic piano music filled the theatre. I know, I know, I should have acted really cool and laid back and let my mates watch the film in peace, but I just couldn't help interrupting. I kept going, "Oh, that's Clem with the puppy. Mr Mantovani hated that poor animal. It kept widdling on his shoes," and, "Rose could have been a famous celebrity, you know, but she wanted to be an intellectual, so what can you do?" I was so proud that I had actually been with them while this film was being made.

"Oh, you've got to watch this bit," I said suddenly. "This is where they tied poor Rose to the train tracks. Honesty was convinced she was going to be mashed by an express train. I wasn't too happy either, so I surrounded Rose with— *Omigosh*!"

Lola laughed. "Hey, Boo, you're a celebrity!"

I gazed in pure astonishment at the screen.

The scene was very nearly as I remembered it, with Rose miming wide-eyed terror, and the villain pulling evil expressions.

But now three people were in shot: the heroine, the villain, and a girl in a pink Kung Fu Kitty T-shirt and boot-cut jeans.

"But how…?" I breathed. "I wasn't even visible, not then."

"This is the heavenly copy," Reuben said softly.

"But I look – I look…"

I was so happy, I'd lost the power of speech.

Like an angel, I thought. I look exactly like an angel.

Fogging Over

With thanks to Australian angels Kerry Greenwood and Jenny Pausacker for helping me with Mel's trip to the Northern Territories. Thanks also to Viv French for helping me find my way round Victorian London. And a special thank you to my daughter Maria for her totally luminous inspiration!

CHAPTER ONE

Once upon a time, I lived on a gorgeous blue-green planet called Earth. I didn't stay long, thirteen years and twenty-two hours max. But it often felt a whole lot longer. That's because I was in a perpetual state of panic. It would take too long to list all the things I was scared of. There were all the normal human anxieties obviously: spiders, dentists, exams. Plus those typical teen twitches, worrying that I looked fat or had evil-smelling breath or that I'd been walking around the school with my skirt trapped in my knickers. These were just my background worries! The bass line for the heavy stuff.

But one fear was so humiliating that I never admitted it to anybody.

I was petrified of being by myself. I knew it was nuts, even at the time. Loneliness can't actually kill you, right? But the minute I was alone, I literally felt myself dissolving with terror. My home felt SO empty. Even with the TV on full blast. Even when I called my mates and kept them talking for hours on the phone. Even if I made butterscotch-flavoured popcorn and pigged the lot. Even – well, you get the picture.

It all started when my dad walked out. Naturally I started worrying that Mum would be next to abandon me. Every time she left the flat, I knew she was going to get mashed in a road accident and I'd be taken into care. But she didn't and I wasn't, and eventually she met my lovely stepdad Des. After we all moved in together I let myself relax for a whole twenty-four hours. Ohh, it was bliss! But next day, EEP! I was back on Red Alert. Only now I was panicking about Des dying in the same tragic car wreck. Plus a few months later, my baby sister was born, so then I had to add her to my panic list too.

But that's all ancient history. These days you'll find me living happily on the other side of those famous Pearly Gates. I know! Unbelievable isn't it? It was actually me who died, which is about the one scenario that never occurred to me! I just wish I could go on *Oprah* and broadcast an inspirational message to the stressed-out Mel Beebys of this world.

"Go with the flow, babes," I'd tell them. "No matter what happens, you can handle it. You're ALL going to be fine!" And to prove it, I'd show them some feel-good footage from my personal video diary.

To a cool hip hop soundtrack, you see this like, MTV montage of me and my mates, shopping in our favourite department stores, paddling on the seashore and dancing the night away at the Babylon Café. At the end I'm by myself. The camera pulls back to show my friend Lola Sanchez watching as I sashay through the school gates. "At first glance, Melanie Beeby looks like any normal schoolgirl," she tells the viewer. "But appearances can be deceptive and this is no ordinary school."

The camera focuses on a sign saying *Angel Academy* in shimmery letters, then zooms in on the angel logo on the gates. Next minute there's a new close-up of the identical logo, only this one is on my cute midriff T-shirt. I go floating through the school in graceful slow-mo, chatting and laughing with my mates.

Then CUT! Lola and I are sipping strawberry smoothies at Guru, our favourite student hang-out.

"I used to think of death as the ultimate tragedy," I confide in my friend. "Like this scary black hole that swallowed you up for ever? But the fact is, dying totally improved my life. Naturally I was upset to leave my family," I add hastily. "But at my old school I'd got this reputation for being a real bimbo. One teacher called me 'an airhead with attitude'."

Lola pulls a face into the camera. "Yeah, Miss Rowntree!" she says cheekily. "And look at her now!"

"I was so amazed when I got to Heaven and found I'd won a scholarship to the Angel Academy!" I giggle. "Someone must have thought I had hidden depths!"

Now Lola and I are walking past the school library. It's made of glass and looks a bit like a lighthouse, only with magic cloud effects scudding over the walls.

"We don't think of ourselves as pupils," I say into the camera. "We're trainees. And if we make the grade we'll be the celestial agents of the future, which has to be the coolest job ever."

The scene dissolves, and we're in the middle of a science class. Mr Allbright is demonstrating a new technique for beaming celestial vibes. After a few attempts, everyone successfully materialises a wobbly sphere of golden light above his or her cupped palms. We all look v. intellectual, especially Lola, who's wearing cute little gold glasses.

This time it's my voice on the soundtrack. "Lollie is my best friend," I tell the world happily. "She's the soul-mate I've been longing for my whole life, which is incredible as originally she's from my future! Angel trainees can come from every period of Earth's history. Oh, except for pure angels like my buddy Reuben here."

The camera drops in on a martial arts class, where a skinny, honey-coloured boy is performing a sequence of ninja angel moves. He looks focused, yet v. endearing with his little dreads whipping around his head.

CUT! It's sunset and the whole class is sitting on the beach in the lotus position. The sun slips down into the ocean, beaming rosy rays across our faces. A musical throbbing builds on the soundtrack, sounding like some huge divine humming top.

I say, "This is the first sound I heard after I left my body and found myself in Heaven. I call it my cosmic lullaby, because it makes me feel really safe and secure. You see, life really doesn't end when you die! The truth is, it just gets better and better!"

At this point though, my video diary totally runs out of steam.

Diaries are meant to tell the truth and I'm not sure mine is giving a true picture. Perhaps you didn't notice, but in trying to focus on the bright side, I accidentally make my school look like a Pepsi commercial. Like, I never *once* mention the Dark Powers. I also give the impression that I'm finally sorted (yeah, right!).

But like our teacher says, being an angel is not about being perfect. It's about being real. So I want you to forget all about that phony Pepsi Heaven, because I'm about to tell you the uncut, unvarnished, totally unglamorous story of my last assignment.

But first, to help you understand what happened, I've got to tell you about Brice.

I ran into Brice on my very first trouble-shooting mission to Earth. At that time he was working for the PODS (that's what my mates and I call the Powers of Darkness). I won't lie to you, I hated him on sight. It didn't help that this cosmic low-life was the exact double of a really buff boy I once fancied at my old school, right down to the bleached hair and bad-boy slouch.

Anyway, without going into the sordid details, I got the better of him. After that Brice became like, my evil nemesis or whatever, because he turned up again on our mission to Tudor England. This time he beat our buddy Reuben up so badly that Reubs had to be airlifted back home. He's still got a huge scar.

Now I've convinced you that Brice belongs firmly on the dark side of the cosmic fence, right? Unfortunately, it's not that simple.

You see, once upon a time, Brice was an angel like me.

I know, it's too disturbing for words. I don't understand why it seems more shocking for a Light Worker to go over to the Opposition than if he'd been bad from the beginning, but it does.

I'm not going to get into why Brice sold his soul to the PODS. But the Agency obviously believed there were extenuating circumstances, because last term, after complex negotiations with the Opposition (that's the official Agency term for the Dark Powers), they brought Brice in from the cold. And next thing I know, bosh! He's back at school. They actually had him working on the Guardian Angel hotline, would you believe!

Our headmaster explained that the Agency has to take the long-term view. He also said a heap of other stuff, about Eternity and how if you wait long enough trees sometimes evolve into diamonds. It was an excellent speech, but I still thought Brice was a jerk.

Luckily he was keeping totally out of my way. I'd catch glimpses of him at various student hang-outs, but he was always on his own and never stayed longer than a few minutes. Once I bumped into him mooching around the stacks in the school library. And another time I saw him on the beach, chucking pebbles at the sea, looking incredibly depressed.

The boy's a freak, I thought smugly. He can't hack the Hell dimensions and he can't stand Heaven. I bet he won't make it to the end of term.

Basically I couldn't wait for Brice to let everyone down again and go slinking back to the Opposition. Then I could pretend the creep never existed and life could go back to how it was before.

Then summer came and things took a totally unexpected turn.

I only have myself to blame for what happened. Lola was desperate for me to spend the holidays with her, in the heavenly interior doing adventure activities. "Everyone says you come back totally transformed," she enthused. "We'll be like angel warriors! The PODS won't know what hit them!"

But I'm not the bungee-jumping type, and anyway I'd promised to help out at the preschoolers' summer camp. So at the end of term, we went our separate ways.

For the first few days I literally felt like I was missing a limb.

Every time I went into town I'd leave a message for Lollie on the Link – the angel internet. But days and weeks went by and she still didn't reply.

I told myself she must be holidaying somewhere remote, where they hadn't even heard of internet cafés. But I wasn't convinced. I mean, we're both angels, right? Normally I know the instant she's thinking about me. Yet I was getting this permanently 'ENGAGED' signal, as if my soul-mate's thoughts had drifted totally elsewhere.

Luckily with thirty hyperactive angel tots to take care of, I didn't have time to mope. Days whizzed by in a blur of activity: picnics on the beach, treasure hunts among the dunes, trips to the Sugar Shack for home-made ices. Until finally it was our last day. Since we'd worked so hard, Miss Dove told us we could have a couple of hours off.

Picture me lying in a hammock in the afternoon sunshine, listening to the soothing whisper of waves from the beach below, my eyes glued to a spine-chilling novel I'd found in our holiday cottage. From nearby came a babble of excited little voices as the toddlers tried to guess the mystery objects in Miss Dove's special magic bag.

I heard the creak of a hammock and Amber sat up. "Boy, you've really got the bug," she yawned. You were reading Sherlock Holmes last time I looked!"

"Finished it last night," I mumbled.

My reading marathon started out of sheer self defence. After a hard day keeping up with the tinies, I needed to flake out and relax. Unfortunately Amber and the other volunteers were bursting to hold lengthy midnight discussions on various deep angelic issues. I didn't want to hurt their feelings, so I had to pretend to be fascinated by the mildewed book collection in my attic bedroom. I guess I must have been quite bored, because one book led to another and I was now shamelessly addicted – my current read had me totally mesmerised! You would not *believe* the things that happened to that heroine. First both her parents die in a storm at sea. Then her relatives pack her off to a typhoid-ridden boarding school on the moors, so they can cheat her out of her rightful inheritance. I was desperate to know how it would turn out.

Suddenly shrieks of excitement made me look up.

"YAYY!! I guessed right!" Next minute little Maudie landed on top of me. My hammock wobbled madly, tipping both of us on the ground, and I found myself buried under a heap of giggling preschool angels.

But finally the day was over and my fellow volunteers and I tottered back to our cottage at the top of the cliffs. It was still really warm so we ate outdoors, watching the lighthouse wink on and off across the bay.

Out of the blue, Amber said, "So have you guys decided where you're going yet?"

For the second time that day I came back to reality with a bump.

"Omigosh!" I gasped. "I can't believe I forgot!"

Mr Allbright had announced that the History students would be going on a field trip at the beginning of the new term; a trip with a twist. We had to pick an era in human history which interested us. If the Agency approved, we'd be assigned a suitable human from that time period and we'd go to Earth to study them in their natural context.

That's what I think is SO cool about my school. We don't just learn history from books, we visit historical eras for real. I'm serious, we literally travel in Time!

This time we were supposed to be working in groups of three, something to do with power triangles or whatever. I naturally assumed I'd be in a three with my fellow cosmic musketeers, Lollie and Reuben. But it had been a v. stressful term and my frazzled mates couldn't seem to agree on anything.

Lola had insisted we went back to ancient Persia where she'd done her Guardian Angel module. And Reuben had this bizarre fixation with King Arthur and his Round Table.

"I hate to burst your bubble, hon," I said, "but the King Arthur thing is just a story. Camelot never actually existed."

As a pure angel Reuben often finds it hard to grasp quite basic concepts, such as the difference between human history and fairy tales. In the end my mates grumpily informed me that they'd leave our destination entirely up to moi. And I'd immediately put it to the back of my mind. After all, I had the whole summer in front of me.

Only now the holidays were over and I still hadn't thought of a destination. You see, I wanted it to be somewhere truly amazing. I mean, I wanted my mates to have a great time, but most of all I wanted to wow them with my super de luxe five-star decision-making. Unfortunately under that kind of pressure my mind turns to pink bubblegum, incapable of making even weedy one-star decisions!

Yikes! I wasn't even back at school yet but my stress levels were soaring dangerously. So I took myself off to have a calming read in the bath.

I lit a small army of candles, climbed into the old-fashioned tub, lay back in the hot water and settled down to finish my mystery. The pages started going wavy in the steam, but I refused to budge until the evil rellies got their just desserts. At last I closed the book with a sigh of satisfaction. Then I shot bolt upright, sending bath foam everywhere. I'd had the most fantabulous idea!

I towelled myself dry, put on my cute *Treat me like a Princess* T-shirt and flew into my room to investigate my antique book collection.

Every title gave me goosebumps! *The Story of Dr Jekyll and Mr Hyde*, *The Woman in White*, *Collected Ghost Stories* by Charles Dickens, and most spine-tingling of all, real-life reports of the case of Jack the Ripper! And all these books were written in the exact same era. Victorian times. Well, was that a sign, or was that a sign?

I grabbed the Ripper book and screwed my eyes tight shut. "Just give me a date," I muttered. "Any date will do." I opened the book at random and peeped out from under my lashes.

There it was, bang in the middle of the page. 1888!

By total fluke, I'd found the perfect destination for our time trip. Lola, Reubs and I could do a spot of enjoyable time-tourism, plus we'd collect enough info on social conditions and whatever to satisfy our teacher.

Now I could relax and enjoy the last few hours of my holiday with a clear conscience. I was so impressed with myself, it never occurred to me that my mates might not be as thrilled with my idea as I was!

Have you noticed how the moments you most look forward to are so often the ones that are a total let-down?

The instant I got back to school, I hurtled along to Lollie's room to tell her the good news, but she still hadn't returned from her adventure holiday. So I dashed along to my room and called Reuben's number. Reuben *had* to be back. Only he wasn't.

I collapsed on to my narrow bed and gazed out over the heavenly rooftops. It was evening and lights were coming on all over the city, like sprinkles of little stars. But tonight this beauty just made me feel depressed. "Hi, I'm back," I told my empty room. And then I said, "Well, can't sit about here all day."

I unpacked my bags, singing along to my current fave single, a sweet little hip hop track called *True Colours*. After that, I had a shower, drying and conditioning my hair slowly and carefully. And after that, I gave my little orange tree some overdue TLC, lovingly polishing every leaf with Leaf Shine. But there was still no sign of Lola.

"I'll lie down for a minute," I told myself. "I won't go to sleep. I'll just rest my eyes."

But the next thing I knew, my room was full of dazzling celestial sunlight. Someone had posted a message under my door while I was sleeping. With a rush of happiness I recognised Lola's handwriting.

Yo! Sleeping Beauty! We're having breakfast at Guru to celebrate our last hour of freedom!
Big love,
Lollie xxx

My soul-mate was back in town!

Guru's chef must have been making their special chocolate brownies when I arrived, because the café smelled divine.

I heard a husky chuckle and spotted my friend's mad dark curls over by the window. She was chatting to some real outdoor types, looking incredibly pretty in a cute red dress I'd never seen before.

Pure happiness fizzed up inside me. I planned to sneak up and put my hands over her eyes. Ta da!

Before I could reach her, Brice burst through the kitchen doors, waving a bottle of maple syrup. "Here you are, princess! You can't eat pancakes without maple syrup." He sat down beside her, draping an arm round the back of her chair.

I couldn't believe what I was seeing.

"This isn't happening!" I whispered. But it was.

My best friend and my old enemy were an item.

CHAPTER TWO

I wanted to run but I was totally paralysed. Anyway, it was too late – Lola had already spotted me.

"Boo!" she shrieked. "Omigosh! I've missed you so much!"

I have no idea why Lola calls me Boo. She loves giving her friends crazy nicknames.

Lola poked Brice in the ribs. "Don't just sit there, you monster! Find her a chair!"

My soul-mate seemed to think everything was quite normal. Like, "It's no big deal. I've just spent my entire holidays with a cosmic juvenile delinquent."

Well, it *was* a big deal. I was completely

traumatised. So much so that I behaved like a complete child, blanking Brice and babbling to my friend as if we were alone.

"Guess what, babe!" I wittered. "I had this brilliant idea for Mr Allbright's time project. And I'm thinking Victorian times, because they—"

"That's great," Lola said politely. "Though I have to tell you, after the summer we've had, schoolwork seems kind of irrelevant. Oh, Mel, I wish you'd come with us! We had such a fabulous time, didn't we?" She beamed at Brice. "You should have seen us canoeing down that waterfall, babe! Omigosh, those canoes are SO tiny, I don't know how we both—"

"OK, tell me the details later," I said hastily. "Look, about that project—"

"You've got to come with us next time!" Lola interrupted. "It's SO sublime. We used to take our sleeping bags outside and just lie staring up at the stars. Oh, but one night, something really funny happened." Lollie gave her husky chuckle. "It makes me laugh just thinking about it!"

Just then Reuben came in. Unlike me, Reuben has a forgiving nature. So when he saw our best friend openly sharing maple syrup with the thug who'd put him in the hospital, he didn't seem to think anything of it. Brice also seemed to think it was all water under the bridge.

"Have my seat, mate," he told Reuben. "They're expecting me down at the Agency."

"Why? Got an appointment with your probation officer?" I said spitefully.

Brice just blew me a kiss on his way out.

Good riddance, I thought. Lola had started chatting to someone else about her holiday, but I didn't want to hear about her and Brice gazing up at the stars, so I hooked my arm through Reuben's. "Reubs, I was just telling Lola about this idea I had for our project."

"Melanie!" he protested. "I just got back five minutes ago!"

"I know, babe, but they're expecting us at the Agency any minute and they'll ask us where we're going, so you've got to back me up and say we want to go to London in 1888."

"Why, what's so special about 1888?"

"Oh, loads of stuff," I said enthusiastically, to cover the fact that my mind had gone embarrassingly blank.

"Name one," he insisted.

"Well, erm – for one thing, Jack the Ripper was still stalking the streets!" I remembered triumphantly.

"Doing what?" Reuben couldn't have looked less impressed.

"Duh! Murdering people, what else!"

My angel buddy shook his head. "I don't get it."

"Oh come on," I groaned. "The Ripper has to be the most famous serial killer in history."

Reuben's expression went from blank, to confused, to totally appalled. "You're kidding? They made someone famous because he *murdered* people?"

I took a deep breath, reminding myself that Reuben often finds it hard to understand human behaviour. "I suppose it's because he was never caught," I explained. "It makes him seem immortal, kind of. Like he's still out there somewhere."

"But that's really sick."

"Well, don't blame me," I said defensively. "It's history, OK! You can't just pick out the pretty bits."

"Whatever," said Reuben. "Anyway, you'll have to count me out. I promised I'd help Chase with this tiger conservation thing."

I was genuinely shocked. I couldn't believe Reubs was ducking out.

"But you have to come!" I wailed. "Mr Allbright said we had to work in threes!"

"Then find someone else." Reuben glanced at

his watch. "We'd better run. We're due down at the Agency in five minutes."

The Agency, if you hadn't guessed, is the angelic organisation which keeps the whole of Creation running smoothly, so the Agency building is kind of Angel HQ.

There are gorgeous buildings everywhere in this city, but the Agency Tower is truly fabulous. Sometimes I get the feeling it's alive. It's made of special stuff that changes colour constantly. And with that high-level cosmic activity going on inside, you feel the vibes when you're still like, streets away.

On the way downtown, Reuben and Lola swapped holiday stories, but I didn't join in. Helping at a preschool camp doesn't exactly compare with canoeing down waterfalls or saving tigers. And anyway, they were meant to be my best friends and they had totally let me down.

We went in through the revolving doors, flashed our IDs at the guy on the desk, and took the lift up to the floor where we have our Agency briefings.

Trainees were already crowding into the hall, and I lost my mates in the crush. I spotted Orlando in front of me and felt a blush creeping up my neck.

Officially Orlando still goes to our school. Unofficially, he does a lot of hush-hush assignments for the Agency. Orlando's a genius basically – not a twisted genius like Brice, the real thing. Ohh, and he is SO cute! He literally looks like an angel; the gorgeous kind you see in old Italian paintings.

Hmmn, I thought. Maybe I could persuade dishy Orlando to be in our three? I was just about to take the plunge when Lola came dashing up.

"Boo, I'm so sorry! I didn't have my school head on back there," she said breathlessly. "Look, I trust you, OK. I'm sure we'll have a great time in 1880 or whenever, and don't worry about Reuben dropping out. It's all sorted!"

"It is?" I said.

"Totally. I told Brice and he insisted on taking Reuben's place. Isn't that SO sweet!"

"Well, actually," I croaked. "I don't know if I—"

"Mel, relax. It'll be great! Brice has changed. He really has!" She beamed into my eyes.

But I wasn't sure I wanted to go to Jack the Ripper's London any more. Especially not if I had to go with Brice.

Then I suddenly saw how this could work out to my advantage.

Right now Lola was seeing Brice through a holiday glow, which was partly my fault. I hadn't been around to give her regular reality checks, which is what good mates are for, right?

But if the three of us went on the same time trip, the cracks would start to show, and she'd have to see him for the charmless yob he really was. OK, this might not be much fun for Lola, but she'd thank me in the end.

"That sounds like a fabulous idea," I said brightly. "Let's sign up!"

We joined one of the queues of trainees, waiting to register their choice of destination with junior members of staff. Yet again I found myself wondering why all the younger agents look so poker-faced. Would it kill them to smile once in a while?

The agent looked startled when I told him our destination, but he dutifully typed our data into his laptop and said it would take an hour to match us with a suitable human.

I was going to suggest that Lola and I spent the time shopping for new outfits. But before I could get the words out, Brice came schmoozing up, and Lola said apologetically, "Oh Mel, you don't mind do you? I said I'd help Brice find some new jeans." And before I could say, "Actually, I do mind," the two of them headed out of the door hand in hand.

I stared after them. Don't over-react babe, I told myself shakily. Lola is a very tactile person. She'll hold hands with anyone. It doesn't mean a thing. There is no reason for your feelings to be hurt.

Luckily I remembered how in magazine advice columns they tell you to do something v. positive for yourself, so I took myself into town for a spot of v. positive retail therapy. And guess what! I went into The Source and found the most delicious little vintage top which would give my hipster jeans and boots the perfect retro twist.

But when I walked back into the Agency Tower, I couldn't believe my eyes. My soul-mate was waiting for the lift, wearing an identical top to mine! We stared at each other. "How totally luminous!" she screamed. "You got the same one!"

I went weak with relief. This was ultimate proof that Lola and I are spiritual twins, which meant that nothing and no-one could ever come between us.

"Where's Brice?" I asked casually.

"Still shopping," she said. "I've been telling him he should get some new stuff. His old clothes kind of smell."

"Oh, right," I said politely.

Lollie wrinkled her nose. "Yeah, some of the Hell dimensions are really whiffy, and it doesn't wash out apparently. Anyway, fill me in on these Victorians, *carita!* Michael is sure to ask questions."

By the time Michael buzzed us in, Brice still hadn't turned up, which put me in a real quandary. On the one hand I wanted Lola to know what a scumbag he was. But if he let us down, our Victorian trip would have to be called off.

Suddenly he came panting along the corridor.

"You're late," I said.

"No, sweetie, you're early. I'm totally on time."

I was going to tell him where to get off, but Lola said quickly, "You got that Diesel top after all. It looks great on you."

Brice looked down at his grey hoodie as if he had no idea where it had come from. "What, this?"

"Come on, you guys, Michael's waiting."

I was genuinely shocked when I first got here and heard all the kids referring to our headmaster by his first name. But I soon discovered that Michael is not your average headmaster. In fact he's an archangel, one of the immortal beings who oversee the running of Creation. The poor sweetheart has permanent jetlag from zipping between Earth's major trouble spots. But no matter how tired he is, Michael is totally with the programme. And when he looks at me with those scary beautiful archangel eyes, it's like he literally sees into my soul.

As usual he went straight to the point. "I won't deny that I was slightly concerned at your choice of era. I gather it was your idea, Mel, and I wasn't sure you'd realised all the implications?"

I'd been thinking the same thing, but now Michael had put it into words I felt really offended. He thinks I can't hack it, I thought, but I hid my hurt feelings with a little airhead joke. "No way are we backing out," I giggled. "We might get to meet Sherlock Holmes!"

"Hate to shatter your illusions, sweetheart," Brice murmured, "but Holmes was a fictional character."

I gave him my most poisonous look. "I did know that, actually."

Michael was constructing miniature steeples with his fingers. "I felt much better when I heard you were going to be the third member of the team," he said to Brice. "I seem to remember you spent some time in this era."

Brice just nodded expressionlessly. I guessed this was some oblique reference to his murky PODS past.

"I'll be frank," Michael said. "If it wasn't for you, I'd be asking the girls to reconsider. But if you're going along, I know they'll be in experienced hands."

Oh, this is great, I thought. Not only had my enemy been reinstated in Heaven, now I was meant to look up to him for his dodgy past!

Michael began shuffling the papers on his desk, a sign our interview was coming to an end. "This is an ideal opportunity for you to understand what makes this era tick. But as you know, some eras are especially tough to handle, so try to stay centred and alert, won't you? I'm expecting you to take good care of them," he said to Brice.

He flushed. "I'll do my best."

I gave Michael my sweetest smile. "Oh, we'll be fine! We're big girls now."

As usual, the Departures area was a hive of mad activity. We queued for our angel tags, then we queued all over again for our Agency watches, then we had to hang about waiting for the maintenance staff to finish servicing our portal. But finally we stepped inside and the glass door slid shut.

I always get serious butterflies at this point and no wonder. We were going to be blasted from a world of divine beauty and harmony into the bubbling stewpot of History. Lola normally relieves the tension by singing the tune Reuben wrote for us. It starts, "You're not alone, you're not alone," and it always makes me feel better. But today she seemed to forget about our little departure ritual. She just kept glancing nervously at Brice, like, "Oh, I hope he'll be OK." He seemed totally oblivious, listening to his headset.

So I sang our theme tune to myself in my head. "You're not alone, You're not alone." I kept on singing it until we took off.

The portal lit up in a blue-white blaze of cosmic light, and the heavenly city fell away as we blasted through the invisible barrier which divides the angelic fields from the beautiful unpredictable fields of Space and Time.

Centuries of history flew past in minutes, making gorgeous coloured patterns in the dark. As we drew closer to our time zone, the colours grew more and more intense. This time we made an impressively smooth landing. The portal door slid back and we stepped on to my favourite planet. Or rather, we floated.

I stared around me in shock. "What in the world—?"

We were in a desert so red it seemed to glow. The vegetation was like nothing on Earth. Spiky bushes with pink berries that looked fake. Stunted trees with pale papery leaves. A flock of birds flew past, their marshmallow-pink feathers perfectly matching the waxy pink berries. All the birds landed on the same branch, chuckling to themselves like birds in a cartoon.

The desert air smelled scorched and deeply alien, like I imagine it might smell on Mars. Perhaps it *was* Mars. That would explain the surprising lack of gravity.

Brice blew out his breath. "All right, I give up. Anyone know what we're doing in Australia?"

"Australia?" I gulped. "Are you serious?"

The pink cartoon birds suddenly decided to turn themselves the wrong way up. They just hung there, chuckling, letting the blood rush to their heads.

"I think those are galah birds," said Brice. "And the trees are definitely eucalyptus. So somewhere in the Northern Territories is my guess."

"But it feels so strange," said Lola. "I feel like I could just float away."

"Me too," I agreed.

Even our voices sounded floaty, like voices in a dream.

"The Agency must have miscalculated," I said in my floaty voice. "We'd better call them so they can get us back on track."

Brice shook his head. "They don't make that kind of mistake."

"But Michael agreed we could go to Victorian London," I protested childishly.

"So? For some reason they wanted us to come here first."

"But why would they send us somewhere uninhabited?"

Brice sighed. "This land is not uninhabited, sweetheart. Aborigines live here for one thing. Plus there's a road." He pointed through the shimmering heat haze.

"I'd call that a track," I said sniffily.

"Call it what you like. People made it and people use it. All kinds of people. Herders looking for work on cattle stations, missionaries looking for converts, hunters, trappers, telegraph workers—"

I was just wishing I had something to throw at him when I heard rustling and panting sounds. A demented-looking figure came stumbling through the bush. For a minute I actually thought it might be a mirage, but suddenly he gave this heart-rending cry, "Someone help me!" Then he crumpled across the track and went totally still.

We went skimming over to him, our feet barely touching the ground. I'd have worried about this normally, but we had a human emergency to attend to.

I stared down at the wild old man and felt myself shiver.

Something terrible had happened to him. I don't mean just physically. He was like those trees you see that have been struck by lightning, all blasted and hollow inside.

I saw a tiny muscle move in Brice's cheek. "Poor guy must have got close to the PODS."

Lola's eyes went dark with distress. "You think the PODS did that?"

"Oh, yeah. They use you up. Then when there's nothing left, they shed you like yesterday's trash." He tried to laugh.

The old guy's hair and beard had grown so long and messy that tiny life-forms had set up home there. He must have been wandering around out here for weeks. Once Miss Rowntree read us a v. depressing poem, *The Ancient Mariner* it was called, about a sailor who stupidly shot an albatross and was doomed to wander the seven seas for ever. I thought maybe he'd looked like this.

Lola had put her hand on Brice's sleeve. "But that didn't happen to you. You got away. Plus you've got friends who really care about you."

They'd obviously forgotten I was there, so I coughed. "At least we know we've come to the right time." I pointed at the old man's shredded sun-faded garments. "Those fastenings are typically Victorian." I knew my fashion, if nothing else.

"Well, if someone doesn't get him out of the sun, this Victorian's a goner," said Brice.

Lola sucked in her breath. "Oh, no, his poor leg!"

The old man's tattered trousers had split at a side seam, exposing a hideous scar around his bony calf.

Brice whistled. "He probably came over to Australia on a transport ship. They used to keep the convicts in leg irons until they got to Botany Bay," he explained.

I stared at him. "A convict? Are you saying he's a criminal?"

"Not necessarily. In his day, just stealing a loaf of bread is enough to get you transported."

"Does it matter, Boo?" said Lola. "He asked us to help."

She's right, I thought. We'd heard his SOS, which made us kind of responsible.

"What can we do, though? We can't exactly move him," I objected.

"We can keep beaming vibes," she suggested.

"If we boost his energy levels, it'll be easier for the Agency to send this guy the help he needs."

We sat down in the desert and beamed vibes until I felt dizzy.

The old man started mumbling to himself. "I put it in my pocket," he blurted suddenly. "I put it in my pocket!"

After half an hour or so, I saw Lola shading her eyes. "Is that a dust devil?"

A huge cloud of dust was travelling towards us. But it wasn't some kind of home-grown Australian whirlwind; it was a wagon pulled by sweating horses.

"Whoa!" The driver jumped down from the wagon and knelt beside the old man. "Wonder how long you've been here, you poor old devil?"

He unstoppered his water bottle and tried to drip some water down the old man's throat, but it ran away into the sand.

"I can't just leave you here," he muttered. The driver was a really sweet guy, also *très* muscly. He lifted the old man easily and laid him in the back of the wagon.

"We'd better go with him," said Lola at once. "To make sure he's OK."

Distances in Australia are really something else.

We went bumping down that track for FIVE hours. Was this really the nearest place the driver could think of? The old man was still raving deliriously about his mysterious pocket.

Poor darling, he's lost it, I thought. I won't pretend I was thrilled at this unexpected diversion, but when you're an angel you have to take the yin with the yang and whatever, and I did feel genuinely sorry for him.

"Yikes, tingles!" squeaked Lola suddenly. "I'm getting major tingles all over."

"Me too," I murmured. "What's doing it?"

"I should imagine it's that rock," said Brice. "Over the rise there."

The glowing red rock formation looked practically extraterrestrial. It was huge, like some massive crouching animal.

"It's out of this world," breathed Lola.

"It is in a way. It's sacred to the Aborigines, so it exists in multi-dimensional reality as well as the three-D kind," Brice told her.

We all gazed at the awesome rock. It was a really special moment. But then Brice had to spoil it. "Oh, the Aborigines are the original Australians, Melanie," he added patronisingly. "The people who don't live here, remember?"

I spent the rest of the journey in huffy silence.

At last we spotted a big plantation of eucalyptus trees. Behind the trees was a wooden church, and beside the church was the mission house, a white-painted building with a large shady verandah.

The driver reined in his team and bellowed a greeting. Two serving women appeared, looking stunned to see another human being.

"Got an old timer in my wagon, half-dead with sunstroke," he told them.

The older woman climbed up and laid her hand on the old man's forehead. "You could fry eggs on him," she muttered.

She frowned as she registered the scars. "You can't bring him in the house," she told the driver. "Convicts make the missus nervous." She gave a rasping laugh. "They made an exception for me. Good cooks are hard to find, eh!"

Luckily the driver was a real charmer and he managed to persuade the women to make up a bed on the verandah. The driver carried the old man into the shade. "I put it in my pocket," the old man moaned. "I put it in my pocket."

"Never mind, grandad," said the woman. "You'll be out of it soon."

"He's had it hard," said the younger woman timidly. "You can see it in his face."

The other servant snorted. "Him? He didn't have to slave in the prison laundry for five years. And he didn't live with a drunken bully and lose two precious little babies to the diphtheria, so don't tell me he's had it hard."

But she wasn't as cynical as she pretended, because with her next breath she told the driver to come round to the kitchen for a feed of boiled mutton and some strong tea. They went into the mission house, leaving the old man alone.

"I can't believe those missionaries won't let a dying man in their house," I said. "I thought Christians were supposed to like, forgive people."

"I'm not convinced he is dying, actually," said Lola. "I'm not getting that death vibe, are you? I don't think he's ready."

I knew what she meant. You could feel the old man's spirit hanging on grimly by its fingernails.

It's almost like something won't let him die, I thought. Like that guy in the albatross poem. A shiver went through me. "Can the PODS do that?" I asked in a panic. "Can they make someone stay alive even if they don't want to?"

"Definitely not," said Brice. "He has to be doing it himself."

*   *   *

Hours passed and still the old man hung on. The fierce heat began to lose its sting and at last the sun went down like a great ball of red fire.

We were watching our human so anxiously that we didn't notice the old Aboriginal woman come out of the bush. She was just suddenly there, padding silently up the wooden steps and on to the verandah. She went straight to the old man, squatted down beside him and started giving him a real telling-off!

As you know, angels understand every human language going, and her scolding went something like this.

"I know why you can't die, you wicked old white fella. You still got work to do. You got a terrible wrong to put right."

It was amazing. The old man instantly calmed down. It was like he actually understood what she was saying. Brice and Lola looked as astonished as I felt.

"That's better," said the old woman. "You been a loud-mouth your whole life. Now listen to someone else for a change. That's good! Now you get to hear the Earth singing to you. You didn't know everything got its own song, even a no-good white fella like you? Well it has." The woman's eyes flickered slyly in our direction. "And these Shining People, they came out of the Dreaming to help me sing it to you."

Omigosh, she must mean us! I thought.

The old woman had begun to chant aloud in her own language.

"Well, show some respect, will you," said Brice impatiently. "She said we'd come to help. So help already!"

That's the amazing thing about the angel business. You never know what's going to happen next. You set off to Victorian London, and before you know it, you're in Australia taking part in a tribal chantathon on a Christian verandah.

But actually it was kind of cool. And after a while this mystical thing happened. I felt the night literally come alive around me. The coolest thing was that I was a part of it. Angels, sacred rocks and eucalyptus trees, mad men and wise old women, we were all a part of the same living, breathing, star-spangled web, and for just a moment we seemed to share one heart and one mind.

Quite suddenly we all stopped chanting and my head filled up with this vast silence. We just sat there without speaking, or even thinking, and it was so peaceful I can't tell you.

The chanting must have been *très* powerful too, because when the sun rose next morning the old man was sleeping like a little baby, and the old woman was nowhere to be seen.

Lola did one of her catlike stretches. "Time to hit the road, guys. Our human's out of the woods. Now it's up to him to sort his life out."

Brice grinned at me. "Are my little Shining People ready to beam themselves to London?"

Beam ourselves! I thought. Omigosh, do we have to?

Brice has this unnerving ability to sense my weaknesses. "Erm, angel tags, sweetheart?" he said sarcastically. "Remember those? You use them to connect with your cosmic power source, blah blah blah."

"I know how angel tags work," I said sniffily. "But what if we end up in the wrong place?"

"Relax, Boo," said Lola. "We've done it before."

Yeah right, from like, a street away, I thought.

Brice's smirk made it clear he thought I was chicken.

"OK, fine!" I said. "Let's beam ourselves to completely the other side of the world. I mean, why worry?" And I grasped my tags and concentrated like crazy.

There are places on Earth where it's almost impossible to get a decent angelic signal, and there are others where the atmosphere is so pure that the connection is instantaneous. The Australian outback is the second kind.

The power surge totally lit up our surroundings, and next minute the glowing desert with its trees and rocks began to stream away from us like flowing lava.

Oh-oh, this is way too mystical for me! Suppose they go and leave me alone in the Dreaming? I panicked. I'll be floating around for ever all by myself.

I was so scared that I just grabbed for Lola's hand and shut my eyes.

To my huge relief, the terrifying cosmic rushing sensation stopped almost as soon as it had begun.

After a few seconds I dared to peek and saw Brice rubbing the feeling back into his fingers.

"You should take up arm-wrestling, sweetheart," he quipped. "You've got quite a grip."

It wasn't Lola I'd clutched in my terror. It was Brice.

Chapter Three

"It seems very different. From Elizabethan times, I mean."

Lola's obvious disappointment penetrated my blur of shame. She hates it, I thought. She thinks I've screwed up big time. And now I came to take in my surroundings, so did I.

We were on a street corner in the East End of London, just before dawn. An old-fashioned gas lamp made a wobbly halo in the fog. Figures toiled past like grey ghosts. They all seemed to be struggling with things that were too heavy for them, lugging baskets or bundles, or patiently dragging home-made carts and trolleys. Soot-blackened tenements loomed over the street, shutting out the sky.

I swallowed. It isn't like this in Sherlock Holmes, I thought.

"Hey, we just went from summer to winter in twenty seconds. That's enough to make anyone feel strange," I said brightly. "The sun will come up in a minute. Then we'll see how cool this is."

Brice pulled his hood over his head. "I wouldn't hold my breath."

A young girl trudged by. "'Oo will buy?" she called in a harsh voice. "'Oo will buy my sweet pippins?"

I saw Brice examining his watch with a baffled expression. It just showed a bizarre row of zeros. So did mine and Lola's.

"Maybe the Dreaming confused them," Lola suggested.

Trainees don't strictly need the Agency's hi-tech watches to monitor the local thought and light levels, or to signal the approach of humans assigned to them. Angels functioned for centuries without the aid of technology and so could we. But the technical hitch made me feel scarily far from home.

Without a word, we set off down the street. Brice was visibly cheesed off, and Lola kept darting him worried looks, like, "Oh, no, poor Brice is in a bad mood."

I scowled to myself. Why did he have to be here? OK, maybe Victorian London wasn't as buzzy and atmospheric as I hoped. But if Lola and I were by ourselves, we'd still be having a laugh. She's not giving it a chance, I thought. She's under this like, sinister Brice spell and she's seeing everything through his eyes.

It wasn't light yet, but all around us Londoners were grimly starting the new day. Shutters went up with a clatter, and sleepy shop assistants came out and started sweeping the pavement, getting ready for business. Since we'd arrived, traffic had been trickling steadily into the city and horse-drawn cabs, carts and omnibuses began to fill the narrow streets.

I noticed Lola peering into a dingy shopfront. Over the door was a painted sign showing three golden balls. The shop window was crammed with old tat: tarnished jewellery, broken clocks, a pair of faded leather gloves worn into holes. Who'd be desperate enough to buy that? I thought.

"What does this shop sell?" Lola asked in a puzzled voice.

"It's a pawnbroker's, sweetheart," Brice told her. "People only come here when they're stony broke. They leave an item as security, a few teaspoons, a necklace or something, and the pawnbroker lends them some cash until they can afford to buy it back. Only mostly they can't, which means the pawnbroker gets to collect."

I quickly moved away. It was the gloves. The thought of anyone wanting to buy them. The thought of anyone being that poor.

I'd pictured Victorian London as scenery basically; a colourful backdrop for a little spot of angelic tourism – the sound of trotting hooves on cobbled streets, hot buttered muffins by the fire. I hadn't thought what it would feel like for humans living there.

A terrifying figure emerged from an alleyway with a bundle of filthy brushes on his back. He was dragging a little boy by the arm. Both man and child were totally black with soot, except for their red-rimmed eyes. The little boy was crying in the hopeless way kids do when they know no-one cares.

"Stop your bleedin' row!" the man yelled. "Or I'll stop it for ya!"

Lola looked shocked. "What's he doing with that little kid?"

"Providing him with a career opportunity," said Brice. "Giving him a chance to be an honest tax-paying citizen."

"That child is tiny. What can he possibly do?"

"He'll fit very snugly inside a chimney," said Brice. "Especially if that nice gentleman gives him a good kicking to help him on his way. Everyone has coal fires these days. Haven't you noticed the soot everywhere? And if you don't sweep your chimneys regularly, darlin', they catches on fire, don't they?"

Lola stared at me. "Boo, tell me he's joking?"

Unfortunately I had to tell her the truth. "He's not. They really do put little boys up chimneys. It's in *Oliver Twist*."

"And this is like, legal?" My mate's eyes were dark with distress.

"You bet," said Brice. "Since the Industrial Revolution, kids are a vital part of the economy. They work as fluff pickers and mud larks and—"

He's doing this on purpose, I thought miserably. He's brainwashing Lola, making her think coming here was a mistake.

It was so unfair. Brice was supposed to look bad, not me.

By this time crowds of office clerks were hurrying through the streets. They were on their way to work, but in their gloomy suits and high stiff collars, they looked more as if they were going to a funeral.

Brice was still reeling off facts.

"Most of these sad characters work in the counting houses in the city," he said. "What a way to spend your life, copying figures into ledgers all day."

But I didn't need an ex-PODS agent to tell me how hard these people's lives were. I could see it in their bleak expressions and their unhealthy complexions, as if they rarely saw daylight.

It's like they're trapped in some nightmare machine and don't know how to get off, I thought. I was feeling fairly trapped myself.

Lola gave me a searching look. "Did you do that protection thingy?" she murmured. "Because you look a bit rough."

Oh, no wonder! I thought. What with my little hand-holding humiliation earlier, and the watches malfunctioning, I'd forgotten to do my usual landing procedure. Which meant that basically since I got here, I'd been soaking up negative vibes like a sponge.

I mentally instructed my angelic system to protect itself from any cosmic toxins in the locality.

"Shouldn't we be running into our human at some point?" I said aloud.

"You'd think," said Lola.

A horse-drawn cab pulled up to the curb. A middle-aged lady got out carrying two carpet bags.

The street was really busy by this time, so she started off towards the crossing. I don't know if it was her crinoline or the corset underneath that made her take such little steps, but it made her look like she was on tiny wheels! When she reached the crossing, I saw the lady crinkle her nose. There were piles of horse manure everywhere.

Suddenly a little boy appeared, flourishing a bald-looking broom. He made a bow to the lady and grandly swept all the poo out of her path.

The lady fumbled in her purse and gave him a very small coin.

"I'll carry them bags for yer, if you like, lady!" he said eagerly. "I'll carry them to Timbuctoo if you just says the word."

She clutched her bags. "Certainly not! Such impudence! Run along, you little guttersnipe. Shoo!"

"Stop thief!" An older boy came haring across the street complaining at the top of his voice. "Turned me back for a second and the little tea-leaf swiped me broom!" he panted.

"Call that a broom?" jeered the little urchin. "Where I come from, we calls that a stick." He flung down the broom and legged it down the nearest alleyway.

For no obvious reason we all went chasing after him.

The people in the tenements had strung their washing across the alley. Victorian pantaloons, nightgowns and petticoats hung limply overhead in the stagnant London air.

In mid-sprint, Lola and I exchanged glances.

"It's him, isn't it?" I panted. "He's our kid?"

I saw Brice grinning to himself.

"What's so funny?"

"Nothing," he smirked.

"Can you believe that!" said Lola breathlessly. "We went all the way to Australia and we still hooked up with our human!"

"Agency timing is quite cool," Brice admitted.

"What about PODS timing?" The remark slipped out before I thought.

"Also excellent," he said coldly.

Lola gave me a look. Like, how could you be so mean? So I gave her a look right back. Like, was I being mean?

Our human slowed down to a leisurely amble, but you could see he didn't totally relax. He was like an animal in the wild, noticing the smallest sound or movement, alert for trouble.

They've picked us a real character this time, I thought.

He wore a battered stove-pipe hat and a

swallow-tail coat at least two sizes too big for him. The coat was full of holes which he'd tried to mend with jazzy remnants, including a bit of old curtain. But he had this air of genuine dignity, as if his hand-me-downs were just a costume he was wearing for the time being.

We trailed our little urchin through a maze of sleazy courts and alleyways and finally emerged in a street market.

It was completely mad. Stall holders competing for who could yell the loudest. Two women having a cat fight, literally pulling out clumps of hair! Plus a driver was backing a brewery wagon into a very narrow entry, while bystanders yelled contradictory advice.

But the little boy in the patchwork coat just sauntered through the mayhem, dodging all the slippery cabbage leaves and fruit peel underfoot, and cheerfully scuffing up dirty hay with his boots as if it were autumn leaves. He was having his breakfast on the move, helping himself to a bread roll when the baker's boy wasn't looking, sneaking a quick dipper of milk from under the milkman's nose.

He strolled up to a stall selling the lurid Victorian horror comics known as Penny Dreadfuls and started reading furtively, while he munched away on a stolen apple.

Eek, I should be taking notes, I thought, and I fumbled in my bag until I found my notebook.

Our human is probably about ten years old, I scribbled. *But v. undernourished, so looks younger. He can read though he doesn't seem to go to school.*

The comic stall was next to a stand serving freshly-made coffee and cooked breakfasts. An elegantly dressed gentleman stood apart from the regular customers, self-consciously turning his coffee cup in gloved hands, looking as if he'd been up all night.

"Slumming," said Brice knowingly. "You get a lot of that here. Toffs coming down to get their thrills."

"Toffs!" I mimicked. "Who are you? The Artful Dodger?"

I'd become vaguely aware of a news vendor bawling on the other side of the market. I don't know why I suddenly felt so sick. I couldn't even hear what he was saying at first. It was just another raised voice, competing with the voices of barrow boys and costermongers yelling about fresh fish and shallots. And even when I managed to make them out, the words still didn't really register.

"Another murder in Whitechapel. Read all about it!"

I saw people gasp and turn to each other to make sure they'd heard correctly.

"Omigosh," I said. "The Whitechapel Murderer! That's what Victorians called Jack the Ripper."

Lola's face went white. "The Ripper was in these times? Why didn't anyone tell me?"

Brice sounded stunned. "I assumed you knew. That's why I—"

And suddenly I felt as if I was falling through space.

I had actually chosen to come here. I'd even imagined it would be fun, like when my mates and I used to watch dross like *Jeepers Creepers* to scare ourselves into hysterics. But it wasn't thrilling to be on Jack the Ripper's turf for real. It felt unbelievably sordid and scary.

And suddenly I knew what was wrong. It wasn't the fog and soot that made Victorian London so dark and brooding. It wasn't even the poverty. Plenty of times are poor and dirty, but only a small handful are a breeding ground for cosmic evil. And for shallow and pathetic reasons which I was totally ashamed to remember, I had brought my lovely soul-mate to one of them.

CHAPTER FOUR

I'm not going to try to justify what I did next.

OK, so maybe my angelic system was affected by its brief exposure to those negative Victorian vibes. Maybe that clouded my professional judgement. But that's no excuse.

I should have called the trip off then and there. I was going to, I was, honestly. I opened my mouth, drew a big breath – and did absolutely nothing. I pictured Brice smirking to himself as I mumbled my way through my apology, then I pictured Lola and him exchanging glances over my head, and I couldn't do it. I just couldn't give him that kind of satisfaction. There was this crucial split second when I could have, *should* have, done the right thing and I fluffed it. What can I say?

I promised to tell you the whole truth and here it is. Uncut, unvarnished and as you see, deeply unflattering to yours truly.

"He's on the move again," hissed Lola.

Our human was making for a stall, where a woman in a filthy bonnet had various hot suet puddings for sale. "Well, it's my little Georgie," she said. "'Ow's tricks?"

I was still inwardly freaking at what I'd done, but I couldn't bear to think about it, so I whipped out my notebook and scribbled frantically, *Our human's name is Georgie.*

Georgie produced a coin from an inside pocket. "I'll have a ha'porth of the plum," he shivered. "But I want it hot, mind."

"I don't blame you, dear! Perishin' today, ain't it?" The pudding lady gave him a toothless grin. "I'll tell you what I'll do. You run and fetch me a drop of what does your 'eart good!" She gave him a conspiratorial wink. "And I'll give you a bit of plum duff for nuffin'."

"Is that code?" whispered Lola.

Brice grinned. "She's sending him to buy gin. Gin is the poor man's tipple," he explained. "Life doesn't seem quite so bad when you see it through a boozy blur."

The gin shop was in the most depressing street I have ever seen. The houses were all on the verge of falling down. People had stuffed old rags and newspapers into the cracks in an attempt to keep out the cold. I couldn't believe anyone really lived here, but if you listened you could hear them clattering cooking pots and soothing crying babies inside.

In these surroundings, the gin shop, with its fancy sign and plate-glass windows, stood out like a palace. Inside everything was bright and gleaming: the polished mahogany of the bar, the brass rails, the giant gin casks painted glossy green and gold. The barrels were labelled with enticing names, like Real Knock-me-down, and Celebrated Butter Gin.

It seemed early to be knocking back the hard stuff, but some of the customers already smelled of drink. One half-starved woman was shushing a toddler.

"Never mind, dearie," cackled an old lady. "A few drops of gin in 'is bottle and 'e'll sleep good as gold."

Georgie bought something called Regular Flare-up. As soon as he was outside the shop, he took a furtive swig. He shuddered, wiped his mouth then raced back to claim his free plum duff.

I was starting to feel as if I was trapped in the opening scenes of *Oliver!*. Georgie ran about the streets for hours, running errands, taking messages, carrying parcels for toffs.

Wherever we went, Londoners were talking about the Whitechapel murders. I began to know when people were going to bring it up. They all had this same expression on their faces, a scared, sick fascination. They were Jack the Ripper addicts, swapping the latest lurid rumour, endlessly rehashing horrific details. It's like they couldn't stop talking about it.

Georgie stood in the barber's for ages, waiting to deliver one of his messages. He kept clearing his throat, waiting for someone to notice him, but everyone was too busy speculating about the Ripper's true identity.

Someone's cousin had seen a suspicious figure with a doctor's bag, fleeing the murder scene. Others had heard of a foreigner with a gold-topped cane in which he concealed his deadly weapon. One customer swore it was the killer's perfume that marked him out. "Sweet, like lily of the valley. It's to cover the smell of the blood," he explained with relish. "It's that scent what'll give him away, mark my words."

"Nuffin' won't give 'im away," the barber chipped in. "Our Jack's too clever for 'em."

"I heard that Scotland Yard know who it is," said his customer through a froth of shaving foam. "I heard, they'd been asked to hush it up."

The barber stopped with the razor in his hand. "Why would they do a thing like that?"

"It's obvious, isn't it? It's got to be a member of the Royal Family."

In the street outside, some guy was buttonholing anyone who'd listen. "It's a Hebrew conspiracy!" he shouted, spraying spit. "Send them murdering Jews back where they come from. Coming here, taking food out of our children's mouths!"

I think that was too much for Georgie. Without any warning he bolted into a side street. Outside a tumbledown tenement, two kids, brother and sister, were crouching in the gutter. They looked blue with cold. Drunken shouts drifted from an upstairs window.

Yet only five minutes' walk away everything was peaceful. I could hear a little winter bird tweeting, and the sound of someone busily scrubbing something with a brush.

Georgie turned into somewhere called Milkwell Yard. The houses were small and narrow but well cared for. Outside Number 7, a maid was polishing a brass knocker.

"Hello, Ivy," said Georgie.

She beamed at him. "Why it's Georgie Porgie! Haven't seen you for days. Too busy kissing the girls, I suppose!"

"You suppose wrong," he said cheerfully. "I've got business to attend to."

Ivy laughed. "'Ark at you! You sound just like a gent on the Stock Exchange! Go round the back, lovie, but keep your voice down. The mistress had another bad night." She gave him a grin. "If you ask me, the spirits are getting their revenge!"

I assumed this was another reference to gin, but then I saw the name on the brass plate. *Miss Minerva Temple, Medium.*

I nudged Lollie. "Is that cool or what!"

She looked uneasy. "Doesn't that mean she talks to the dead?"

"Yeah, Victorians were really into it. We are going to get so many brownie points for this. Mr Allbright is going to love us for ever!"

We followed Georgie down some steps.

A fair-haired girl rushed to open the door.

"Georgie! Where have you been? I was worried something had happened to you."

Georgie's sister was so pale, you could see daylight through her, except for her cheeks which were bright pink. In her lavender gown and button boots, she looked like a little china doll.

She dropped her voice. "We'll have to be quiet," she whispered. "Miss Temple is feeling fragile this morning."

"She still treats you well I hope, Charlotte?"

Hello! I thought. Georgie had completely changed his way of talking. He sounded almost posh.

"Oh, no, she is really kind," his sister reassured him. "She's extremely satisfied with my work. She says my face is wonderfully ethereal!" Charlotte's giggles turned into a long coughing fit.

"I'm afraid you are getting ill, Charlie," said Georgie anxiously.

She shook her head. "Don't be silly! I just catch my breath sometimes."

As the children chatted, I noted down useful facts for Mr Allbright. Georgie and Charlotte were orphans. Their mother had died only a couple of years ago. Until recently, both kids were surviving on the streets, by selling matches and bootlaces. It was

Georgie who had found his sister her unusual post as a medium's assistant. Georgie was the youngest, yet he was fiercely protective of his sister, wanting to know if Miss Temple was working her too hard.

Charlotte said the hardest part was trying not to laugh when Miss Temple pretended the spirit guides were speaking through her. "She sounds exactly like a bullfrog!" She broke off to cough, and this time she couldn't seem to stop. It sounded like rusty machinery rattling inside her.

"The poor kid's got TB," Brice said in a low voice.

"Don't be stupid!" I hissed. "Charlotte's fine. Look at her pink rosy cheeks."

"That's what TB looks like in the early stages," he said grimly. "Until they start coughing blood."

I forced myself to count to ten. I knew what he was up to. He wanted to make me look bad in front of Lola.

"Victorians didn't all have TB," I muttered.

Brice heard. "No, some of them died of diphtheria and typhus and cholera. Also polio and scarlet fever and pernicious anaemia—"

"Give it a rest!"

"Boo, chill out! Brice knows what he's talking about."

Yeah, but why did he have to keep ramming it down my throat?

Georgie fetched his sister a glass of water and she gulped it down. He sat down beside her and they leaned their foreheads together like two babes in the wood.

"Your cough's not getting any better," Georgie said in a worried voice. "I'm going to see our uncle."

Charlotte looked panic-stricken. "Georgie, don't, not after last time."

"I'm going. I don't care," he said. "We've got to get you to a doctor."

She threw her arms round his neck. "Oh, Georgie, I wish we had someone to turn to!"

"We have, stupid, we've got Uncle Noel," he said stiffly. "It wasn't him who tried to have us sent to the workhouse. He was horrified when he heard what Aunt Agnes had been up to. He's a good man, Charlotte, and he has suffered a great deal."

"Has he?" said Charlotte doubtfully. "He seems fortunate to me. He is a very successful lawyer, and they have that fine house."

"He has done very well for himself," Georgie agreed. "But it must have been terrible when he was growing up, having to pretend his mama was a respectable widow, when she wasn't even married. Then Grandfather refused to acknowledge him as his son and heir. My uncle had nothing but bad treatment from our family, Charlie, yet he feels responsible for us. He said he would have us to live with him at Portman Square, if Aunt Agnes wasn't such a witch."

His sister laughed. "He didn't call her a witch!"

"No, she's more like his gaoler!" said Georgie. "He can't spend a farthing without having to account to her. It must torture him seeing us living from hand to mouth, when he has the means to help us. I'm sure that's why he sends me on these strange errands to Newgate. It's just an excuse to give me a few pence."

"How *is* Mr Godbolt?" said Charlotte.

"He seemed frail last time I was there, but then he must be quite old by now."

"Did our uncle ever tell you what Mr Godbolt did to get put in prison?" Charlotte asked.

"He just says, 'Edwin Godbolt made one fatal mistake. But he was a faithful employee for many years and though the law has found him guilty, I will not abandon him.' You see what a fine man he is, Charlie?"

A clock began to strike somewhere in the house. Charlotte jumped up. "I must go! Miss Temple is holding a seance in a few minutes."

"This we have to see," I said to Lola.

She looked uneasy. "I don't know if I want to see a woman pretending to talk to the dead."

"Oh, come on, babe, it'll be *très* educational!"

Her lips curved into a wicked smile. "OK," she agreed. "So long as we don't have fun."

We left Georgie drinking cocoa with Ivy and followed Charlotte into the back parlour. She immediately started peering under tables and into light fittings.

"Yikes!" I said. "This house needs some serious Feng Shui!"

"What's Feng Shui?" Lola said.

"It's basically Chinese for chucking out your clutter," I explained.

I have never seen so much stuff in one tiny room. I don't know how Charlotte managed to move around without knocking anything over.

Like, the table was covered with a fringy chenille cloth. The sideboard had lacy doodads on it, and there was a bigger lacy doodad draped over the back of an armchair. There was a bowl of artificial fruit under a glass dome, plus there were real ferns inside a big glass bottle. And I haven't even got round to the footstools or the embroidered fire screen, ornamental photograph frames or the potted aspidistras!

Having checked that her spirit FX equipment was in working order, Charlotte dragged the heavy curtains across the window, plunging the parlour into artificial twilight. A few minutes later Ivy showed a middle-aged couple into the parlour. I noticed that Charlotte greeted them in a hushed tone quite unlike her normal voice. "Mr and Mrs Bennet, please take a seat. Miss Temple will be with you shortly."

"Hope she doesn't cough," Brice said under his breath. "A coughing medium's assistant wouldn't be nearly so ethereal."

I'd expected Minerva Temple to be got up like a fortune teller with tinkly beads, but when she came in she was dressed really tastefully in a plain black gown and a pretty lace cap trimmed with ribbons. Her voice was low and thrilling. In fact she'd have made an excellent stage hypnotist, which she kind of was in a way.

Minerva set about lulling her victims into a receptive state, reassuring the couple that their daughter was now happy in the fields of Eternal Summer. Mrs Bennet gasped but her husband just fiddled with his collar, looking really uncomfortable.

Everyone held hands around the table and Minerva went into a trance. At least she did some bizarre writing and heavy breathing, which apparently meant the spirits were trying to get through.

Minerva had obviously coached Charlotte to produce 'psychic phenomena' on cue. So when her employer cried, "The veil between the worlds is growing thin!" Georgie's sister pulled a secret handle, releasing a blast of cold air from the cellar, to give the impression that spirits had wafted in from the other world.

Of course, typical Melanie – when I suggested gatecrashing these people's seance, I hadn't actually thought it through. I just wanted to tell my mates I'd been to a bona fide Victorian seance. But I began to feel terribly sorry for those grieving parents. The woman was clearly desperate for reassurance that her daughter still survived, even if it was on the wrong side of the 'veil', and I think the husband only came because of his wife.

The worst moment was when this like, radioactive green stuff started oozing out of Minerva. It flowed out of her mouth and nose, even her ears, and collected in a glowing green puddle on the table.

The husband instantly reached out to touch it.

"Don't!" Charlotte said in a warning voice. "Ectoplasm is harmful to the living. The spirits send it only to reassure you of their existence."

"It's actually cheesecloth and luminous paint," Brice told us in a stage whisper. "She'll make it disappear again in a sec. That way no-one can examine it too closely."

I was still in shock from the ectoplasm when I realised we were not alone. I'm serious – some real ghosts had turned up to Minerva's seance!! They were kind of sepia-coloured and flickery, like figures in old movies. A few of the livelier spirits hovered over the table. The rest just hung around in the background looking depressed.

I gave them a little wave. "Oh, hiya!" Then, "How come they're here?" I hissed to Brice.

"Who did you expect to come to a seance?" he muttered. "Living people?"

It's not just embarrassing watching someone conduct a phony seance with disapproving real-life spirits looking on, it's totally excruciating. Also Mr Bennet was looking increasingly fidgety. Eventually he couldn't contain himself, and cut right across Minerva's gushy portrait of their daughter's lovely personality. "You could be describing any young girl!" he objected.

Minerva's otherworldly expression made it clear she was above such petty remarks, but after a while she began to jerk around in her chair going,

"The spirits are saying there's a doubter in our midst."

Under cover of darkness, Charlotte activated another device, and the table started to jump around as though the spirits were having a tantrum. The real spirits looked more depressed than ever.

Brice hooted with laughter. "Oh rock'n'roll! This woman is outrageous."

I thought I saw Minerva's eyelids quiver then, but next minute she was going on about someone with the initial A, so I decided I'd imagined it.

I think everyone was relieved when that seance was over, including the spirits. Charlotte hurried back to her brother and they talked for a while. Then Georgie said he had to go.

"You will remember to come tomorrow?" Charlotte said anxiously.

Georgie's face suddenly went all pinched. "You needn't keep on. I said I would, didn't I?"

It was the first time he'd sounded like a whingey little kid, and I wondered what had upset him.

Outside, veils of yellowish-green fog swirled through the dusk, reminding me unpleasantly of ectoplasm.

Lola sighed. "I felt so sorry for that Mrs Bennet."

"I kept thinking of my mum. I hate to think what a medium would say about me," I said gloomily.

Lollie squeezed my hand. "She'd say, 'I've got this cute hip hop chick here in a vintage top and she wants you to know she's totally totally fine'!"

I felt a rush of affection for my lovely friend.

I wanted to tell her how I was kicking myself for insisting on coming to a time that was mainly notorious for a pervy killer. But most of all I wanted to say how crazy it felt to be missing her like this, when she was actually right here beside me.

Unfortunately, Brice was there too, mooching along with his hands in his pockets, so I swallowed down my feelings and the words went unsaid.

CHAPTER FIVE

The rattle of late-night sewing machines came from an upstairs sweatshop just off Brick Lane. It was eight o'clock in the evening, but for these Londoners, the working day still wasn't over.

Georgie had run his final errand of the day, rushing two hot kidney pies (euw!) to a reasonably famous Victorian comedian called Dan Leno. Mr Leno was doing a gig at one of the music halls in Curtain Road. We actually caught some of his act.

Then we hitched a lift in a brewery wagon and now we were walking along in the gaslight, enjoying the scene. The streets were crowded with Cockneys out to have a good time. For once, the atmosphere was really mellow. In some streets people had set up shooting galleries and sideshows. There was a guy selling something advertised as 'Wizard Oil' and I could hear a voice bawling, "Step right in and see Hercules, the world's strongest man!"

Further down the street were booths advertising unusual sights for people to marvel at, like 'A Genuine Mermaid', and 'The Dog with Lion's Claws'. But I wasn't seriously tempted, until I saw the big queue forming outside the peepshow. I'd heard about these Victorian entertainments, where you paid your penny to see a magic, or maybe a v. saucy scene.

The party mood was infectious, so I decided to take a look.

To my annoyance Brice yanked me out of the queue. "Where do you think you're going?"

"Well, duh! Obviously I want to see the peepshow."

"Trust me, you don't," he said firmly.

When Brice explained that people were queuing to see waxworks depicting the Ripper's crimes, I felt sick to my stomach. "Little kids are in that queue," I said in horror. "Mums with *babies*."

But Georgie quickened his pace just about then so we had to go hurtling after him. The bustle and noise faded behind us, and we were in the back streets of Whitechapel where street lights were few and far between. Lollie and I had already agreed that Victorian gaslights were just a leetle bit too atmospheric. They made this creepy hissing sound, plus they cast disturbing shadows, which made every harmless passer-by look like a leering assassin. But it was the areas of total darkness that really gave me the chills.

When I saw the poster in the pub doorway, I looked away as soon as I'd read the part about Scotland Yard offering £100 reward. I knew it must be for anyone who would lead them to the killer. I just didn't want to see it in black and white, not now we were on the Ripper's home territory.

I wondered how Georgie dared to walk these streets alone. It wasn't just the dark and the fog and the creepy gas lamps; it was something in the air, a lurking menace you could almost taste. I was quite glad of Brice slouching beside us, doing his 'don't mess with me' walk.

In a little lane off Gower's Walk, several heavily made-up girls hung about under a street lamp, shivering in their scanty clothes.

Respectable Victorian women hid their bodies totally from view. What with the corsets and petticoats underneath and the bustles on top, you almost forgot they had normal bodies.

But let me tell you, the Gower's Walk girls were a different species. One was literally spilling out of her blouse, and each time a potential punter came by, they'd all give him a naughty flash of silk stocking. "Take me 'ome with you, mister," one girl called. "I'll show you a good time."

Lola looked distressed. "She's just a kid," she said. "She can't be more than fourteen."

"It's all perfectly legal," Brice told her. "Victorian girls can marry at that age."

"It might be perfectly legal, but it's also perfectly sick," said Lola.

"Well, my stars! Look who the cat brought in!" said a husky voice.

A girl with rouged cheeks and a pink feather boa was grinning unmistakably at Brice.

No way! I thought. NO way!

It's not that I'm a prude. It had just never occurred to me that an Earth angel might hang out with, you know, tarts. Which might be why I'd failed to register the cosmic tingles that let us know when other Light Workers are in the area. Stranger still, this particular angel and Brice were old acquaintances.

"Well, you look in better shape than what you did last time you was here, darlin'," she said. "Go on, introduce me to your pretty girlfriends!"

It was the first time I'd seen Brice blush. "This is Ella," he told us awkwardly. "Ella, meet Mel and Lola."

"Pleased to meet you," she beamed. "I knew this one would come right in the end," she added in a stage whisper. "'E 'ad sumfin' about 'im, know what I mean?"

"So do you work erm, in this lane every night?" Lola asked.

"Someone's got to do it, darlin'. If nuffin' else we can keep the fear levels down."

Ella explained that the dark powers were actively feeding the public's obsession with the Ripper. With the help of the press, they'd turned a sick killer into a bogeyman, a demon almost.

"Sorry, Ella, we've got to go." I'd spotted Georgie's coat-tails disappearing into the dark. Calling hasty goodbyes, we sped down the street, catching up with him outside a huge derelict building.

Georgie climbed on to a sill, stealthily prised up a sash window, squeezed himself through the gap, and landed softly on the other side. I was just about to jump down after him, when a boy stepped out of the darkness, brandishing some kind of weapon.

"Oi! What's your game? These are prime lodgings! If you want to come in, you gotta show me the colour of your tin."

We climbed in after Georgie, wondering what was going on.

"I ain't got any tin," lied Georgie. "But I got this." He delved inside his coat and brought out half a cigar, which someone had thrown down on the street. "Best Havana," he said enticingly. "Same as they smokes in the 'Ouse of Lords."

The boy examined the cigar critically, then fished out some matches and coolly lit up. "Want a pull?" he offered. "It's a good 'un."

"No thanks, I'm giving 'em up." I could see Georgie was trying not to yawn.

His new landlord tossed him an indescribably filthy blanket. "You're kipping in the Royal Suite tonight," he said loftily. "I do 'ope as the tinkling of the chandeliers won't keep you awake."

I was stunned. Not only had this homeless kid got the nerve to take over an abandoned building, he was actually renting out floor space to other waifs and strays. In every room exhausted children huddled under any covering they could find: a coat, a torn curtain, old newspaper. Georgie was lucky to get that blanket.

I pictured Jade, my little sister, in her twenty-first-century bedroom, with its glowstars and Barbies and stuffed toys. Then I imagined her in this stinking hellhole with cockroaches scurrying over her in the dark, and my throat ached. How could Victorian adults let this happen?

Georgie was so tired that he could hardly stand by this time, but he stumbled around until he found a patch of floor out of the draught. Then he wrapped himself in his blanket and fell asleep in seconds.

"I'm going for a walk," Brice said abruptly. Without any explanation he vanished into the night.

I was just going to say, "Ooh, was it something we said?" when we heard whimpering sounds. Lola and I looked at each other. Officially this was a field trip, not a mission, but you can't ignore a frightened kid. So we went tiptoeing through room after horrible room until we found the little girl who was having a bad dream.

She had sores on her face and her hair was all matted. I don't think anyone had washed or brushed it in her life. "Don't 'urt me!" she pleaded in her sleep. "Please don't 'urt me."

Maybe it was her own personal bogeyman the

little girl was dreaming about, but I doubted it. It was like Ella said, a human killer had become an evil demon. By daylight people's fears were just about manageable. But in the hours of darkness, the spirit of the Ripper terrorised London, turning it into a city of nightmares.

Sometimes Lola and I don't need to speak. We just crouched on the bare boards and comforted the little girl with the gentlest vibes we knew. Very gradually her whimpers stopped.

Lola stroked her dirty hair. "Sweet dreams, little one," she whispered. "Only sweet dreams from now on."

We moved among the sleeping children, doing what we could to heal and comfort them. But I knew it wasn't enough. Depression washed over me. Some of these kids were younger than Jade. They needed homes and parents and a good bath. They shouldn't be living like this.

"This universe sucks," I blurted suddenly. "No-one cares about anyone else, not really."

I was shocked at myself actually, but Lola just looked surprised.

"So why are we here then?" she said.

"Because of our stupid pointless pathetic school project."

And because I screwed up, I added silently.

Lola gave me one of her wise smiles. "You don't believe that, babe."

I felt a microscopic prickle of hope. Maybe my friend wasn't mad with me. Maybe I hadn't screwed up. Maybe, just maybe, this could turn out OK?

Oh, get real Mel! I thought despairingly. This is the first time Lollie and I have been on our own since we got here. We wouldn't even be having this conversation if Brice was here. He has to ruin everything.

Then a shameful thought slithered into my mind. Maybe Brice wouldn't come back. Maybe he'd defected to the PODS, once and for all, and vanished from our lives for ever.

CHAPTER SIX

The night sky outside the windows was fading to the colour of grubby smoke. Lola and I were taking a break, sharing a pack of angel trail mix. It was almost like old times. Just being in that rat-infested house with her, munching and scribbling notes for school, not even talking that much, made me ridiculously happy.

Then suddenly Brice was lounging in the doorway with that twisted smile on his face. "How's it going?" Despite the cold he was just wearing jeans and a Bruce Lee T-shirt.

"We're good!" Lola beamed. "As you see, we're stuffing our faces." She rattled the packet. "Want some?"

He shook his head. "No thanks. It feels much better in here, by the way. You two did a great job with the light levels."

"Yeah, thanks for helping. Not!" I scowled. "So where've you been?"

"Oh, you know, checking out the sights."

"In the dark?" I said disbelievingly. "Yeah right."

Lola noticed him shivering. "Babe, what happened to your hoodie?"

Brice shrugged. "Must have left it somewhere."

All around us, kids were surfacing from sleep. The younger children still looked soft-eyed and dreamy. The older ones immediately snapped into survival mode, stowing their pathetic bedding out of sight, stuffing scraps of food into their mouths.

Georgie had been using his coat for a pillow, but when he tried to put it back on, his arm got stuck in the torn lining of his sleeve. He had to rip the lining out to free himself. Perhaps it was because he wasn't totally awake that he looked so sad and bewildered. But as I watched him struggling into his outsized coat, I felt this unbearable pity well up inside me. I couldn't take it, and tried to laugh it off.

"What's up with our little Master Sunshine today?" I asked the others.

"Isn't it obvious?" said Brice. "The kid's life stinks!"

"Presumably it stank yesterday, but he was as lively as anything," I objected.

But as I watched Georgie drearily fastening his buttons, I wondered if this was true. Maybe his cheeky Cockney routine was something he put on to survive, like his badly-fitting clothes.

We followed him back into the street and were instantly engulfed by a billowing snot-green cloud. I've never seen fog like it. This must be what they mean by a Victorian pea-souper, I thought.

"It's been like this for hours," said Brice.

Lollie covered her nose. "It smells rank!"

Victorian London had a really peculiar pong: a mix of bad drains, terrible Victorian cooking and leaking gas, plus the suffocating stink caused by Londoners burning coal twenty-four seven. Unfortunately the dense fog was preventing these toxic smells from escaping into the upper atmosphere.

The Hell dimensions can't smell any worse than this, I thought. The topic of hellish smells naturally led on to thinking about Brice. He could have spent the night plotting with his old PODS cronies and we wouldn't be any the wiser. Well, he'd better not be plotting to hurt me and Lola, or he'd be sorry.

The lonely sound of a foghorn floated out of the murk. I couldn't believe people would take boats and barges out in this weather – the visibility was practically down to zero. If we let Georgie get more than a few inches ahead, he totally vanished from view. We blundered past looming shapes which I guessed to be warehouses and cranes. I'd assumed Georgie was carrying out one of his errands, but as we trudged on and on, I began to suspect he was just walking aimlessly.

We followed him under a dank old bridge and came out opposite a park. After a nervous look round, Georgie nipped through the gates, darted to the nearest flower bed and started picking Michaelmas daisies, which happened to be the only plants in flower. When he had a sizeable bunch, he made a speedy exit.

"What is the boy up to?" Lola said.

"I don't know, but he looks seriously stressed," Brice said.

By the time we'd reached the medium's house in Milkwell Yard, we could see Georgie visibly bracing himself for some major ordeal.

Ivy met him at the back door, with her finger to her lips. "Your sister says she hopes you don't mind waiting," she said in a hoarse whisper. "But a client turned up, total stranger, he was. Just rang the bell, bold as you like. Says his name's Smith." She gave a disbelieving snort. "I said, 'I'm sorry, sir, but Miss Temple won't see you without an appointment, not if you was Prime Minister.' But he comes out with this cock and bull story about his dead granny and how he needs the spirits to help his family find her will."

She leaned closer. "I think he's one of those whatsisname, investigators, trying to catch her out. I said to her, 'Madam, you don't have to see him.' But she says, 'Ivy, my professional reputation is at stake!'"

Ivy noticed Georgie anxiously clutching his daisies and her eyes filled with pity. "Oh, bless," she exclaimed softly. "And here's me rabbiting like it's just an ordinary day."

She suddenly took in his bedraggled appearance. "Tell you what, 'ow'd you like a nice wash, while you're waiting?" she said briskly. "I'll fry you some bacon and eggs and you have a little clean-up, how about that?"

Ivy seemed to know about Georgie's forthcoming ordeal, and was reminding him, in the kindest possible way, that he should make himself look more respectable.

"Let's give the kid his privacy," Brice suggested. "We can have fun with Minerva's paranormal whatsisname while we wait."

Lollie shook her head. "One seance was enough."

"Oh, come on. This one will be a blast," he insisted.

"You're a bit confident, aren't you?" I said.

"I'm totally confident, sweetheart, and I'll tell you why." Brice paused for dramatic effect. "Minerva Temple heard us talking last night!"

We stared at him.

"I'm serious. She has a genuine psychic gift. You saw what happened yesterday. She's a spirit magnet. They can't keep away from her."

"But that doesn't make sense!" I objected. "If she's for real, why go in for fake ectoplasm and funny voices?"

"Because the spirit world is unpredictable, and if you don't give the punters what they want, they won't pay up. Faking it is a safer bet."

"Well, I don't think we should get involved," I said in my prissiest voice. "She's conning vulnerable people. This guy should just go ahead and expose her."

"Maybe you should see what's going on, before you make up your mind," Brice said.

We argued for a bit, but I admit I was a leetle bit curious to see this mysterious Mr Smith myself, so I eventually let myself be persuaded. We crept into the purple twilight of Minerva's parlour. The bored ghosts were killing time playing a game of ghostly noughts and crosses. They didn't have a pencil or paper, so they took it in turns to draw on the mirror with a spooky sepia finger.

Minerva, Georgie's sister and Mr Smith were holding hands in hushed silence, waiting for the fake spirits to show.

After the usual heavy breathing, Minerva announced that Mr Smith's dead grandmother was standing by her side. "She is showing me a beautiful brooch," she said in her hypnotist's voice. "A very old cameo brooch. She tells me she was very fond of it and sometimes used it to fasten her shawl."

Mr Smith shook his head in mock amazement. "What are the chances of anyone guessing that an old lady would wear a shawl and a cameo brooch? Could you ask her if she ever owned a pair of spectacles?"

Brice's instincts were right about this guy. Most paranormal investigators are genuinely after the truth, but this guy wasn't one of them. He didn't just want to expose Minerva and put her out of business. He wanted to destroy her, as a person.

He sat forward and I saw his eyes glitter in the twilight. "Perhaps you could ask my grandmother about someone who used to work in her kitchen? A workhouse girl. I think her first name was Minnie," he mused. "And her last name began with T. It was strangely similar to your own, Miss Temple. Could it be Tuttle? Yes, that's it. Could you ask my dear old granny whatever happened to little Minnie Tuttle?"

Minerva's voice sounded strained. "I don't appear to be getting anyone of that name," she said bravely.

Omigosh, I thought, the poor darling. It's her! *She's* Minnie Tuttle.

This guy had evidently been digging around in her past, a past Minerva found so painful that she'd invented a whole new identity for herself.

"Figured out whose side you're on yet?" Brice whispered.

"Yeah, this creep's got it coming," I agreed. "But what can we do? We're totally not meant to interfere."

He grinned. "And we're not going to." He nodded at the ghosts. 'What do you say, guys? Shall we make it a team effort?"

They looked stunned. One spirit asked Brice something, in a distorted underwatery voice.

"No, seriously," Brice said. "You're the experts. We're just here to help you do your stuff."

It would be completely unprofessional of me to reveal what happened next, so I'll just tell you that ten minutes after we hijacked the seance, the paranormal investigator bolted from the house. The final straw was definitely when Minerva's spirits told her to ask him about an important public examination in which a pupil with the initials O. D. did something he shouldn't.

I know! You have to ask yourself, how do ghosts get hold of this information? How could they possibly know that Mr Smith's real name was Obadiah Dunhill?

I was on such a high that I slapped Brice's palm and said, "Yess!"

"Didn't I tell you it would be a blast?" he boasted.

Lola just beamed at us, like, "You see! These kids can play together nicely if they try."

Minerva was lying back in her chair, sniffing at a bottle of smelling salts. Her spirits hovered solicitously in the background. She looked tired and overwhelmed, but deep down I think she was actually relieved to be back in the bona fide psychic bizz.

Charlotte was pulling back the heavy curtains, letting in what little daylight there was. Then she turned and I saw her face, and my elation died away.

"May I leave now, Miss Temple?" she asked timidly. "You said I could have the morning off? My mama died two years ago today and my brother and I are going to visit her grave."

Lola gave me a helpless look.

So that's why Georgie stole the flowers.

Georgie was waiting in the kitchen, looking astonishingly different without his grime. In fact, he had surprisingly delicate features for a boy. He silently handed half his flowers to Charlotte, and they set off down the street.

Georgie didn't say a word as they walked along. Charlotte kept giving him worried glances, but after ten minutes she couldn't stand it any longer and said, "We must try not to be sad, you know, Georgie. Mama and Papa's troubles are over now. They are with the angels, watching over us from Heaven."

For the first time since we'd met him, Georgie lost his temper. "There IS no Heaven, Charlotte!" he yelled. "The angels didn't help you when you were living on the street. It was me who found you that job. We're on our own. There's just you, me and Uncle Noel, no-one else."

He stormed ahead, leaving a pathetic trail of petals.

Charlotte went hurrying after him. "Wait! Georgie, wait for me!"

"I used to feel like Georgie," Lola murmured. "Didn't you, Mel?"

"Totally," I admitted, "and I didn't have it as hard as these kids."

A fit of violent coughing had stopped Charlotte in her tracks. Georgie ran back looking totally stricken. He waited anxiously until she'd recovered, then he silently took her hand and they walked on together to the church where their mother was buried.

We'd agreed the children should visit the grave on their own, so when we reached the church, we tactfully went off for a walk.

The weather had improved slightly, but left-over fog still clung here and there, wreathing atmospherically around the stone crosses and headstones. Some of the graves had statues of angels watching over them, which Victorians seemed to picture either as big girls with wings, or chubby little cherubs. Lola and I started doing mad angel statue imitations but then a funeral procession came through the gates, so we hastily stopped.

The hearse was a horse-drawn coach, drawn by four black horses in blinkers. Through the window, the polished gleam of the coffin was just visible under heaps of white flowers. A father and his small daughter walked slowly behind, followed by grieving friends and relations. All the women wore long black veils.

Brice was mooching around, examining inscriptions on headstones. I wondered what people would think if they knew a dodgy angel in a Bruce Lee T-shirt was prowling around their graveyard.

The funeral coach went slowly past us, and we all bowed our heads in respect, even Brice. The hollow rumbling of the wheels and the clipping horses' hooves sounded dreamlike and muffled in the fog. One of the horses gave a nervous snort and tossed its ebony plumes.

"I want my mama," the little girl was saying. "Where's my mama?"

I can't handle this, I thought. There's too much death and dying in these times.

I must have looked upset because Lola asked, "Are you OK, hon?" Then I heard her voice change. "Mel, look, there she is!"

A little way off, under the trees, a young woman was watching the funeral. She held a tiny new-born baby in her arms. The mother and baby weren't see-thru and sepia like the spirits in Minerva's parlour. For people who'd so recently died, they looked spectacularly full of life. You could see that dead woman really felt for her husband and daughter, yet her face was filled with utter peace and love.

When will you get it into your head, Melanie? Dying is not the end, I reminded myself. It's not a big hole or a terrifying bottomless pit or a cartoon cliff edge that characters vanish over for ever. It's a portal into a totally limitless, indescribably beautiful universe.

I noticed Brice giving me a funny look, almost but not quite a smile.

"What?" I said. Brice has this annoying habit of spoiling my mystical moments.

"I think the kids are almost finished," he said gruffly.

Georgie and Charlotte had pulled up the weeds growing over their mother's grave. Now they solemnly laid down their flowers. Charlotte said a prayer, stopping once to cough into her handkerchief. Georgie just chewed his lip furiously, but when his sister finished, he muttered "Amen."

The dead woman waved serenely as we left and I waved back.

The children said their goodbyes outside the churchyard. Charlotte wanted her brother to come back to Milkwell Yard, but he said he had something to do. I guessed Georgie planned to drop in on his uncle.

It was a long walk, even with Georgie's impressive knowledge of shortcuts. But I cheered up when I realised Portman Square, where Georgie's uncle lived, joined on to Baker Street. I was walking down the actual street where Sherlock Holmes and Watson hung out solving mysteries! I didn't mention this though. Brice would only try to make me look small.

Sherlock Holmes lived in a flat. I don't think he cared much about worldly goods. Uncovering the truth, that's all he cared about. But Georgie's relations had a big posh house, set behind iron railings.

The maid who opened the door only looked about nine years old. She must have just started working there and obviously didn't recognise Georgie. When she saw him on the step, she clasped her hands behind her back like a child in a talent show.

"The mistress says no hawkers, no traders and no workhouse riffraff," she recited in a pleased voice.

"I'm not selling anything and I'm not riffraff," said Georgie with dignity. "My name is Georgie Hannay. Please tell my uncle I wish to see him, and that it's a matter of life and death."

A few minutes later the maid flounced back, and showed Georgie in to his uncle.

He was sitting by a crackling fire, apparently reading *The Times*. He had long dark hair with dramatic silver streaks. He was actually quite handsome, in a slightly haunted way. A little spaniel was sitting at his feet, longing to be noticed. It gave a joyful bark when we came in and Georgie's uncle looked up.

"Georgie! What is this 'matter of life and death' you have to see me about?"

Georgie stammered out his story. He explained that Charlotte's cough was getting worse and that she urgently needed a doctor. "But we can't afford his fee, so I wondered if you could help us. I promise I'd pay you back," he said anxiously.

The whole time Georgie was talking, his uncle was searching his face with a strangely hungry expression. It wasn't like he was seeing Georgie, so much as looking *through* him to someone else.

"I thought of asking Miss Temple," Georgie babbled nervously. "But if she suspected my sister was ill, she might put her back on the street. I am so afraid Charlotte may have tuberculosis, like mama." His lip trembled.

"You do realise that before I do anything, I must first consult with your aunt, Mrs Scrivener?"

"I understand—" Georgie began.

His uncle cut across him. "I'm afraid you don't. Mrs Scrivener is a formidable woman, some might say frightening, and it is she who holds the purse strings. The fine things you see around us here are mine only through marriage. Your grandfather did not leave me a fortune to squander as he did your dead papa, and if your aunt suspected I was spending her money on my half-brother's brats—"

He saw Georgie go red and added in a gentler voice, "Those are her words, my dear. Your aunt does not feel for you as I do."

Georgie nodded miserably.

"I'm sure this house seems very pleasant, doesn't it?"

"Oh, yes uncle—" Georgie began but his uncle was still talking.

"Well, let me tell you, when Mrs Scrivener has one of her rages, it is a purgatory, a real Dante's Inferno."

"Yes, sir," mumbled Georgie.

Mr Scrivener shook his head, as if he'd just remembered something. "Poor child. How could you have heard of Italy's greatest poet? You don't even go to school. Come, your aunt will not be back for some time. We must have tea before you go."

I've always adored real fires, so I went to warm my hands at the flames. The spaniel immediately came over and lay down beside me. That's one cool thing about being an angel – animals totally worship you.

While they waited for the tea to arrive, Georgie told his uncle about visiting his mama's grave.

His uncle's handsome face flushed. "I believe that your mama's delicate constitution was fatally weakened by that business with your papa."

Georgie looked wistful. "How did Papa die? Mama would never tell us."

His uncle avoided his eyes. "It is better that way," he said. "We must simply pray the weakness has not been passed on to you."

Georgie looked bewildered. "Yes, Uncle."

The tea came and Georgie's uncle plied Georgie with muffins and seed cake and kept refilling his cup with hot sweet tea. The room was very warm, and once Georgie's stomach was full, he had to struggle to stay awake. After a while he began to snore, and his uncle sat watching him with that same strangely hungry expression. I got the feeling Georgie reminded him of someone, someone completely unlike his scary wife.

A new, darker expression came into Georgie's uncle's eyes. He got up abruptly and went to sit at his desk, where he began to compose a letter.

The spaniel couldn't settle with so many angels in one room. It went trotting over to Lola and Brice, wagging its stumpy little tail.

"Nice dog," said Brice softly. "Pity about your psycho master."

The dog gazed at them, as if they were the most wonderful beings it had ever seen. They smiled at each other and their hands touched as they stroked its silky ears.

I was suffering from serious jealousy, I admit that now. But at the time I totally couldn't, so I took my feelings out on Brice. "It's not the uncle's fault he's married to a mean old harpy," I snapped.

"Mel, just ask yourself how two kids from a well-off family came to end up on the streets," Brice said angrily.

"Stuff happens," I said. "You of all people should know that. Anyway, you heard what the uncle said. Georgie's father squandered the family fortune.

Maybe he was a gambler. He obviously had mental problems."

I was horrified at myself. Stop defending this guy, Mel, I thought. You think he's a psycho too.

Brice made a sound of disgust. "That's what Uncle Noel wants people to think. I can't believe you fell for it."

"Even if their dad was a gambler," he said, turning to Lola, "which I doubt, it's likely some of the money was put in trust for them. I have a feeling that nice, caring Uncle Noel used his legal eagle know-how to divert their inheritance to his own personal bank account. Maybe he got himself made executor, so he could 'look after' Georgie and Charlotte's dosh until they come of age. *If* they come of age," he added darkly.

"You mean, Uncle and Auntie Scrivener would prefer it if neither kid survived?" Lola's eyes widened. "Omigosh! Do you think he's psycho enough to kill them?"

"I think he's probably been hoping they'd just die naturally of hunger and neglect. Sounds like the aunt got impatient and tried to have the kids put in the workhouse. Charlotte wouldn't last long in there."

This is so unfair, I thought. I was the Sherlock Holmes fan, not Brice. How come he got to play detective? And how come he and Lola were talking to each other over my head as if I wasn't even in the room?

"Well, I think an angel should always give a person the benefit of the doubt," I said prissily. "Plus you two seem to have forgotten this is only meant to be a field trip. We're not supposed to get involved."

Lollie put her finger to her lips. "Something's happening."

Uncle Noel had finished writing his letter. He slipped it into an envelope, sealing it with hot wax. Then he reached into a money bag hidden at his waist and extracted a shiny silvery sixpenny bit. At last, he went to wake Georgie.

"I want you to take another letter to our old friend in Newgate Gaol. Here is money for a cab and sixpence for yourself. You are to hand this personally to Mr Godbolt. Can you remember my message from last time?"

"I am to tell Mr Godbolt that you have not forgotten about him or his sister," Georgie echoed blearily. He was still half-asleep, but his uncle must have been scared his wife would come back because suddenly Georgie was outside on the doorstep, still struggling into his coat.

He hailed a passing horse-drawn cab and we rode all the way to Newgate Street in unusual style. Georgie was obviously familiar with the drill, and just marched up to the prison door and tugged the bell pull.

I've never seen such an ominous door in my entire existence. The wood was studded all over with iron nails and bound with huge iron bands. The massive bolts were iron too. And this was just the door!

I gulped. We're angels, I reminded myself bravely. We can leave any time we like.

I heard heavy footsteps and the jangling of keys. It was a horribly claustrophobic sound which totally explained why Victorian prison warders used to be known as 'turnkeys'.

A grating slid open. "State your business," growled a voice.

"I'm to take a letter to Mr Edwin Godbolt," said Georgie.

"'I'll see as he gets it."

"It's from 'is brief," said Georgie in his street voice. "I'm to put it in 'is 'and, or I don't get paid."

The bolts rasped back, and a weary looking turnkey let us in to a grim stone hallway. The only source of light came from the glimmering oil lantern in his hand. He was just a tired bloke in a black suit and broad-brimmed hat, but you could see that having those keys made him feel seriously in charge.

The turnkey led us down steps and along twisty passages and through a series of yards, each one guarded by gates with iron gratings. We had to stop at each one, while he put down his lantern, hunted for the right key, unlocked and then relocked the gate after us. The further we went into the prison, the more stale and smelly the air became, as if all the gaol's actual oxygen had been used up years ago.

We came to an immense dank stone room, a cellar basically, with dripping sounds and slimy stuff growing on the walls. The smell was so gross I had to hold my breath. Unbelievably, there was just one toilet bucket for twenty or more convicts to use. Some convicts were trying to sleep on thin mats on the floor. The rest paced or leaned blankly against the walls. One made coaxing noises to Georgie, as if he was a cute little pet. "Come over here, laddie." He leered at the little boy, exposing broken teeth, and Georgie backed away.

The turnkey held up his lamp. "Message for Edwin Godbolt from 'is brief," he said in a bored voice.

An elderly man moved forward into the light. He was pale and painfully thin, but he had the sweetest expression I've ever seen on a human adult. "Georgie, how kind of you to visit me in this fearful place."

"My uncle sent me. He has written you a letter, sir," Georgie explained.

I saw a flicker of emotion in the old man's eyes. "Oh, yes, I should have realised," he sighed. "I haven't received one of those for some time. Thank you, child." Mr Godbolt quickly slipped the envelope inside his thin shirt.

"Don't you want to read it?" asked Georgie in surprise.

The old man smiled. "I have all the time in the world to study its contents. But you are here in person, you precious child, and it does me good to see your face."

"'E looks a bit young to be a solicitor though," someone shouted.

Georgie grinned. "It's my uncle who is a lawyer, not me!"

"No offence to your uncle, nipper, but 'e can't be up to much," said the same joker, "or this old darlin' wouldn't be languishing here along with all us villains. I've been banged up with real forgers, right? And this one don't have the look, know what I mean?"

"'E's like our dear old Granddad, Mr Godbolt is," said a young inmate unexpectedly.

"Yes, yes, he's a regular Saint Francis," said the turnkey gruffly, "and all the mice do little tricks for him on Sundays. Have you finished your business, lad? I've got a nice lamb chop going cold in my office."

"No, sorry," said Georgie. "Mr Godbolt, my uncle says I am to tell you that he has not forgotten about you or your sister." He smiled at the old man, clearly proud of his uncle's generosity.

The old man closed his eyes and took a breath, and when he opened them his voice was almost completely steady. "Thank you very much, child. Take care of yourself, won't you, until we meet again."

It should have been a relief to hit the streets, but no matter how fast I walked I couldn't shake off that icky prison vibe.

No-one in this city is free, I thought miserably. Victorian London is just one big fogbound prison. Normally I'd have squeezed Lola's hand for comfort, but Brice was in between us. So we just kept walking in grim silence until we'd walked all the way back to Whitechapel.

Then I heard Brice say, "I can understand you being upset. Newgate kills me every time." And the creep put his arm through Lola's.

I'd had about enough of being invisible, so I grabbed Lola's other arm and started wittering about how the fog was making my hair frizz.

With a swift movement, Lola pulled herself free. "Stop this, both of you!" she blazed. "You haven't even noticed that Georgie's upset!"

At that moment I couldn't have cared less about him. I was totally not in angelic mode. Lollie had just yelled at me, ME, her best friend! Plus she'd bracketed me unforgivably with Brice.

I glowered resentfully at Georgie. He was standing absolutely still under a street lamp, clutching a silver locket and peering at it in the flickery light with a weirdly intense expression. I'm ashamed to say I assumed that he'd stolen it from his uncle, because of Charlotte. Then I noticed that Georgie had his back to an alleyway, and I thought, this kid's too savvy to check out stolen goods in public. And then I saw a tear tracking down his face, and I thought Lola's right. I never even noticed.

The little boy shut his eyes and pressed the cold silver to his lips. That's when I knew for sure that the locket must be his. His hand shook slightly as he opened the locket, and when he saw the picture inside, a sob burst out of him.

"I'm trying to be strong, Mama," he whispered. "I try, but I get so scared."

At that moment someone came out of the alley and went hurrying past. For an instant I saw a blurred figure, sharply outlined in the gaslight. Then it melted back into the darkness.

Afterwards, the others asked me to describe what I'd seen. Had I seen a surgeon's bag, or an exotic gold-topped cane, that might have concealed the lethal knife? Did I notice an overpowering scent of lily of the valley? But all I could remember was the shadow of a hat and cloak flowing along the wall, monstrous and distorted in the gaslight, and the sensation of something soft and velvety brushing against my energy field.I pulled back. I remember that, but it was pure instinct. I wasn't consciously paying attention to the stranger in the cloak. I was angry with myself because Lola was right about me, plus I was angry with *her* for exactly the same reason.

I put my hand to my face. Something was wrong.

Something had disturbed my energy field so badly that I thought I might actually faint.

"Lola," I began. "I need to sit d—"

Bloodcurdling screams came from the darkness. A girl shrieked, "Get the police!"

Scared faces appeared at windows all along the street.

Someone blew several blasts on a whistle and I heard the pounding of feet as Victorian bobbies ran to the scene. There was a babble of voices, inarticulate with horror.

"Omigosh, Georgie!" said Lola. "Mel, Brice, quick!"

Georgie's face was deathly pale in the gaslight. "He walked past me," he whispered. "Jack the Ripper just walked right past me."

CHAPTER SEVEN

When a defenceless kid has just bumped into Jack the Ripper, the question of breaking cosmic rules doesn't really apply.

"There's a pub down the road, you can see it from here, The Three Cripples," said Brice. "It's basically a dive but the landlady's sound. She'd probably let Georgie stay the night."

We clustered round the traumatised Georgie, and told him firmly and clearly to get himself to Brice's dodgy pub right away.

"You need to be where there are lights and people, kiddo," said Brice.

I felt a zing of angel electricity inside my heart as Georgie got the message. He looked wildly up and down the street and I could hear him thinking, "Lights, people!" He spotted a faint gleam from the pub across the street, and set off at a trot. I heard him repeating Brice's words out loud. "I've got to be where there are lights and people."

The pub door stood slightly open, leaking smells of mice and old beer and stale cooking. Inside a man with multiple tattoos was telling some equally scary men about the latest killing.

Georgie slid around the customers, edging as close to the fire as he dared. He was shivering uncontrollably by this time. A bald-looking dog came to sniff at his hands. "Good dog," Georgie said shakily. "Who's a good dog."

"Are you all right, nipper?" called the tattooed guy. "You looks a bit green around the gills."

A tremor ran through Georgie. "I seen Jack," he said in his street voice. "But I never knew I seen 'im, if you know what I mean. That's why I come here where there was lights and people. I couldn't stand it out there alone in the dark." Georgie buried his face in his hands, and the ugly dog tried to lick him through his fingers.

The landlady had heard Georgie's distraught explanation.

"You stay where you are, littl'un," she said. "As it happens I've got some victuals need eating up, and, well, if you happens to fall asleep by the fire, I'm so rushed off me feet, I probably won't notice till morning."

Lola gave a sigh of gratitude. "You're right, she's a total sweetie. It's so great you knew about this place, Brice."

"Yeah, well, any time you need a criminal hangout, just ask Brice," I said sarcastically.

I could see Lola inwardly counting to ten. "That's not what I mean Boo, and you know it."

"So why do you reckon Uncle Noel is blackmailing Mr Godbolt, Lollie?" Brice asked her over my head.

"Hello!" I said. "You have absolutely no evidence for that accusation. For all you know, Georgie's uncle genuinely wants the guy to know he hasn't abandoned him, even though he's a convicted criminal."

"Hello!" Brice mimicked. "That message about the sister sounded like a nasty little threat to me."

"Not everyone is a nasty little double-crosser, you know, hint hint," I told him.

Lola shook her head. "There's no need to be mean. And actually I agree with Brice."

"Oh there's a surprise!" I was practically spitting with rage.

"I'm just telling you what I think, Boo! Georgie's uncle knows something he's not saying. And that sweet old guy in the prison KNOWS the uncle knows something, and he isn't saying either, but for a totally different reason."

I stared at her. "Lollie, I have NO idea what you're talking about."

"Oh there's a surprise!" Brice imitated my voice again. "Our cute little airhead hasn't a clue what's going on!"

And suddenly my soul-mate went ballistic. "Will you two just stop!" she yelled. "I have totally had enough of being fought over like a bone!"

She glared at Brice. "You are driving me nuts!"

I felt a smug grin spreading over my face but my friend turned on me in a fury. "As for you, *carita*, you seem to have forgotten what angels are actually for."

"But I just—" I began.

"You don't get it, do you?" Lola shouted. "We're professionals, Boo. We can't let our personal business get in the way."

"But I just—" Brice began.

"I'm still talking actually," she told him. "Now here's the deal. You two go back to Uncle Noel's house to do some serious investigating. That should give you a chance to sort out your differences. I'm going to stay with Georgie. Is that clear?" she demanded.

"Crystal," we said nervously.

Brice and I beamed ourselves sulkily to Portman Square. We arrived just as Uncle Noel was going out for the evening, looking seriously spruced up and spiffy. He hailed a cab in Baker Street.

"Take me to Boodles in Marble Arch," he told the cabbie.

I was convinced this was some kind of Victorian strip joint, plus Brice and I were grimly ignoring each other, so I had a really nerve-wracking journey. I was incredibly relieved when Boodles turned out to be a respectable gentleman's club. Though personally I thought it could do with major refurbishing. The walls and ceilings had gone the colour of old tea from the constant puffing of cigars, and the rugs were so faded you couldn't even guess what colour they'd been.

We followed Uncle Noel upstairs into a smoky room full of Victorian gentlemen going "haw-haw-haw", like those depressing debates in the House of Commons. Some of the members had pulled their leather chairs into huddles to make it easier to chat. Others were lounging about with their feet on tables, or blatantly warming their backsides at the fire. They were all really old, like in their forties and fifties. And judging from the conversation about crown courts and plaintiffs and whatever, most of them were barristers like Georgie's uncle. I think a couple were even judges.

For the first hour or so, Uncle Noel circulated and made polite chit-chat like agony aunts tell you to do at parties. Then someone said, "Ah, Scrivener, tell us what you think about the stinking masses? Haw-haw-haw!"

This was so outrageous that I couldn't help catching Brice's eye. To my relief he didn't look away.

"They should put these guys in a museum for boring old bigots," he said.

"It's a shame we're not ghosts," I sighed. "At least we could play noughts and crosses on the mirror."

It was amazing! Those old buffers were so vile that Brice and I were actually bonding!

Brice gave me a grudging grin. "So how does Uncle Noel strike you, now he's in his natural habitat?"

"I think he seems totally ill at ease."

"That could be why he's drinking too much," said Brice.

"And have you noticed how that old guy with the sidewhiskers always pretends not to hear what he says?"

"Our Noel is a self-made man," explained Brice. "In their eyes, that makes him an upstart and a bounder."

The man with the sidewhiskers was thumping the table. "The urban poor breed like rabbits and we've got to put a stop to it!" He went into this long rant about the poor spreading their disgusting diseases, and pushing up crime rates. "By the end of the century we'll be overrun!"

Georgie's uncle seemed increasingly uncomfortable. "You all speak as if the poor are incapable of feeling as we do, as if they have no dreams or ambitions."

"That's true," I hissed to Brice. "The bit about them speaking, I mean, not the poor," I added hastily.

But old Sidewhiskers completely ignored Uncle Noel's outburst. "This so-called Whitechapel murderer is a prime example," he said. "The man's obviously a complete degenerate. I'd be very surprised if he even knows who his father was!"

I don't know if it was the old buffer's words or the approving haw-hawing that upset Georgie's uncle so much. Plus remember he'd really been knocking back the booze. But suddenly he just exploded with rage.

"Are you saying that a man has no right to better himself?" he burst out. "Must he then stay in the situation he was born to, no matter how degrading?"

"Dear, dear, we seem to have touched a raw nerve," someone muttered.

"Yet with education and a sincere desire to improve himself, a poor man can change beyond recognition!" Uncle Noel was almost shouting now. "Such a man might even come and mingle with you gentlemen in your precious club and you would be none the wiser!"

And dashing his glass to the floor he stormed downstairs and out into the street. We had to hurtle after him.

"I thought all Victorian guys were supposed to go in for stiff upper lips and repressing their feelings," I panted.

Georgie's uncle was barging drunkenly into other passers-by. He was so pickled that his thoughts were clearly audible. *I'm twice the man they are.*

No-one ever gave me so much as a helping hand. My father grudged every paltry penny he gave my mother. I was his by-blow, his bastard, so I had to make do with second best; a second-best school while my brother went to Eton, living in that poky house while they lived in luxury.

"Why is he so obsessed with his parents not being married?" I asked Brice. "Loads of my mates' parents weren't."

"It's different in these times," Brice explained. "If a Victorian was born on the wrong side of the blanket, he was considered to be disreputable, a really bad lot."

Georgie's uncle flagged down a passing hansom cab. We climbed into the high unsprung vehicle, with its smells of leather and horses, and went clipping through the foggy streets.

'Try harder, Noel,' Mama kept saying. Uncle Noel was still fuming to himself. *'Pass your exams, show him how clever you are, and you'll make your father proud of you.' There was no money to send me to university, so I worked as a legal clerk by day, and sat up all night studying for the bar. Papa will be proud of me when I get my articles, I thought.*

"Don't you feel just a *leetle* bit sorry for him?" I whispered.

Brice shook his head. "This guy is quite sorry enough for himself."

When we got back to Portman Square, Georgie's uncle went straight to his study and poured himself a generous glass of booze. Then he stumbled to a curtained alcove and pulled back the curtain. Behind it was a painting of a young fair-haired woman in a white dress.

"Haven't we seen her before somewhere?" Brice sounded puzzled.

"Omigosh," I gasped. "It's the woman in Georgie's locket!"

We stared at each other as this sank in. Then Brice gave an evil chuckle. "Well rock'n'roll! Uncle Noel had the hots for Georgie's mama!"

"Second best, always second best in everything." Uncle Noel was really working himself into a state. "Then I met you, Marguerite, and I thought my luck had changed."

He went on rambling drunkenly about how he'd loved Georgie's mama at first sight, but he was poor and illegitimate so he hadn't dared approach her.

"Perhaps you could have grown to love me," Uncle Noel sniffled. "But before I could pluck up courage to speak, my half-brother stole you away from me."

Brice's eyes widened. "Oh – that could be a motive!"

The uncle opened a drawer and took out a framed miniature of the widowed Marguerite with her two small children. I was startled to see they were both wearing dresses!

"Oh my poor darling," he groaned. "Little Georgina gets more like you every time I see her."

My mouth dropped open. Georgina! NO way!

No wonder him mum had put him in a dress. Tough streetwise cigar-smoking Georgie was really a girl!!!

I saw Brice's smug expression and realised he'd known all along.

"You rat!" I said. "Why didn't you say something?"

"I knew you'd figure it out eventually," he grinned.

The door opened and a tiny woman came in, wearing a full-length nightdress and a prim little bedcap with trailing ribbons. "Do try to control yourself, dearest," she said sharply. "The servants will hear."

Uncle Noel's wife might have been pocket-sized, but she was totally deadly. The room was suddenly crackling with ruthless vibes.

Her husband guiltily went to cover the portrait, but Aunt Agnes smiled. "I am not jealous of your Marguerite, beloved," she said with poisonous sweetness. "For she is dead and I am very much alive."

"You are indeed a formidable woman!" He tried to embrace her but tiny Aunt Agnes ducked neatly under his arm.

"Formidable, some might even say 'frightening'," she quoted.

"My love, I didn't mean – have you been spying on me, Agnes?" he asked in dismay.

"You bet your life she has," Brice muttered.

"Purely for your own good," Aunt Agnes said calmly. "You lack the necessary steel to follow our plan through to its conclusion. Luckily I am strong enough for us both."

"But when I think of Marguerite's daughter ending her days among drunks and pickpockets," he blubbered. "I have such nightmares, Agnes...!"

"It's only seeing her which upsets you," she interrupted swiftly. "Once the brats are out of harm's way, you'll feel better."

I heard Brice breathe in sharply.

"I bet she's got a fur coat made from baby Dalmatians, don't you?" I whispered.

Aunt Agnes poured them both a drink and raised her glass to the portrait.

"Silly girl!" she said in musing voice. "She might still be alive if she had married you. Indeed, dearest, she would have married you, if it hadn't been for your half-brother's selfishness. Wasn't it enough that he stood to inherit the law firm and all your father's money? Did he have to break your heart too?"

"Georgie's right. She *is* a witch!" said Brice.

"He was so cold and cruel that he left me no choice. I had to become cruel just like him, or go under," Uncle Noel sniffled.

Aunt Agnes gave a low chuckle. "But what a sweet moment it must have been, when you saw that proud old man standing in the dock like a common criminal."

I was shocked. She was shamelessly manipulating him, constantly reminding him how he'd suffered, trying to make him feel like this money was actually *owing* to him.

Uncle Noel gave her a watery smile. "Yes, yes, a very sweet moment."

"And the ripples go on and on. First your father's public shame, then your brother discovering that the man he so worshipped was a liar and a thief.

They died broken men, Noel. They tried to destroy you but you broke them!"

"But my brother suffered for so many years before he died, and then Marguerite—" he began.

"Don't interrupt, dearest," she said coldly. "The force of your revenge has reverberated through three generations of Hannays. It needs only one more act of courage, and they'll be gone for ever. Then all your father's money will be ours."

"But what if someone finds out? I had my own father accused of embezzling...!"

"Who is going to tell?" she said contemptuously. "Not that fool Edwin Godbolt. He is terrified you will harm his sister. And the man who forged those false documents, Alfred Rose—"

"Lilly," her husband corrected her. "Alfred Lilly."

"Lilly is in the Union Workhouse, and the matron says he has only days to live. That leaves Lovelace, and by now that old villain is either dead or committing new felonies on the other side of the world. For all we know he died of typhus on the transport ship, like your father."

Uncle Noel gazed at his wife with a kind of awe. "You make everything seem so simple, my love."

"But it is dearest, it is," Aunt Agnes said triumphantly. "Wonderfully and exquisitely simple!"

They left the room arm in arm, leaving me and Brice totally stunned.

I gulped. "This isn't just a field trip any more, is it?"

"No," he said.

"It's a mission, isn't it?"

"Yes."

Chapter Eight

"Let's get out of here," said Brice. "This house gives me the chills."

I naturally headed for the door. Brice grabbed my arm impatiently. "You will keep forgetting you're an angel!" And he pulled me through the wall into the cold dark street outside.

Melanie, that was so groovy – you just shimmered through a wall! I told myself. It was actually quite a cool sensation.

Brice was still ranting. "And that aunt is pure evil. Her husband practically destroyed an entire family and she's just cheering him on to the finishing post!"

I gulped. "She was talking like she wanted him to make them, you know, disappear."

"Noel Scrivener knows some unsavoury Victorians," he said grimly. "It wouldn't be hard for him to find someone to bump his nieces off, no questions asked."

"We should go back and tell Lollie and start figuring out what to do," I said.

I saw Brice's expression change at the mention of Lola. "Actually, I could do with a few minutes to get my head together."

"Oh, that's OK," I said hastily, "I'll beam back by myself."

To my surprise, he said, "No, don't rush off. Let's just walk around the square for a bit, see how the rich live."

It was well past midnight and the square was almost deserted. Outside one brightly lit house a coachman was dozing in his coach, waiting for someone to finish socialising inside. Most of the windows were dark. The fog had practically gone, there were just drifty veils here and there, but the air felt damp and raw. After a while I noticed Brice shivering in his T-shirt.

"You don't have to freeze, or did you forget you're an angel?" I teased.

"Oh, yeah." He genuinely hadn't noticed.

I could see this struggle going on inside him. He

seemed desperate to get something off his chest, and suddenly he just blurted it out. "I was just trying to take care of her. Guys are supposed to do that. Then she accuses me of acting like a dog with a bone!" He swallowed. "Was that how I seemed to you?"

"Do you want the honest truth?" I asked.

"Well, I certainly don't want you to lie," he said scathingly.

"Well, you have been acting a bit possessive." I took a breath. "We both have."

Babe, what are you doing? I thought. You almost apologised to Brice!

Just then a little grey cat came running up to us. Reuben is teaching me this cool angel language which is understood by practically all animals, so I petted her and tried out my phrases.

I noticed Brice darting sideways glances at me. Suddenly he said, "I think I'm a bit out of my depth with this boy-girl business."

"Hey, hold it right there," I said nervously. "Is this going to get embarrassing? Because if so I'm beaming out of here pronto."

He grinned. "I'm not going to ask you about the angels and the bees. It's boy-girl feelings I'm having trouble with."

I shrugged. "Yeah well, you're a guy. What can I say?"

"I wish that's all it was," he said. "Mel, can you even imagine what my life was like before the Agency took me back? I've been hanging out with some really dark characters, you know. I feel like one of those kids raised by wolves, except with me it was demons and ghouls."

"I know! It must have been a total nightmare." I pulled an embarrassed face. "That sounded really dumb. You're right. I can't even imagine what the Hell dimensions are like. I don't know how you survived."

"I don't know if I did, not totally," he admitted. "But Lola seems to think – she's so amazing, isn't she?"

"She's the best," I said softly.

"I guess I got a bit carried away." He took a deep breath. "Sorry if I acted like a jerk."

"Yeah well, I wasn't exactly behaving like an angel." I paused and shook my head. "Did I really say that?"

I held out my hand to show him it was starting to rain. "Have you finished soul-searching now? Because I am dying to see Lollie's face when we tell her Georgie is actually a girl!"

Back at The Three Cripples, we found a truly touching scene. Georgie was curled up on the floor fast asleep, cuddling the ugly dog for comfort. Around her in a protective circle were dozens of raidiant little globes of rose-coloured light.

Lola had been reading her Angel Handbook while Georgie was sleeping. When we came in, she whipped off her glasses, smiling. "Hi."

"Pink lights," said Brice. "That's nice."

I knew he was thinking, pink for a girl.

"I thought they'd help him feel safe," Lollie explained.

"Help *her* feel safe," I corrected demurely.

Lola's eyes widened. "*She*? Omigosh, you're kidding!"

"It's true," said Brice. "Young Georgie Hannay here is actually Georgina. You can't blame her for disguising herself as a boy, living on the streets and with the Ripper on the loose."

We scrutinised Georgie's face by the glow of Lola's angel lights.

"I can't imagine how I ever thought she was a boy," I whispered.

Lola shook her head in wonder. "That's one brave little human."

I went to sit by the hearth where a few embers

still gave out heat. "Brice knew straight off," I said in a casual voice.

I saw my sharp-eyed friend register that Brice and I had made a truce, but she just said, "So what else did you guys find out?"

We explained how Georgie's uncle had developed this major grudge because his favoured half-brother had married the girl he loved.

"So Scrivener decided to take revenge on the entire Hannay family," said Brice. "He used his dodgy contacts to acquire forged 'evidence' that would make it seem as if his hugely well-respected old man, Charles Hannay, had embezzled his clients' money. It was obviously a brilliant forgery, because the judge sentenced him to be transported – only he died of typhus before he reached Australia. Are you going to eat all that trail mix, Mel?"

"Oh, no, sorry!" I took over the story while Brice munched.

"It looks like Georgie's papa never got over the shame of having his father publicly humiliated. He and Marguerite eventually had kids, but I think the foundations of his world had like, crumbled." It was only now I was explaining it to Lola that I totally understood this.

"So Georgie's dad gradually gave up the ghost

and died of a broken heart," said Brice. "And a few years later, their mama followed."

Lola shook her head. "So Uncle Scrivener is indirectly responsible for these kids being orphaned."

"He's *totally* responsible." Brice sounded furious. "Not only that, he makes it seem as if Georgie's parents left their two little girls destitute. Then this guy has the nerve to whinge about having nightmares!"

"Someone must have known what was going on," Lola said.

"Yeah, Edwin Godbolt, who was conveniently sent to gaol for a crime he didn't commit," said Brice. "Also Scrivener's threatened his sister, so while she's still alive, he can't tell what he knows."

"There's one other witness," I reminded him. "That old forger, Alfred Lilly. But the aunt said he could pop off any minute." I yanked at my hair. "It's SO frustrating being invisible. If we could just materialise for five tiny minutes we could go to Scotland Yard—"

"No way!" Lola said sternly. "Last time you pulled that stunt you almost got expelled."

Brice looked interested. "Why haven't I heard this story?"

"Omigosh," I shrieked. "OMIGOSH, guys! I know what we're going to do!!"

I was so overexcited, I literally had to fan myself with both hands before I could get the words out. "We'll go to Minerva's first thing and Brice can ask his spirit buddies to tell Georgie and Charlotte what their evil rellies are up to. If the girls can get to Alfred Lilly in time, he can maybe make this like, deathbed confession to the cops or whatever." I beamed at them. "Well, what do you think?"

"I'm grudgingly impressed," Brice admitted.

I blew on my nails. "Not bad for an airhead, huh?"

"It'll mean giving Georgie a cosmic nudge," said Lola. "She might have her own plans."

Brice emptied the last of my trail mix into his mouth. "Sweetheart, if the Agency wanted to play it by the rules, why would they send *us*?"

Lola and Brice started swapping trouble-shooting stories, but I moved closer to the fire, staring into the dying embers.

Brice had made it sound like this had always been a mission, a mission that just happened to be in educational disguise. This bothered me, because deep down I knew I'd let Georgie down. Not only had I allowed my personal business to get in the way, but I'd deliberately distanced myself from her. Georgie's life was unbelievably tragic and I hadn't been able to stand the thought of how painful it must be. So to protect myself, I'd made her into this quirky little Victorian character I was studying for a project.

But now I took a proper look at Georgie, I mean really looked at her vulnerable sleeping face, and I thought, in another life she could be me and I could be her.

And you know what? I felt really moved to think that after all my stupid mistakes, I'd been given another chance to help her.

Then I thought – omigosh, how karmic is that! Like, before I could help Georgie, I had to learn all this heavy stuff about myself. And *then* I thought, it's true what they say about the Agency. It does move in mysterious ways.

Next morning, Georgie had dark circles under her eyes. She was so exhausted she could hardly drag her clothes on.

"Have you got somewhere safe to sleep tonight, dearie?" the landlady of The Cripples asked her anxiously.

"I've got dozens of places I can go," Georgie boasted, but I felt her terror go through me like a blade. Because since her mama died, she didn't have anywhere safe to go, not tonight, not ever.

It was wet and windy outside and Georgie had to stop on the doorstep to turn up her collar. Two grim-faced bobbies stood guarding the alleyway, where the girl had been murdered.

It made me shudder to think that we'd been in the next street when it happened. We should have helped her, I thought miserably. What's the use of being an angel if you can't save someone's life? And then I thought, but we can still save Georgie.

Georgie didn't need nudging in the direction of Milkwell Street. She went there all by herself. The poor kid had totally lost all her confidence and didn't know where else to go. She managed to keep it together, up to the moment when Ivy opened the door, and then she burst into tears, babbling hysterically about her brush with the Ripper. Charlotte came running, wide-eyed.

"I can't do this any more, Charlie," Georgie sobbed. "What's going to happen to me?"

Her sister looked genuinely scared. She was used to Georgie being the strong one. "Tell us exactly what happened," she said bravely.

Minerva appeared in the kitchen doorway. "Is something wrong?" she asked. Several concerned-looking spirits followed her in. Brice immediately nipped over to do a bit of cosmic networking.

"I hope you don't mind Georgie being here, Miss Temple. He didn't know where else to go." Charlotte sounded flustered.

I saw a spirit say something to Minerva, and she made a sound of genuine dismay. "I am being told that someone has been menacing this child," she said anxiously. "Have you any idea who it might be?"

"Oh, yes, Miss Temple," said Charlotte. "A poor girl was killed in Whitechapel last night, and the Ripper ran right past Georgie in the street."

Minerva shuddered. "I'm not talking about that fiend in human form. This is someone close to you, someone who did you both a great wrong many years ago. You pose a threat to this person and you are in very great danger."

Georgie backed away, with the tears still trickling down her face. "I've heard about your seances," she burst out. "All those levers and pulleys and ectoplasm and I don't want nothing, anything I mean, to do with any of your 'spirits'."

Charlotte flinched, obviously fearing she would lose her job, but Minerva just settled herself into a chair.

"Now listen to me, dear," she said. "I will not deny that I have occasionally contrived a few atmospheric effects to further my own ends."

"You cheated people," said Georgie, who was so upset that she had totally forgotten to be polite to her elders and betters.

"Yes I did," said Minerva. "Maybe I should have trusted the spirit world to take care of me, but I was afraid of – well, never mind what I was afraid of. But you must believe me, child. The spirits have been talking to me ever since I can remember, and they are insisting that someone intends to harm you and Charlotte. And stop pretending you're not listening, Ivy," she added calmly. "We're going to hold a little private seance for these girls."

Georgie sounded frightened. "Why did you call me that? I'm not a girl."

Minerva clicked her tongue. "It's not like the spirits to slip up about something like that!" She smiled into Georgie's eyes. "I know this must be upsetting, dearie. But I think we should know what kind of villain we're dealing with."

I could see Georgie still didn't believe in Minerva's powers, but she was too shattered to argue.

All the humans sat at the kitchen table and held hands, slightly awkwardly because of the table being square. All the invisible beings stood around them, with our angel contingent standing close to Georgie.

With our help, Minerva described the big house where the Hannays used to live, and how they used to go flying kites on Hampstead Heath, until Georgie's dad's nerves got so bad he stopped going out at all.

"Charlotte could have told you that," Georgie growled.

"That's true," Minerva agreed.

"Ask Georgie why she was looking at that silver locket in the lamplight," I said impulsively. I felt a zing of cosmic electricity as Minerva heard my words.

"But she didn't tell me about you standing under that street lamp last night, gazing at that silver locket," Minerva said smoothly. She smiled at the stunned Georgie. "Thought you were all alone in the world, didn't you? Well, you aren't, you see."

Georgie was making little gasping sounds, as if she might be crying.

"You think I'm talking about my spirits, don't you?" said Minerva. "But I'm not."

"Who then?" whispered Georgie.

"Angels, lovie," Minerva told her. "You've got three angels standing behind you now. I can't see them, but I know they're there."

Tears spilled down Georgie's face. "I want to believe you," she wept, "I really do. But I don't know if I can!"

"Do you need a tissue?" Lola whispered.

"No, I'm fine," I sniffled.

My plan was succeeding beyond my wildest dreams. After we hit Georgie with the locket message, she became a total believer. She was naturally distressed to hear that a dark-haired male relative, with the initials N.S., intended to harm her and her sister. But as it sank in, Georgie seemed strangely relieved, as if the pieces of a confusing puzzle were finally coming together.

"Some nights, I'd be trying to sleep in a doorway, and I'd tell myself stories to help myself drift off. I'd imagine how Uncle Noel would come riding up in a hansom, telling me he didn't care what Aunt Agnes said, he was going to have us to live with him." The memory made Georgie turn red with shame. "But when I was with him, he'd always make me feel all mixed up inside. He'd seem so kind, but then he'd deliberately say things to hurt me, as if he wanted to punish me for some reason."

She clutched at her sister. "What is he going to do to us, Charlie? I'm really scared."

This was our cue to tell Minerva about Alfred Lilly. The spirits relayed the relevant info, and to start with everything went like a dream. Then Georgie said eagerly, "So where can we find this old forger?"

I saw Minerva's eyes cloud over. "I'm not sure," she said in an anxious voice. "The spirits seem to be fading away."

The spirits turned to each other in a panic, like: well, I'm sure I'm not fading. Are you fading?

"She's blocking," hissed Brice.

Omigosh, I thought, what are we going to do if she won't give Georgie the message?

And then I remembered. Minerva Temple, the successful medium, had once been Minnie Tuttle, a defenceless workhouse child. Apparently her experiences had scarred her so deeply that she couldn't even hear a message that had the word 'workhouse' in it. Without thinking I moved round to Minerva's side of the table and put my arms around her.

"Don't be scared," I whispered. "Those workhouse people hurt you because they were bigger than you and you were young and helpless, but now it's these little girls who need help."

I hadn't actually given any thought to the effect an angelic hug might have on a gifted psychic, but let me tell you, it was pure dynamite! Minerva shot out of her trance like a rocket.

"Charlotte, fetch your coat and bonnet," she said briskly. "It's bitterly cold out. I don't want you setting off that cough."

Charlotte was bewildered. "But you didn't tell us where the old man lives?"

Minerva had started rummaging on the kitchen dresser. "The worst place this side of Hell, lovie," she told her.

I heard the dread in Georgie's voice. "You mean the Union Workhouse."

"I vowed I'd never go back," said Minerva, still rummaging among the bottles and jars. "But the spirit world has other plans." She found a green bottle, uncorked it and took a good swig.

"Dutch courage," she said bravely. "Now I'm ready to meet this old rascal. And if he has any breath left in his body, he's going to tell me everything he knows!"

CHAPTER NINE

The Union Workhouse was actually several grim small-windowed buildings, set behind tall iron gates like an army garrison. On the other side of the gates, I glimpsed drab figures listlessly sweeping paths in the drizzle.

"They make them wear uniform," I whispered. "Like prison."

Brice's tone was savage. "This *is* prison, for people tried and found guilty of being poor. Can you believe husbands and wives have to live in separate parts of the workhouse? The authorities let them meet up on Sundays if they're good."

I understood now why Minerva hadn't dared to rely on the spirit world to keep the money rolling in.

She was terrified of falling back into the grey Hell dimension of the workhouse.

An expressionless porter let us in through the gates. We had collected a police constable on the way, a stout fatherly man, and seeing Minerva falter, he immediately took charge and asked where they could find the matron.

The porter silently pointed out a path leading to one of the staff cottages.

A scared little maid in a badly-fitting workhouse gown showed us in. The matron had been having her elevenses: cold roast beef, pickled onions and a pint of porter to wash it down. She listened with growing astonishment as the constable explained that they needed to talk to one of the workhouse inmates. "We have reason to believe Mr Lilly has vital information about a serious miscarriage of justice," he said solemnly.

She gave an outraged snort. "I don't care how serious it is. My inmates follow an orderly routine and I can't allow them to be disrupted."

But the policeman stood his ground, telling her that if she didn't cooperate, he would have to charge her with obstructing the due process of the law, and the matron eventually gave in.

"Though how a senile old man can help you with

your inquiries, I don't know!" she said spitefully. "He don't know what day of the week it is, most of the time."

We were so proud of Minerva. As she walked into the dreadful institution she'd vowed never to enter again, she looked totally composed. No, better than composed. She looked like a queen. The echoey bile-green corridors and those nauseating whiffs from the kitchens must have seemed like a bad recurring dream, yet her face showed no trace of the childhood terrors churning underneath. "We'll just be a few minutes," she told the girls reassuringly. "We'll be outside in the fresh air in no time."

"We will if that matron woman's got anything to with it," muttered Brice.

Keen to finish her morning snack, the matron was rushing her visitors through the wards.

One room still stands out in my memory. It had a smell I associate with shipyards, and you could hardly see the inmates at first because the air was bewilderingly full of tiny floating fibres. Men in skimpy workhouse coats and trousers were sitting around a vast table, patiently teasing apart strands from apparently endless coils of industrial-type rope. All the wards were unheated and their fingers, already raw and blistered from the ropes, were blue with cold.

"It's called 'picking oakum'," Brice whispered. "The idea is that people aren't supposed to get something for nothing. They have to earn their bowl of watered-down gruel, otherwise everyone will want to come. Joke," he added quickly.

You'll think I'm dense but until then I genuinely hadn't realised why they called it a 'workhouse'.

We never saw the children's ward and I was grateful. Georgie and Charlotte totally didn't need to go through that.

At the far end of the very last ward was the door to the infirmary. I saw Minerva and the policeman brace themselves before they entered, so I was already expecting the worst.

I'm sorry, but there are no words which adequately describe the horror of that ward. It was a place of pure despair. Inmates were only brought here when they became so ill that it was pointless trying to squeeze any more work out of them; when they were on the brink of death, basically. Many were so ravaged by illness that if it wasn't for their clothes, you couldn't have said if they were male or female. You could hardly even tell they were human.

I was deeply grateful to Mr Allbright for teaching us a new technique ideal for use in this type of harrowing situation, when you can't stop and help each human individually. You connect with your cosmic energy source and command, "Stream!" and immediately uplifting celestial vibes stream out of you to everyone who needs it. OK, so it's not much, but like Reuben always says, better to light one candle than to curse the dark.

The matron stopped beside an iron bedstead. "Well here he is," she announced. "And much good may it do you," she muttered as she bustled away.

We all looked down at the shrunken old man under the faded quilt.

Brice shook his head. "Damn. Too late."

"I felt it as soon as we came in," Lola sighed.

When a human is getting ready to leave the Earth, there is an unmistakable vibe; a kind of intense, almost unbearable, sweetness.

"Mr Lilly," the policeman was saying doggedly. "We need to ask you a few questions. Have you ever had any connection with a gentlemen called Noel Scrivener?"

Minerva shook her head. "He can't hear you."

The policeman sounded offended. "He's responding to my voice."

The old man's watery unfocused eyes had widened with surprise. He broke into a tremulous smile, and we heard his thoughts. *I can die happy now. I'll never get to Heaven, old sinner that I am, but now I've seen the angels, I can die happy.*

Brice's expression was unreadable. "This is just incredible."

"I know," I said sympathetically. "I hate how they teach humans that stuff, about having to be good to get into Heaven."

"Actually I was talking about Agency timing," Brice explained. "Here's an old man dying alone, scared he's too wicked to get to Heaven. Now suddenly there are three angels in the vicinity. How do they do it?"

Lola was stroking the old man's knobbly hand. "Forget about the past, *amigo mio*," she whispered lovingly. "Let it go. Focus on what happens next." My friend trusts her instincts more than any angel I know, and she had instantly recognised what we had to do.

I knew we were just about to lose our one witness to Noel Scrivener's crime, but that seemed suddenly irrelevant. Like getting born, dying is intense for everyone involved. There's just no room to think about anything else.

There was a beautiful moment when the

forgotten angel inside Alfred Lilly finally slipped free and stood beside the old man's worn-out body. And suddenly the room filled with luminous figures who had come to guide him to the next world.

"I'm glad we could help him die in peace," Lola whispered.

"Me too," I whispered back. "I just wish we'd got there sooner so we could have talked to him. Then those poor girls could have got what's rightfully theirs."

Minerva gently closed the corpse's eyes. Her voice was full of sorrow. "He's gone," she told the girls. "I'm so sorry."

I was sorry too, but I was also mesmerised by what was happening to the spirit of Alfred Lilly, who seemed to be getting younger every minute. His face lit up with joy as he recognised the old friends and relations who had come to meet him.

"Hope you really enjoy Heaven, Mr Lilly," I whispered.

The forger turned to smile at me. "Lovelace," he said clearly, and he touched his chest. "The letter's in his pocket."

And he'd gone, leaving me in a blur of astonishment.

Lovelace. That was the name of the villain Aunt Agnes believed had died on the transport ship to Australia; Noel Scrivener's accomplice!

Scenes flashed before my eyes at lightning speed. Red dirt, pink cartoon birds, silver eucalyptus trees and an ex-convict with a guilty secret. *I put it in my pocket, I put it in my pocket...*

Omigosh, I thought. OMIGOSH!! Because I suddenly knew exactly how Sherlock Holmes felt when he solved a case.

Mr Lilly had just given me the crucial information we needed to restore Georgie and Charlotte's stolen fortune. And it totally didn't worry me that our witness was on the other side of the world, in the middle of the red Martian desert of the Northern Territories. Because when you're in full angel mode, you just know with every shimmery angelic cell that miracles can happen.

"*Carita?*" said Lola anxiously. "Are you all right?"

"I'm better than all right," I burbled. "I might even be a genius!"

I turned to Brice. "Do you think your spirit buddies would do us one final favour?"

*   *   *

OK, I admit to a bad moment when Ivy showed the Scotland Yard detectives into Minerva's parlour. But it was just a bad moment.

We had seances down by this time. First we softened them up with titbits of relatively trivial personal info; the name of one detective's favourite childhood dog, that time the other detective nicked money from his mama's purse and blamed it on the gardener's boy.

After that the cops became a great deal more open-minded and listened to our revelations with increasingly attentive expressions. The younger one was taking notes laboriously. "So your, erm, spirits think Mr Scrivener's accomplice may have been transported to Australia?"

With the help of her team of angelic researchers, Minerva gave a detailed description of the area where we'd found the old convict, including the sacred rock and the mission house.

The detectives were sufficiently perturbed by what they heard to pay a visit to Uncle Noel's house that afternoon, taking Charlotte and Georgie with them. Naturally we tagged along.

When Uncle Noel saw the girls' accusing faces, it was like a dam burst inside him. He cracked and tearfully confessed what he'd done. As Brice said later, Uncle Noel just wasn't cut out to be a villain. He wanted all the perks, but he wanted to be Mister Nice Guy at the same time. No wonder he made Georgie feel so confused!

The next twenty-four hours brought all kinds of satisfying changes for the Hannay girls. Scotland Yard sent a telegram to the cops in Alice Springs, asking them to track down a transported criminal called Sid Lovelace for questioning. And Edwin Godbolt was released from Newgate. Can you believe that old sweetheart immediately came round to Minerva's house to volunteer to be the children's legal adviser, for free? He brought his twin sister too. She looked exactly like him, except for being female.

There was quite a party by that time. The two detectives had popped back, with a police photographer. I think he was hoping to capture Minerva's spirits on one of his photographic plates.

I remember looking around the parlour and just feeling so honoured to be part of this happy ending.

"It's so cool that Minerva wants the girls to come and live with her," I said to Lola.

My friend was watching Brice chatting to his see-thru buddies in the corner. "Wouldn't you love to know how he learned to speak Spook?" she grinned. "Now that has to be a good story!"

Suddenly Lollie's face took on a listening expression. "I can't believe it's that time already!" she groaned. "I was just getting into the Victorians."

I couldn't believe it either, but when the Agency want you to move on, they totally let you know about it.

"This is so unfair," I complained. "I mean, I know things will work out but I wanted to SEE them work out."

Brice looked over. "You still can, you ditzy angel," he called. "And when we get back I'll prove it to you."

Then the entire parlour lit up and we blasted off back to our heavenly home.

"There'd better be a very good reason for dragging us down to the Angel Watch Centre at this hour," I yawned.

I'd been hoping for a nice lie-in the next morning. Instead we were tiptoeing past flickering booths where AW personnel were working vigilantly at their computers.

Brice let us into a private cubicle usually reserved for Agency staff. "Stop moaning, Beeby." He slid a glittering disk into the machine.

A screen lit up and a familiar scene appeared; red dirt and eucalyptus trees wavering in a heat haze.

"I can't believe you were able to swing this!" Lollie gasped.

He tapped his nose. "Inside information," he said smugly.

Somehow Brice had acquired one of the cosmic recordings the Agency uses for training purposes. From an angelic point of view, Earth's past, present and future all occur simultaneously. So it was technically possible for us all to see what had happened after the telegram arrived at the police station in Alice Springs.

We watched in total silence as Aussie cops in sun helmets finally tracked Sid Lovelace down at the mission house. The missionaries must have taken pity on him after all. Lola and I gasped as the old man, still weak from fever, reached into his pocket and pulled out a letter so old it had almost disintegrated. The writing was only just visible, but after Brice had enhanced the image, we just made out the incriminating passage requesting Alfred Lilly to falsify certain legal documents. At the bottom of the letter was a signature. *Noel Scrivener.*

Lovelace handed the letter to the police, and I felt the terrible weight roll off him, like the lifting of a curse.

This is SO cosmic, I thought. We saved him, and now he's saved Georgie and Charlotte, so he can start to forgive himself.

"That's it. Show's over!" Brice said brusquely. "I'd better get this back before anyone notices."

Lola and I agreed to meet up with him later at Guru. By this time we were totally wide awake and extremely peckish.

"Do you believe he actually stole that disk?" Lola giggled as we breezed into our favourite breakfast hang-out. "The guy's a total maverick!"

"I'll say. I'd love to know what he was up to that night, when he left us with those kids."

Lola's expression changed. "Actually, Boo, I do know, but you've got to promise not to tell him I told you."

I was covered in shame when Lollie told me that Brice had gone to help the spirit of one of the Ripper's victims. The poor girl had been so traumatised that she needed angelic assistance to help her cross over to the Next World.

"Why ever didn't he say?" I exclaimed.

"I guess he thought you wouldn't believe him," Lola said. "You do tend to be a bit hard on him."

And suddenly Lola and I were having our first proper conversation in months. I told her how jealous I'd been when I realised she and Brice were together, and she was astonished.

"Together! We're not 'together', Boo! No way! He needed a friend and I really like bad boys, OK? Babe, you're my soul-mate! I wouldn't drop you for some – guy!"

I was stunned. "Like, you didn't ever kiss?"

Lola gave a wicked giggle. "Now, did I say that? It gets v. romantic under the stars, you know!"

We were still having a giggly heart-to-heart over our breakfast pastries when Brice came in with Reuben and his bizarre mate Chase. "Brice has been showing us a picture of your Minerva," Reuben beamed. I got the funny feeling he knew something we didn't.

"Don't ruin my story," objected Brice. "I found a book on Victorian mediums and there she was. She became quite famous. Here's a picture."

Time is so weird. It seemed like only yesterday when that photograph was taken, and in my time scheme it was. Yet here it was in a book written more than a century later, by a sceptical academic who thought all mediums were frauds and charlatans.

The black and white portrait showed Minerva looking v. stern and Victorian. Light seemed to have leaked into the camera, inadvertently creating some weirdly extraterrestrial-type FX.

I stared at the three featureless blobs beside her. The photographer had snapped us at the exact moment we beamed back to Heaven.

"This is my favourite bit!" Brice pointed to the caption.

"Minerva Temple and her angelic advisers," I read. "The heavenly trio famously helped Scotland Yard solve the notorious Scrivener case." Underneath the author had written, "An obvious fake."

We all howled with laughter. It is so cool to be back, I thought. This is one of the happiest moments of my life!

"So what was it like, going on a mission with your evil nemesis, Mel?" asked Chase.

The entire café went silent. Chase, otherwise known as Mowgli, mostly hangs out with the animal kingdom and is not known for his tact. I really wished the ground would open up and swallow me. Everyone was staring at me, waiting to hear my answer. I felt my face grow bright red.

"Well, actually—" I began.

I stopped. This matters, Melanie, I thought. It matters what you say here. Don't wriggle out of it.

Don't try to please anybody. Just answer him truthfully.

Brice was trying to look as if he didn't care what I thought.

I forced myself to meet his eyes.

"It was educational," I said finally. "Unexpectedly educational."

Fighting Fit

This book is dedicated to Terri, Toni and Steph, for inspiring the plot of *Fighting Fit*, to Amber, for showing me round Bath's Roman baths, and to Maria, for everything. My grateful thanks to Vivian French, Derek Levick, and Liz Nair, for suggesting such wonderful books and research materials on Ancient Rome. Any major bloopers are purely the responsibility of the author.

Chapter One

I used to think that being an angel was going to be all sweetness and light. I pictured myself zipping off to Earth, bringing peace, harmony and whatever to humankind. Then I'd zoom back to the Angel Academy, jump out of my combats, fling on a sparkly midriff top and swan off with my mates to dance till dawn. If only...

I adore my work, don't get me wrong. But the angel business has a definite downside. PODS are never off duty. They sabotage our missions constantly and it really gets to me sometimes.

The official term for the Powers of Darkness is the Opposition. But my mates and I just call them PODS. PODS agents are opposite to angels in every way. Unlike us they have no bodies or personalities of their own.

You think this is a drawback, right? Wrong! Over the centuries, PODS have developed the creepy ability to morph into any shape they like. But though PODS can disguise their appearance, their vibes are a dead give-away. To us anyway. Angels can suss out Dark agents immediately. So can sensitive humans; kids especially. But most people think if it looks human and acts human, it HAS to be human. They don't notice how this 'person' makes them feel.

If you're exposed to PODS toxins for any length of time, you become poisoned. Life feels like hard work. You'll go, "Life is pointless. Why should I care what happens to this stupid planet? Turn up the TV and let someone else worry."

See what I mean? That's not you! That's PODS talk. They want you to think life on Earth is ugly and meaningless. They want you to be depressed. When humans despair, it's MUCH harder for us to get through to you.

So far I've come back from Earth unscathed. But from time to time agents do get seriously injured. Angel trainees are especially vulnerable. That's why our school makes Dark Studies compulsory.

I HATE Dark Study days. We're cooped up inside the Agency building for hours, while professional celestial agents put us through one simulated PODS encounter after another. These PODS set-ups are the safest way to train inexperienced angel kids and teach them to deal with the real thing. But the simulations are just SO real. By the end of the day you feel as if you've literally been dragged through the Hell dimensions and back.

After the last D.S. day, we didn't get back to our dorm until the small hours. I had a long hot shower to wash off any lingering PODS pongs (I told you simulations are realistic) and threw on my old T-shirt that says *You're no Angel*. I felt too hyper to sleep, so I went along to Lola's room to see if I could beg a mug of her special hot chocolate.

Before I could even knock, the door flew open. Lollie popped her head out. Her face was scarcely recognisable under her spooky face-pack. Without a word, she pulled me into her room, plunked a steaming mug of hot chocolate in my hand, plumped up my favourite floor cushion, so I could sit down, then calmly got on with her beauty routine.

Lola Sanchez, Lollie to her friends, is the soulmate I've been looking for since the universe began. We're so alike it's unbelievable. We both have long legs and hair that refuses to be tamed. We have almost the exact same taste in music. We even dress similarly, though being from my future, Lola is that bit whackier. She has this mad habit of giving her friends nicknames. Our big buddy, Reuben, is Sweetpea and I'm Boo. I have no idea why!

I curled up on my floor cushion, sipping my drink and moaning about my life. "You never get any time off in this business. It takes over your ENTIRE existence."

"That's because we're on the fast track, babe." Lola had to mumble through stiff lips because of her face-pack.

"The fast track to what exactly?" I asked her.

"The fast track to evolution, stupid."

"I am SO sick of that word!" I complained. "Why does everything have to keep evolving into something else? Like forests turn into coal and coal turns into diamonds. And humans turn into angels and angels turn into – whatever angels turn into. Talk about a hyperactive universe. Why can't it just chill out for a change!"

"You know what Mr Allbright says," my mate said in her face-pack voice. "'Don't knock evolution, it's—'"

" '–the only game in town!'" I quoted gloomily.

Lola went into the bathroom to wash her face. "Heavenly vibes don't just make us peachy on the outside," she called through running water. "They're transforming us on the inside. This school is basically a cosmic hothouse. That's why it gets so intense."

I sighed. "I don't feel like I'm on the fast track to anywhere, Lollie. I feel a complete fake."

Lola is the kind of girl who says exactly what she thinks. "OK, as a human, maybe you were a bit of a ditz," she agreed. "But you've changed a lot, Mel Beeby." She came out blotting her face with a towel.

"Orlando doesn't think so," I sighed. "We were in the same group all day and he totally ignored me."

My friend gave me a severe look. "How did Mr Cutie Pie sneak into this conversation? I thought we were having a serious discussion about angelic stress."

"I'm an angel aren't I?" I sighed. "Plus I'm seriously stressed!"

I was beyond stressed actually. I was terminally confused.

You see back on Earth, I always knew I was going to meet this special somebody. You know how the story goes, one day our eyes would meet and it'd be like DING! Now your real life can begin!!

But thanks to a hit and run joyrider my 'real life' ended dramatically the day after I turned thirteen. On the upside, all my human problems instantly became irrelevant. What I didn't reckon on, was a whole new set. For example, Dating in the Afterlife is not a subject teen advice columns tend to cover.

That's why I had no idea what to do about Orlando. Even Lola admits that Orlando is the most gorgeous boy in our school. He literally looks like an angel in one of those old Italian paintings: olive skin, dark eyes and a smile so sweet it ought to be illegal.

And this is a problem? you're thinking.

Er, no! My problem is that Orlando is a genius. Lola told me from the start that all Orlando thinks about is work. "He has NO idea of the effect he has on girls," she warned.

I remember watching Orlando walk through the library, soon after I started at the Academy. I'm not exaggerating, every single girl turned to look at him. They were like sun-starved sunflowers yearning after the light. Like Lola said, Orlando didn't even notice!

I despise girls who whinge on about boys who don't know they exist, and I was determined I would never join Orlando's sad little groupies.

But then I got all confused. You see sometimes Orlando *did* seem to notice me. I *wasn't* imagining it, I swear. And each time it happened, my heart totally stood still. That has to be love, right?

Just thinking about it made me sigh heavily into my frothy hot chocolate. "I just don't know where I am," I whimpered. "Remember the night before our guardian angel assignments? Orlando went out of his way to walk me back to the dorm. He was SO sweet! But today I might as well have been invisible."

My friend was brushing her glossy black curls so hard, I could see sparks. "Mel, this is driving me nuts. There's a big beautiful universe out there. And you're boringly fixated on one good-looking boy."

"Hello! One drop-dead gorgeous boy, thank you."

"One drop-dead, gorgeous, mysteriously unavailable boy," Lola pointed out brutally.

I stared at her. "I don't believe you said that! That is SO callous!"

"It's the truth! You're obsessed, girl. Every time

we have a conversation it always comes back to Mr Cutie Pie. We could be talking about cats and you'd go, 'Do you think Orlando likes cats? Maybe I could give him a sweet little kitten? Perhaps he'd notice me then?'"

"You're right. I'm hopeless," I sighed. "Do you think I need help?"

"I think you need a boot up your sorry angel behind," she told me. "Come to the gym with me, Boo!! Wake up those dozy celestial cells!"

"I keep telling you, I'm not a gym kind of girl."

"Correction," Lola said. "You WEREN'T a gym kind of girl. But in your new incarnation they will call you the Workout Princess!"

Since she got back from her adventure holiday last summer, my soul-mate has totally converted to the healthy life. I had to admit her fitness regime was paying off. Angels always have a special glow, but my friend looked stunningly healthy and toned.

Miaow! I thought. Exercise really does make a girl look good!

A glorious fantasy flashed through my mind. A new dynamic *moi* hurrying across the campus, sunlight glinting on my hair. Suddenly Orlando catches sight of me. I have been SO blind, he thinks. This is the girl I've been waiting for. And he rushes up to me and – well I'm sure you get the picture!

"Sweating into Lycra isn't normally my idea of fun, but I suppose I could give it a try," I sighed.

Lola was delighted. She threw her arms around me. "You won't regret it, Boo! Today is the first day of the rest of your life!"

I felt a twinge of guilt. My motives were nowhere near as pure as she thought.

The workout routine was agony to begin with. Lola literally had to drag me out of bed the first few days. But after a month or so, a miracle happened. I started waking up before my alarm went off. And check this – I was actually looking forward to my morning run!

I LOVED it. Isn't that unbelievable? I truly loved that moment when Lola and I sprinted out of the door into the pearly light of early morning and jogged down to the beach. I loved running along by the water's edge, feeling tiny shells scrunch under my trainers, then looking back and seeing our two sets of footprints in the damp sand. I even loved the ache in my muscles afterwards that told me I'd worked them to the max.

Now I'd started, Lola refused to let me slack. At lunchtime we'd grab a salad from the cafeteria, then head for the gym. She even got Reuben to make us a hip hop remix of her singing *Sisters are Doing it for Themselves*. Maybe I didn't tell you, but Lola literally sings like an angel. "We can listen to it on our headsets," she beamed. "It'll give us added motivation!"

We got so carried away that we started singing aloud while we were working out. All the kids in the gym started clapping and cheering. "Look out PODS!" one boy yelled. "The sisters are coming to get you!"

Lola decided I was ready for the advanced martial arts class she goes to with Reuben. All trainees study martial arts as part of their angel training. Like Mr Allbright told me when I first got here, "You can't just charm your way out of a sticky cosmic situation, Melanie. There are times when you have to fight back."

But with Reubs, martial arts is more than a module on the heavenly school curriculum. It's a way of life. Our buddy got talent-spotted back in kindergarten and he's been training at a dojo in the Ambrosia district in every spare moment ever since.

The dojo is the simplest building in the city. It's

basically a roof, supported on carved wooden pillars made from some heavenly wood that smells totally sublime. Bamboo blinds keep the dojo blissfully shady. Banners of gold and crimson silk flutter in the breeze. Some have mantras painted on them in an old angelic script. One just says *Breathe*.

The dojo master stepped out of the shadows to greet us. Reuben introduced us and we bowed respectfully to each other. Students in baggy fighting clothes were arriving in twos and threes. They bowed to the master too and silently got on with warm-up stretches.

Omigosh, I thought. I want to wear karate gear and be calm and pure just like them.

I started going down to the dojo twice a week after school.

Brice came along some nights. Lola said it was part of his rehabilitation programme. I was getting used to seeing my old enemy around the campus these days. I'll admit to a bad moment when I found out he and Lola had got alarmingly close, on holiday. But in a way I could understand it. Lola has a warm heart and as you know, a bad boy with a past is incredibly hard to resist. What I could NOT understand is why Reuben and Brice were such great mates.

"You do remember that he beat you up?" I asked him one night, when we were working on my sword-fighting technique.

Reuben shook his dreads out of his eyes. "Yeah, I remember. I'm not stupid!" He assumed a defensive crouch.

My angel buddy doesn't look that tough. He's just this skinny honey-coloured kid. But studying angelic martial arts has given him this genuine inner strength.

"But don't you mind seeing Brice every day?" I asked.

Reuben looked blank. "Why should I mind?"

"Erm, because he tried to destroy you?"

"He did what he had to do." Reuben made a lunge with his sword and pierced me efficiently through the chest.

"Hey, I wasn't ready," I complained.

"Try telling that to the PODS," he grinned.

Heavenly swords have light-beams instead of blades, so Reuben and I were able to slash at each other quite merrily; we just got a temporary light overdose and went dizzy. If you used the same weapon on the PODS, however, they'd dissolve into mush.

"He left scars, Reubs," I persisted.

With a lightning move my buddy captured my sword arm. "I got caught off-guard," he said. "I won't do that again in a hurry. Brice taught me a valuable lesson."

I freed myself with a new gravity-defying jump and was impressed to find myself hovering over Reuben's head. "Don't you worry he might, like, defect back to the Dark Powers?"

"No," said Reuben in a firm voice. "Now drop it, OK?"

"OK," I agreed reluctantly.

Unlike me and Lola, Reuben is pure angel and has never lived on Earth. Human concepts like holding a grudge are completely alien to him. So far as he was concerned, Brice had turned over a new leaf and that was that.

He grinned up at me. "Are you planning to stay up there all night?"

"I'm not sure," I said anxiously. "I can't seem to get back down."

Reuben gave me a mischievous smile. "Seen Orlando lately?"

I went crashing painfully to the floor. "You big pig!" I complained. "That was SO mean!"

"Focus, Melanie-san," the dojo master said sternly. "An angel warrior must be empty like the wind. No past. No future. Only NOW."

My conversation with Reuben reminded me that I hadn't seen Orlando for weeks. Officially he's still at school, but like I said, the boy's a brainbox and the Agency regularly sends him on solo missions.

Next day followed the new hectic pattern: running at dawn, followed by a healthy breakfast and lessons, a quick salad and gym at lunchtime, then afternoon school. I was going to have to skip the dojo that evening. Mr Allbright wanted to talk to me about my progress. I felt a familiar sinking feeling as I went into our classroom.

I was not a big success at my Earth comprehensive and I still can't quite believe my new life is for real. It's like, deep down, I'm secretly waiting for my teachers to find out I'm a fraud.

But to my relief it was all good news.

"I'm impressed," my teacher beamed. "If you keep this up, you could find yourself in line for a HALO award one of these days."

"You are kidding," I breathed.

Mr Allbright's praise made me glow all the way back across the campus. I practically danced down the path towards our dorm, singing a happy off-key version of *Sisters are Doing it for Themselves.*

Suddenly my heart gave a skip of surprise. Orlando was walking towards me. He looked incredibly glad to see me. "I've been looking for you everywhere, Mel!" he said. "Where've you been?"

Was I dreaming, or had my luck finally changed? Could destiny really be this kind?

I was in a total daze. I vaguely heard Orlando ask me to meet him at the library later so we could talk. And I vaguely heard myself gasp out some pathetic reply. Then I flew upstairs to my room going, "Omigosh! Omigosh!" It was official! Orlando had asked me out!!

Chapter Two

I immediately flew into a major panic. It was the most important day of my angelic existence and what I really needed was a style consultation with my soul-buddy. Unfortunately, Lola was at the dojo. But after a nail-biting half hour, I managed to come up with the perfect romantic look. Denim capri pants, and a white off-the-shoulder gypsy top embroidered with tiny pink butterflies. I put on the sweet silver charm bracelet Lola gave me, splashed on my fave heavenly fragrance (it's called Attitude) and I was ready to go.

I was going on my first ever date with the most beautiful boy in our school. OK, so the school library isn't the most thrilling venue. But who knew where we'd end up after that!! Don't get ahead of yourself, Melanie, I warned myself. Take it one step at a time.

When I walked in, there was some big meeting going on. The ground floor was jam-packed with trainees. I assumed Orlando was waiting for me upstairs. I started elbowing my way through the crowd, going, "Excuse me. Sorry, was that your foot? Erm, excuse me."

Then I heard a familiar voice coming from the front. "You can't believe how bad it is, until you see it for yourselves. Nero's time is basically just a PODS' playground."

It was Orlando.

I closed my eyes as the humiliating truth sank in. Orlando had not invited me to the library for a talk. He'd invited me to A TALK at the library.

Someone tapped me on the shoulder. "Did I miss much?" Reuben was still in his martial arts clothes. He must have rushed over from the dojo.

"I couldn't tell you. I just got here."

"Cool outfit," said my buddy. "Going somewhere special?"

"Not really," I said in a dull voice.

"Could you have this conversation somewhere else?" said an irritated trainee. "Some of us are trying to listen."

"Sorry man!" Reuben gave him an apologetic grin. "I'm surprised to see you here, Mel," he whispered. "I heard they just needed guys."

For the first time I registered that everyone in the audience was male. What was going on? We edged towards the front. Orlando was standing on a makeshift platform, looking tired but determined.

"I literally got back from Ancient Rome a few hours ago," he was saying. "In forty-eight hours I'll be going back, and I hope to be taking a team of volunteers with me."

I felt a prickle of shock. Angelic missions are coordinated by the Agency. I'd never heard of agents getting their own missions together before. Orlando wasn't even a real agent, he was still only a trainee.

"I stumbled on some alarming information during my last mission," Orlando went on. "I passed my findings on to the Agency. They admit they're concerned, but apparently the twenty-first century is draining most of their resources."

I felt myself cringe with shame. Just once, could it please be someone else's century giving us all this heavenly hassle?

"I'm going to level with you," Orlando said. "This feels very weird. Every day, trainees are told that the essence of good troubleshooting is team work. Nine times out of ten I'd agree with this. And in the past I've given some of you a hard time for trying to go it alone."

I felt myself go red. I knew Orlando was remembering the big fight we had on my first ever time trip to Earth. I defied him and broke a major cosmic law and came close to getting myself expelled.

"But there's always that tricky one time out of ten," Orlando was explaining earnestly. "I believe this is one of those times."

He looked embarrassed. "Listen, you guys, I have absolutely no desire to be a hero. It's not my style. But the Agency's hands are tied, so I feel it's my responsibility to bridge the gap. I asked the Agency for permission to take a trainee task force back into the field. They agreed."

"But what would we be doing exactly?" asked a nervous trainee.

"I can't go into details at this stage," Orlando said. "You'll just have to trust me. I promise to keep you informed on a need-to-know basis."

I heard guys muttering, "Fair enough."

"Will we get basic training?" someone asked. "I know zip about the Romans."

"Sure you do, they're the ones who wore togas," quipped his mate.

"That's not actually true," I told him snootily. "Generally only men wore togas. And that was just for formal occasions."

I hate speaking out in public as a rule, but fashion is one topic about which I am one hundred percent confident.

Orlando smiled. "Volunteers will undergo a forty-eight hour intensive training course. This is a ridiculously short time to train anyone for such a dangerous mission, but it's the best we can do."

I'd totally forgiven Orlando by this time. My dearest wish had come true. He'd finally noticed me. But he didn't only like me for my looks. He respected me. Enough to want me to fight alongside him, as an angelic equal. All these months I'd worried I wasn't good enough for this amazing boy. Then out of all the girls in our school, he picks me for his personal task force!

"So do we have any volunteers?" he asked hopefully.

A forest of hands shot up, including mine and Reuben's.

Orlando looked relieved. "That's fantastic. Thanks guys. Erm, are there any questions?"

"What should I wear?" I asked anxiously.

Some of the guys laughed, but Orlando took my inquiry seriously.

"You'll be visible throughout the mission, so obviously the Agency will provide suitable clothes."

Reuben and I exchanged startled glances. Trainees are rarely permitted to materialise. I'd materialised three times at most since I'd started my training, and one of those was an accident.

When the meeting was over, I raced along to Lola's room and hammered on her door. She came out, wearing puffs of cotton wool between her toes and clutching a bottle of bright pink nail varnish.

"Boo, you look totally luminous!" she exclaimed. "Who's the lucky guy?"

"Reubs and I are going to Ancient Rome," I said breathlessly.

My mate blinked. "A bit sudden, isn't it?"

"I know," I beamed. "I thought Orlando and I were going on a date but he really wanted volunteers for a dangerous mission."

Lola's eyes went wide with sympathy. "You must have been upset."

"I was," I admitted. "Then I told myself that a

warrior must be like the wind with no past or future, only now."

My mate gave a disbelieving snort. "You mean you looked at Orlando's eyelids and thought, 'I will follow you to the end of Time!'"

I felt myself go bright red. A telepathic soul-mate is all very well but sometimes a girl needs her privacy.

"So why didn't I hear about this big meeting?" she asked.

"It was just for guys," I explained. "Except for me."

"You're the only girl he asked!"

I tried to look modest. "Apparently."

"He must have his reasons," she said in a doubtful voice.

My heart did a little somersault. "I think he loves me, Lollie."

She gave me another searching look. "Are you sure about that, babe?"

I felt a twinge of dismay. "What do you mean?"

"It's just that Orlando is a really advanced being."

"You mean I'm not good enough," I said in a huffy voice.

"That's not what I meant," said Lola. "Sure

Orlando loves you. He also loves trees and humming birds and head-lice. That boy loves the cotton-picking cosmos, Melanie. But he lives for his work!"

I told myself that Lola hadn't seen Orlando's face as he came towards me or she wouldn't have made that hurtful head-lice comparison.

"I know he does," I agreed. "That's what's so incredible about him!"

"But you think he sees things like you do, *carita*, and I'm not sure he does."

"He chose me, Lola," I said pathetically.

Lola sighed. "Look, just don't expect too much, OK?"

"I won't," I promised. "I just want to help him. You should have seen him tonight at that meeting. He's SO committed. The Agency couldn't spare the agents to deal with this Roman problem, so he's getting a team together off his own bat. Can you believe that!"

"What era are you going to exactly?" she asked.

I frowned. "Orlando said something about Nero."

Lola looked appalled. "No way! That's a cosmic war zone. I can't believe the Agency's letting him take trainees!"

"He warned us it could get hairy," I said defensively. "How come you know so much about Ancient Rome anyway?"

"Brice used to go there on business for the PODS. He said Nero was about as psycho as a human psycho can get. Half Nero's advisers weren't human, Melanie."

Lola's warning had the opposite effect to the one she intended.

"Angels are *supposed* to go into war zones, when humans need us," I said stubbornly. "That's what we're for."

I was disappointed in my friend. It was thanks to her that I'd got myself fighting fit in the first place. She should have been thrilled I was putting my new abilities to good use.

A thrilling picture flashed into my mind. Orlando and me, fighting side by side to save the Earth from an unknown cosmic catastrophe. Maybe Lola was right. Maybe I didn't know what I was getting into. But I knew one thing. This was the proudest moment of my entire angel career.

Chapter Three

"You're picking this up really quickly, sweetie. Shall we just try once more to make sure?"

I nodded dumbly.

Tia whipped half a dozen bronze hairpins out of my crown of braids and my hair tumbled loose around my face. "Try plaiting it tighter this time," she suggested brightly. "We're aiming for a lovely basket-weave effect."

It was the second day of our Ancient Roman intensive and I was totally confused. Until a few hours ago, I'd been soaking up Roman survival skills alongside the male trainees. The first part of the course was mostly theory: Roman beliefs and superstitions. And curses. Cursing was HUGE back then. If someone stole your new bracelet, you didn't call the cops. You wrote a curse, calling on the gods of the underworld to punish the thief.

We were all fascinated by Roman beliefs about the Afterlife. Like, after they died, Romans would expect to be met by a strong silent ferryman called Charon. For a couple of denarii he'd row you across an underground river called the River Styx, and deliver you to your specially designated area of the Underworld. Heroes went to the Elysian Fields. Ordinary folk wound up on the Plains of Asphodel. Villains were whisked off to a Hell dimension known as Tartarus.

"But what *really* happened to Romans when they died?" I asked the instructor.

"They got what they expected, naturally," he grinned. "Until they'd had time to adjust to life up here and realise there was more to the Next World than they thought."

After Beliefs and Superstitions, we had practicals. How to conduct ourselves at banquets, appropriate behaviour in Roman temples. We had to learn about the local currency for this mission. We'd be posing as humans and like other humans we'd need to pay for the facilities – the baths for instance.

I still couldn't believe I'd be expected to bathe in public! Apparently if I refused, people would think I was a barbarian.

"Barbarian" was about the worst insult a Roman could throw at you. They applied it to anyone who didn't think or behave the way they did. To them, a barbarian was everything that was despicable in the human race.

As an angel, I would never diss another person's culture, but the fact is Romans had some pretty barbaric attitudes themselves.

Did you know it was perfectly acceptable for a Roman dad to reject his newborn baby, especially if it was female and he'd wanted a son? I couldn't believe it when the instructor told us that. And twin infants were routinely put out of the house to die. Romans considered twins to be bad luck. This struck me as deeply strange, considering:

1. Their capital city was founded by a pair of twin brothers, and

2. Two of their own gods were twin brothers – Castor and Pollux the Heavenly Twins.

Talk about a double standard!

It was a lot to take in in a short time, but, if I say so myself, I kept up with the guys pretty well. Then halfway through the second morning, a new instructor took over. His muscles bulged under his fighting clothes and he had a scar on his cheek: a souvenir from some close cosmic shave with the PODS.

"By this time you all think the Romans were insane for holding such bizarre beliefs," he said.

Everyone looked sheepish. That's exactly what we were thinking.

"What you need to understand is that Romans lived in constant terror. They weren't just scared of being overrun by barbarians. They were paranoid about their own people. Life was harsh for the majority and there was a real danger the starving masses would rise up and murder their rich masters in their beds. The rulers decided it would be wise to divert the peoples more violent tendencies into safer channels. This is why they invented the Imperial Games."

The instructor said these weren't what we would think of as games, but horrifying, bloodthirsty spectacles held in an arena, a kind of humungous circus ring. The Games were sometimes used to dispose of unwanted Roman citizens: convicted criminals, political troublemakers, or prisoners of war.

"But the most popular games featured

professional fighters known as gladiators," the instructor explained. "A gladiator's life was brutal and short. He had probably been sold to the ludus – the gladiator school – as a slave. Or maybe he was a criminal who fought so bravely that his life was spared by the crowd. A few became real celebrities and had hordes of female fans, a bit like rock stars in other centuries."

We all tittered but it was mostly to relieve tension. This was unbelievably dark stuff.

"You all have some experience of martial arts," the instructor went on. "So, if you should end up in the arena for any reason, you'll all be able to handle yourselves. Now there's not much time, so I'll only be able to teach you the most common fighting style. I want four volunteers to come down to the front."

I eagerly jumped out of my seat. Finally some action!

"Not you, Melanie," Orlando called. "There's an agency stylist waiting for *you* upstairs."

Can you believe that? The guys get to acquire gladiator skills and I'm sent to the makeover department. I felt SO humiliated.

I'd now spent six hours out of my precious forty-eight, mastering Roman hairdressing skills. And I'm sorry, I could *not* see the relevance. Was I supposed to zap the PODS with my hairpins? I don't think so!!

Whatever, it wasn't Tia's fault, so I did my best to follow her instructions. Finally, she was satisfied with my plaiting. After that she showed me how to mix a home-made face-pack, and helpfully suggested Roman household ingredients I could use in place of modern eye make-up and blusher.

"Now we've got to teach you to dress like a real Roman girl," she beamed.

When she'd finished my historical makeover, Tia led me in front of a full-length mirror. I gazed at my reflection in astonishment. Over my tunic, I wore an outer garment known as a stola, which fell in soft folds to my ankles. Draped around my shoulders was a pretty light shawl. This was called a palla. A pair of leather sandals completed my Roman outfit. I put my hand to my throat.

"It needs something here."

"Oops, I forgot to give you your bulla!" Tia held out a bizarre little charm.

I giggled. "I can't wear that! It looks like a willie!!"

Tia explained that bullas were charms worn by freeborn Roman children to protect them from evil spirits. Girls wore them until they were married. On the day of her wedding a girl would sacrifice her bulla to the god of the crossroads, to show she was now a woman.

"Most of them were pretty rude, I'm afraid," she admitted.

Tia let me hunt through her charm supply. Finally I found one I could have shown my nan without blushing, with a sweet little bee design.

Reuben popped his head around the door just as Tia was fastening it around my neck.

"We need you downstairs," he said. "Michael's here."

"We're all done now, anyway," Tia told him. "I hope you enjoy your trip, Mel. If you get the chance, try that little pastry shop near the Temple of Vesta. Their walnut tarts are to die for!"

I stared at her. "You lived in Nero's time! I had no idea!!"

"Yeah, well it's all ancient history now," she laughed.

I raced after Reuben, skidding slightly in my sandals.

Michael looked up and smiled as we came into the hall and I felt a familiar prickle of awe.

I don't think I'll ever completely adjust to having a headmaster who is also an archangel. Though, unlike the other archangels, Michael genuinely has the human touch. Lola thinks it's because he has special responsibility for Planet Earth. His workload is so ridiculous we don't see him for days on end. Then suddenly there he'll be, strolling across the campus, chatting to some awed little kid. He'll be absolutely shattered: dark shadows under his eyes, a suit that looks as if he's slept in it. The guy doesn't take care of himself at all. He's even developing a bit of a podgy belly, which makes him look exactly like a big bear. But when Michael looks at you, it's like he's looking into your soul.

"As I was saying," he went on humorously, "hopefully, you all know a little more about Nero's Rome than you did before. But there are things we can't prepare you for, and if it's your first visit to this era, you can expect a certain amount of culture shock."

Michael gave us the usual warnings about keeping our eyes peeled for PODS. "As you know, the Opposition constantly bombards Earth with negative thoughts and energy. Even professional celestial agents can find themselves adversely affected. Once you leave the safety of Heaven, it's easy to lose focus.

So you must keep reminding each other why you are there, and what you came to do. Try to remember that no matter how it seems, you're always connected with your heavenly source. Good luck."

That was it – we'd graduated! Tonight we'd be in the decadent world of Nero's Empire.

There was a sudden clatter as two Roman hairpins dropped to the floor. I'm not ready! I panicked. It was like those exam dreams, I used to have on Earth. That paralysing terror when you know you just haven't put in the hours. I fiddled frantically with another slipping hairpin. "I can't even control my own hair," I whimpered.

As I grovelled on the floor collecting hairpins, a new worry occurred to me. "Omigosh!" I wailed. "They forgot to tell me what I'm supposed to be called. It's bound to be some weird name and I won't be able to remember it."

"Your name is Mella," said a voice.

Michael crouched down beside me on the floor. He touched my little bee charm with a fingertip and I felt angelic volts shimmer through every cell.

"It's Latin for 'Honey'," he told me. "So you see, you chose the right charm quite by instinct."

"I did?" I whispered. "Omigosh, I did!"

Isn't that incredible? When I chose that bee

design, I had NO idea my Roman name was going to be "Honey"!!

Suddenly I didn't give a hoot about my hair. How can you fail when your charm has been personally touched by an archangel?

Chapter Four

In Departures, no-one turned a hair at our Roman costumes. It's always mad down there, even in the early hours of the morning. Agents milled around making calls. One girl was sitting in the lotus position beside her backpack, meditating while she waited. A group of trainees were playing a card game just inches away, but she was oblivious.

Our portal needed some last-minute TLC, but eventually we all squeezed inside. Al, my fave maintenance guy, closed the door with a thunk. Michael gave us a reassuring smile through the glass. This was huge for Orlando, and Michael wanted him to know he had the Agency's blessing.

The last moments before take-off always make

me nervous. I wish Lollie was here, I thought. It feels weird going without her.

I think Reuben read my mind. In a husky, not entirely in-tune voice, he started to sing our private theme tune. It goes, "You're not alone. You're not alone." One by one everyone joined in. Some of the more musical guys even put in harmonies. We were still singing as our time portal lit up and we blasted through the invisible barrier that divides the timeless angelic fields from the unpredictable world of human history.

En route, Orlando filled us in on a few essential details.

"We're going to Ostia, a Roman port, a few miles from the capital. I did tell you we'd be posing as slaves?" he added anxiously.

He hadn't, but by this time Orlando could have told us we were walking into a fiery furnace and we'd have followed him like lambs. That's the kind of angel he is.

Reuben patted my shoulder. "May the gods protect you, my little honey bunny," he whispered in Latin.

"You too, Sweetpea," I answered fluently. Being able to understand every language going is one of the cooler perks of being an angel.

I noticed my buddy scratching absently at the collar of his rough woollen tunic. I fingered the fine white cotton of my stola. How come I'm the only one on this mission wearing good clothes? I wondered. But there was no time to puzzle about this. Outside the portal, the colours had grown unbearably intense. We were coming in to land.

Seconds later I stepped out into a crowded Roman market place. I could smell fish and sewage and something that might be incense. Hungry white seagulls wheeled over my head screaming. Hello seagulls, I thought lovingly. Hello icky smells.

I was back on my favourite planet.

I don't know about you, but when I feel happy, I immediately have to tell someone!

"I think there's still a part of me that really misses being human," I burbled. "Like, here we are in a totally unknown sea port, in a totally unfamiliar century, but something inside says, 'I'm home!'!!"

"Mel, shut up and move your angel butt, NOW!" Reuben ordered.

This was SO not the reaction I expected. Next minute my buddy practically threw me into a very smelly doorway. A shaven-headed guy in a tunic came striding past with a big stick, whacking anyone in his path. "Make way, scum!" he bellowed, only in Latin obviously.

People scattered as a curtained litter carried by two male bearers came swaying into view. A warm salt breeze was blowing off the sea. Suddenly it lifted up a corner of a curtain, revealing a middle-aged Roman inside, lounging on piles of cushions. He glared at us and twitched the curtain closed.

I felt really shaky. I'd been in Nero's time for less than sixty seconds and I'd almost got my skull bashed in already! "Thanks Reubs," I said.

My buddy looked traumatised. "That human saw us," he said. "That feels so weird."

When you're invisible, you have time to adjust to being back in the material world. But if humans can SEE you, it's full-on right away.

I've been to a few eras now, but I've got to say, Ancient Rome was different right from the start. It wasn't any one thing that blew me away. It wasn't the towering public buildings of stone and marble, or the grimy Roman flats, where poor people lived packed like sardines. It wasn't the spicy whiffs of unfamiliar hot snacks, or even the babble of voices talking Latin and other ancient languages that had been totally forgotten by my time – it was everything. *Everything* was different. Even the sunlight on my skin. It seemed clearer, brighter. To me it felt like the world was still new. As if all its colours hadn't totally dried yet.

I love those first moments of a mission when you're still sussing out humans, wondering who you'll really get to know, and who'll be like, cosmic extras.

Take that girl sitting at a table outside a bar called *The Shower of Gold*. She's got an unusual face, I thought. She was loads paler than the olive-skinned locals I'd seen so far. That must mean she was wealthy enough to stay in the shade while slaves do her dirty work. The tiny rubies at her earlobes were another giveaway. That girl's been treated like a princess her whole life, I thought. You can just tell nothing has ever happened to her.

Tough-looking slaves stood by with cudgels, keeping a wary watch on the family's luggage. The girl was fussing over a fluffy little dog in her lap. It was so fluffy, in fact, you couldn't tell where its eyes were. "Minerva's been stung, Pater," the girl said to her dad. "She whimpers when I touch her paw."

Minerva, I thought. Now that IS weird. On a mission to Victorian times we met a fake medium who called herself Minerva. I'm not sure I'd have named that puppy after the Roman goddess of wisdom myself. Goddess of fluff maybe.

"It seems really swollen," the girl persisted.

Her father didn't answer. He was gazing confusedly around at the buildings, as if he feared this was all a strange dream from which he might wake any moment.

At that moment I heard Orlando calling to us on a wavelength used only by angels. *Mel, Reuben! Get over here now!*

We hurried through the crowded forum following Orlando's vibes. Suddenly a gap appeared in the crowd and I saw the slave market.

The slaves in the slave market at Ostia were mostly barbarians, white-skinned tribes-people. They peered out fearfully through matted hair, shivering in their filthy rags.

We nervously joined Orlando and the others.

Typical Melanie, I hadn't thought how it would feel to be this close to half-naked humans who'd been cooped up in slave ships for weeks. For one thing, they didn't smell very nice, though this was hardly their fault. But it wasn't just the smell that made me feel ill. The air was thick with human fear and hatred. The kind of vibes that make it hard for an angel to breathe.

The dealer was chalking prices on crude wooden tags. He'd glance along the line of slaves, do a quick calculation, scribble a price and matter-of-factly hang it round someone's neck.

In the forum a shoe mender went on mending a broken buckle. The fishmonger roared out the price of his freshly-caught squid, and the owner of *The Shower of Gold* came out to place olives and fresh bread in front of the girl and her father.

It didn't seem to trouble them that dozens of fellow humans shivered a few metres away, with price tags round their necks. I'm not going to pretend I know how it feels to be a slave. This was my first ever glimpse of slavery. But when I looked into the eyes of these sullen, shivering men and women and children, I felt ashamed for humankind.

I was standing beside a hairy little barbarian, who was covered with tribal tattoos. His hair and beard were grey and his face was lined with age. But he was only about as tall as the average six-year-old.

"We'll get a good price for you," the dealer said approvingly. "You dwarves are worth big bucks. Can you juggle?"

The man shook his head. "No juggle."

The dealer sighed. "Give me a break, sunshine. Even boneheaded barbarians can juggle a few oranges."

"I am not Sunshine. I am Flammia," the man said with dignity. "I swallow fire."

The slave dealer broke into a delighted grin. "Well well, a fire-eating dwarf. Some days you just know Jupiter is on your side."

When the dealer reached me, he looked me up and down as if I was a calf in the livestock market. He immediately registered the bulla. "Hmmm, freeborn," he muttered. "Tall for a girl. Nicely turned-out. Quite pretty. Make someone a good ornatrix. Might get seven sestercii if I'm lucky."

He scribbled a Roman numeral on a wooden tag and hung it round my neck. For the first time he noticed I wasn't shackled. He clicked his tongue with annoyance. "Now how did that happen," he grumbled and hurriedly found some rusty old shackles.

"Please don't," said Orlando. "She won't try to escape."

I was SO touched. It's like, even though we weren't real slaves, Orlando totally couldn't bear to see me in chains.

The man gave a derisive laugh. "A slave's promise, now that's really worth having!"

"None of my friends are chained," Orlando pointed out. "We're here of our own free will."

The dealer shook his head. "I hate to hurt your sensitive feelings, sunshine," he sighed, "but I'd prefer a little bit of insurance."

He went hurrying along the line of angel trainees, hanging inflated prices round their necks and securing them with chains. "Don't know where you came from," I heard him saying. "But you've been well cared for. I'll get a fortune for you beauties."

"This is sick," Reuben whispered.

"Isn't it?" I said. "What a way to run an empire!"

I was totally off the Romans by now.

"Be fair," said a trainee, "they've got incredible ideals."

"Ooh, absolutely, plus they invented central heating!" I said sarcastically. "I'm sorry, a civilisation built on human misery sucks."

Just then someone came limping up to the dealer. He was really alarming looking. He'd lost part of one ear. He wore an eyepatch over one eye, and he had horrific scars on his legs. To judge from his limp, one of them was still giving him trouble. I decided he must be an old Roman legionary who'd received his injuries fighting the barbarians in some distant corner of the empire.

He must have been a good customer because the dealer was instantly all over him. "Festus

Brutus – good morning! How have the gods been treating you?" And he went into a spiel about this special purchase deal he could give him.

"That guy must be a lanista," whispered Reuben.

"Very probably, but I don't know what that means," I hissed back. It must be something they'd covered while I was perfecting my plaiting skills.

"It's Roman slang for 'butcher'," Reuben explained. "He's on the lookout for raw recruits he can train up for the arena."

OMIGOSH! I thought. Suddenly everything made sense. That's why Orlando picked me for his task force! This butcher person was going to buy us for his ludus and turn us into gladiators. OK, so this might be a bit of a challenge, but if Orlando thought I could handle it, I was up for it, no question. Admittedly, you don't tend to hear about girl gladiators, but like Lola says, if you relied on history books for your info, you'd think girls didn't even exist in some time periods!

I shut my eyes and beamed a grateful message to my soul-mate. I owe you babe! All that fitness training you made me do, all that martial arts – it's finally coming together!

Next minute, it all fell apart.

The girl with the lapdog had left the bar to wander around the slave market. Now she was heading purposefully in my direction. Keep walking, I prayed. Pick someone else.

The girl walked right up to me, and looked intently into my face, almost as if she knew me from somewhere. I felt angelic tingles shimmer through my bones.

Don't do this, I pleaded silently. I'm sure you're a sweet human but I can't be your personal angel, OK? I'm on a v. dangerous cosmic mission.

The girl was a year or so older than me, but not nearly so tall. Up close I could see her eyes were grey and when she smiled I saw she had a dimple in her cheek. My nan would have said that was where she'd been touched by an angel. I had to admit there was something appealing about her. In another time, or another place, I'd have been delighted to get to know her. Just not here and now.

"This must be horrible for you," she said quietly. "I've always thought it strange that a country which thinks itself civilised, should be dependent on slave labour. My name is Aurelia Flavia, by the way."

"You don't introduce yourself to slaves!" Her father had caught her up. But there was no real energy to his words. It was like he was going through the motions. "She probably doesn't even speak Latin!" he added in a tired voice.

I unfocused my eyes, willing them both to go away.

Aurelia didn't take the hint. "We've been living in Britain for years," she explained. "My father thinks I've gone tribal!"

I was genuinely shocked to hear her mention my country.

Aurelia saw it. "She understood, Pater! You can see how intelligent she is. Her soul shines out of her eyes."

Her father sighed heavily. "Souls," he muttered. "Just like your mother. She talked of souls."

"Please, may we buy her?" Aurelia pleaded. "You agreed I needed an ornatrix. She does her own hair beautifully."

A distressing thought flitted into my head and once it was there, it refused to go away. He wouldn't, I thought. Orlando wouldn't do that to me. Omigosh, he *had*! Was that why I didn't need gladiator training? Was that why I got the deluxe Roman makeover treatment, while the others had to make do with hessian? I'd even got my own personal Roman name...

"Your hairstyle is so pretty!" Aurelia was prattling. "My hair is impossible. Every slave I have just despairs."

I wanted to howl with disappointment. Festus Brutus was prowling down the rows of slaves, checking us out for gladiator potential. If Aurelia kept chatting to me about hairstyles, he wouldn't think "Feisty fighting girl", he'd think "Personal maid".

Go with her, Melanie!

I heard Orlando's voice as clearly as if he'd spoken aloud. He didn't say that, I thought. He didn't say what I thought he said. Oh, but he did.

Aurelia needs you, Orlando told me. *It's why I brought you.*

You brought me to Rome so I could be some rich girl's hairdresser!

I was so upset, I only just stopped myself from stamping my foot.

All my foolish fantasies had crumbled into dust. To think I'd imagined he saw me as an equal. A bimbo, that's all I was. A joke. I felt totally betrayed. I wanted to crawl into a hole and never come out. I was dangerously close to tears.

Bottle it up, I scolded myself. Swallow it down. Whatever. Don't let Orlando see you cry.

But just then the universe supplied an unexpected distraction. Our teachers are constantly telling us that the Agency works in mysterious ways. Like, one tiny thing can change the whole course of human history. Even a silly little fluffball of a pooch.

While I struggled with my feelings, Minerva suddenly noticed Reuben. My angel buddy has an affinity with all furry or feathered creatures. Birds, bees, dancing bears, universally adore him.

With a weird whimpering sound, the little dog jumped out of Aurelia's arms and went wriggling up to Reuben, holding up her injured paw.

Disregarding his chains, Reuben stooped down and began to pet her, talking so softly that no human would guess he was speaking in a very ancient language we use for communicating with birds and animals. I'm not nearly as fluent as my buddy but I got the basic gist.

"Did the wasp sting you?" he was saying. "Do you want me to take the hurt away?"

Reuben touched her paw with a gentle finger. I saw an arrow of glowing pink light beam from his heart into Minerva. By the time Reubs straightened up, her limp had totally gone.

I don't know what Aurelia saw, but she was looking totally amazed. "I want to buy the boy too," she told her father. "Minerva will need a kennel slave and he's obviously wonderful with animals."

"I'm also wonderful with plants," Reuben said shamelessly. "Give me a free hand in the garden and you'll think you're living in paradise."

My buddy never gets caught up with his emotions the way I do. He didn't give a hoot about missing out on gladiator school. Kennel boy, gardener, beggarman, thief – it was all one to him. He didn't need to be told that Aurelia needed us. Pure angels tend to go with the flow.

"Sixteen sestercii for the pair," said the dealer promptly.

Aurelia's father opened his mouth to protest.

"It's a good price," said Aurelia quickly.

Her father counted out coins with a dazed expression.

I gave Orlando a hurt look. "I can't believe what you just did."

"Melanie, I needed a way to get an agent into Aurelia's house. This was the obvious solution. I don't see why you're so upset. Being her ornatrix is not who you are. It's your cover."

"It is?" I quavered. I SO wanted to believe him.

"I keep telling you, she needs your help." Orlando said.

"Yeah, after all she's totally alone," I said. "Ooh, except for her rich daddy and a gazillion slaves. Not to mention helpful angels falling over themselves to heal her little puppy!"

The dealer was coming back with the lanista.

Orlando looked genuinely worried. "Promise me you'll look after her?" *Please, Helix?* he added silently.

Helix is my angel name. Orlando was appealing to me as a fellow professional. So I had to say yes, didn't I?

The lanista and the slave-dealer were closing their deal. Any minute now, Orlando and I would be taken off to our different destinations.

My throat ached with misery. It wasn't meant to be like this.

"You could have explained," I told him reproachfully. "Did you think I was this little airhead who wouldn't understand?"

Orlando seemed shocked. "Of course not! I told you at the start, you'd have to trust me."

"Do you even know where they're taking you?" My voice cracked with distress.

But before he could answer, Orlando, the rest of his task force, plus Flammia and five regular-sized barbarians were all led away in chains by the lanista.

Aurelia was watching with a sympathetic expression. "It's too soon for you to trust me, but maybe one day, you'll tell me your story."

The stupid thing is, I'd sensed a bond with Aurelia from the start. I think Aurelia sensed it too. Maybe she wasn't as ordinary as I'd thought.

"Will you tell me your name?" she asked gently. I touched my bee charm and reminded myself that I was always connected with my heavenly power source.

"It's Mella," I said huskily.

Aurelia's father hired horse-drawn wagons to transport us and their possessions back to Rome. Reuben went up front with Aurelia's dad.

As vulnerable females, Aurelia and I had to travel in the middle of the convoy. I thought these precautions were a bit extreme, but she explained that there were bandits on some stretches of the Via Roma.

It wasn't far to the capital city in miles, but in a Roman-style wagon train, the journey seemed to go on forever. But it gave Aurelia and me the opportunity to get to know each other. I tried not to tell too many lies. My mistress assumed I was a freeborn girl who'd fallen on hard times and been sold into slavery, and I just went along with it. To explain my unfamiliarity with Roman ways, I said I'd grown up in Carthage. Our instructors had mentioned this mysterious ancient country, and it had stuck in my brain. Mostly I got Aurelia to talk about herself.

Aurelia was born in Rome, but when she was a few months old, her dad had been posted overseas to administer Roman law to the bolshie Brits. Aurelia said she'd been happy, but there were very few Roman kids in her area, and she'd often felt isolated. "This is the first time I've had a person of my own age to talk to in a long time," she told me.

We both went back to gazing out of the window. The scenery was gorgeous: shady cypresses, lush vineyards and peach groves. Now and then we'd glimpse a small red-roofed farm among the olive trees.

"My mother described this countryside so vividly that I feel as if I remember it myself," Aurelia said in a wistful voice. "My mother died when I was ten," she explained. "People say you'll get over it but you never do."

"True," I agreed. "But it stops hurting so much."

Aurelia's grey eyes went soft with sympathy. "Did you lose your mother?"

I swallowed. "And my little sister."

The night before I died, Jade sat up in her sleep and said, "You're my best sister in the universe."

I said, "I'm your only sister you nutcase." Well, I didn't know it was our last conversation.

I hastily cast around for a different subject. "I guess you must look like your mum. You certainly don't look like your dad."

She smiled. "I don't look like either of them. I'm adopted."

"Oh, I'm sorry! I didn't know!" I said.

Luckily Aurelia didn't seem at all offended by my remark.

"Except for my older brother, Quintus, none of my parents' natural children survived more than a few hours after birth. When my mother's last baby was stillborn, she told my father she no longer wanted to live if she couldn't give him any more children. Next morning a slave found me on the doorstep. My mother thought it was a miracle and begged my father to adopt me. My father was so grateful to see her happy again that he agreed, even though I was only a girl."

I couldn't imagine how it would feel, not knowing who your real parents were. My dad left us when I was six years old, but I knew him at least.

"So you have no idea who you really are?"

"No," she said cheerfully. "I'm a complete mystery."

"Wow, that must be so weird. You could have other brothers and sisters somewhere."

Aurelia laughed. "When I was little, I was obsessed with the idea that I had a missing twin. I used to see her in my dreams. She looked exactly like me, but did all the naughty things that I was too scared to do! We would have these really long, complicated conversations."

"You won't believe this but I had a twin fantasy, too," I told her.

Aurelia smiled. "Probably all lonely little girls have it."

Inevitably, we got on to boys. Aurelia asked mischievously if anyone had ever wanted to marry me.

"In Carthage, we think thirteen is too young to marry," I told her. That sounded snotty, so I said quickly, "Has anyone asked to marry you?"

She blushed. "Once."

"Oooh!" I giggled. "Was he a barbarian with tattoos!"

Aurelia took a breath. "Gaius was Roman."

My smile faded. She said "was".

"He came to Londinium from Rome on the Emperor's business. We entertained him at my father's villa." She glanced at me from under her lashes. "He was very handsome."

Was, I thought.

"He visited us several times after that. He hated British weather. All those low clouds. But I said mist could be romantic." She darted me another look under her lashes. "I really liked him. He was homesick and I'd make our cook prepare his favourite dishes." She pulled a face, "You can't imagine how disgusting most British cooking is. He started dropping in when my father was out. He was always very respectful," she added hastily. "We'd just talk and read together. One day we hired a boat and took a picnic on the river. There was white mist hanging in the willow branches. It looked like bridal veils. Gaius said, 'You're right, mist is romantic.' And he asked if I'd be his wife."

The memory made Aurelia go dreamy-eyed.

I don't care how romantic it was, I thought. Gaius had no right proposing. She was just a kid. Then I remembered our instructor saying the average Roman woman wouldn't live beyond twenty-eight. Maybe Roman girls knew they didn't have much time. Maybe they had to grow up fast.

"Did you accept?" I asked.

"I had to say no. My father has not been himself since my mother died. I thought perhaps when we came back home." Aurelia's voice shook slightly. "And now it's too late."

I waited.

"He died," she explained huskily. "Just a few hours after he returned home. My brother, Quintus, told us it was a sudden illness, but I fear—" she faltered. "I fear he may have been poisoned. Oh, Mella, these are dangerous times."

"I'm so sorry," I told her. "But who would—?"

I could see this subject was too painful for Aurelia. "It's all in the past now," she said quickly. "Did I tell you I *am* to marry? Quintus has found me a suitor."

"Oh," I said. "Erm, congratulations."

Aurelia explained that she didn't exactly know Quintus. He was fourteen by the time she came along, almost adult by Roman standards. When their father got his British posting, Quintus had chosen to stay behind.

"These days he's one of Nero's most trusted senators. You will meet him, Mella. He still uses my father's house for entertaining important guests. It is supposed to be very beautiful."

It was evening by the time the jumbled rooftops

and towers of Rome came in sight. To get to the city gates, we had to drive through the necropolis. Romans were forbidden to bury their dead inside the city and a vast graveyard had grown up outside the city walls. It went on for miles. Sometimes I saw the flicker of camp fires, as a homeless person settled down to sleep among the dead. I saw my first Roman spook, flitting among the burial urns wearing a ghostly laurel wreath. Brice would want to stop and chat to him, I thought.

Brice has this bizarre empathy with ghosts. I suppose if you hang out in Hell dimensions long enough you'll talk to anyone. This led on to worrying about what was happening to Orlando and the others...

Some time later I felt Aurelia gently shaking me. I couldn't believe I'd dozed off! A fine angel you are, Melanie! I scolded myself.

A slave helped me down from the wagon and I stumbled sleepily after Aurelia. Her dad was banging wearily on a bronze knocker, calling to the porter to let them in. This house hasn't got any windows, I thought in surprise. A peephole slid back and a wary eye looked out. I heard someone gasp, "Thank Jupiter! The master's back!"

An elderly watchman let us in, beaming all over

his face. "Dorcas dreamed you'd come, master! She's been cooking all day long."

Slaves came hurrying to welcome us, helping us off with our sandals, bringing jugs of warm scented water for us to wash off the dust, offering us honeyed wine.

I'm in a Roman house, I told myself. But I couldn't quite believe it.

We were in the atrium, a large central space with rooms leading off on all sides. There was a skylight in the roof to let in air, and light during the day, I guessed, because of the lack of windows. By night, oil lamps gave off a soft amber light, which reflected back from a gleaming marble floor. The furniture was minimal: a couple of couches, woven wicker chairs and a stone bust of the Emperor Nero. A fountain tinkled into an indoor pool, with gold sparkles in the marble basin.

The actual decor was totally alien to modern tastes. Three walls were painted blazing red. The fourth featured a large mural of a horribly realistic battle scene – noble-looking Romans in armour, versus hideous barbarians in chariots.

I noticed Aurelia's father look up hopefully every time someone came in. Finally he asked a slave if his son was expected home that night.

"Quintus Flavius is very busy," the slave said tactfully. "He sometimes finds it more convenient to stay at the palace."

"Pater, let's go and see if mother's quince tree is still alive," Aurelia pleaded. "She talked so often of that tree."

"You go, child," he said in his tired voice. "I am going to rest."

"Mella can come with me." Aurelia seized my hand and pulled me into a room with couches arranged around a low round table. The mural in the dining room showed gods and goddesses feasting in flowery meadows.

On the far wall, beyond the open door, I was amazed to see waterfalls of white roses glimmering in the dark. Then I remembered that Romans put their gardens inside their houses! This one was completely enclosed by a beautiful stone walkway with doors opening into yet more rooms and apartments. Aurelia's house was the closest thing to a palace I had ever seen.

To her delight, the quince tree was still alive. It was old and bent but I could see tiny baby quinces gleaming faintly in the moonlight. I glanced up through the leaves and was thrilled to see stars.

Stars inside your house, now that IS cool! Then I noticed Aurelia furtively wiping her eyes, so I tactfully slipped off to find Reuben.

Reubs and I had our supper in the slave quarters. The food was actually not bad: a kind of Roman sausage, followed by small deep-fried pastries, dipped in honey. But Reuben isn't big on Earth food, so he sneakily fed most of his sausage to Minerva, who was now his faithful shadow. The other slaves stared at us quite openly while we were eating.But suspicious slaves were the least of my worries. For absolutely no reason, I was deeply depressed.

Reuben put his arm round me. "You forgot your protection procedure didn't you?" he said sternly.

"Might have done," I admitted.

"Well do it now. This house is seriously toxic."

It was a relief to know these weren't my personal bad feelings. But where were they coming from?

"You think there are PODS, here in this house?" I asked nervously.

My buddy shook his head. "Something isn't right. You should stay with Aurelia tonight."

That was easy to arrange. When I told my mistress I was too scared to sleep by myself, she said I could sleep on a couch in her room.

"Won't the other slaves think it's strange?" I asked.

"Of course not," she laughed. "But if it worries you I'll say you're my personal bodyguard!"

As Aurelia's ornatrix, I had to unpack her clothes and put them away in the cedar-wood closets in her room. Then I carefully set out all her little perfume bottles, tweezers, brush, comb, pretty hairpins and so forth on her dressing table. Before she went to bed, I had to help her remove her jewellery and lock it in a special casket. You couldn't be too careful in Roman times, even in a house full of watchful slaves.

When I went to take off her bulla, Aurelia suddenly jerked away.

"Leave it on please, Mella. I *never* take it off."

"I didn't know, sorry," I said apologetically. I could tell I'd genuinely upset her. Romans are SO superstitious, I thought.

I helped Aurelia into her night-gown, then brushed her hair until it was smooth and silky.

"Your hair isn't so bad," I told her. "It's out of condition that's all. Perhaps we can buy some almond oil tomorrow. That's what Lola uses."

"Is Lola your friend?" Aurelia asked.

"She's more like my spiritual twin," I said truthfully.

My mistress looked wistful. "So you actually found your twin, Mella?"

Oh yeah, I thought. So I did!

Two slaves came in, lugging a small couch between them. They solemnly positioned it to form a solid barrier between my mistress's bed and the door. They bowed to Aurelia and backed out, looking faintly puzzled. I heard one mutter, "She's a bit small for a bodyguard."

"Size is irrelevant with Carthaginians," hissed his companion. "All Carthaginian girls carry knives, it's a known fact."

Aurelia was asleep minutes after we blew out the lamp.

I lay awake going over the events of the past few hours. I still had no idea why I was posing as a slave in Ancient Rome. But the Agency had gone to a great deal of trouble to establish my cover. For some reason Aurelia was important to them. I decided I was honoured that Orlando trusted me to take care of her. *I won't let you down, I swear,* I told him silently.

Suddenly my mouth went dry with fear. Unsteady footsteps were coming towards our room. The door opened very softly and someone came in, stumbling in the dark. My heart gave a massive thump as I felt the intruder lean over me and peer into my face. I could smell his breath, a suffocating mixture of garlic, fish and alcohol. This isn't a burglar! I thought in a panic. This is deeply creepy!!

"Pollux!" he muttered in disgust. "It's only her slave."

For Aurelia's sake, I had to control my terror. I made my breathing deep and regular. I'm just a slave girl, I told myself, not even worth bothering with. I'm a tired slave girl dreaming whatever Roman slave girls dream about. It worked. After some minutes, whoever it was stumbled away.

I was trembling with shock. Omigosh, what was that about? I was almost positive the intruder wasn't PODS. But from the vibes, he wasn't totally human either.

There was no way I'd be able to fall asleep now. I lay clutching my bee charm in the dark, jumping out of my skin at every tiny household creak.

I remembered Aurelia saying, "He may have been poisoned."

"That girl needs you," Orlando had said. And now I knew why.

CHAPTER FIVE

I felt so responsible for Aurelia's safety that two weeks later, I was still suffering from major angelic insomnia. At night, that is.

In the day, I only had to sit down in the sunshine to shell a few peas to find myself dropping off! One afternoon I actually dozed off at the baths.

Unlike other rich Romans, who took hordes of slaves everywhere they went – one to unbuckle your sandals, one to help you into your litter, a third to run ahead clearing the rabble out of your way – Aurelia preferred a democratic approach. On our daily visits to the baths we took it in turns to guard our possessions. I'd watch them while she bathed and had her massage, then she'd do the same for me.

Apart from the constant risk of robbery, the atmosphere was really relaxing. I tucked my feet under me, leaned my head against the tiled wall and settled down happily to wait.

I was now a complete convert to Roman-style bathing. It was the most *sublime* experience. First you washed off the dust from the street, then you were slathered in scented oil and massaged v. vigorously by a trained masseuse. Then all the oil was scraped off with a cunning little gadget called a "strigil". After that you went through warm pools and sweltering steam rooms and icy plunge pools, until every last speck of dirt had been extracted from your pores. By the time you floated back on to the street, you were so clean you could hardly speak!

I watched dreamily as half-naked girls and women wandered to and fro between the steam rooms and the plunge pool. The humid air was full of soothing scents, jasmine, rose and sandalwood oils, perfumed creams and Roman shampoo. The sounds were soothing too. The whoosh of steam, the swoosh and bubble of water, the murmur of voices.

I felt safe in this scented female world. Safe enough to risk a teeny little snooze...

My eyes flew open in terror! I'd felt someone brush past. A pale blue robe was disappearing around the corner. Omigosh! I panicked. Aurelia's jewellery!! But to my huge relief, my mistress's possessions seemed undisturbed.

It was mid-afternoon by the time we went back out on to the street. After the languid atmosphere of the baths, the heat and noise outside seemed tremendous. A new temple was going up across the road and the air was thick with dust. Armies of sweating slaves in filthy rags, wrestled massive blocks of stone into place, as an overseer bellowed instructions.

While we looked around for our litter bearers, a guy tried to get us to buy a carpet. "For such pretty ladies, very special price."

Another guy was trying to sell us a jar of rejuvenating oil!

"Cheeky thing!" I fumed.

"Do you know where they get that stuff?" Aurelia grinned.

From the glint in her eye, I knew this was going to be gross.

"It comes from the gladiator schools," she told me. "The masseurs save all the dirty oil they scrape off the gladiators and sell it on."

I stared at her, open-mouthed. "Who in the world would buy dirty massage oil?"

"Deluded women," she said. "They believe gladiator sweat will keep them eternally young!"

"Euw," I said faintly. "Bottled gladiator sweat! That is so icky!!"

We eventually spotted our bearers squatting by the roadside. They'd been waiting patiently in the heat for hours.

Most upper-class Romans wouldn't even register a bearer as a human being. But Aurelia was such a sweetie. "These men look half-starved," she said in a low voice. "Give them a few denarii to buy food. We'll wait here."

While we were waiting, I spotted a poster advertising the next day's Games. I was stunned to see a *girl* gladiator amongst the attractions. So girls really do fight in the arena I thought wistfully. This one was known as Star. Someone had added a drawing of her in a tiny leather skirt and boots, wielding a short curved sword. Her face was hidden behind a spooky metal mask.

"Have you heard of this girl?" I asked Aurelia. I turned to see her furtively examining a scrap of papyrus. I just had time to glimpse a childish drawing of a fish and what might have been a name and address, then she hurriedly slipped it inside her stola, looking flustered. "Did you say something, Mella?" she said in an innocent voice.

Don't say Aurelia's got a new love interest already, I thought. She's only been in Rome a couple of weeks! How did that happen?

It turned out that my mistress knew all about the gladiator girl. She'd got the local goss from her masseuse at the baths. Star herself had only arrived in Rome a few weeks ago, but she was already becoming a bit of a celeb.

"You'd have to be a special person to be a girl gladiator," I sighed enviously. I couldn't imagine where anyone would find that kind of courage.

"Gladiatrix are really just novelty acts," said Aurelia. "Like dwarves and exotic beasts. No-one takes them seriously."

"They're taking this one seriously," I pointed out. "It says here she's mastered three different fighting styles."

Aurelia shook her head. "It doesn't matter if she masters three thousand. Romans admire gladiators in the ring, but they fear and despise them in real life. This girl will be an outcast all her days. When she dies, her body will be thrown in a pit with the corpses of criminals and suicides."

"That's terrible!" I gasped.

"We Romans are a terrible people." Aurelia looked upset. Her hand strayed to her bulla. "Mella, do you believe—" she began.

At that moment we heard a polite cough. Our bearers had devoured their hard-boiled eggs and lentil porridge and were ready to take us home.

As we swayed and jolted through the city, tremendous waves of sound washed over us: chanting from the temples on the Via Sacra, and the tramp of hobnailed sandals as the Praetorian guard marched through the narrow streets, grimly maintaining Rome's precarious law and order. Occasional bursts of sexy music pierced the din, as we passed bars featuring saucy barbarian dancing girls. But behind our drawn curtains, Aurelia and I were in our own intimate little world.

"So who's coming to this big banquet again?" I asked with interest. "Your brother, Quintus. Titus whatever his name is, the guy who wants to marry you. And who else?"

Aurelia sighed. "A great many important Roman citizens and their wives. I won't know what to say to them." She looked embarrassed. "Actually I needed to talk to you about that. I'm afraid you won't be able to recline with us, Mella. Quintus has rather strong opinions about the status of slaves. If it was up to me—"

"Don't worry about it," I told her. "I'm not used to eating lying down. I'd probably choke and humiliate myself."

"I may humiliate myself, too," sighed Aurelia. "My brother is making Dorcas prepare some very strange dishes."

My mistress found her life in Rome as bewildering as I did. I'd only had a two-day intensive at the Agency and she'd spent most of her life as a foreigner amongst hostile British tribes.

In normal circumstances, her parents would have helped Aurelia learn the ropes. Unfortunately her mum was dead, and her dad was having some kind of breakdown. We'd see him first thing in the morning, making offerings to the household spirits at the family shrine. Then he'd disappear into his library and stay there, rustling through his scrolls, until a slave took him his evening meal. Just once I saw him in the garden, staring at his dead wife's quince tree with a haunted expression. He wants to die too, I thought, so he can be reunited with her on the Plains of Asphodel.

I think his son was also a major disappointment to him. Quintus Flavius still hadn't shown up at the house, so Aurelia's father sent a messenger to Nero's palace. Quintus eventually replied, sending his respects to his father along with a note to Aurelia, welcoming his sister to the Eternal City, hinting that her admirer was longing to meet her. But it seemed like he couldn't be bothered to drop in to say "hi" in person.

Then out of the blue he sent instructions for a huge banquet to be prepared in their honour. At first, I thought he just wanted to welcome his father and sister home, in true lavish Roman style. Which was nice, if a bit late in the day. Then Quintus sent another message to Aurelia, saying she'd better buy herself a new dress, because he was bringing her future husband to meet her.

The whole thing made me deeply uneasy. All Aurelia knew about this Titus Lucretius guy was that he was one of Nero's closest advisers. Even her father hadn't met him, which seemed really disrespectful. I mean, officially her dad was still head of the household.

I looked up to see my mistress absently sliding her gold bangle back and forth on her wrist.

Quintus must know how vulnerable Aurelia is, I thought. And he's deliberately taking advantage. If you ask me Quintus has way too much influence in this house.

I accidentally blurted my thoughts aloud. "Wouldn't you rather meet this Lucretius guy before the banquet?" I would hate to meet my future husband, plus an unknown brother, in front of important Roman senators and whoever.

"Quintus sent word to say they'll be at the amphitheatre tomorrow," she said.

I gasped with surprise. "You're actually going to the Games?"

Aurelia looked queasy. "My brother says it's my duty as a Roman citizen. I was going to ask if you and Reuben would keep me company?"

Reuben was well in with the other house slaves by this time, and he was always telling me horrific stories of the mistreatment of slaves. Reuben and I must be the only slaves in captivity whose mistress actually ASKED them if they'd like to do something! So of course I said yes.

But I wasn't just going for Aurelia's sake. My reasons were mostly personal. On the same poster that featured the gladiatrix, there had been another name in tiny print. *Flammia the Fire-eating Dwarf.*

If Flammia was performing, chances were the lanista's other recruits weren't far away. And that meant I'd *found* Orlando!

Chapter Six

Next morning I felt incredibly jittery. Seeing humans hack each other to death is not a thing I ever hoped to have to see. Plus I wasn't at all sure my pure angel buddy would hold up under the strain.

On his first ever Earth mission, Reuben saved a dancing bear who was practically being beaten to death. This experience made him incredibly ill.

Reuben insisted I had nothing to worry about. "I'm not saying I'll enjoy it," he added hastily, "but I'll handle it, same as you, Melanie."

For space reasons, as well as decorum, he had to travel to the Games in a separate litter. This particular day, traffic was even worse than usual. There was some big ceremony going on at the

Temple of Vesta. At one point our bearers had to stop to let a procession cross the Via Sacra. We weren't going anywhere, so I peeped round the curtain and watched.

All the devotees of Vesta were girls and women. They wore dazzling white stolas and wreaths of white roses in their hair, and carried small offerings for the goddess. As I watched them making their way towards the Temple of Vesta, chanting and swaying to the beat of a drum, I felt a tingle go down my spine. Vesta's temple was a genuinely sacred place, no doubt about it.

"Which goddess is Vesta again?" I asked my mistress. The Romans had so many gods and goddesses, it was hard to keep track.

Aurelia explained that Vesta was a particularly important goddess to Romans. "She's the goddess of the hearth. Her temple is regarded as the hearth of Rome."

"Is that where those girls tend the sacred flame?"

My mistress nodded. "It's seen as a great honour to serve the goddess in this way. Vestal virgins are chosen when they're only nine or ten years old. They're taken to live in the Palace of the Vestals, where they undergo years of training. You sometimes see them being carried through the city. They wear white veils to show they are the brides of Rome. I used to dream about becoming one myself."

"Can't they ever get married for real?"

"When their period of service is finished. But they rarely do." Aurelia looked wistful. "I used to think it would be wonderful to be a Vestal, then I found out what happens if you let the flame go out."

"What happens?"

"You're stripped and beaten," she said sombrely. "The flame is supposed to be the spirit of Rome. If it goes out, Rome itself will fall."

She suddenly made an irritated noise. "I could walk to the amphitheatre faster than this! Can't the bearers take a shortcut!"

Aurelia seemed unusually stressed, but I assumed my soft-hearted mistress was dreading sitting through so much violence.

Our bearers dropped us off outside the amphitheatre. To our surprise, Aurelia gave me and Reuben our tickets, little clay counters, and told us to go ahead. "I'll find you inside," she said firmly. Before we could follow her, she'd vanished into the crowd.

Reuben and I stared at each other.

"The little minx just gave us the slip!" he said. "Do you think she's gone off to see this guy?"

I'd told him I thought someone had smuggled a note to Aurelia at the baths.

"You can't exactly blame her," I said. "She's going to be married off to some wrinkly old senator any day now."

Reuben looked uneasy. "I still don't think Aurelia should be meeting someone on the sly like this. She'll get into big trouble if she's found out."

"I'm sure it's just a harmless flirtation," I said. "Aurelia's not the type to take silly risks."

Reuben shook his head. "You know her better than I do."

Not that well, I thought wistfully. I'd genuinely believed we were friends. Well, as friendly as a mistress and her slave can be. Yet Aurelia hadn't breathed a word about this exciting new crush.

Reubs and I fought our way into the entrance of the amphitheatre. It was seething with fast-food and souvenir vendors.

"Sorry, man," Reuben told one guy. "Your little gladiator lamps are cool but we're really just passing through."

"Why not just come out and tell him you're an angel?" I said.

"You think I should?" he said anxiously.

"I was joking, Sweetpea!"

We showed our tickets and a slave took us down a long corridor to the VIP enclosures. We emerged blinking into the sunlight and the noise of the amphitheatre.

I almost bolted when I saw how many people were inside. There must have been fifty-thousand Romans crammed in there, at least. A red awning had been unfurled over the arena to protect them from the sun. The fabric rippled in the breeze, sending waves of coloured light over the sand. Fast-food vendors went up and down the rows of seats. Officials with banners reeled off the names of which gladiator would be fighting who. Bookies were taking bets. It was mad.

Our seats were right at the front. A wooden barrier separated us from the arena. At opposite ends of this massive circus ring were pairs of ominous-looking gates. I found myself imagining the scene on the other side. Terrified prisoners of war, trained fighters in armour, bewildered slaves; all praying frantically to their gods to help them survive this savage entertainment.

Aurelia came hurrying towards us, looking slightly pink. "Sorry, I was going to buy us some stuffed dates, but the queues were impossible."

Yeah, we believe you, I thought. People were craning forward, watching the gates with avid expressions. My palms went clammy. Something was going to happen. A herald in a white tunic ran into the arena blowing terrific blasts on a horn. The musicians struck up and the amphitheatre filled with military music. The gates burst open, and the crowd roared with excitement as the gladiators came marching out. They might be outcasts in the world outside, but here, in the arena, they were kings and they knew it. They looked amazing, in their swirly purple cloaks and gleaming helmets with nodding peacock plumes.

The gladiators' armour and weapons varied according to their fighting style. The crowd's favourite was the retiarius, the Fisherman. When he strode out with his giant fishing net and trident, all the girls and women screamed like fans at a concert. The two girl fighters, their faces hidden by strange bronze masks, also raised a big cheer.

The gladiators marched into the middle of the arena, then they formed a double line, standing back to back, raised their clenched fists and shouted out, "We who are about to die, salute you!"

My hair practically stood on end. "How can anyone be that brave?" I whispered to Reuben.

"It's the training," he explained. "Even in his death throes, a gladiator will try not to make a sound."

"Reubs, are you sure you can cope with this?" I asked anxiously.

"I told you, I'll be OK," he said calmly. "Anyway we're not alone."

I thought he was quoting his own lyrics, then I realised Reuben meant it literally. Every row of seats had at least one Earth angel in Roman costume. If I hadn't been so preoccupied, I'd have noticed the tingly cosmic vibes.

"Omigosh! There's so many!" I whispered to Reuben.

"Yeah, and we're going to need them," he said grimly.

To my relief, the first part of the programme was quite tame: there was an elephant who wrote numbers in the sand with his trunk, with a bit of prompting from his minder, followed by a team of dwarves, who did mad acrobatics.

Flammia rode into the ring standing in a tiny

chariot pulled by a Shetland pony, and brandishing a burning torch. The crowd loved this pocket-sized fire-eating barbarian. At the end of his act he rode out in a blazing chariot, like a miniature fire god, yelling with triumph.

Next they had warm-up fights between pairs of trainee gladiators. As each pair ran on, bravely waving their wooden swords, I felt a rush of hope. This one had to be Orlando. But it never was.

The crowd was getting restless. "It's time they cut some throats around here!" yelled someone.

"Keep the action going!" someone else bellowed. 'We want real swords and real blood, not this kids' stuff!"

All around us people started to boo and hiss. It was the first time I understood why our teachers constantly go on about evolution. In my century, you'd never get fifty-thousand humans howling with excitement, purely because they wanted to see blood spouting from other people's internal organs.

A rotten apple whizzed past my ear, followed by a flying egg. Frustrated Romans were pelting the recruits with any missile that came to hand. The recruits ran off. Shortly afterwards another gate burst open. Twenty or thirty terrified men were forcibly dragged and prodded into the arena by amphitheatre officials.

I remembered that the Roman authorities regularly used the Games to dispose of unwanted troublemakers. These guys were probably all convicted criminals. They could handle themselves in a street brawl, but had absolutely no experience of this kind of fighting. They'd been given weapons but no armour or protective padding. But this was never intended to be a fair fight. The audience wanted to see blood flow. Well, now they were going to get it.

I won't go into details. No human should have to see the suffering we saw that day. Anyway, Reuben says it's always better to light one candle than to curse the dark, so I'm going to tell you about the angels instead.

When the killings began, the Earth angels totally disappeared from the stands. It felt like lights going out all around the amphitheatre. For a few chilling seconds, I saw this terrible place in all its gory blood-soaked darkness. Then all the lights came back on, only now they were inside the arena.

To some humans, love is just a word. You love your cat. You love chocolate. But to angels love means something quite different. To us, it's a power: a totally impersonal force that recreates the cosmos every single day. Think about it. Every moment love is creating brand new birds, and stars and blades of grass and amazed new humans to enjoy them.

You don't have to 'deserve' this love. It's just there for free. And no-one is allowed to die alone.

What we witnessed that day in the arena was desperate, but it was also inspiring. During their last agonised moments on Earth, dying humans were shown pure love by unknown angels. And you know what? It gave me new courage. Those angels reminded me who I really was. I wasn't really a part of this human drama. I was just an angel passing through. But that was no reason not to help.

Reuben and I had joined in with our Roman colleagues, beaming loving vibes. For obvious reasons this took all our concentration. Then suddenly I thought to check on Aurelia. She'd gone as white as a sheet. She was clutching her bulla as if she was terrified to let it go, whispering something over and over.

But all nightmares end eventually, even this one. The mutilated bodies were dragged out of the arena. Slaves raked fresh sand over the bloodstains. But they couldn't hide the smell. It simmered in the steamy summer air like something from a Hell dimension.

I don't know what made me look behind then. It's as if I knew Orlando would be there. He was talking to the lanista, looking tired and pale. I went weak with relief. He was here, and he was OK!

Aurelia was trying to pull herself together. "Mella, your gladiatrix is on next," she said bravely.

Star had been paired with Juno, the only other girl fighter on the programme. Probably Star and Juno ate the same rations at the same table, slept in the same room and borrowed each other's perfume and hairpins. Now they had to try to kill each other or they wouldn't get paid.

The girls hurtled towards each other from opposite ends of the arena, swords flashing in the sun. Guys yelled obscene comments from the stands, wanting the girls to show them what they had under their leather chest bands. But they were immediately shouted down. Star and Juno were big favourites, and I soon saw why. If gladiators were kings of the arena, these girl fighters were warrior queens. And Star was just amazing.

Juno was stronger and more cunning, but Star was lighter, faster and more graceful and took crazier risks.

You know how a great dancer can make you feel as if she's dancing for you? Like she IS you, almost? That's how I felt watching Star. It was me with the sun beating on my bare neck. It was me out there on the burning sand with leather thongs tied round my bare arms and an intricately plaited hairstyle. Star was an artist. A fabulous, daring, totally lethal artist.

Aurelia was totally entranced. "I feel as if I know her." She put her hand to her heart. "I know her in here."

"I know!" I said. "Me too." I suddenly heard what I was saying. Melanie this is outrageous! I scolded myself. Star's a killer. You've got no business admiring her!

It was like I'd hexed the gladiatrix with my thoughts, because the very next second, Star's foot slipped from under her. Juno pounced, slashing at her with her sword. Star faltered, then renewed her furious attack. She didn't seem to notice the blood seeping through her short leather skirt. Star was fighting for her life and there was no room for anything else.

The dojo master would love her, I thought in awe. When Star fights, she's like the wind, totally empty. No past, no present, only now.

So I wasn't surprised when a sweating, bloodstained Star finally stood over her opponent, the point of her sword blade triumphantly grazing Juno's throat.

"Kill, kill, kill!" chanted the crowd. Star had been fighting for them too. Now they wanted her to kill for them.

The gladiatrix stared calmly around the arena, as if she was genuinely considering the crowd's demands. Then she threw her sword down in the sand and raised a clenched fist. "This is not Juno's day to die, citizens!" she cried in heavily accented Latin. "She fought well. Spare her to fight another day!"

Reuben gave a gasp. I saw a bright drop of blood fall from Star's leather skirt into the sand; and another and another.

The gladiatrix swayed and clutched her side. She glanced down and looked astonished to see the spreading crimson stain. Without a sound, she crumpled to the ground, and lay totally still.

"NO!" I yelled.

I was on my feet before I'd thought. I was beside myself with distress. I'd just seen dozens of people senselessly murdered. But I didn't know them. I'd felt a connection with Star. She couldn't be *allowed* to die.

But someone was already vaulting over seats to get to her. It wasn't the lanista or a uniformed official. It was Orlando.

When I saw the look on his face, I felt myself falling through space. All these months I'd been waiting for this beautiful boy to realise I was his special someone. But he'd found her already and it wasn't me.

CHAPTER SEVEN

I hurled myself over the barrier and raced across the arena. I could feel grains of burning-hot sand stinging my bare legs as I ran. Down here, the smell of blood was suffocating.

Orlando was already kneeling beside Star. The lanista, Festus Brutus, limped hastily down from the stands to join Orlando. A doctor attached to the gladiator school hurried after him.

Star was trying to lift her head.

"Lie still!" Festus growled.

Orlando looked appalled to see me. "Mel, what are you playing at? You're not supposed to be here."

"Will Star be OK?" I asked in a small voice.

"Too early to say," he said tersely. "Now go and take care of Aurelia like you're supposed to." A flicker of worry crossed his face. "She's OK, isn't she?"

As OK as you can be when you've just watched thirty human beings slaughtered in public, I thought. But I just said huskily, "She's fine."

"Well, you shouldn't leave her too long."

Star didn't look like a warrior queen lying there on the sand. She looked small and vulnerable. She's no taller than Aurelia, I thought.

But the gladiatrix was a warrior to the max. When the doctor ripped her blood-soaked skirt, Star didn't murmur, even though the leather was sticking to an open wound. The doctor began to probe the wound with metal instruments, trying to discover the extent of the damage. It must have been agony but she didn't flinch.

Up close I saw that Star's arms and legs were peppered with bruises and tiny healed scars. Through the slits of her mask, her closed eyelids were deathly pale.

"We should get her back to the barracks," the doctor told Festus. "She's lost a lot of blood."

Orlando hovered anxiously. I wanted to believe his concern was strictly professional, but paranoid suspicions swarmed through my mind.

Had Orlando met Star on his previous trip and fallen head over heels-in-love with her? Did he organise his task force purely to save her from a bloody death in the arena? Was that why he couldn't tell us the purpose of the mission?

I stared down miserably at my rival. You were right, Melanie, I thought. Star's everything you'll never be. Sexy, fearless, mysterious...

Reuben came up behind me. "You should come back," he said. "You can see Orlando's busy."

"Give me a minute," I pleaded.

Orlando and the lanista were helping the dazed gladiatrix to her feet, with some assistance from Juno. Between them they half-lifted, half-supported Star out of the arena. There were confused murmurings from the crowd.

I went back to my seat like a zombie.

"You missed my brother," Aurelia said in a bright voice. "He brought Titus Lucretius to meet me."

"Didn't stay long, did they?" Reuben murmured in my ear. "You'd almost think they'd been waiting to get her by herself."

"So who was that beautiful boy you were talking to?" Aurelia asked me with that same fake brightness.

I could tell she totally wasn't thinking about what she was saying. She didn't know how I felt about Orlando. She couldn't know the last thing I needed right now was for him to have another female admirer.

Through my fog of misery I sensed that Aurelia's meeting with her future husband had distressed her. It was sweltering in the amphitheatre, but I saw her shiver. She drew her thin shawl more closely around her, and for the first time since I'd known her, she spoke like a haughty mistress addressing her slave. "Find our bearers, Mella. I wish to leave. At once!"

That night I helped my mistress get ready for the banquet. I helped her put on her new silk stola. I arranged her hair and secured it with ornamental hairpins, making it look as if her complicated braids were studded with tiny pearls. She looked lovely when I'd finished, except for being so pale. She'd hardly said a word since we came back from the Games. I knew I should get her to open up and tell me what was wrong, but I was in a total daze. I was just going through the motions.

Being an angel isn't that different from being a gladiator, I thought bleakly. You might be bleeding inside, but you keep going. Your heart might be breaking, but you can't let it show.

Later, I ran about with the other house slaves, making our guests welcome. I brought warm scented water to wash the dust from their feet. I took ladies' shawls and gentlemen's cloaks. I plumped up the cushions on the couches, so our guests could recline like gods and goddesses, wearing their ceremonial crowns of leaves and flowers.

But none of it seemed real. Not like Orlando's face when he saw Star's blood soaking into the sand.

In the kitchen Reuben and two other slaves were helping with the preparations. Like all Roman kitchens, this one was a soot-encrusted hellhole. Can you believe Dorcas had to cook this entire banquet over a wood fire, with no windows for ventilation? Plus the dishes Quintus had selected for his guests were just *bizarre*: peacock eggs in pepper sauce, milk-fed snails sautéed with garlic, stuffed dormice. It was pretty obvious that Aurelia's brother hadn't designed his banquet to be enjoyed. He just wanted to impress his guests with how rich and important he was.

Reuben grabbed me as I tottered past with a

huge wine jug in each hand. "OK, so Orlando has other things on his mind," he said in a firm voice. "And OK, so you're upset. But get over it. You're no good to Aurelia in this state and *she's* the one Orlando wants us to watch.

"I can't help it, Reubs," I wailed. "It hurts so much."

My angel buddy made me look at him. "Maybe Mel Beeby can't get over it, but Helix can."

Sometimes I think Reuben knows me better than anyone else in the universe. It's like he knew exactly the right thing to say. As he spoke my angel name out loud, my buddy's voice took on an amazingly powerful vibe. To my astonishment, I saw my name forming in the air in glowing letters, right there in that horrible kitchen. No one but Reubs and I saw, but I gasped. And guess what? I was over it! I snapped out of my self pity just like that. I wasn't Mel-with-a-broken-heart, I was an angel with a job to do. Reuben's right, I thought. I can do this. I'm going to do this.

I gave his hand a squeeze. It felt rough and calloused from his gardening, but still deeply comforting. "Thanks, Sweetpea. I owe you."

"I know," Reuben agreed smugly. Without thinking he popped a nibble in his mouth and choked. "What was that?"

"I hope it's not a stuffed dormouse!" I giggled.

I reached the dining room to hear a slave announcing solemnly, "Quintus Flavius and Titus Lucretius!"

I'd had my suspicions about Quintus as you know, and the minute he walked into the room, I knew I'd been right. Quintus was handsome, even charming, but you could see an unmistakable glint of cruelty in his eyes.

Aurelia's future husband followed him in. He was short and squat and his lips looked unpleasantly red through his beard. He handed me his cloak. "Well, well. It's the little slave girl," he said in a high thin voice.

I almost fainted with terror. I knew this guy. I'd breathed his icky alcohol fumes. I'd felt his pervy vibes touch my angelic energy field. Omigosh! I thought. Titus Lucretius was our intruder!!

I wanted to grab Aurelia and run right out of that creepy house and keep running until we ended up somewhere nice and normal.

I was scared and disgusted, but I was angry too. Titus could have arranged to meet my mistress, if that's all he'd wanted. But he didn't want to get to know Aurelia as a person, did he? He wanted to creep up on her in the dark like she was his helpless prey. He wanted power over her.

Aurelia's brother must have been in on it, I thought in horror. That's how Titus got past the watchman. Ugh, this era is SO sick!

I was so upset I had to rush off to update Reuben.

Dorcas was standing over the hearth, simmering what looked like little grey bird-tongues in some kind of strange spicy sauce. The slave woman turned in surprise as I burst in, and saw my stricken expression. "You've seen The Knife then," she said grimly.

It turned out that Dorcas knew exactly what was going on, and it sickened her to the core. "Titus Lucretius is the head of Nero's secret police," she told us in a low voice. "We call him The Knife because he's had so many people murdered."

"Aurelia can't possibly marry him," I gasped. "Someone's got to stop it."

Dorcas shook her head. "Everyone's too scared of him. I just thank the gods my mistress never saw this day. She loved that poor girl like her own." She wiped her eyes on her apron. "You two genuinely care about her, don't you?" she said in a puzzled voice.

I nodded. "Yes, we do."

"You'd better go back before anyone gets suspicious. Here, take this to Titus Lucretius." The slave woman ladled out more mulled wine. Then she pursed her lips and spat deliberately into the jug. "A little present from the people," she whispered.

Quintus and his guests were tucking into their peacocks' eggs. The guests had brought their personal slaves to wait on them. If they didn't like something they simply threw it on the floor and the slaves obediently swooped and picked it up.

Once I looked up to see Aurelia's father in the doorway in his freshly-ironed toga, looking dazed. But when he saw his adopted daughter reclining on a couch next to the chief of Rome's secret police, he went away.

I'd have been ashamed too, if I was him. Aurelia's dad was the one person who could have put a stop to this, but he'd given away his authority to his son, and everyone knew it.

My mistress had left her huge egg untouched on her plate. She didn't eat any of the next course either. She looked dangerously close to tears. This feast was meant to be an opportunity for her and Titus to get to know each other, but both he and

Quintus were treating her as if she didn't exist. They just giggled together at private jokes, like cruel little schoolboys. It's like they were deliberately trying to humiliate her.

I went to take Aurelia's plate, thinking I could whisper something comforting in her ear. Suddenly Titus caught my wrist in his clammy grip. I noticed guests watching us with unpleasant expressions. For a moment, their faces seemed to distort in the lamplight, as if they might be going to morph at any moment into something totally evil.

I went utterly cold. Brice had been telling the truth. Some of these Romans weren't actually human.

"Your mistress doesn't seem to be enjoying her flamingo tongues," Titus was saying in his high voice. "Perhaps she's grown too used to barbarian cuisine. Has Aurelia Flavia turned into a barbarian? What's your opinion, girl?"

The PODS guests waited with interest to hear what I'd say. They knew who I was and I knew who they were. But they couldn't exactly blow their cover, and I certainly couldn't blow mine, so we all kept up the pretence that everyone here was human.

"My mistress is not hungry," I told him defiantly.

Titus and Quintus looked at each other. "Then maybe your mistress is thirsty!" Giggling like a spiteful little kid, Titus lifted his goblet and threw its contents all over her, absolutely soaking her dress.

For a moment Aurelia just stared blankly at the spreading crimson stain, and I knew she was remembering Star, bleeding from her wounds in the arena. Then with great dignity, she drew her silk shawl around her. "And you want me to marry this man?" she said to her brother in a trembling voice. She rose from her couch and left the room. As I rushed after her, shouts of laughter followed us.

Now I knew why Orlando had planted me in this house. The PODS wanted to destroy Aurelia. They didn't just want to harm her physically. They wanted to kill her spirit.

But why on earth would they bother, unless she threatened their own malevolent plans in some way? And that was just ridiculous. Aurelia wasn't a threat to anybody. She's just a sweet girl, I thought. A sweet, harmless little rich girl.

I shot out of an uneasy doze to hear my mistress moving around in the dark. I opened my eyes as she crept softly out of the room. Probably just going to the latrine, I thought drowsily.

Erm, so why is she wearing her cloak, Melanie? I asked myself.

I was off my couch in a flash. I was Helix, an angelic trouble-shooter on a mission that was just about to go seriously pearshaped.

You should have seen this coming, babe, I scolded myself. That banquet gave Aurelia a nightmare preview of her future. Now she's rushing off to the arms of her secret love.

I beamed urgent signals to Reuben as I threw on my clothes.

Meet me under the quince tree, Sweetpea. NOW!

Outside, the warm night air smelled of roses. A perfect full moon sailed over the quince tree. Reuben came hopping out of the slave quarters, still trying to buckle his sandals. "I'd have been here quicker but I had to shut Minerva in her kennel," he whispered. "What's up?"

"Aurelia's running away. I think she's going to this guy. We've got to follow her."

We slipped out of the slaves' entrance and raced along the dark street. "This is terrible, Reubs!" I panted out. "You heard what Dorcas said. Anyone who gets in Titus's way ends up seriously dead. If he finds out about her boyfriend, Aurelia could be next."

"We don't even know she's got a boyfriend," Reuben objected breathlessly. "This might not be what you think."

"Why else would a nice Roman girl be out in the streets at night? She's not likely to be going clubbing!"

"There she is!" said Reuben suddenly.

Aurelia had stopped to peer at a piece of papyrus in the moonlight. We silently caught her up.

"Right at the crossroads," she murmured. "Take the third on the right by the olive mill. Go to the old aqueduct and wait."

And she was off again.

When we reached the aqueduct, someone stepped out of the shadows. With a flicker of alarm, I saw other figures moving behind him. I heard someone whisper, "Bless you little sister," then they all set off together down the street.

Hello, I thought. "This isn't about some boyfriend is it?" I whispered to Reubs.

"Doesn't look like it," he agreed.

Other anonymous humans joined them as they

hurried along. It went on like this, a growing crowd of silent men and women, all heading for the same unknown destination. Now and then one would stop and listen intently, to see if they were being followed, then they'd hurry on.

Finally we reached open ground. There had been houses here once, but they had crumbled into rubble years ago. We trailed Aurelia and her companions through the moonlit ruins until we came to an overgrown fig tree. The gnarled branches partly concealed a low archway, which had once been part of a temple. Everyone silently filed inside. When we were quite sure the coast was clear, we followed.

On the other side of the arch, a flight of steep stone steps disappeared down into the dark. On every sixth or seventh step, someone had placed a lighted clay lamp.

Helix might be up for it, but Mel Beeby wasn't too keen to go exploring some crumbly old crypt in the dark, so I quickly helped myself to a lamp.

It's lucky I did. At the bottom we found ourselves in a low stone tunnel with dozens of other tunnels going off. It was a total labyrinth.

"Now what do we do?" My voice echoed spookily around the tunnel.

Reuben pointed at the wall. "We could always follow the fish."

By the flickery flame of my lamp, I saw a crudely painted fish daubed on the tunnel wall. "That's like the one I saw on Aurelia's letter," I said in amazement. Reuben had been right, as we crept along the tunnel the fish symbol reappeared at intervals, wherever the tunnel branched off.

"What's that sound!" my buddy asked.

I strained my ears. It sounded like the blurry murmuring of bees. What IS going on down here, I wondered nervously?

The tunnel went on and on. Sometimes the murmuring seemed quite close, then it would fade again. Each time it grew louder, the back of my neck went strangely tingly.

All at once I smelled incense. Not the stuff Romans used in temples. This was musky and sweet like burning pine cones. The bee-sound was getting really powerful now. In fact it was giving me goosebumps. For the first time I realised the murmuring had words. It wasn't Latin. It was unlike any language I'd ever heard.

Next minute the tunnel opened out into an underground chamber. I glimpsed more wall paintings, strange and richly coloured. Then I saw the rapt lamplit faces of hundreds of humans.

My heart practically jumped into my mouth. I'd seen people in this state on TV: eyes closed, hands raised, chanting, swaying. And if it wasn't drugs, a fake guru was always involved. I scanned the ecstatic faces, anxiously, until I found Aurelia. Don't let this be happening, I prayed. Then I saw her, swaying and chanting along with everyone else.

"This is SO much worse than I thought!" I gasped.

I grabbed Reuben's hand and dragged him out.

"What are you so upset about?" he asked in a grumpy voice. "The chanting was cool. The total opposite of that arena."

"Sweetpea, I'm not being horrible, but you haven't been to Earth that often, so you've probably never heard of religious cults. Well what we just saw, that's a cult. I don't know how Aurelia got sucked into it. Maybe they had a secret chapter in Ancient Britain or something. But she's in real danger. We're in way over our heads, Reubs. We've got to tell Orlando."

"You're the expert," he sighed.

"This incense is making my nose run," I said. "Let's wait outside."

Next day, using the excuse of taking Aurelia's wine-stained stola to the fullers, (a kind of Roman dry cleaners) Reuben and I hired a litter to take us to the ludus.

The gladiator school was basically a kind of Roman boot camp, with high walls set with metal spikes and broken pottery, and prowling heavies everywhere. Few people actually wanted to be gladiators, so to stop his protégées escaping, Festus Brutus had them watched twenty-four seven.

We found Orlando and the lanista behind the barracks, drilling a sullen group of human recruits in a make-shift arena.

Everyone but Orlando and Festus had thick protective padding tied around their arms and legs. The recruits were supposed to charge at straw men, with wooden swords, and pretend to disembowel them. Under Festus's scowling gaze, Orlando made them charge again and again, until he was satisfied with their technique.

"Orlando is something else," grinned Reuben. "He's been here two weeks, max, and he's already like Festus Brutus's right-hand man."

"I don't know how he does it," I agreed.

Reuben and I rushed up to Orlando at the end of the session.

"I don't believe you two," he sighed. "You'd better have a really good reason for coming here. It's taken days to get Festus Brutus to trust me. If he sees you guys, he'll go up the wall."

"We have got a good reason," I babbled urgently. "Aurelia's joined a dangerous cult."

Orlando didn't react at all how I'd expected. In fact he laughed with pure relief. "You followed her to the catacombs, right?"

I stared at him in consternation. "You know about that place?"

"Of course!" he said. "It's the only place Christians can meet in safety. Practising the Christian faith is illegal in Nero's time."

My mouth dropped open. "Those people were Christians?"

"They can only meet in secret. That's why they use symbols, like the fish, so only insiders understand what's being passed on."

My cheeks burned with embarrassment. You are SO ignorant, Melanie! I scolded myself. Kindergarten angels know more than you.

Reuben looked worried. "What would happen if they were found out?"

Orlando glanced away. "They'd be put to death."

"Are you serious?" I gasped. "That girl is in enough trouble as it is! We just found out her brother is marrying her off to this evil secret police chief."

Orlando nodded. "The Knife."

"Omigosh, you knew!" Of course he did, you birdbrain, that's why he asked you to take care of her, Melanie, I reminded myself.

I suddenly remembered something. "Erm, how's Star?"

Orlando's eyes softened. "She's making a good recovery. Festus Brutus took her into his own home, so she can be cared for properly."

Well, he wouldn't want to lose his investment, I thought darkly.

All the way home, I thought about how I'd underestimated Aurelia. "A sweet harmless rich girl", I'd called her. My prejudice had blinded me to all kinds of obvious clues. Her hatred of all forms of cruelty. Her kindness to people worse off than herself. Her talk of souls.

I waited until bedtime, when Aurelia and I were alone together in her room, and then I told her that Reubs and me knew her secret and would do everything in our power to protect her.

My mistress jumped up in terror, knocking over the jar of almond oil, and spilling the sweet-scented oil everywhere. "You've been spying on me, Mella! I trusted you and you betrayed me."

"You still can trust me, I swear!" I told her. "Reuben and I only followed you because we were so worried about you." And I explained how we'd decided she had a secret sweetheart.

Aurelia must have sensed that my words came straight from the heart, because she looked deep into my eyes and it was a total replay of our first meeting at the slave market. It was like she *knew*. But at the same time she didn't. My mistress sat down again without a word, and I continued brushing her hair.

"Your mum was a Christian too, wasn't she?" I said.

"She gave me this." Aurelia took off her bulla. "Look at the back."

On the reverse of her charm was a tiny mother of pearl cross.

My eyes filled with tears. Aurelia has picked a really lonely way to be true to herself. Then I thought, but she's not alone any more.

I caught Aurelia watching me in the polished bronze mirror. "I never knew there were friends like you," she said softly. "One day I'll give you your freedom."

My freedom wasn't in her hands, but Aurelia wasn't to know that.

We talked into the night, and as I blew out the lamp, we agreed that we were both happier than we'd been for days.

We weren't to know that every word of our conversation had been overheard by Aurelia's brother, adviser to the Emperor Nero and faithful servant to the Powers of Darkness.

Chapter Eight

I woke to find lamplight flickering confusingly in my eyes.

Dorcas was shaking me. "Get dressed!" she said in a fierce whisper. "Leave this house and take Aurelia Flavia with you."

Aurelia rubbed her eyes drowsily. "Is there a fire?"

"You've been betrayed, little mistress," Dorcas told her. "Your brother has found out you follow the teacher from Nazareth."

We jumped up and began to fling on our clothes.

"Why are you helping me, Dorcas?" Aurelia said from inside her tunic. "You still follow the old gods."

"I follow my heart," said Dorcas in a low voice. "They say a teacher who says such things must be insane. But I say his is a better madness than Nero's."

We were still dressing frantically, when we heard the sound of tramping feet outside. The Praetorian Guard, Nero's police, had come to arrest us.

Reuben came running as soon as he heard the commotion, so they arrested him too.

Aurelia's father watched it all from the door of his study. "I showed her nothing but kindness and she betrayed me," he said in disgust.

"I love you, Pater," Aurelia called desperately. "I always loved you!"

I heard desolate howls from Minerva's kennel as we were led away.

The guards marched us through the early morning streets, I could see Aurelia was in a state of shock. She kept looking around, wide-eyed, as if she totally hadn't realised how beautiful the world was until this moment. The sun was rising and birds sang joyfully from hidden gardens. The air was full of scents, roses from the flower market, eye-watering fumes from the street of the leather workers, burning incense from a shrine. I was trying hard not to think about what would happen when we stopped marching and reached our destination. I just put one foot in front of the other; left right, left right.

People called out to know why we'd been arrested. "We bagged a few more Christians!" a guard shouted back cheerfully. The mood immediately darkened. "Filthy vermin," a woman screamed. One man spat in our faces. "You're going to die today, Christian scum!"

Outside one semi-derelict apartment block, people pelted us with rotting fruit, and someone started throwing stones. Everyone loathed and despised us, the guards included.

"I don't understand people like you," a guard said contemptuously to Aurelia. "We've got perfectly good Roman gods and goddesses. But you have to have your own special god, it makes me sick."

"Why do you care which god she worships, man?" Reuben asked. "She's not dissing yours, is she?"

"Reuben!" I hissed. "You're not meant to hold philosophical discussions with the guards."

"All Christians are in league with the barbarian hordes," the guard ranted on. "You want to burn

Rome down around our ears."

When we reached the amphitheatre, crowds of Romans were already queuing to go in. We were taken to a row of cells and a guard booted us in through a door. I just had time to see the gruesome straw on the floor, then the door slammed behind us and we were plunged into total darkness.

We're going to be fine, I told myself bravely. Any minute now that door will open and Orlando will walk in.

But when we finally heard the bolts being dragged back, some hours later, a security guy stood in the doorway, grinning unpleasantly. "Let's be having you!" he said. "Mustn't keep those hungry pussy cats waiting."

"No," leered his mate, "we've been starving them specially."

Other Christians were being dragged from neighbouring cells. We were chained together like dangerous criminals and kicked and prodded along a low gloomy tunnel. We stumbled along, our eyes fixed on the white blaze of sunlight at the far end. Fifty-thousand brutal voices surged to meet us. They were all chanting the same word over and over. "Kill! Kill! Kill!"

Aurelia stumbled and Reuben and I quickly steadied her. "I know it doesn't seem like it, but we're going to be OK," I told her.

My mistress's voice trembled, but her face was totally calm. "Other martyrs have died for their faith," she said bravely. "And I know I will soon be reunited with my mother in Heaven."

When the crowd saw us emerge, blinking and confused in the pitiless midday sun, they howled with excitement.

I'd been clinging to the hope that Orlando would stage some fabulous last-minute rescue. If so, he was leaving it desperately late.

I stared wildly around the amphitheatre. Where were all the angels? I wondered.

Two gates flew open and thirty or more lions exploded into the arena. I assumed they were lions. I just heard furious roars and saw a mad blur of gold. Then my world went into slow-mo, and suddenly everything was in nightmare close-up; wild yellow eyes with tawny flecks, fleshy crimson tongues. Bared fangs drooling saliva.

When I smelled their hot breath on my face, I squeezed my eyes shut and flung my arms around Aurelia. It was the only way I could think of to protect her; some crazy idea that I could at least slow the ravenous beasts down. In that moment I relived every piece of wildlife film footage featuring lions and helpless baby animals I'd ever seen on TV. I didn't just see it. I was getting Dolby surround sound. The juicy ripping of muscle. The splintering of bone...

But the seconds ticked by and there was no ripping or splintering.

The crowd had gone oddly silent. Even the lions had gone quiet. Their roaring had been replaced by a bizarre rumbling, like the throbbing engines of a very old bus. Amazed laughter rippled round the amphitheatre.

I opened my eyes. It was like a scene from a particularly magical dream. My angel buddy was standing in the centre of a circle of lions, completely unharmed. The beasts gazed back at him with adoring expressions. The rumbling was the purring of thirty blissed-out lions.

Aurelia was trembling with awe. "It's a miracle!" she breathed.

When will you ever learn, Mel Beeby? I asked myself. We ARE the angels. We didn't need any help.

And at that moment the audience went wild. All around the amphitheatre, Romans jumped to their feet: slaves, citizens, senators, men, women and children. And all because of a honey-coloured angel-boy with dreads. Omigosh, they love him, I thought tearfully. They love him even though they think he's a Christian!

Hang on? A worrying thought occurred to me. Shouldn't all these people have their thumbs UP?

But no matter where I looked, people were jabbing their thumbs in a sharp and quite unmistakable downward direction.

They still want us to die! I thought in despair.

Then my heart gave a leap as I heard everyone yelling. "FREE THEM! FREE THEM!!"

That's when I found out the Hollywood movies got it wrong. In Roman times, the thumbs-*up* gesture actually meant, "Stab him in the jugular!".

An official in a toga approached the barrier, keeping as far away as possible from the lions. "Hey, you kids! Get over here," he called. "His Imperial Majesty wants to meet you."

"Omigosh, Nero's here at the Games!" I squeaked.

Normally I'd have panicked at the prospect of meeting a real live emperor, particularly an emperor as cruel and decadent as Nero, but we'd just survived wild lions, as you know, so we were up for anything.

We were marched into the Emperor's presence between hefty Praetorian guards.

Considering he was the head of the biggest empire the ancient world had ever known, Nero wasn't actually that impressive. He had practically no chin to speak of and his eyes were such a pale blue, that you could hardly detect the colour. He was wearing what appeared to be an old dressing-gown spattered with stains and crusty splodges of food.

He might not have the looks or the gorgeous robes, but Nero had the imperial attitude all right. His gaze flickered over me and Aurelia, as if we were little dung beetles, unworthy of his attention. Then he saw Reuben, and a greedy glitter lit up his eyes. "We live in strange times," he said. "So strange that the mighty Nero is willing to make a bargain with a Christian slave boy. Teach me how to make lions love me, and I'll let you and your little girlfriends go free."

I understood where Nero was coming from. He'd just witnessed a despised slave perform a feat that no ordinary human could possibly have done, not even an all-powerful emperor. Now he wanted this magical gift for himself. If Nero could get wild lions to worship him, his people would think he was some kind of god!

Of course, that was never going to happen. Reuben was firm in the way only a pure angel can be. "Sorry, that won't be possible," he said politely.

I'd have said the Emperor was borderline normal up till this point. But the instant Reubs turned him down, I felt him switch.

Nero didn't froth at the mouth, or rant, he just went very very still. But you could feel this terrible darkness seething inside him.

"Take them out of my sight!" he commanded the guards. "They bore me."

Aurelia gasped. "But what will happen to us?"

"I haven't decided," said the Emperor in an irritated voice. "But throwing you to wild animals is obviously out. What do you think, my friends?" he called over his shoulder.

My heart sank as Titus and Quintus hurried forward. Nero drew them into a huddle. "How shall I kill the Christian children?" he asked petulantly.

"Easy!" said Titus in his high voice. "Put them in the ring with trained gladiators!"

The Emperor let out a mad titter of laughter. "Excellent! Take them to the dungeons. Tomorrow the gods can decide their fate."

CHAPTER NINE

The sun was setting as the guards marched us through the city. In households all over Rome, people were cooking their suppers. The air was hazy with wood-smoke and I kept catching savoury whiffs of frying fish and onions. Once I saw a woman on a balcony, hushing her new baby to sleep.

As we tramped through twilit streets, the Christians sang to keep up their spirits. Early Christian hymns were v. uplifting, nothing like the dirges we sang at my comprehensive. Reuben and I totally couldn't help joining in. Then we taught them Reuben's song, *We're not alone*. The Christians soon picked it up and put a cool little

Roman spin on it. But we were starting to attract attention and the guards got nervous and told us to shut up.

As we were passing the Temple of Vesta, I felt an unmistakable mystical tingle. A door stood open between two lofty stone pillars. I caught a glimpse of a rich velvety darkness inside, and the golden flicker of the sacred flame. The sweet smell of incense wafted towards me.

Suddenly, I had to pinch myself. Coming down the steps towards me in the tunic and veil of a Vestal virgin, was ANOTHER Aurelia!

For an instant everything seemed to shimmer: the girl in her gauzy white veil, the beautiful temple, the violet sky with its pinpricks of stars – then Aurelia's double vanished into the crowd like a dream.

Typical Melanie, I had to blurt out what I'd seen. "Omigosh, Aurelia! I've just seen your absolute spitting image!!"

"No talking!" barked one of the guards.

Aurelia looked bewildered. "You saw someone who looks like me?" she whispered.

"She's so like you it's spooky," I whispered back. "And she's a Vestal virgin, just like you once wanted to be. Isn't that amazing?"

She stared at me wide-eyed.

"That must be why you always felt something was missing," I told her excitedly. "Perhaps you really are a twin!"

Aurelia's eyes brimmed with tears. "Perhaps," she said softly. "But even if you're right, I'm not going to live long enough to meet her."

"No, it's all going to work out, I swear!" I promised. "I can feel it, Aurelia! It's like, there's this beautiful mosaic forming and we're all a part of it, but we're too close to see the pattern."

I really meant it. I could feel all the gorgeous multicoloured pieces coming together around us. Of course, I had no idea how complex this particular mosaic would turn out to be...

That night Orlando sprang us from the dungeons. I have NO idea how he got hold of those Praetorian guard uniforms but my angelic colleagues made brilliantly convincing guardsmen.

No one even challenged us! The real guards were totally convinced that their dungeons were impregnable, so they were just chilling out in the guard-room, drinking wine and playing backgammon. We basically sneaked out right under their noses!

The Christians naturally assumed that Orlando and his team belonged to the early Christian underground. They thanked him and quickly melted away into the night.

"We'd better lie low," I told Orlando. "By tomorrow every Praetorian guard in this city will be looking for us, not to mention Nero's secret police."

"We're taking you back to the ludus with us," said Orlando. "We've got a wagon waiting a couple of streets away."

"But the minute Festus Brutus sees us, he'll turn us over to the authorities," I objected.

"You're wrong," said Orlando. "It was Festus who lent us the wagon. He might seem rough and ready, but his heart is in the right place."

Aurelia was chatting to some of our rescuers, so I took the opportunity to tell Orlando about my amazing discovery. "I saw this girl on the way here," I said eagerly. "She's a Vestal virgin at the temple and I'm not exaggerating, she could be Aurelia's identical twin!!"

My voice faded as I saw Orlando's expression.

He knew, I thought. Orlando had known Aurelia had a twin all along.

The lanista lived in a comfortable apartment behind

the training school. A slave showed us into a brightly-painted room where Festus Brutus was doing Roman-style calculations at his desk. A grizzled old dog lay at his feet, looking as bad-tempered and battle-scarred as the lanista himself.

"Just a minute," Festus barked as we came in. "These taxes will be the death of me."

We waited while he finished scribbling numerals on a wax tablet with a sharp metal stylus. I looked around with cautious interest. There was a couch heaped with leopard and zebra skins, probably booty from various games. All around the walls, an artist had painted scenes of gory gladiatorial combat. Alongside the usual offerings in the household shrine, was a simple wooden sword. I knew from Reuben that this was a "rudis". A lanista would give this symbolic sword to a gladiator on the day he finally bought his freedom.

You're such a ditz, Mel, I told myself. Festus Brutus wasn't wounded on the battlefield at all. He got those injuries in the arena. Festus had been a gladiator too!

He looked up at last, rubbing bloodshot eyes. "Well, well, if it isn't the lion children!" he growled. "The city is buzzing like a beehive with news of your—" He broke off abruptly. He was staring at

Aurelia with a stunned expression. "But she's exactly like—"

Orlando quickly shook his head and Festus checked himself.

"My friends would like to see Star," said Orlando. "If it isn't too late."

The old gladiator gave an amazed laugh. "I'm getting senile," he muttered. "Aiding and abetting religious dissidents. Giving new cadets the run of my ludus. Next thing I'll be turning Christian."

You couldn't blame him for being confused. He had no idea why he'd allowed this barbarian slave to wander freely around Rome, instead of keeping him chained in his barracks like a dog. But we did.

Festus, like Aurelia, was deeply susceptible to angelic vibes. Plus, I have to say, Orlando is excellent at his job!

We followed Festus Brutus across a moonlit courtyard to the small apartment where the gladiatrix was convalescing.

"Is Star any better?" I asked.

"For someone who almost bled to death, she's alarmingly well," he said in a grumbling voice. "That girl has unnatural powers of recovery."

Beside the open door was a peach tree so weighed down with fruit, that its branches almost touched the ground. Soft voices floated out of the house into the evening air. Star sat with her back to us in a flood of lamplight. Juno stood behind her, plaiting Star's hair.

It's never one thing that makes you recognise a person. It's more like lots of small things. A tone of voice. A gesture. The texture of someone's hair.

Festus gave a last baffled glance at Aurelia. "Strange times indeed," he murmured. He picked up a fallen peach, dusted it off on his tunic, and took a bite. "You have a visitor!" he called to Star.

"I am not interested in visitors," the gladiatrix called back in her foreign-sounding Latin.

"You'll be interested in this one," said Festus.

There was a strange excitement in his voice.

But by this time I knew. I hadn't been looking for similarities before. I'd been confused by Star's mask and her sexy fighting costume, not to mention my own mixed-up emotions. But now I knew with absolute certainty what I'd see when Star turned to face us; a girl with grey eyes, flyaway brown hair, and a dimple in her cheek.

My mistress wasn't separated from one sister at birth, but two. The Christian girl, the Vestal virgin and the feisty gladiatrix were identical triplets!

I'll probably never see two humans more

astonished than Aurelia and Star when they finally set eyes on each other.

First they were stunned, then disbelieving, then shocked. Then they flew to each other, squealing like little kids on Christmas morning. They hugged and cried all over each other, kissing each other's hands and cheeks.

"I used to see you in my dreams," Aurelia wept.

Tears streamed down Star's face. "I saw you too!" she sobbed. "I knew you were real. But they beat me and told me it wasn't true!"

"Omigosh," I whispered to Orlando. "They've been communicating telepathically all these years!!"

"Let's leave them," he whispered to me and Reubs. "They've got some serious catching up to do."

Festus Brutus had vanished tactfully into his house, loudly blowing his nose.

The three of us went to sit under an olive tree in a white pool of moonlight. At first we were all too moved to talk. It felt a bit weird sitting so close to Orlando in the dark, but I just looked up at the night sky and listened to the cicadas singing somewhere in the bushes. I sensed that Orlando had something on his mind. Eventually he cleared his throat. "I think it's time I told you about the curse."

My mouth fell open. "No way! There's a curse? As well as triplets!"

I think I already mentioned the Roman tendency to curse everyone and everything that annoyed them. But the curse Orlando was talking about was in a totally different league.

"Ancient Romans see signs and portents in everything, as you know," he told us. "If you spill wine at a banquet, you'll have bad luck in business. If your child is born with a harelip, it's because you're being punished by the gods. In such a superstitious climate, even the birth of twin babies is seen as alarming. Surviving triplets are so unique that their very existence seems unnatural."

I could tell we were going to be here quite a while, so I made myself comfortable against the nubbly trunk of the olive tree and listened to Orlando's story.

"Fifteen years ago, in the poorest part of Rome, a woman gave birth to three identical baby girls. After a long, difficult labour she was too weak to hold her baby daughters in her arms. She died only hours after giving birth. These children weren't just linked by the circumstances of their birth," Orlando explained. "Their souls were connected too."

"Omigosh, they were spiritual triplets!" I gasped. "That is SO special!"

Orlando nodded. "Our Agency had been expecting three very special children to show up during this era. They just didn't know exactly where or when. Unfortunately the local Opposition agent was quicker off the mark, and he grabbed the opportunity to do major cosmic damage."

A passing moth brushed against my bare arm, making me shiver. "Go on," I whispered.

"OK, now you guys know from Dark Studies that a curse is basically a negative thought, delivered with intense force?"

Reuben and I nodded nervously.

"But if enough humans feed it with the energy of belief, a curse can become a kind of black hole, sucking in more and more negativity, until eventually it takes on a demonic life of its own."

Reuben swallowed. "That sounds dark."

"It gets darker, believe me," said Orlando. "Like most uneducated Romans, the triplets' grandmother was terrified of what she couldn't understand. She had been jealous of her daughter-in-law, and was furious that her son expected her to feed and care for these three freakish infants. This made her a perfect target for the Opposition."

"Oh-oh," I said.

"This jealous old woman was convinced that the triplets' mother must have offended the gods, and she made up her mind to free herself and her son from this bad luck. She bought a live chicken and took it to the shrine of a particularly unsavoury underworld god. A Dark agent, posing as a priest, accepted her offering. She started to weep and wring her hands, so he made her tell him what was wrong, and after he'd heard her story, this fake priest told her that he knew a way to divert the bad luck from her son's house."

"Don't tell me – with a curse," said Reuben.

"Yes, with a curse. Since the old woman was illiterate, he promised to help her word the curse to make it binding."

Orlando described how the fake priest scratched the words on a special curse tablet made of lead, and watched with a strange eagerness as the triplets' grandmother placed it in the bloodstained shrine.

"What did the curse say?" I whispered.

"That the unnatural babies must be taken from the house and abandoned in three different areas of the city, where they would be exposed to the elements and left to die. If the old woman did everything exactly as she was told, she and her son would prosper in all their dealings. But if the girls were ever *reunited*, not only would this good fortune end, Rome itself would fall.

"While her son was sleeping, the grandmother took the new-born girls out of the house under cover of darkness and abandoned them in different areas of the city, as she'd been instructed. By this time, the local light agents had got their act together. With a little celestial help, two of the triplets quickly found new families. But despite our agents' best efforts, the third – Star – was left crying in an alleyway for three days before any human noticed."

Reuben was horrified. "It's a wonder she survived."

"You'd be surprised. New-born humans are surprisingly tough," said Orlando.

Orlando described how Star was eventually rescued – if you can call it that – by the owner of a sleazy public house called *The Pomegranate*. But when she was three years old, this charming guy sold her on to a slave dealer. After that, Star basically had spent her childhood running away from abusive owners, and being recaptured.

It's not surprising that she grew into a little female hooligan, who hit first and asked questions afterwards. Yet like her sisters, she had a strong spiritual side. She had vivid dreams and saw strange visions. But Star learned it was unwise to talk about these things. She decided it was better to be laughed at for being a feisty tomboy, than stoned as a witch. When she was ten years old, she stowed away on a ship bound for Carthage, to seek her fortune.

I shivered when Orlando told us this. How weird is that? It's like when I made up my fictional life-story for Aurelia, I had somehow tapped into Star's real life-story.

Star did find her fortune; kind of. Soon after she arrived, a sharp-eyed local lanista noticed a wild-haired ragamuffin defending herself in the street from some older boys. He was impressed by her spirit and thought it would be amusing to train her for the arena.

Reuben looked disgusted. "He wanted to put a ten-year-old girl in the arena? That is SO sick."

Orlando shook his head. "Star doesn't see it that way. She says it was the first time anyone ever believed in her. Festus Brutus saw her fight a few weeks ago and decided to buy her for his ludus. To begin with he was just exploiting her like everyone else, but now I think he genuinely wants to help Star to buy her freedom."

"Who gave her that name?" I asked curiously.

"Star was called dozens of different names while she was growing up, but none of them were her own. So when she needed a stage name, she decided to call herself Star, her private name for herself when she was a small slave girl," Orlando explained.

I felt my eyes prickle with tears. I couldn't imagine how that unloved child had survived such a harsh life.

"What about the other sister? The temple girl?" asked Reuben.

Orlando smiled, "Lucilla is something else. Her foster parents never told her of the circumstances of her birth, yet she always knew that she had an unusual destiny. From the age of three or four, she'd plead with her parents to take her to the Temple of Vesta. If they refused, Lucilla ran off there by herself, taking offerings of flowers and cakes. She told her parents she felt peaceful there. No-one was surprised when the temple authorities sought her out to train her as a Vestal virgin."

"So now all three sisters are in Rome," Reuben remarked. "Star returned from Carthage or wherever. Aurelia just got back from Britain, and Lucilla was here all along."

"Lucilla will be so amazed when she finds out she's got two long lost sisters," I said excitedly.

Reuben frowned. "But won't it be dangerous to bring them together?"

"Omigosh, the curse!" I gasped. "I forgot about that."

Orlando shook his head. "The three sisters are supposed to be reunited. That's been our objective all along."

"Orlando, that is SO cool!" I was practically hugging myself.

Orlando had the funny look he gets when I've missed the point. "This isn't some family reunion, Mel," he said in a patient voice. "Or the Agency would never have backed our mission."

"No, of course not," I said hastily.

"It's an event of major cosmic significance," he explained. "Individually, all the girls have wonderful qualities, yet until now they've been incomplete. But once they are reunited, their inner light will become so powerful, that it will shine down the centuries." Orlando fixed me with his most intense expression. "These girls will transform history, Mel."

Reuben looked nervous. "Do the PODS know about this?"

"Why do you think they tried to keep them apart?" said Orlando softly.

I felt a sudden pang of worry. "We should go to the temple," I told him. "We should go and find Lucilla now!"

The Powers of Darkness had other ideas. On the way to the Temple of Vesta we ran into every Roman obstacle imaginable: builders' wagons blocking the street, floods from burst water pipes. We even got stopped by two night watchmen with leather buckets, wanting to know if anyone had reported a fire. But finally we were racing up the long flight of temple steps, taking them two and three at a time.

When we reached the top, a shiver went through me as if someone was walking on my grave. The door to the temple stood wide open. We rushed inside, but Lucilla and the other Vestals were nowhere to be seen. The shrine to the goddess was in darkness, its sacred flame totally snuffed out.

CHAPTER TEN

Vesta's lamp lay smashed into pieces at the far end of the temple. It was obvious it had been hurled there by a supernatural force.

Reuben silently collected the glimmering gold fragments and returned them to the altar. It was a sweet Reuben-type gesture, as if he was apologising personally to the goddess.

Without her sacred flame burning on the altar, Vesta's temple felt like a lifeless shell. Orlando gazed around him in despair. "It's over," he said in a dull voice.

"It isn't over," Reuben comforted him. "It's just a – a bad setback."

"It's a disaster," said Orlando huskily. "The Dark

forces got Lucilla and it's all my fault."

"We'll find her," I said, with more confidence than I felt.

Reuben shook his head. "We can't leave the temple like this. Every evil entity in Ancient Rome will think they've got squatter's rights."

But Orlando was on his way out of the door. "Sorry, I've got to go," he said miserably. "I've got to figure out what to do next." He hurried off into the night.

Until this moment, I'd put Orlando on a pedestal. Now for the first time I saw how vulnerable he was.

"It's no wonder Orlando's stressing out," I said miserably. "This mission is too much responsibility for one trainee."

Reuben squeezed my hand. "He just needs to clear his head. He'll be back on track by the time we get back to the ludus, I bet you. Now, let's get to work."

To my astonishment he calmly sat down in the dark. After a few seconds, rays of pure white light started streaming from his hands and heart. Apparently Reuben intended to spring clean the whole temple!

"OK, angel-boy, I get the message," I sighed.

"But can we make it quick?"

But my buddy refused to budge, until we'd neutralised every speck of PODS contamination, and filled the space with uplifting vibes.

As we left, I caught a flicker of movement in the porch. I thought it was some old rags blowing in the wind, then I looked again and saw a beggar huddled in the shadows. You couldn't really tell how old he was. He was little more than skin and bone. But something in his eyes made me look twice.

"Excuse me," I said. "We're looking for a Vestal called Lucilla. You don't know what happened to her, do you?"

The beggar's voice was so quiet, I had to crouch down to hear him.

"They took her to the Field of Sorrows."

I didn't like the sound of this. "Where on earth is that?"

"It's where they take Vestals who offend the goddess. They're going to bury her alive," the beggar said sombrely.

I gasped with horror. "Just for letting the flame go out! But that wasn't even her fault!"

"Lucilla is charged with a second offence," said the beggar in a low voice. "A temple elder accused her of meeting a young man in secret."

"But she didn't, right?" said Reuben.

"Lucilla has served the goddess faithfully since she was ten years old," said the beggar. "She would never do anything to dishonour her."

"Can you tell us where to find this field?" Reuben asked.

The beggar gave us detailed directions.

"You've been really helpful." I started fumbling in the purse at my waist and held out the usual small coins.

To my surprise, he waved them away. "It was my pleasure to help you. Thank you for cleaning up in there, by the way. It didn't go unnoticed."

I stared at him. This was not normal behaviour for Ancient Roman beggars. Plus there was something about his eyes. "Omigosh!" I gasped. "You're an—"

The Earth angel quickly put his fingers to his lips. "When you see Orlando, tell him what happened here was not his fault," he whispered urgently. "But he has to hurry. He's running out of time."

I was still beside myself with embarrassment. "You must think I'm so rude – I had NO idea!!"

The Earth angel gave a soft laugh. "You weren't supposed to recognise me. We try to tread carefully in Dark eras. Most of us cloak our vibes to keep the Dark powers off the scent."

"But not at the Games," said Reuben.

"No, not at the Games." I saw the angel's teeth flash in the shadows. "We also give the occasional cosmic nudge!"

We found Orlando back at the gladiator school, battering the daylights out of a straw target in the dark.

"We know where they've taken Lucilla!" I panted out. "Plus we've got a message for you."

The Earth angel's message had a totally luminous effect. Orlando immediately threw off his depression and beamed telepathic signals to the rest of the task force. Dazed-looking angels emerged from their sleeping quarters to join us under the stars.

"What's going on?" asked a confused trainee. "Are we going home?"

"I wish," someone sighed. "I've had enough boiled barley to feed a Roman legion."

"Barley's good for gladiators. It makes your blood clot," said another trainee in a cheerful voice.

"It makes *everything* clot," said the second trainee darkly.

Orlando waited until everyone had settled down, then he started to talk. He was one hundred percent back in leader mode; calm, collected, totally focused. First Orlando had to fill everyone in about Aurelia and her long lost sisters.

"The aim of this mission was to bring the three girls together," he explained. "But the Agency advised me not to make this generally known. They said there were cosmic spies on every street corner in Nero's Rome, monitoring conversations, even thoughts." Orlando gave a rueful laugh. "I thought this was paranoid to be honest. But it looks as if their caution was justified. A few hours ago we went to make contact with the third triplet. Somehow – I've no idea how – the Opposition found out and got there first."

I was glad it was dark so no-one could see me going red.

"That might have been my fault," I mumbled.

Orlando looked startled. "What do you mean?"

"I saw Lucilla coming out of the temple, when we were being taken to the dungeons. I was so stunned by her resemblance to Aurelia, I just blurted it out. One of our guards must be a spy for the PODS. I'm sorry, everyone," I said humbly. "That's the only way it could have happened."

Reuben was twiddling one of his baby dreads. "No way was this your fault, Mel. You had no idea then that Aurelia *was* one of triplets. And you definitely didn't know she and her sisters were caught up in a cosmic tug of war."

"It IS my fault," I said miserably. "I'm a total motor mouth."

"I agree with Reuben. You shouldn't blame yourself," said Orlando. "But unless we get Lucilla back, this mission will be a write-off."

"So let's get her!" called someone.

"This isn't going to be like sneaking prisoners past drunken guards," Orlando told him. "We'll have to fight."

"Surely we aren't allowed to use angelic fighting skills on humans?" said a trainee in alarm.

Orlando's reply chilled me to the bone. "The beings who took Lucilla from the temple aren't human."

Just occasionally you find an Earth location that feels like it's twinned with a Hell dimension. The Field of Sorrows was one of those.

It was the dead of night when we rumbled up in Festus's wagon, but the air was so thick with human despair, you could practically taste it. We'd arrived just as the tail-end of a silent torchlight procession was disappearing in through the gates.

I could sense Orlando psyching himself up. "Once we're in there, there's only one way out – the hard way," he said tensely. "So put up your energy shields and keep them up. I don't want you guys contaminated with evil energy. I don't want any casualties tonight. Good luck everyone."

We slipped through the gates and began to mingle with the crowd.

"What are all these people doing here?" I whispered nervously.

"It's a public ritual," Orlando said. "Anyone can come."

After the Roman Games you'd think I'd be unshockable but the idea that humans would trek out to this desolate place in the dark, to gawk at a teenage girl being buried alive, left me speechless.

They weren't all sightseers. At the head of the procession, priests, senators and government officials walked ceremoniously behind a curtained litter. The sight made me shiver. Lucilla was by herself in there, waiting to go to her death, and these people were just going to stand and watch it happen.

The procession wound its way to higher ground.

In the flickering torchlight, I noticed ominous mounds like giant mole-hills.

Reuben went wide-eyed. "Is that where—?"

"I don't want to talk about it," I said huskily. It was hard to talk in the Field of Sorrows actually. The terrible vibes made the words dry up in your mouth. The only sounds were the hypnotic tramp of people's sandalled feet over strangely hollow-sounding ground and the occasional phlegmy cough of one of the litter bearers.

This is a funeral march, I thought in horror. It was like Lucilla was officially dead already.

The flaring torches cast dramatic shadows on people's faces. Most of them had the sharp cheekbones of the chronically poor, yet their eyes glittered with excitement. Probably the temple scandal and Lucilla's gruesome punishment were the most thrilling events to have happened in ages.

At last the procession stopped beside a newly dug pit. When I saw the rungs of the crude wooden ladder protruding from the earth, I had to dig my nails into my palms. I couldn't believe these people were actually going through with this.

The bearers set down the litter at the edge of the pit. Two temple flunkeys drew back the curtains and lifted Lucilla out, bound and gagged and still dressed in her white tunic and gauzy bridal veil. I tried not to imagine how terrified Aurelia's sister must be.

It seemed the authorities couldn't just dump a dishonoured Vestal virgin in a hole and leave her there. First they had to blow horns and chant, and a priest had to say pompous words in Latin about how wicked and sinful she was.

The dreary ritual seemed to go on for ever, yet Lucilla stood perfectly motionless, with her bound hands clasped in front of her, looking completely serene. Even her thoughts were serene. I know this because I could hear them as clearly as if she'd spoken them aloud. *Mother goddess, you know I am innocent. Give me the courage to bear my fate.*

At the end of the ceremony, five women stepped forward, looking as if they were going to a bizarre Roman housewarming. Two were clutching dishes of food, a third carried a jug of wine and the fourth hugged a folded blanket in her arms. The fifth woman held a lighted lamp, and seemed to be having trouble sheltering the flame from the wind that blew over the open ground.

"They have to leave Lucilla enough provisions to last twenty-four hours," Orlando whispered.

"Otherwise it's sacrilege."

"But it's OK for her to be suffocated from lack of oxygen, is it?" I hissed angrily.

"No, of course it's not OK. But most of these people believe she insulted the goddess. To them that's like insulting Rome. They think she's a traitor to Rome. The way they see it, if they don't punish Lucilla, Vesta will withdraw her protection and the Roman Empire will fall."

People were crowding closer to the pit. I could feel their excitement rising. I broke into total goosebumps as I recognised the PODS who'd been at Quintus's nightmarish banquet.

Why are you surprised, Melanie? I thought in disgust. They framed this innocent girl to stop us reuniting her with her sisters. Naturally they'll be in at the kill.

For PODS this was like the ultimate cosmic joke. And as always, they'd manipulated gullible humans into doing their dirty work for them.

One of the flunkeys started to untie Lucilla's ankles. I felt myself go dizzy with horror. They were going to make Aurelia's sister climb down into her own grave!

Then Orlando's signal flashed through me like volts down a wire.

Go go go!!

In that confused nanosecond, before mixed-up Melanie Beeby turned into Helix, the heavenly whirlwind, I relived my fantasy: me and Orlando fighting bravely side by side. Well, now it was happening for real. And it *wasn't* thrilling and it certainly *wasn't* romantic, and it *totally* didn't matter how I looked. The world had narrowed down to a single urgent thought. Saving Lucilla.

I have a theory about what happened. I think these particular PODS had been sponging off Ancient Roman humans for too long. They'd got the impressive spy network, plus they could bump off inconvenient humans if they had to, and they thought that was enough. They'd lost their edge, basically. It just didn't occur to these creeps that a ragtag bunch of unarmed celestial trainees would charge out of the crowd and put a stop to their murderous plans! And as every warrior knows, surprise is the best weapon.

OK, so I might have squealed like a girl when my first Roman lookalike melted in front of my eyes, but then my angelic training kicked in and I focused like I've never focused before. Fighting PODS is unbelievably hideous. One minute I was kicking the sassafras out of something that looked like a human. Then, euw! I was grappling with a slimy monster from my darkest nightmares. Plus, whenever I glanced up, I'd see my fellow angels doing battle with their own horrors.

But that wasn't the worst thing. The worst thing was having to get up close and personal to beings who are basically pure evil energy.

This full-on cosmic combat lasted ten minutes max from start to finish. For the *bona fide* humans in the crowd, it must have been a horrifying spectacle. Most of them fled in terror including, it has to be said, the priests. But one by one the PODS were beaten back, their human forms dissolving into the earth. The only signs they'd ever existed were these like, glistening trails of slime.

Reuben and I immediately started to untie Lucilla.

Orlando sounded so calm, you'd think we'd just completed a successful Dark Studies exercise back home. "Excellent work, team. Now let's get out of here. We've won the battle, but that doesn't mean we've won the war. Next time they'll be ready for us."

"Did the goddess send you?" Lucilla asked us in awe.

"Just think of us as your friends," grinned Reuben.

"And your sisters' friends," I said impulsively.

Lucilla gasped. "My sisters? But I don't—"

"It's a long story," Reuben said. "We'll tell you on the way."

On the way back to the gate, Lucilla kept glancing back uneasily, and I heard her whisper a prayer to the goddess. She was remembering those terrible mounds, the graves of Vestals who were not so lucky.

I linked my arm through hers. "Come on," I said. "This is the first day of the rest of your life."

And we walked away from the Field of Sorrows.

Chapter Eleven

Lucilla said very little on our journey back. She mostly rested with her eyes closed. A few times I saw her snatch a shy peek around the crowded wagon. I think she needed to reassure herself that we were real, that she wasn't actually down a pit, just hallucinating being rescued. Once she said, "What did you say their names were?"

I patted her hand. "Star and Aurelia."

"All our names are full of light," she said softly. "What does Aurelia mean?"

"The golden one." Lucilla closed her eyes again.

"This has to be the longest night in history," I said to Reuben. "I feel like I've been charging about Ancient Rome forever."

"Well it's nearly over now," he said comfortingly.

I put my lips close to his ear. "Am I the only person here who thinks this is a teeny bit scary?" I whispered. "Orlando is defying a seriously evil curse. Remember all that stuff about cosmic black holes? Who knows what will happen when we put these triplets together?"

Reuben gave me one of his pure angel smiles. "The Agency wants them reunited," he said. "So it'll all work out. Relax!"

We dropped the rest of the guys off at the barracks. Reuben, Orlando, Lucilla and I walked across the courtyard to Star's apartment.

To my dismay someone had broken several branches off the peach tree. The fallen fruit was trampled into mush.

Orlando turned pale. "Festus told two men to watch the door. Where are they?"

Oh no, I thought. Please please no!

The door was open. Inside Juno was trying to comfort a sobbing Aurelia. Festus Brutus hovered unhappily.

"Where's Star?" Orlando said at once.

"Nero sent for her," he growled.

"At this hour?" I said.

"Couldn't sleep apparently," said Festus in

disgust. "His advisers thought a private performance from Rome's most famous gladiatrix would while away the night. I tried to stop them lad, but I'm not the man I was."

I could tell the old gladiator felt ashamed that he wasn't able to protect his protégée.

"You've been a good friend to Star," said Orlando. "You mustn't reproach yourself."

Aurelia was still sobbing with her hands over her face. She'd got to the stage where you can hardly breathe. Lucilla went to kneel beside her. She gazed at this unknown sister in awe, as if she was afraid she would vanish. With a trembling hand, she reached out to stroke her hair. "My sister," she said softly. "The goddess showed you to me in visions, but I never thought we would meet in this world."

Aurelia's face was red and swollen from crying. She peered at Lucilla incredulously. "You're the temple girl! Mella found you!"

"Not just me," I said awkwardly.

"Oh, this is so strange! I just found and lost one sister. Now you—" Aurelia broke off and gave a slightly hysterical laugh. "I can't take it in. I feel deranged. I don't know if I should tremble, weep, or jump about with happiness!"

Lucilla sat beside Aurelia and took her hand. Her eyes sparkled with tears. "We should be happy," she said softly. "A Dark power forced us to travel this life alone. Now the gods have brought us back together and we can fulfil our destiny."

Woo! I thought. This triplet was totally luminous! She practically had her own personal hotline to the gods. She knew exactly what was going on!!

Unfortunately we still only had two triplets in our possession.

"The PODS really shoved a spanner in the works this time." I sighed to Orlando.

But now they'd taken Star, he was like this unstoppable force. "They slowed us down a bit, that's all," he said. "We know Star is at Nero's palace. We'll reunite them there."

Personally, I would not have chosen an imperial palace full of PODS, plus their human sympathisers, for the triplets' reunion, but I suspected there was a crucial element of cosmic timing, which Orlando was keeping to himself; so for once I decided not to argue.

Nero's palace was in the super deluxe area of Rome, high on a leafy hill, well away from the noise and smells of the common people. It wasn't too hard to sneak into the palace grounds. No CCTV cameras or electric gates in those days.

The trouble started when we tried to get in through the kitchens. We'd forgotten that all Nero's slaves were dressed in identical livery, to show they belonged to the imperial household. A slave sussed us the instant we put our noses inside.

"What's this? The cabaret?" he said sarcastically.

The cheeky answer just jumped out of my mouth. "Yeah, we're the dancing girls, and these are our body guards."

I heard Orlando making choking sounds.

The slave grinned. "Then you won't mind letting me see you dance."

"No problem," I said confidently. Well, raunchy dancing is universal, right? I showed him a few sexy dance moves.

He shook his head. "All young girls can dance. So if you're the cabaret, where are your costumes?"

"Oh, duh," I said. "Like we could walk through the streets in those without being arrested. We sent them over earlier. With, erm, the musicians," I improvised hastily.

The slave laughed. "Nice try, darling. Now get out before someone from Security sees you and things get nasty."

But I had no intention of leaving. This was absolutely the only way I knew to reach Star. "Look, ask the Emperor, if you don't believe me!" I said desperately.

The slave shook his head in mock despair. "There's no helping some people." He bellowed into the distance. "Guards!"

Orlando and Reuben were looking at me as if I'd lost my mind.

"I know what I'm doing, OK?" I hissed. "You want to get the sisters back together don't you? What does it matter if we're taken before Nero as prisoners or, like, his naughty hoochy-coochy dancers?"

A look of grudging respect came into Orlando's eyes. "Melanie Beeby," he murmured, "you are something else."

Nero's household guards marched us down gleaming corridors, through a pair of gigantic doors, and into a marble dining hall filled with loud drunken voices and the busy clattering of cutlery. The smell of complicated Roman sauces floated through the air. The Emperor had insomnia, so naturally he was giving a nocturnal feast for all his pervy friends and relations.

A group of musicians were playing valiantly at

one end of the hall. You could hardly hear the instruments through the gales of talk and laughter.

Nero himself reclined on a golden couch, among gold tasselled cushions, wearing a white silk toga, with a gold striped border. The Emperor's laurel wreath had slipped down over one eye, and he was smacking his lips over a plate of little roasted birds. I tried not to look too closely, but judging from their size they were blackbirds or thrushes.

On the other side of a low table, Titus Lucretius was tossing raw oysters into that wet-looking red mouth of his. Beside him Quintus steadily knocked back the booze.

The guard cleared his throat. "Your majesty, these children were discovered sneaking into the palace. They claim to be a troupe of barbarian dancers, majesty."

Nero's midnight party had put him in a mellow mood. "But these are the lion children," he said in a mild voice. I saw his eyelids droop briefly as he registered the extraordinary resemblance between Aurelia and her sister. "My, my," he crooned. "One Christian and one Vestal virgin. How enchanting. You came at the right moment," he told them confidingly. "Just in time for the evening's main attraction."

"With respect," Titus interrupted smoothly, "your majesty does remember that these are intruders, not invited guests?"

Nero's face darkened. "Which of us is the *Emperor*?" he demanded.

"You, of course, your majesty, but—"

"Then I think I can decide who to invite into my own palace, Titus Lucretius," said the Emperor haughtily. He jumped up and his plate of little dead birds fell to the floor with a crash. Broken pottery and gravy went everywhere.

"Let me show you my surprise!" he told Aurelia and Lucilla in a conspiratorial voice. Seizing their hands he pulled them over to another set of doors. A slave hastily flung them open.

"Behold!" said Nero proudly.

There's something about madness that makes you feel crazy yourself. And when I saw what was on the other side of the doors, I literally felt dizzy, as if reality was turning inside out.

Nero had built an amphitheatre inside his palace. It was on a smaller scale, but apart from that everything was identical; the tiers of seats, the sand-filled arena. As it was night-time, the arena wasn't flooded with Mediterranean sunlight, but lit by burning torches.

The Emperor's guests filed in to take their seats. Some brought their full plates and goblets with them, and carried on gorging themselves and gossiping loudly. The Emperor made us sit with him in the front row. As his new special best friends, Aurelia and Lucilla had to sit on either side of him.

"They brought a little gladiatrix here for my amusement," Nero drawled. "But ordinary armed combat is so boring. So I decided to introduce an element of surprise." He clapped his hands. "Bring her in!"

When I saw Star led into the arena by the guards, I practically bit through my lip to stop myself crying out. She'd come to fight, yet they'd taken away her sword, her shield and all her protective armour. In her white linen tunic she looked desperately small and vulnerable.

But when Nero set eyes on her, he looked totally stunned. His eyes swivelled nervously to Lucilla and Aurelia, then returned to the gladiatrix.

Omigosh! I thought. It's the first time he's seen her without her mask! Beads of perspiration appeared on the Emperor's forehead and he began to breathe in panicky gasps. I felt almost sorry for him. Hanging out with PODS was doing absolutely nothing to improve Nero's mental health.

"It's OK, your majesty," I said in my most gentle voice. "You're not imagining things. The girls *are* identical triplets. This is the first time they've been together since they were ba—"

"Silence, foolish girl!" barked Nero. He hastily blotted his sweaty face with the silken hem of his toga. "Obviously I realised they're triplets!" he hissed at me. "Do you think I'm insane?"

Oops, I thought.

The PODS in the audience looked visibly disturbed when they saw Star separated from her sisters by just a flimsy wooden barrier and a few metres of sand. This was something they definitely hadn't bargained for. And then two concealed gates burst open, and ten fully-armed gladiators stormed in.

This was the Emperor's surprise element. Nero wanted to see the gladiatrix fight for her life against impossible odds, and finally expire in a pool of blood. So did all his sick cronies. The amphitheatre erupted into hyena-type whoops of excitement.

But when Star saw what entertainment Nero had laid on for his guests, she did something extraordinary. The girl who'd had to fight to survive for practically her whole life, silently knelt down in front of the Emperor, bowed her head, and totally refused to fight.

Nero was beside himself. "Get up, get up!" he screamed.

Star didn't move.

The gladiators came to a stumbling halt. They were the kind of guys you'd hate to meet in a dark alley: scary professional killers, skilled in every fighting style going, and proud of it. But murdering a kneeling girl requires no skill whatsoever. They stared at Star like puzzled bulldogs.

The sweethearts, I thought deliriously. They totally can't do it!

But the mad Emperor wasn't going to be cheated now. A creepy smile spread over his face. "Guards!" he bellowed. "I'm introducing one last challenge for the gladiatrix."

He jerked Lucilla and Aurelia to their feet. "Take them into the arena to join their sister!" he announced.

CHAPTER TWELVE

Aurelia gave me a beseeching look as she and Lucilla were led away.

I could feel the air seething with dark vibes. The PODS were seriously alarmed. No way did they want these sisters in Nero's arena. But the Emperor had spoken and he had to be obeyed.

Orlando had gone totally white, and Reuben was frantically twiddling one of his dreads. This was so not how any of us had pictured this reunion.

Like Brice said, the Emperor was seriously psycho. He was determined to force Star to perform, and he'd come up with the perfect scenario. The gladiatrix could never stand by and watch as her sisters were slaughtered. She'd rather die defending them.

For the first time since they were babies, the triplets were only metres apart. For a moment no one moved, and then in one supple movement Star rose to her feet and she did this really touching thing. She walked right up to her long lost sisters and looked wonderingly into their eyes, the way a trusting small child would do, and her sisters gazed wonderingly back at her.

I thought my heart was going to burst. "That's SO sweet," I whispered.

"They're remembering each other's vibes," Reuben said softly.

Star briefly closed her eyes. I saw tears spill down her face. Aurelia and Lucilla spontaneously reached for their sister's hands and as the three girls touched, a shiver of cosmic electricity went through me.

Orlando sighed with pure relief. We'd done it.

The amphitheatre was in total confusion. Some gladiators charged at the triplets, then thought better of it. Others just gave helpless shrugs and let their swords fall to the ground. The audience was outraged. They started stamping and chanting, "Kill! Kill Kill!"

The girls were oblivious to all of this. Their rapture at finding each other had enclosed them in a kind of joyous force-field. To them, nothing else existed. The mad Emperor, this toy arena and the audience of baying upper-class Romans, was a meaningless illusion. Only their love was real.

When human love is that pure, it can move mountains. It can stop the murderous onslaught of trained gladiators. It can send such beautiful, electrifying shock waves through the air, that an evil dynasty finally begins to crumble.

I became aware of disturbing grinding sounds far beneath the earth, as if the tectonic plates or whatever, were shifting. Hairline cracks appeared in the palace walls and a marble statue of the Emperor wobbled unsteadily on its plinth. None of this cosmic upheaval registered with the humans. Not yet. It was more like an angelic trailer of things to come.

Omigosh! I thought. Is this what happens when you reverse a hideous Ancient Roman curse?

I glanced at Orlando for reassurance, but he was watching the reunited sisters with a dreamy expression. His mission had worked out just like it was supposed to. Against all the odds, we'd succeeded in getting these three extraordinary sisters into the same space, and let me tell you, their combined energy was awesome. I could literally feel it pulsing through me like light from a star.

Aah, I thought blissfully. This is just the best job in the universe.

That's one major difference between us and the Dark agents. PODS operatives are never moved by human emotions. And by this stage in his career, Titus Lucretius was three-quarters of the way to being a POD. I vaguely registered him edging stealthily towards the barrier, but I didn't see him reach inside his toga.

My angel buddy did. Frantic thoughts flew from his mind to mine. *He's got a dagger*! *He's going to kill Aurelia*!

Vaulting over anyone in his way, Reuben launched himself wildly at Titus. In my desperation to reach Aurelia, I hurled myself over the barrier into the arena and fell heavily on my knees, taking off a layer of skin.

Star was faster than any of us. She saw the dagger flash towards her sister and simply stepped in front of her to block the blow.

I wanted to scream at the top of my lungs, but somehow all my pain and shock stayed trapped inside.

Titus's dagger had pierced Star through the heart. It looked all wrong sticking out of her body. Stupid, grotesque and wrong. A crimson flower of blood came welling up around the hilt of the dagger, soaking through the white linen of her tunic.

The gladiatrix quickly pressed her hand to the wound and tried to smile. "I thought it would be today," she managed to say. "I told Juno I would die today. Don't look so sad," she told her horrified sisters softly. "I'll be waiting for you in the Elysian fields." Then she crumpled in sickening slow motion.

Lucilla and Aurelia tried to catch her, but Star sagged emptily in their arms and all three of them ended up sprawling on the ground.

There was a silence so total, that it was more shattering than any sound. I felt as if I'd been murdered too. I couldn't believe this vibrant beautiful girl was dead. Then just as I thought my head would explode with horror, the scene became oddly fixed and silent.

It was like in *Sleeping Beauty*, when people all over the castle get frozen in really dumb positions. Romans, wearing laurel wreaths and clutching lumps of roast chicken, craned forward to get a good view of the dead gladiatrix.

Titus was exchanging a frozen grin of triumph with Aurelia's brother. A horrified gladiator continued to stare down helplessly at the stricken girls cradling their dead sister.

Was this some bizarre side-effect of the curse? I wondered. And if so, why weren't we frozen too? I could hear Reuben breathing unevenly. Plus I could feel my own heart hammering behind my ribs.

Someone else was moving too, making his way slowly and shakily past these bizarre human waxworks and into the arena.

Orlando looked like someone who'd got trapped inside a bad dream and couldn't wake up. He knelt beside Star and his face was grey with shock. "Why couldn't I save you? I should have saved you," he whispered.

My throat ached so much I could hardly speak. "You couldn't know," I told him painfully. "They were so happy. It just didn't seem possible anything bad could happen."

Reuben was looking around him nervously. His sharper angelic senses had picked something up.

"What's happening?" I asked in alarm.

I felt a powerful disturbance in the air, like the beating of invisible wings. A shaft of light came down and Michael appeared beside us. Wouldn't you know it, I thought bitterly, now it's too late, the Agency's stepped in.

I wanted to throw myself into Michael's arms and beg him to take me home. I wanted to kick and scream like a bratty little girl. "Why did you let it happen? Why did you let Star die?!"

But my inner angel refused to let me give in to these immature impulses. She just watched and waited to see what would happen next.

In his despair, Orlando didn't seem to register Michael's arrival.

When he didn't look up, Michael touched him very lightly between the shoulder blades. The whoosh of cosmic energy seemed to jolt Orlando out of his trance. "They were together for less than three minutes," Orlando's voice was flat with misery. "And now she's dead. I didn't even see it coming."

"There was nothing you could have done," Michael said softly. "I know how it seems, but everything is completely as it should be. Now we have to get these two girls to safety."

Michael bent over Lucilla and Aurelia. I saw a flicker of light go through them. If I had been them I'd have wanted to stay frozen forever. When the surviving two sisters saw Star still lying dead in their arms, their faces were pitiful.

"I have to take her now," Michael told them.

I heard Aurelia gasp and their eyes filled with awe. I wondered what the sisters were seeing. Could they see Michael's crumpled suit and his beautiful archangel eyes? Or did they see some anonymous figure with wings?

Michael lifted Star's lifeless body in his arms. A pearly haze of white light began to form. It softly enfolded the sisters, growing brighter and more intense until they were completely hidden from view.

Once again I felt that odd thrumming disturbance as Time switched back on. But by this time Michael and the girls were nowhere to be seen.

There was major pandemonium as the amphitheatre returned to life. Obviously the humans didn't suss that an angel had spirited the sisters through a gap in time. But they knew they'd witnessed some kind of supernatural event.

Nero became totally unhinged and started screaming at the guards. "It's sorcery! Taming lions! Vanishing triplets! I won't allow it! Search the palace from top to bottom!"

Guards came running. Gee thanks, Michael, I thought nervously. How do we get out of this?

"Go through every box room and latrine until you find those two sorceresses," Nero was ranting. "And those other prisoners!" he added vaguely.

Other prisoners? I glanced down at myself in confusion. Could he possibly mean us?

Orlando gave me a wan smile. "Relax. We dematerialised a few moments ago."

Reuben sagged with relief. "Then let's get out of this hellhole!"

But someone had stepped in front of us, deliberately blocking our exit. Even in our non-material forms Titus Lucretuis could see us perfectly. "I'll find them if I have to move Heaven and Earth!" he hissed. "Make no mistake, those sisters will die and their blood-line will die with them."

"Time for a reality check, Titus," Orlando said quietly. "Haven't you noticed? You and your masters lost this one."

Titus turned purple. "Haven't YOU noticed?" he raged. "I killed the gladiatrix, fool! The sisters have been separated for ever. WE defeated YOU!!"

Orlando shook his head. "You're still part-human, though not for much longer at the speed you're mutating," he added drily. "So you don't understand that Time essentially has no meaning."

"Oh please!" groaned Titus. "Spare me the angelic hogwash!"

Orlando smiled. A real full-on smile. I could still see the shock and sadness in his eyes, but our boy was back.

"You really should get your evil masters to educate you," he said calmly. "From your limited human point of view the sisters' reunion was so brief as to be meaningless. But from a cosmic perspective, this event will resonate through human history until the end of Time itself."

Titus stared at him open-mouthed.

"I'll explain," said Reuben in a friendly voice. "What Orlando means is that Star might be dead, but she still changed the world. Love is cool like that!"

"Come on," said Orlando. "Let's go home."

Three days after we returned from our Roman mission, I scored a professional first and ended up in the hospital.

I was suffering from a massive overdose of PODS toxins, but I didn't know that, so after a hot shower and a change of clothes, I just went straight back to school. That's what you do when you're a professional. In my opinion I was the same as normal, better actually.

OK, so it was harder to sleep at night since I came home, and when I finally managed to drop off, my dreams were v. disturbing. And OK, so for some reason it felt as if there was a sheet of frosted glass between me and my mates. But that didn't mean anything was wrong with me.

The bad nights meant I persistently slept through my alarm. Three mornings in a row, Lola went jogging on her own.

"Why didn't you wake me?" I complained when I caught up with her after morning school.

"I figured you needed the rest, Boo," she said.

I gave her my brightest smile. "I need to wake up my dozy angelic metabolism, that's all. Let's grab a salad, then we can at least go and work out in the gym."

"Babe, don't take this the wrong way, but I think your tank is running on empty," Lola said in an anxious voice "No, actually I think you're running on pure fumes. You should slow down. Give your energy system a chance to recover. You guys went through a lot."

"Hey, there's nothing wrong with me," I told her huffily. "If you don't want to come that's fine. I'll go by myself!"

And that's what I did.

I was doing all right, until I went on the treadmill. There's something v. hypnotic about running on a never-ending conveyor belt. Maybe that's why I started having Ancient Roman flashbacks. Strangely, most of them were flashbacks to experiences I hadn't registered at the time. Like I could hear the exact tune the musicians played for the dancing girls as our litter bearers carried me and Aurelia past a sleazy bar.

And I kept seeing all these unknown Roman faces. The sunken eyes of an exhausted slave, as he used his last ounce of strength to help fellow slaves winch a slab of marble into place. The animated expressions of teenage girls at the baths, as they argued about which of their fave charioteers was the best looking.

Then I'd see my own hands fastening pearl hairpins into Aurelia's hair, as I dressed her for that horrible banquet. I never said goodbye, I realised. Aurelia was my human and I really respected her and *I never even said goodbye.*

But the disturbing flashbacks still kept coming: bloody executions, Christians chanting, the rungs of a wooden ladder sticking out of a newly dug pit. They came faster and faster and they wouldn't stop. I totally couldn't take it. My heavenly surroundings began to whirl around me, then suddenly, like the fadeout at the end of a movie, everything went black.

When I came round, I was lying in a white bed, surrounded by gauzy white curtains. An angel in pastel-coloured scrubs was calmly checking my pulse.

"You'll be fine," he told me. "You just need to rest, but we'd like to keep an eye on you for a couple of days. Would you like me to leave the curtains open?"

I tried to nod.

Drawing back the curtains, he went back out into the garden.

Sunlight and air came streaming in through the stone pillars and I could hear birds singing. I lay back weakly on my pillows and felt a soft breeze blow over my face. For the first time since I came back, I could smell the heavenly air, with its scent that is almost, but not quite, like lilacs. For absolutely no reason, tears began to seep from under my eyelids.

I cried on and off all the rest of that day, as distressing Roman memories floated to the surface. When I started crying about Star, the angel came in from the garden, smelling of rain and flowers, and silently held my hand.

I slept all night without moving. I didn't even wrinkle the sheets.

I was woken by sunlight glinting in my eyelashes. When I opened my eyes, Lola was sitting by my bed, rosy-faced from her early morning run. I threw my arms around her. "I missed you so much!"

My soul buddy freed herself apologetically. "Me too, Boo. But I am also a *leetle* bit sweaty as you can probably tell! You might want to leave the hug till later."

"Lollie, after Ancient Rome, angelic sweat smells like roses!" I giggled.

On the last night of my PODS detox, Michael dropped by to see how I was getting on. By this time I was ready to talk about things that still bothered me. The curse for instance.

"That curse said if the triplets came back together, Rome would fall," I said earnestly. "Well, we got them back together, Michael, and I literally felt Rome's foundations shaking. I don't know how it seems to you guys, but I got the definite impression that Nero was, erm, *toast*."

"And you're worried you might have done some harm."

I chewed at my lip. "Well, yes," I admitted.

Michael smiled. "Melanie, you helped to turn an evil curse into a blessing. Have you any idea what a rare and wonderful event that is?"

"A blessing?" I said dubiously. "Are you sure?"

"I'm one hundred percent sure!" Michael flipped open his cool little laptop and set it up where I could see the screen. "You might want to take a look at these."

He started to scroll through a huge picture gallery of human faces. To me it seemed like they came from every race, era, and civilisation. Male, female, black, white, golden and brown, the faces flowed on and on.

Now and then Michael would single one out, like: "Of course if Marie hadn't shown such exceptional courage, radium would never have been invented." Or: "Rosa's refusal to be a second-class citizen, helped to give birth to the American civil rights movement."

I was baffled. "I don't get it. What have these people got in common?"

"I've been waiting for you to ask me that," he beamed.

Michael tapped a key and made the portrait gallery disappear.

Now only two faces gazed out at me. I felt the slow dawning of recognition. They were older in these pictures, but the strength and beauty of Aurelia and Lucilla's faces shone through, totally unaltered.

"All those humans were descended from just two sisters?" I said in amazement.

"Every last one," he said firmly. "And they all did these incredible things?"

"They were all incredible people, which isn't quite the same thing. The kind of humans who change the atmosphere of the planet for the better, just by being themselves."

Michael gave me an unusually mischievous smile. "In fact if you yourself were to trace your human family tree all the way back to Roman times, you might get a surprise, Melanie!"

"Yeah, right," I grinned. "Which Ancient Roman triplet am I descended from?"

"Aurelia, obviously," said Michael in the same light-hearted voice. "There's a very strong connection between the two of you, which I think you noticed."

This idea was way too fanciful for me. I was just happy to know that Aurelia and her sister survived to live happy productive lives. Plus it gave me a definite buzz to know we'd had a hand in such significant historical events, however indirectly.

Next morning, Lola came to take me home. "I thought we'd drop into Guru on the way back," she said. "My treat."

I felt a flicker of panic. "I don't know if I'm ready to see people yet, Lollie."

"Sorry Boo," said my soul-mate in a firm voice. "You won't be fully recovered until you've had Guru's infallible chocolate brownie cure."

"Lola, that is SO low!" I giggled. "You know I can't resist!"

It felt strange walking through the lively streets of the Ambrosia quarter, after the blissful peace of the sanctuary. When we eventually reached Guru, I saw a familiar figure slouched at an outdoor table.

Brice whipped off his shades and gave me a cool stare. "Hi, Melanie, how was Ancient Rome?"

"Excuse us," I said politely. I dragged Lola into a huddle. "I really appreciate you inviting me out," I hissed, "but I'm not playing cosmic gooseberry to you and lover boy. I'll wander back to school, OK? And you and Brice have a brownie for me."

"Sit," said Lola threateningly.

"Yeah, Melanie, sit," said Brice. "You might have to wait a while. The new waitress is still learning the ropes."

It was unexpectedly nice sitting in the sun in my

fave student hangout. I even found myself telling Brice about stuff. Stuff that to my surprise, he seemed to understand.

"What I don't get is what made them change," I said. "Like, we hear about major cosmic events shaking up Planet Earth's climate, thundering great meteorites, ice ages and whatever. But they never tell you what it takes to shake up human hearts. I mean how did humans get from the Field of Sorrows to, well – Greenpeace and Save the Children and whatever."

"Evolution?" Brice suggested wickedly.

I put my hands over my ears. "Aaargh! That word drives me nuts. No, it had to be a miracle. It's the only possible explanation."

Brice gave me a funny grin and began whistling to himself. After a while I recognised the tune. It was *Sisters are Doing it for Themselves.*

I stared at him in bewilderment. What was it Reuben told Titus? That Star might be dead, but she'd still helped to save the world.

"Omigosh," I breathed. "The sisters did that? They changed the hearts of the whole world?"

"The sisters and their children and their children's children," said Brice carelessly. "You could call it a miracle. Or you could just call it evolution. Our order's taking a long time," he called to Mo as he zipped past with a tray of smoothies.

"Sorry, our new girl is still finding her feet," he explained. There was a loud crash from inside the café. Mo hastily excused himself.

"Uh-oh," said Lola under her breath.

Orlando was standing by our table. "I heard you'd been ill," he said shyly. "Are you OK now?"

"She loved the flowers you sent her," said Brice mischievously.

"Shut up!" I hissed.

Orlando ignored him. "You and Reuben really did great work."

Lola gave him one of her looks. "Boo's the best," she said.

The new waitress came backing out through the door with her tray.

"Wait!" called Mo. "You forgot the forks!"

Poor girl, she's really struggling, I thought.

Then I saw her face and the entire café went shimmery. It's no wonder I was shocked. The last time I'd seen her she'd had a knife through her heart, though it would have been really tasteless to mention it. Plus, in her new heavenly surroundings, Star's life as a gladiatrix seemed oddly irrelevant, like old clothes she'd totally outgrown.

She looked incredibly stylish actually, with her cool haircut, and her black and white waitressy outfit. The only reminder of her old life was the charm around her neck: a silver charm in the shape of a star.

"I'll see you when you get off work then," Orlando told her softly.

Star glanced at him from under her lashes. "Maybe," she said in a considering kind of voice. "If I'm not busy."

To my surprise, it hardly hurt at all; though I couldn't explain this, even to myself. I still thought Orlando was the most beautiful boy in the universe, but after our Roman mission, I seemed to be seeing him in a less adoring light. Plus I liked Star. I liked her a lot. I wanted to get to know her better.

Wow, I've really changed, I thought.

Ahem, said my inner angel. You mean you've evolved.

Omigosh! I thought. It's true! Like, all this time, I'd been waiting for somebody (OK, Orlando!) to make me complete. But I didn't need Orlando, or any boy, to complete me. I had my fabulous mates, my totally luminous angel career, and best of all – I had ME!

Mel Beeby, feisty girl warrior, time-travelling stylist and celestial hip hop chick, was finally ready to move on!

STOP PRESS!

COSMICALLY MIND-BLOWING NEWS!

We, that's me and Lollie, have started a newsletter:

COSMIC BUZZ!

Subscribe now and we'll send you all the hot goss, including the Heavenly Top Ten; the coolest beats reverberating in Heaven; gourmet Guru food; celestial recipes to share; super-sparkly fashion tips; hair tricks straight from the Academy and even sneaky peaks into our secret, special diaries. Also, don't miss the chance to win some completely divine prizes!

To subscribe just log on to
www.angelsunlimited.co.uk

Get all the fab news on looking good, feeling good and having a totally luminous time – straight from the chic-est chicks in Heaven!

Love, Mel Beeby
a.k.a. the trouble-shooting, trouble-making angel!